Coming Undone

"Sixteen, seventeen, eighteen, nineteen," Remington finished aloud.

"I beg your pardon?" she said hoarsely.

"Your buttons . . . nineteen on a side. That makes a total of thirty-eight. Thirty-eight on one dress . . . it's enough to make a man wonder." He paused and watched her fighting the urge to look at him. She needed a bit more incentive.

"What are you afraid of?" he asked with a low, husky laugh. "That something will get out?" She whirled on him, her eyes flashing.

"Or perhaps you're afraid something else will get in." He lowered his head, feeling her allure curling through his blood. "Ah, Antonia. Buttons aren't much of a barrier if a man is truly determined."

Tilting her backward as she strained to avoid contact with him, he impulsively picked up the scissors in her lap. She gasped as he opened and slid them around her top button on one side, shearing it off. A heartbeat later, he slid them around a second . . . a third . . . and a fourth. It was an outrage, but she couldn't bring herself to stop it or even to protest it . . . not when he was so near and her blood was surging against her skin in eagerness for his touch. She couldn't move, could only watch as her buttons rolled and the top of her bodice began to slide. . . .

Betina Krahn

The Last
Bachelor

Bantam Books

NEW YORK · TORONTO · LONDON · SYDNEY · AUCKLAND

THE LAST BACHELOR
A Bantam Book / September 1994

ISBN 0-553-56522-2

Published simultaneously in the United States and Canada

Bantam Books are published by Bantam Books, a division of Bantam Doubleday Dell
Publishing Group, Inc. Its trademark, consisting of the words "Bantam Books" and the
portrayal of a rooster, is Registered in U.S. Patent and Trademark Office and in other
countries. Marca Registrada. Bantam Books, 1540 Broadway, New York, New York
10036.

PRINTED IN THE UNITED STATES OF AMERICA
RAD   0 9 8 7 6 5 4 3 2 1

 *For Don,*

the partner of my journey

*May He raise you up
on eagles' wings*

Prologue

She lowered her lashes.

He nuzzled her ear.

She sighed.

He smiled.

Nervous.

Eager.

Kisses drifted and laces slid. Modesty reeled, dizzy from the twirl of buttons, and respectability fled as its guardians were peeled away . . . skirt and bodice, petticoats and bustle, corset and high-button shoes. Hard boning, volumes of lace, flounces of muslin and sateen, and black silk stockings—so many fastenings, hooks, and tapes—with reluctance yielded, revealing tantalizing glimpses of pale flesh at the center of an unfolding blossom of womanliness.

In the glow of the down-turned gaslight, the lovers left garments like puddles on the floor, marking their passage toward a thick feather mattress and bared linen. Sinking one knee into the soft bed, he drew her against him, savoring her sweet hesitation. She ran her tongue over her lip and braced the heels of her palms against his bare chest as his arms encircled her. Her eyes darted toward the door of the rented room, then back to his, searching, uncertain.

"Don't be concerned, dearest," he murmured, lifting her hand to his lips. He shot a lidded glance toward the door that seemed to be troubling her and smiled knowingly. "No one knows of this place . . . the innkeeper is most discreet. You're perfectly safe with me here."

"I trust you with all my heart, my love," she said on a quivering, indrawn breath. "It is only that . . . it has been such a long time, and I am so fearful. . . ."

"Surely not of me, sweetest," he said, coaxing her averted eyes back to his with a squeeze of her waist. "You must know that I would die before causing you the slightest distress or discomfort."

"It is not that. I am just so afraid of . . ." She lowered her lashes and her cheeks filled with becoming color. "My late husband was not a passionate man."

"Ahhh." He smiled knowingly and tilted her face toward his once more. "You need not fear, my lovely angel. Your willingness to come to me like this is proof you have given me your heart." He spread his hand over her chest and gazed heatedly at the erotic bump nudging the fabric just below it. "And if I have your precious heart, what more could I possibly ask?" He slid his fingers onto her thinly veiled breast and closed them over it, wringing a gasp and a shiver from her.

In the throes of the next deep kiss, her eyes fluttered open, tracing his brow with adoring strokes, then closed again. His eyes opened an instant afterward, focusing with satisfaction on the delicate skin and silky blond hair of his partner in passion, then on the linen waiting below.

"Tell me, my darling, that we shall be together like this . . . always," she murmured as he pressed her back into the soft bedclothes and slid his chest over hers.

"Always?" he murmured against her throat as he tried to insinuate his knee between her tightly clamped legs. After a slight pause he added the persuasion of: "But of course, my dearest. *Always.*" When those words melted the resistance in her knees, he poured still more into her ear. "Together forever, my angel. From this day forward we shall find sweet solace in each other's arms, shall ease each other's burdens and delight each other's heart."

Through a sweet flurry of limbs and covers, as he drew back to dispose of the last of her garments and inhibitions, the sound of voices reached them. At first neither paid much heed; both her chemise and his control were sliding. But the sounds increased and finally intruded on their idyll.

"You are quite sure this is the room?" came a woman's impassioned tones from just outside the door. Beneath them the innkeeper's voice rumbled; whether in protest or reassurance, it was impossible to tell. "You, in room two twelve . . . open this door, immediately!" the woman addressed the pair in the bed. When they did not respond, the heel of a righteous fist was laid to the door. "Open, or I shall be forced to have the innkeeper admit me."

The lovers lay frozen in horror as the heavy wooden panels vibrated under the sharp raps, the jingle of keys was heard, and metal scraped ominously in the lock. When the door banged back against the wall, the lovers scrambled to pull the bedcovers up around them. The door frame filled with the outline of a feminine figure swathed in black silk and dark veiling.

"Lady Antonia!" the young woman in the bed gasped, and the name hovered on the hush of the chamber.

Lady Antonia surged into the chamber amid rustling skirts, then caught herself back a step, recoiling from the sight of the wayward pair. She turned to the innkeeper, who was loudly professing both indignation and ignorance of all such infamous goings-on in his establishment, and declared in a choked voice, "This is a painful and private matter, sir. I fear we are at the mercy of your discretion."

When the door closed behind the relieved innkeeper, Lady Antonia turned on the couple in the bed, straightened, and lifted back the heavy veil that shrouded her head and shoulders. Beneath a broad-brimmed hat, framed in a swirl of black silk, was a strikingly beautiful face set with such fierce determination that its loveliness became secondary. Her youthful, fashionably clad figure was transformed by her outrage into an ageless, towering presence. And at the center of her countenance, light and expressive eyes were sharpened to pale, hot points of emotion.

But whatever feelings the interruption of this tryst had roused in Lady Antonia, shock was certainly not among them. This was not the first—nor would it be the last—time she had encountered such a scandalous scene.

"Camille. How could you stoop to such a thing?" she demanded, clasping her hands tightly to constrain them. "This—after all my efforts on your behalf!"

"Please, let me explain," the young woman begged in a voice clogged with rising tears.

"Explain? What is there to explain? What has happened is more than plain to anyone with two good eyes." She waved a black-gloved hand toward Camille's disheveled hair and the bedcovers behind which she cowered. "You have disgraced yourself and violated my trust in you."

"Please, Lady Antonia," Camille pleaded, tears rolling down her fair cheeks as she gripped the bedclothes in whitened fists. "You do not understand. I love Bertrand with all my heart . . . and he loves me." She began to sob in earnest and turned to bury her face in her stunned lover's chest.

The sound of his name and the force of Camille Adams thrusting herself upon him jolted Bertrand Howard—promising young bureaucrat and adamant bachelor—from the haze of disbelief that had insulated him from the spectacle of his own ruination. "See here, Lady Antonia!" he blustered, stiffening and trying desperately to put distance between him and his weeping inamorata. "How dare you burst in upon us like this? You have no right—"

"No right?" Lady Antonia gasped as if struck physically by the fellow's insolence. "I have every right! When Camille came to my house, a new widow, made destitute by vulturous creditors, I embraced her as if she were a part of my family. I gave her my support and confidence. And she repays me"—she transferred a shriveling glare from the weeping Camille to the half-naked Mr. Howard—"by lifting her petticoats for a high-living rogue who will only despoil and abandon her."

"I am not a high-living rogue, nor a despoiler and abandoner of women," he protested, trying without success to get the suddenly boneless Camille to support herself as he edged away from her on the bed.

"Oh? And what did you intend after you had your way with her?" Lady Antonia demanded, watching his retreat from Camille and calling him on it with an accusing finger. "To slink away, that's what." At her charge he halted his flight and reddened prodigiously. "You would have gone back to your high-living friends, leaving her ruined and heartbroken." She looked again at Camille's quaking shoulders, and her manner softened markedly.

"Our poor, innocent Camille . . . without a contriving or deceitful bone in her body. And obviously without a prudent one, either." Her countenance filled with righteous anger once more, and she stalked closer to the bed. "It is clear who is at fault here. Only a callous, loathsome beast would take advantage of a tender-hearted young widow made defenseless by the blows of misfortune."

The accusation and her disdainful scrutiny combined to send the full impact of his rash pursuit of the delectable young widow crashing down upon Bertrand Howard. His eyes flew wide and his skin caught fire.

"What you have done, sir, is unconscionable," she continued. "There is nothing to be done, except make it right."

"M-make it . . . right?" he said, his muscles contracting visibly, bracing for the blow he sensed was coming.

"The immorality of your behavior is so flagrant—" She paused and pressed a hand to her temple as if distressed by having to speak of such matters. Recovering, she leveled a stare on him that turned her next words into a scarcely veiled threat. "I needn't tell you that the foul breath of scandal can topple a promising young career in government every bit as surely as it can ruin a young woman's reputation. There is only one honorable way to recoup such a hideous situation." And she announced it with the finality of a magistrate's gavel sealing a sentence: "You must marry Camille as quickly as it can be arranged."

Marry. It echoed about the chamber and in his ears. He looked down into Camille Adams's tear-rimmed eyes, then up at the implacable bastion of morality who had thrust upon him this reckoning of his carefree and libidinous ways. After a few last futile thoughts of escape—the death throes of his much-prized bachelorhood—he understood there was no other course. He was a gentleman, a man of some connection, a man with a future. He was also caught . . . like a rat in a trap.

Always. His own cozening tongue had pronounced his fate. Closing his eyes, he squared his shoulders to accept the punishment being forced upon them by society's pitiless standards. *Marriage*. He nodded.

Lady Antonia withdrew to the parlor at the end of the hall, to allow the couple to clothe themselves decently. When they emerged from the room, she took charge of Camille immediately, declaring she would send an announcement to *The Times* straight away, and insisting Mr. Howard call on them at her house the following evening to discuss wedding arrangements. He jerked an angry nod and cast the red-eyed Camille a glowering look as they made their way down a discreet set of back stairs to a cab Lady Antonia had kept waiting.

The husband-to-be shoved his fists deep into his trouser pockets and struck off for his club, churning inside at the thought of his conjugal future.

The bride-to-be watched him anxiously from the window as the cab rumbled off into the darkness, and vowed to make him the best wife in all of London.

And their matchmaker, Lady Antonia, drew her veil down over her glowing face and relaxed back against the leather seat with a small, triumphant smile.

Chapter

1

"Champagne, Hoskins!" Lady Antonia Paxton ordered as she swept into the spacious center hall of her house on Piccadilly. She handed the aged butler her gloves and reached for her hat pin. "A whole magnum of it . . . in the upstairs parlor, if you please."

"A celebration, ma'am?" he said, turning to help Camille Adams off with her short cloak.

"Oh, indeed, Hoskins," she answered, scooping her heavy veil up into her hat with a flourish. She was positively glowing. "Felicitations are in order. This evening our Camille has become engaged to be married to that most eligible Mr. Howard."

"*Mr. Howard*, ma'am?" He raised one bushy white eyebrow, glancing between his mistress's radiant countenance and the strained face of the bride-to-be.

"Surely you recall him, Hoskins. Mr. Howard is the Head Assistant to the Undersecretary of the Deputy Minister of the Board of Trade." When he frowned and shook his head, Antonia paused in the midst of unbuttoning her mantle and leaned closer to him. "The tall, dark-haired gentleman who has called for Camille several times of late." Still there was no spark of recognition. "Wears excessively sharp revers and walks with a bit of a swagger."

"Ahhh." Recognition finally flared in the butler's eyes as

he helped his mistress off with her wrap and laid it across his arm. "Him what's fond of striped green cravats."

"The very one. Though, I must say, neither his cravat nor his swagger were much in evidence this evening," Antonia said, with a mischievous smile at Camille, who blushed and looked down.

"Poor bastard," the old fellow mumbled under his breath, shuffling off toward the cloakroom and kitchens. "Marriage 'as got to be a raging epi-demic around this house, of late."

It was true; marriage had indeed become something of an epidemic at Paxton House during the past three years. A seemingly endless stream of women had arrived at the fashionable residence, stayed for a time, and then left to take nuptial vows in short order. And Lady Antonia Paxton, widow of the wealthy and altruistic Sir Geoffrey Paxton, was clearly to blame for the contagion. She had an abiding interest in stray cats, stray widows, and weddings . . . and a firm conviction that every widow, like every cat, should have a home of her own.

Smiling at the crotchet-ridden old butler's reaction, Antonia picked up the branched candlestick on the center hall table and sailed off through the grandly arched hall and up the polished oval staircase at the rear. Camille hurried along after her, but before they reached the door to the upstairs parlor, the bride-to-be pleaded a headache and excused herself to her room on the floor above.

Antonia sighed as she watched her latest matrimonial project retreat up the stairs, undoubtedly to cry herself to sleep. She had been right to tell the girl nothing about her plans this evening. Too softhearted for her own good, that one, she thought. The little thing would have given herself utterly to the slippery and self-indulgent Mr. Howard, with nary a thought for her own security or future. Wagging her head, she turned the other way and continued down the hall to the broad double doors of the upstairs parlor.

The densely furnished chamber was bathed in both the scent and the golden glow of numerous beeswax tapers, the use of which, every evening after nine o'clock, was a custom held over in memory of Antonia's late husband. Heavy, fringed brocades were drawn over the lace curtains at the windows, and a fire had been laid in the iron grate of the marble fireplace to drive out the March chill. In the midst of polished mahogany, gilt-framed portraits, and silk upholstery slathered in crocheted doilies, sat a white-haired woman wearing a knitted shawl and a pair of gold-rimmed spectacles.

"Antonia!" The old lady lowered the book she was holding up to the light of a branched candlestand. "How did it go?"

"An unqualified triumph, Aunt Hermione," Antonia announced, beaming as she went to the fireplace and stretched out her hands to absorb the warmth. "Our little Camille will be the new Mrs. Howard within the month."

"Oh, excellent," Aunt Hermione said, laying her reading aside, her delicately lined face brightening. "Just excellent." She glanced around Antonia, toward the door, with a quizzical look. "And where is the blushing bride?"

"Busy *blushing,* I am afraid," Antonia said tartly, untying the bow at her neck and loosening the top two of her bodice's numerous buttons. "Where is everyone? I ordered champagne."

"Oh, Prudence and Pollyanna had a few things to tidy up. They didn't expect you to return so soon. The others went on to their beds some time ago. Come. Sit." She patted the seat of the chair opposite her. "I want to hear every detail. Where did you find them?"

"The Bentick Hotel, of course. Those bounders from the bar at White's always seem to use the Bentick. Rather makes you wonder if that little weasel of a proprietor gives them some sort of a discount."

"Not very imaginative," Aunt Hermione said with a sniff.

"Men in rut seldom are," Antonia retorted as she settled onto the chair. "But then, it is precisely that characteristic which makes them so marvelously easy to outwit." The doors opened just then, and in hurried two older women wearing identical gray worsted day dresses and lace-edged caps.

"Back so soon? It must be good news!" said one of the Mrs. Quimbys, as the pair set about dragging parlor chairs toward the warm hearth.

"Have ye done it, then? Trapped another one?" said the other, her eyes narrowing behind tin spectacles as she perched on the edge of her seat.

"Yes, Pollyanna, I trapped another one," Antonia replied with unabashed satisfaction, propping her French-heeled shoes up on the fence of the iron fire grate and plumping her well-padded bustle so she could lean back on it in her chair. "Or perhaps it would be fairer to say that he trapped himself, the cad. He certainly wasted no time. They hadn't been gone more than three quarters of an hour, and he had her primed and plucked and pinned on her back in the middle of the ticking." Her eyes shone as she relived the pleasure of witnessing Bertrand Howard's shock. "You should have seen him . . . sitting there half-naked, jaw agape, gasping like a landed trout . . . with the most delicious look of panic on his face."

"Scandalous," Pollyanna said through pursed lips.

"Indeed it was," Antonia agreed, burrowing pleasantly back into her chair.

"I meant your having to see the wretch *bare* like that," Pollyanna corrected with an indignant scowl.

A laugh bubbled up inside Antonia. "Dear Pollyanna,

the sight of a man's bare shoulders is not unknown to me. I am a widow, after all."

"As are we all," Pollyanna said primly, nodding to the others. "But I for one have never seen a man's bare . . . *person* . . . and I hope never to see one."

"Well, sister," Prudence Quimby said with a matronly giggle, "if I had been married to Farley Quimby, I should have been most happy to remain ignorant of such a sight as well."

Hoskins arrived just then, bearing a bucket of chilled champagne and several tall, fluted goblets. As he uncorked the wine and poured, Antonia detailed her part of the encounter: confronting the innkeeper, charging through the door, and expressing convincing horror. Then with relish she recounted Bertrand Howard's reaction and his guilty acquiescence to his nuptial fate.

With a "harumph" and a narrow look at his mistress—his customary protest on behalf of his beleaguered sex—Hoskins handed out the last glass and shuffled back out the door, muttering, "Unlucky bastard." Antonia indulged in a perfectly wicked grin and, when he was gone, raised her goblet to propose a toast.

"Here's to husband number . . . number . . ." She paused, narrowing her eyes. "Good Lord. I've lost count of just how many there have been."

"Twelve previous, dear," Aunt Hermione informed her. "Mr. Howard is your thirteenth victim."

"Thirteenth?" Antonia was genuinely surprised by the number. She lowered her glass to make a cursory count on her fingers, and confirmed it. "Thirteen. Good Lord, it's true. And they call us the weaker sex!" She chuckled, and the old Quimby sisters chuckled and nodded archly to each other in agreement.

"And as to this 'victim' business"—she turned a good-natured reproach upon her Aunt Hermione—"may I remind you, Auntie, that *they* were the ones who chose to seduce or entice the women of my household. I simply took advantage of the opportunity their baser impulses provided to lever them into decent and honorable marriages."

It was true. Each of the thirteen men she had matched with her "protégées" had indeed cut a swath through London's feminine landscape as an adamant bachelor. And it was also true that while she had contrived to introduce the women under her protection to a number of potential husbands, the actual choosing had been the work of the pair themselves. The knowledge that her "victims" always had a hand in selecting their own comeuppance made each bit of matrimonial justice all the more satisfying.

"Here's to our Camille." She raised her goblet again, seeing in the golden glow of the crystal and the wine the promise of her protégée's future. "May she have a house in Mayfair . . . three lovely children . . . and all the pin money she could possibly want."

"And a headache whenever she needs one," Pollyanna added emphatically, drawing surprised looks from Antonia and the others. "Well"—she drew her chin back and frowned—"a woman can never have too many headaches."

"Here, here!" Prudence seconded.

They laughed and drank more toasts: to the groom-to-be; to the toadying and bribable proprietor of the Bentick; to the weaker sex; and to the virtues of a well-made marriage. Then the subject of the date for the wedding came up, and they agreed that a month hence allowed a decent interval between engagement and vows.

"Sweet Camille," Prudence said after a moment. "I shall miss her."

"It's hard to think that in a month she'll be gone." Pollyanna sighed wistfully.

In the brief silence that followed, the same thought struck them all.

"We shall have a vacant room!" Antonia spoke it aloud, snapping upright in her chair and scanning the tea table, the book stand, and the littered writing desk on the far side of the room. "Where is the latest *Cornhill*?"

"Oh, not again," Aunt Hermione said with a groan. "Not already!"

"It's not too early to begin planning our next project," Antonia declared, spotting the magazine and jumping out of her chair to retrieve it from the desk. She thumbed through the pages until she came to the personal advertisements. "Here they are."

She scanned them, her frown of concentration deepening as her eyes fell from one advertised tragedy to another. "Listen to this," she said, positioning herself near the candles and holding up the magazine to read: " 'Mrs. F., thirty, husband in America, appears to have deserted her . . . will do anything.' "

"Oh, but you'll want a genuine widow . . . not the 'grass' variety, surely," Pollyanna offered.

"Then how about this one?" Antonia continued. " 'Mrs. G., aged thirty-seven, clergyman's daughter, governess for seven years. Dislikes teaching. Is suffering in consequence of overwork. Desperate.' Hmmm . . . it doesn't say what happened to her husband. . . ."

"The clergy produce such sour, long-faced women." Prudence frowned, confirming her opinion in Pollyanna's wince of distaste. "I think you'll be wanting someone with a bit of life left in her."

"Oh, dear." The words fairly leaped off the page at Antonia. " 'Mrs. A., widow. Husband speculated and ruined the family, which is now dependent on her. Four daughters, aged fourteen to twenty-three. Not trained to anything . . . imperfectly educated . . .' "

"Oh, that won't do at all. A whole family." Prudence clucked her tongue.

"All those unmarried daughters." Pollyanna covered her mouth, looking genuinely pained. "Quite a tragedy."

Unmarried daughters. A tragedy. That terse assessment caught Antonia's heart unawares, rousing feelings she had thought well mastered. She, too, had been the unmarried daughter of a widow whose husband had "speculated," then died, ruining the family. Her eyes slowly scanned the lines again, then again.

Antonia Marlow Paxton had been born the only child of a wealthy and nobly born financier and had grown up among the wealthy and privileged. But when she was only sixteen, her father was killed in a boating accident, leaving a Gordian tangle of interconnected loans, a mountain of unpaid debts, and a wife who had been lovingly protected from the vulgarities of money and finance.

One by one the familiar comforts of her and her mother's lives had been stripped away: the country estate with its fine stables, the line of credit, the town house with its paintings and furnishings, the family jewels, and soon their fashionable but fickle friends. Totally unprepared for the realities of her diminished life, Antonia's mother gave in to despair and, within months, mourned herself into an early grave. At seventeen Antonia had found herself virtually alone, with the security and the dreams of girlhood lying in ruins at her feet.

Shaking off the effects of that advertisement, Antonia straightened and continued. "Perhaps this one: 'Mrs. R., aged thirty, a widow, lost large property by a lawsuit . . . tried to live by needlework and failed . . . eyesight damaged . . .'"

On she read, giving voice to the desperate pleas of women needing help. Some were widowed, some had never married, and some did not know the whereabouts of their husbands. "Off in the colonies," "lost in foreign service," and "took French leave" were common phrases. Some of the women had dependent children; some were alone in the world. Some of the unfortunates were victims of financial disasters, some had lost loving and protective families to illness, and some were simply advancing in age and had been turned out into the streets by employers desiring younger workers.

The more she read, the more intense her manner became. Her fingers gripped the pages harder and her spine straightened. In her mind's eye she began to see them: their faces haggard, expressions listless, and eyes dulled by deprivation and fear. Then she came to another advertisement that jolted her composure:

" 'Mrs F., aged forty, recent widow and mother, seeks honorable position for daughter . . . dear angel of the house . . . creditors closing in . . . desperate situation.' "

It was a thinly disguised plea to save a daughter from the predations of male creditors who would slyly suggest a man's debts could be paid by his daughter . . . on her back.

Memories materialized through the walls built to contain them in Antonia's mind: her father's business associates paying oddly timed condolence calls, commenting on how much she had grown, making her uncomfortable with their knowing smiles and avid stares. At first she hadn't understood. Before she could suppress it, her head filled again with the scents of brandy and cigar smoke and cloying ambergris . . . with the crude, clandestine caresses of men old enough to be her father . . . with the rasping, suggestive whispers that offered to forgive debts in return for her cooperation. She had soon learned what it was they wanted from her, and why.

She had no dowry and was considered unmarriageable.

Men who only months before had been considering a dynastic match between her and their sons now saw her merely as a vessel of male convenience . . . a depository for their lustful urges. And in those two precarious years between her father's death and her marriage, she had learned well that the only protection, the only security, a woman could expect in life was to be found in marriage.

As Antonia read, Dame Hermione Paxton-Fielding removed her reading spectacles and settled her attention on her niece by marriage, taking in her upswept chestnut hair and glowing eyes, and settling on her flushed face. Antonia's dramatic features—long, straight nose, prominent cheekbones, and generously curved mouth—had seemed too strong and her eyes too large and intense when Hermione had first seen her as a young girl of eighteen. But the years had set and finished her face into a work of unique beauty, and now, at the age of twenty-five, her unusual features, womanly shape, and natural wit combined to make her a stunning young woman.

Not, the old lady sighed, that anyone ever noticed. Until now Antonia had shown a perfect genius for staying in the background of society. Except for her charity work and occasional husband-hunting forays into shops and public events with her protégées, Antonia was something of a recluse. If only she would concern herself less with others' lives, Hermione thought wistfully, and more with her own.

"See here, Antonia," she inserted into the next available pause. "Perhaps it would be best to wait awhile. Give yourself a chance to rest, and give the tongues that may wag a chance to tire. After all, this will be your third wedding since Christmas."

"But the only one for a woman under my own roof," Antonia answered defensively. "No one knows of my involvement in the other marriages."

"No one but the brides and grooms, and whoever else they might have told," Hermione corrected, wagging a cautioning finger. "Thirteen, Antonia. You cannot count on their embarrassment to keep them *all* silent forever."

Antonia could feel heat collecting in her face. She closed the magazine with a flourish and held it up in evidence. "If the entire world knew of my activities, I would still do what must be done to help these abandoned and downtrodden women."

"Yes, yes, I know you feel most deeply about it—"

"Oh, my. Just look at the time." Prudence looked down at the watch brooch pinned to her bodice and pushed to her feet, giving her sister a hand up. "Where has the evening gone?"

"Busy day tomorrow, don't you know," Pollyanna muttered, stealing with her sister toward the door. They knew what was coming.

"It is a hideous injustice, a disgrace upon our land." Antonia scarcely took note of the old sisters' retreat or of the click of the door latch behind them. "These are women of good and decent families who grew up expecting to take up their places and live out their lives as wives and mothers. Now vast numbers—as many as half a million—find themselves unneeded, unwanted. *Surplus.* Can you imagine? That insufferable wretch in the *Spectator* called them *surplus women!*"

"An outrage, I agree," Aunt Hermione said, frowning.

"And there wouldn't *be* a surplus of women if the cursed 'empire' didn't send hordes of British men into far-flung corners of God-knows-where to serve its grand notions of majesty." Propping her hands on her waist, she narrowed her eyes. "Or if the selfish wretches left behind would quit smoking cigars, swilling Scotch, and throwing their money after slow horses and fast women. *Bachelors,* auntie . . . those cold-blooded, tightfisted, self-indulgent creatures who refuse to accept their duty to women and their debt to soci—"

"Antonia!" Aunt Hermione interjected, bringing her up short. "You are only one person. Try as you might, my dear, you cannot save them *all.*"

The old lady's voice, filled with familiar warmth and wisdom, poured over Antonia like a balm. She stared at her dear friend and kinswoman, and knew that if anyone understood both the injustice of the situation and her burning desire to rectify it, Aunt Hermione did. Dame Hermione Fielding was a widow four times over, a woman who knew what it was to be alone and adrift in the world.

Since coming to Paxton House several years ago, when her fourth husband died, Hermione had taken Antonia under her wing and guided her through the marriage in which she matured into womanhood, then through the loss of Sir Geoffrey and into widowhood. Because of their shared history, Antonia could guess what came next.

"Dear girl, you are so absorbed in finding husbands for other women and bettering their lives, that you seriously neglect your own." She raised a hand to ward off Antonia's objections. "Hear me out. I simply think you should wait awhile . . . give some thought to your own life before taking on another matrimonial project."

Antonia vented some of the steam in her blood with a hiss. "That again. I tell you, Aunt Hermione, I am perfectly content with my life as it is. *Perfectly.*"

"*Perfectly Content* does not get up in the middle of the night and rummage about in the kitchen making hot milk with brandy. Perfectly Content does not redden her eyes by reading late into the night, then fall asleep in her kippers and eggs the next morning. And Perfectly Content does not come home after every wedding and closet herself away in her room to cry."

The old lady's perceptiveness momentarily disarmed

Antonia. Her rigid posture melted a few degrees. "Weddings are an occasion for tears, after all," she said, raising her chin to compensate for the slide of her defenses. "What should it matter to anyone that I prefer to shed them in private?"

Aunt Hermione sighed. "You miss the point, my dear. There is more to life than cats, aging widows, and rescue work. When I was your age, I had lived on three continents, buried two husbands, and was being courted by every cock-o'-the-walk in London. I was determined to drain every drop of life I could from this mortal cup . . . attending soirees, staying out until dawn, chatting up the prime minister, and playing footsie with ambassadors under tables. . . ."

"I have no desire to play footsie with ambassadors."

"Nor with anyone else, I take it," her aunt said with an aggrieved expression.

Antonia felt her face redden. "Footsie" was something she refused to discuss with anyone, even Aunt Hermione. Forcing a glare at her insightful old aunt, she turned away to the window and pushed back the lace curtain to stare down into the gaslit boulevard below.

"Geoffrey would have wanted you to get on with your life, Antonia."

"Sir Geoffrey would have approved of my efforts, probably even helped me." A spark flashed in her eyes. "He undertook a bit of rescue work himself, remember."

It was true. And the subject of his noble efforts, they both knew, had been none other than Antonia herself.

While Antonia's only living uncle chafed under the burden of having her added to his household and looked the other way while his male cronies made indecent overtures to her, Sir Geoffrey Paxton—a man of substance and impeccable character—had quietly stepped out of the shadowy circle of her father's business associates to offer her his support and protection . . . an offer that could only be accepted within the framework of marriage. Thus rescued from the life of a demimondaine, or of genteel servitude as an unmarriageable poor relation, Antonia had become a bride at eighteen, and a widow at the age of twenty-two. And since her husband's death, three years past, she had devoted herself to rescuing other women the way she had once been rescued . . . by marriage.

"Well, at least give some thought to putting this mourning business aside." Aunt Hermione tried yet another route. "All this wearisome black and gray and purple—it's quite oppressive. You cannot stay cooped up in this house forever, Toni. You need to get out and about." She flung up a hand in a carefree gesture. "Life is perilously short, my dear."

Antonia turned it over in her mind as she searched the determined look in her aunt's aged but undimmed eyes. This was not the first, nor would it be the last, of Hermione's appeals. The old dear worried about her, she knew, but she couldn't allow Aunt Hermione's grand but impractical notions of life to interfere with her work. After a moment she hit upon what she deemed an acceptable compromise.

"You may be right, Auntie. Perhaps I have been keeping too close to the house." With a mischievous smile she swayed back to the table and poured herself another glass of champagne, raising it in salute to the old lady's suggestion. "The debate on the Deceased Wife's Sister Bill will begin in Parliament soon. Perhaps I'll just go along to Westminster to watch the proceedings." Her smile became a wicked little laugh. "And make sure the gentlemen members do the right thing."

Hermione frowned.

"Oh, dear."

Chapter

2

_____

"Something ought to be done about that woman," Sir Henry Peckenpaugh declared, drawing nods and murmurs from a circle of gentlemen seated in the noisy bar of the renowned White's Club on St. James Street.

"Here, here!" came endorsements from every man present.

It was late in the evening; stale cigar smoke, tension, and the thick redolence of expensive liquors permeated the mahogany-paneled room. In one corner of the bar, under a gaslight, six members had gathered at a table to commiserate the demise of yet another cherished bachelorhood. Bertrand Howard, the dispirited groom, sat with his hands wrapped around a thick crystal tumbler filled with the club's most venerable Scotch. His face was drawn, his eyes listless, and his shoulders sloped in uncharacteristic resignation. He was the man single-handedly responsible for enforcing the Board of Trade's standards of weights and measures throughout the rough world of the London docks, yet here he sat, reduced to a despondent lump by the thought of his nuptials on the morrow.

The men who had gathered to give him a proper send-off watched his dread with genuine sympathy. They knew the pain of saying farewell to freedom and the unencumbered pleasures of the single life, for each of the five had himself been wed within the last three years . . . each to a widow under the patronage of the infamous Lady Antonia Paxton.

"She's a menace, pure and simple," portly Sir Albert Everstone declared, punctuating each word with a jab of his Havana cigar. "A plague upon the future of men everywhere."

"Just when you're all set in a nice, cozy nest," Lord Carter Woolworth said, staring into his glass, but seeing some vividly remembered scene in his mind, "she swoops down on you like the avenging angel of matrimony and—"

He halted; there was no need to say more. They never spoke of it outright. It wouldn't have been gentlemanly for a man to admit untoward circumstances surrounding something so intimately associated with his honor as his marriage. The words "widow" and "Lady Antonia," spoken in association with a man's upcoming nuptials, were all that was necessary to communicate volumes to one who had experienced a similar fate. And in the way of men who suffer together, a bond of brotherhood had developed among her victims at White's.

They shifted in their seats, blew clouds of smoke, and downed searing bolts of whiskey as the clock above the bar ticked away the moments toward dawn.

"I suppose it's only fitting that she always wears black," phlegmatic Basil Trueblood said wearily. He propped an impeccably clad elbow on the scarred tabletop and set his chin on his fist. "I understand it's the customary color for executioners."

Grimacelike smiles acknowledged the dark humor, but more than one finger tugged surreptitiously at a starched collar.

"I say, suppose we get our chaps in the Commons to introduce a bill making it a capital offense to conspire against a man's bachelorhood," Lord Richard Searle proposed, gesturing with his glass.

"Wouldn't help old Howard, here." Everstone gave the overshot bridegroom a cuff on the shoulder that set him swaying. "He's already trapped and trussed and ready for the roasting."

"True. It's too late for the lot of us," Peckenpaugh grumbled. "We've all had to pay our cursed fines to the Bachelor's Club already. But we might find a way to salvage our younger brethren who have not yet been caught in the nuptial noose. A man has a duty to posterity, after all."

"The best thing we could do for posterity would be to put the diabolical Lady Matrimonia out of business . . . get rid of her," Woolworth declared.

"Here, here!" Searle raised his glass and the others joined him.

It was as if the burn of the Scotch and cognac somehow seared Woolworth's words into their sodden minds. By the time they lowered their glasses, the idea had seized their thoughts and sobered their vision. *Get rid of her.* Each of them was suddenly savoring the delicious possibility of revenge in his mind. Was it possible?

"There ought to be some way to put her in her place," Searle mused.

"Some way to make her suffer as we have," Trueblood said with a sigh.

"Humph!" Everstone blew a stream of smoke and rocked forward in his chair. "She ought to be leg-shackled like the lot of us. Find a fiend as foul as herself and chain her up with him for life. Some unscrupulous cad . . . a real blighter."

"As fitting as that might be," Lord Woolworth said, his eyes heating, "I cannot help wishing for a more personal bit of satisfaction."

"Don't we all," Peckenpaugh agreed. "Damme if I

wouldn't give a year's winnings to catch her with *her* drawers down, in some fellow's bed."

Searle hooted a laugh. "The Dragon of Decency in a man's bed? Perish the thought!"

But the thought didn't perish, it lingered. And as the clock ticked relentlessly on, it blossomed into an idea.

"Lady Matrimonia caught with a man," Woolworth said, contemplating it.

"Good God, yes. Perfect bit of revenge. But where would we find a man jack capable of taking her on and then taking her down?" Everstone demanded, rubbing his chin. "He would have to look like an archangel and have the soul of a demon . . . a bloke who despises women every bit as much as she hates men."

There was a small commotion at the far end of the bar, and Basil Trueblood lifted his languid gaze above their circle to see what was happening. A new arrival was being greeted in hearty tones. Blinking and squinting through the haze, Trueblood made out the contours of an angular face, a pair of handsome dark eyes, and a fierce, quixotic smile. He sat a bit straighter, drawn to attention by the force of that countenance. He recognized those arrogant features and that elegant frame, which, even in the simple act of walking, communicated a self-possession that caused other men to step aside.

The object of Trueblood's scrutiny made his way past several fellow club members to the empty end of the bar and answered the barman's greeting with an order for a fire-breathing brandy from the club's select stock. Trueblood sat abruptly straighter in his chair and grabbed the forearms of the men seated on either side of him. They followed his directional nod to the gentleman at the bar, then exchanged looks of puzzlement, then speculation. When the others demanded to know what had caught their attention, they turned and also became riveted on the sight of him.

"Landon," Everstone said on an indrawn breath. "Good God."

"Handsome as Lucifer and tough as teakwood," Peckenpaugh declared.

"A pure devil with the women, when he wants to be," Woolworth muttered. "Which isn't too damned often."

"Not susceptible to muslin madness, that's for certain," Searle added, then frowned. "Runs with the radicals in Parliament . . . hot for that female suffrage business and a lot of other bally-nonsense."

"For which reason the queen won't allow him in her sight," Trueblood whispered with rising excitement. "Says he's godless and subversive . . . antimarriage, antimorality, and against the God-given order of things."

Antimarriage.

They exchanged broadening smiles.

Remington Carr, ninth Earl of Landon, gulped his first brandy without giving it its due, an act that would have been considered barbarous any other hour. But at half past twelve in the evening the members of White's generally dispensed with the niceties of indulgence in the club's bar. And it was precisely that promise of license which had brought the well-heeled and controversial earl here this night. He was seeking a uniquely male preserve, a place where men could still exist in all their raw, uncomplicated splendor, a place where the wretched rules of duty, obligation, and above all, *domesticity,* held no sway.

The brandy carried a splendid burn and filled his head with exquisite vapors, which slowly unwound the coil of tension in the middle of him. As he closed his eyes and paid proper respect to a second brandy, the rigid angle of his shoulders softened, and the muscles outlined in his jaw smoothed. The smells of smoke and hard liquor, the drone of male voices, and the familiar surroundings worked a subtle magic on his senses. He took a deep, liberating breath and felt his internal balance tilting back to equilibrium, unaware that he had collected the stares of a half-dozen men seated just behind him.

"I say—Landon!"

He looked up to find Carter Woolworth, eldest son of the old Duke of Eppingham, approaching with a drink-ruddy face and a hearty smile. Remington straightened and accepted his outstretched hand. "Woolworth. It's been a while."

"Too long. But then, when a man goes into the marital harness, he usually finds himself pulling on a very different course from his old school chums," Woolworth said. "Look who's here: remember Albert Everstone and Henry Peckenpaugh . . . ahead of us at Harrow?" He gestured to a group in the corner. "And Richard Searle and Basil Trueblood, they were behind us. And Bertrand Howard there, somewhat younger still. Come join us, Landon. I believe you'll find the company and the conversation most . . . intriguing."

Remington considered it as he glanced at the men who sat poised on the edge of their chairs watching him with undisguised expectation. Something in their urgent desire for his companionship did indeed intrigue him. When Carter Woolworth clapped a hand on his shoulder and steered him toward the group, he allowed himself to be drawn into their company.

One of the group quickly gave up his seat to Remington and went in search of another. From the moment he eased into the leather-clad chair and saw them inching their seats closer, he knew that they wanted something from him. But he was not at all prepared for the subject of their entreaty.

"Bertrand Howard here," Woolworth announced, "is being married on the morrow." He gave the groom a sympathetic clap on the back. "We're here to give him a final send-off."

"Condolences." Remington lifted his glass, wincing at the snared-rabbit look in the groom's eyes.

"Indeed. And all the more so because"—Woolworth leaned closer and the others followed suit—"*it was not his idea.*"

"Well, I should hope not," Remington said, his mouth curling up on one side as he scrutinized the poor wretch who was about to enter a life of matrimonial servitude. "He looks like a fellow with at least a modicum of common sense." He also looked like a Newgate convict approaching the gallows.

"His dismal fate was engineered by a contriving and unscrupulous woman, you see . . . one Lady Antonia Paxton of Piccadilly," Richard Searle announced, watching him for a reaction. When there was none, he added: "The fire-breathing Dragon of Decency."

"The Medusa of Matrimony," Albert Everstone put in bitterly. "So called because one glimpse of her face turns a man into a husband."

"Especially if that man happens to be sitting buck naked in a woman's bed," Henry Peckenpaugh put in, and the rest grumbled agreement.

"She's got a heathen and malicious mind, that woman," Woolworth said, drawing Remington's gaze back to him. "Sets her treacherous hooks for well-fixed men, baits them with curvy widows"—he made casting and reeling motions—"and then pulls in her hapless victims, smooth as silk."

"And there's naught a bloke can do, once he's caught in one of her traps, but marry the treacherous little piece she's saddled him with," Everstone ground out, his jowls reddening. "I tell you, it's right crimi-nal the way that woman operates. Respectable as cottage pie one minute and devious as the devil's backside the next. . . ."

Remington looked from Everstone to Woolworth to Searle, then to Peckenpaugh and Trueblood. They were taking young Howard's demise hard, quite personally, in fact. It occurred to him that only the flare of righteous anger separated the expressions they wore from the haunted look of the despairing bridegroom. Suspicion bloomed in his mind, and as he looked from one to another, it hardened into certainty. He rolled his brandy snifter back and forth in his hands a moment, then leveled a searching look on his old school friend.

"You were married yourself not long ago, eh, Woolworth?"

The young lord understood the question beneath the question. His face grayed and his jaw set like mortar as he visibly weighed the discomfort of the revelation against a desire for revenge on the cause of the alterations in his life. "I was indeed married some months ago"—he paused and swallowed hard—"after a particularly ugly encounter with the Dragon." The confession, in this brotherhood of ruined bachelors, seemed somehow to lighten his soul. He sat straighter.

Remington turned to the middle-aged Everstone. "And you, Sir Albert?"

The portly MP huddled back in his chair, looking like a cornered bulldog. He glanced around the circle as he gathered the courage to say it. "We're all her victims, every man jack of us. And we're resolved that something must be done about the woman."

In the silence that followed Remington felt the weight of their accumulating stares and finally caught a glimpse of what it was they wanted with him. "So you've some nefarious plot in mind, and you're looking for someone to work out your bit of revenge for you." For one brief moment their eyes lighted with hope. He smiled and let them down as gently as possible. "I wish you luck in finding the right man."

"But we thought . . . p-perhaps you . . . ," Woolworth stammered.

"S-since you hate women and marriage so . . . ," Searle tried to finish for him.

Remington's eyes glinted with amusement. "While it is quite true that I despise the archaic institution of marriage, I must disabuse you of the notion that I also despise all women. I hate only those who insist upon being married and maintained by men."

"Which means virtually every woman in the world," Trueblood concluded.

Remington's shoulders quaked with a quiet laugh. "Very nearly. However, there is a new breed of woman about these days, gentlemen. Women of learning and enlightenment who see the inequity and injustice of the old social order and are ready to embrace new ways. They are fully capable of being educated and employed, and are quite capable of supporting themselves entirely. It is my opinion that we should give them the vote . . . give them places on school benches and in offices, mills, and factories . . . and give them some of the wretched headaches of governance, diplomacy, and commerce that we men have grappled with for centuries."

He had scandalized them; he could see it in their shock-blanked expressions. And it was not altogether unexpected. His radical views on women and conventional morality had earned him a place of infamy among the hidebound upper orders. He made to rise, but Woolworth grasped his sleeve to halt him.

"You see?" Woolworth turned to the others with a wistful expression. "He's perfect!"

Remington felt the coil of tension that had recently

loosened in his gut tightening once more as Woolworth coaxed him back into his seat. He cast a longing glance at the door as they began to relate hair-raising tales of the atrocities Lady Antonia had committed against male freedom. But he listened, in spite of himself, and gradually began to picture her in his mind: a sour, overbearing old crone bent on making the rest of the world as miserable as she had probably made Lord Paxton.

"Paxton . . ." He interrupted their diatribe. "I've never heard of a Lord Paxton."

"Her husband wasn't a lord," Trueblood informed him. "The old boy was knighted years ago for amassing indecent piles of money, then having the good sense to be generous with his bribes. Bought himself a lady wife."

"And what does he think of all this?"

"Nothing at all, I'm afraid. He's dead," Woolworth answered. "Living with the Dragon probably killed him."

"She's a widow, then," Remington mused, painting fusty widow's weeds on the grim portrait forming in his mind.

"And she seems to make a specialty of finding husbands for marriageable widows," Searle said with a sullen tone. "No doubt because they are easier to place. A fellow drops his guard with a widow, figuring she's safe, since there are no eagle-eyed mothers or spotless virtue to bother about. And a widow usually knows what sort of 'comforts' a man likes. This Lady Antonia is diabolical, I tell you."

A diabolical woman. Not a particularly rare phenomenon, in Remington Carr's experience. He'd encountered more than his share of them in recent years and had no desire to get mixed up with another, no matter how deserving a cause it might be. For all the pathos and indignation their stories aroused in him, that single word—diabolical—decided him firmly against becoming involved in their scheme.

"If all is as you say, then indeed, something ought to be done about the woman. However, I must decline to help. I already have a number of projects in the works, and my late father's affairs continue to press me."

"See here, Landon, you've got to help us," Peckenpaugh declared. "If this woman is allowed to run loose, you'll look up one day soon and find yourself the last bachelor in London!"

"Sorry, gentlemen. No doubt you'll find another St. George to slay your Dragon."

They looked positively deflated as he downed the last swallow in his goblet and rose. Avoiding their dispirited faces, he turned away and found the club's steward bearing down upon him with a harried expression.

"Your lordship! Thank God." The fellow fairly ran the length of the bar to reach him. "There is a woman here to see you, sir. Most insistent. I offered to open the annex to her, even at this late hour, so that you might receive her there. But she barged past both myself and the night porter and has ensconced herself in *the window*"—he groaned—"right in full view of the street!"

The pain in the steward's expression was genuine. The strategic ground the audacious female had chosen to storm and seize, the famous bow window of White's, which overlooked St. James Street, was both legendary and revered in the world of London clubs. It was the seat from which the famous and infamous of every generation since Charles II had looked down upon those not privileged to taste the society inside. And now both the club and the window had been stormed and breached by a mere female demanding access to *him*.

"Who is she?" he demanded, knowing her identity didn't matter. Whoever she was, at this hour and in the window of White's, she could be only trouble.

"She refuses to give her name or to move until you

agree to see her, your lordship. Says she's prepared to stay all night if necessary." The steward tugged his waistcoat irritably back into place. "And I believe she means it."

Heat crept beneath Remington's starched collar, as one unpleasant possibility occurred to him. "Is she tall, smartly dressed . . . with a voice like a screeching hinge?"

The steward nodded, then curled one side of his nose as if smelling something unpleasant. "If you know this woman, your lordship, please come and see her off the premises before I am compelled to employ more vulgar means of removing her."

Remington did indeed know her. In point of fact, he had been dodging her for two days. She had besieged his house with missives, sent her personal servants to his offices to insist he call upon her, then, late in the day, had arrived in person at his offices, causing him to have to flee down his own back stairs like a thief trying to avoid detection. Notes, messengers, and even her personal appearance at his office he might have withstood with some grace. But to invade his male sanctum, his club. And White's, of all places! Had the harridan no decency at all?

Roiling up out of his well-controlled depths came a surge of righteous anger. If years of dealing with her and the others like her had taught him anything, it was that decency was usually too much to expect of a woman. And this one was worse than most. He was sick to death of her incessant demands, hysterical appeals, and strident dependence. He paid her bills, oversaw her investments, and even pacified the household retainers who had to put up with her. But it was never enough.

Well, this time she had pushed him too far. He fixed the beleaguered steward with narrowed eyes and a taut half smile that contained equal measures of fire and ice.

"Do what you will with the woman, Richards. It is none of my concern."

Turning a shoulder on the steward's confusion, he settled back in his chair and beckoned to the barman, calling
for a new deck of cards and a fresh bottle of Scotch. He met
Woolworth's startled look with a vengeful smile. "It appears I won't be leaving just yet. Cards, gentlemen?"

The steward came running back moments later, ashen
and wringing his hands. "My lord, my lord! That female
person—"

Behind him, above the drone of voices, came the sound
of a woman's scream. Talk in the bar ceased, play in the
billiards room halted, and every breath in both rooms was
bated in shock.

Remington swore mentally, tightened his grip on the
cards in his hand, and ignored her. But the termagant held
an unexpected trump card: his name. "Remington Carr,
how dare you refuse to see me!" she screamed. "I know
you're in there! Let go—unhand me, you thug! Remington,
you cannot abandon me—ohhh—"

Every eye in the bar turned in his direction, and a
general murmur of outrage rose from the far end of the
room. But he braced to weather the humiliation, telling
himself it could not be the first time a scheming female had
penetrated the club's pristine male provinces. He had to
stand his ground and refuse to allow her outrageous behavior to draw him into a public row. There was nothing for it
but to gut out the embarrassment. He took a deep breath
and steeled his tautly stretched nerves.

"Good God," Everstone said, shoving to his feet when
the struggle made it to the door of the bar. "She's got past
Richards—she's headed in here!" Several of his table mates
lurched to their feet, their expressions ranging from fascination to terror.

"Dash it all, Landon," Woolworth demanded, staring
frantically between the fracas in the doorway and Remington. "You must *do* something, man!"

"So I must," Remington said with seething calm, considering the pasteboards in his hand. "I'll have three cards." Adamantly oblivious to the wild tussle going on just thirty feet away, he laid three cards down on the tabletop and waited for the dealer to fulfill his request.

The others gazed, confounded, between the porters grappling with the woman calling Remington's name and his towering indifference to the spectacle. Never in their lives had they seen a more audacious display of coolness under fire. This incident would undoubtedly go down in clubmen's lore along with the time old Lord Glasgow flung a waiter through a window and gruffly told the club secretary to "put him on the bill."

"Well, gentlemen, are we playing or not?" he demanded, seeming decidedly more concerned with the delay of the game than with the potential ruin of his reputation.

Following his lead, they sank back onto their chairs and glanced at each other in amazement. As the shrieks of the interloping female faded toward the street door, their admiration for the unorthodox earl mounted to worshipful proportions. Here, their looks of shared wonder said, was a man who truly knew how to handle women.

But inside that imperturbable facade, dark fires of anger were scarcely being held in check. For months the heat had been building in him, and this degrading little spectacle—the invasion of his last male sanctuary—had provided the final spark to set his raw pride aflame. Suddenly he was molten, churning inside.

"Women, gentlemen, are indolent, manipulative, and unpredictable creatures at best," he said harshly. "They're also expensive and self-absorbed and devious beyond belief. And it really doesn't matter whether you've wedded them or not . . . they'll have their pound of flesh all the same." The fierce glow in his eyes as he lifted his gaze from his cards made his companions stiffen in their seats. "Console yourself with the knowledge that, as married men, you may have escaped the unpleasantness of dealing with aging mistresses. They're the very devil to dispose of."

He picked up three newly dealt cards from the table, but the fury mounting in him made it all but impossible to focus on his hand. He was seized by an overwhelming urge to strike back, to do something to right the balance scales in him that had been knocked askance yet again by a woman's volatile and demanding nature. He had to do something, to strike a blow for manhood as well as for himself. And when he looked up, he read in the wan and hopeful faces of that company of ruined bachelors the opportunity to do exactly that.

Lady Antonia. A devious and contriving woman. A plague upon the freedom of mankind. A woman in dire need of a comeuppance.

"So, Woolworth," he said, taking a deep breath and feeling fresh resolve pour through his tense frame, relaxing it. "Just what did you have in mind for our diabolical Lady Antonia?"

Chapter

3

The atmosphere was charged in the House of Commons that sultry afternoon in mid-May. The Gothic arch windows set high in the walls had been opened to provide ventilation, but the only air stirring in the great hall came from the heated blasts of the speakers on the main floor itself. The opposing ranks of green leather benches that lined the main floor were crammed with black-coated members, all exercising the long-standing MP prerogative of commenting on the recognized speaker's parentage and sanity, as well as his oratorical style and the substance of his discourse.

Debate on the controversial Deceased Wife's Sister Bill was under way, and tempers were rising apace with the temperature in the stuffy chamber. The measure was an attempt to change the legal code to permit marriage between a man and his deceased wife's sister, a degree of relation both the Church and civil authority had decreed too close to permit a conjugal union. The progressive element in the Commons ranted that the "sister prohibition" was a relic of Old Testament days in which the vice of concubinage was rampant, and that it was badly outdated. The conservatives raved that sin was sin, whatever the era, and that if moral law was to be tampered with, the Ten Commandments would soon be reduced to the Ten Suggestions and the whole empire would go sliding straight into the water pipe.

Neither side bothered to apologize for its scandalous language, even though the gallery that ringed the upper walls of the chamber was overflowing with observers, a number of whom were female. If women took an un-feminine interest in things governmental, both liberals and conservatives agreed, then they had to expect to be shocked from time to time. Still, in deference to those women who might have come with more appropriate *social* motives—say, to hear a husband's speech or to flirt with an eligible MP after the session—a wooden screen had been erected along one side of the gallery to shield the fairer members of the weaker sex.

It was behind that screen of spindles that Antonia Paxton sat, chafing at the restricted view and at the nonsense being bandied about on the floor below. Wielding her fan vigorously with one hand, she dabbed her heated face with the handkerchief in the other. She had chosen to wear her black-trimmed purple silk with its cuirass bodice, stove-pipe skirt, and fashionable bustle, and as the afternoon wore on, she began to feel every prickly lump in her horse-hair-padded bustle and each unyielding stay in her corset. It was a struggle to keep the heat of the chamber and her discomfort from distracting her from her purpose in being there.

She had come to observe the progress of the bill and to take note of which members of the House might be considered friends of the measure, and which were sworn enemies. A fortnight ago she had attended one of the parliamentary hearings on the bill and had come away from the proceedings incensed by many of the members' attitudes toward marriage. As a result she had written impassioned letters to key members of the House of Commons and had importuned one of her former protégées whose husband was an MP to secure gallery passes for her.

She bit her lip and curled her fingers around the railing of the gallery, wishing she could demand to be recognized and speak on behalf of the women she knew would be securely married if not for that cruel and antiquated law. But the smells of stale smoke and exercised male heat billowing up from below underscored the fact that this was an exclusively male arena, and that however informed or powerful a woman's views, she had to rely upon a man to express them here. The combination of her growing personal and political discomfort brought her to the edge of her nerves.

"If old Pickering utters one more 'thou shalt not,' I swear I shall climb out of this balcony and have at him with my purse," she muttered from between gritted teeth. Rearranging herself yet again on her hard seat, she cast a glance at Aunt Hermione, who sat beside her wearing a look of wilted forbearance. "The ripe old cod. Just look at him." With a nod she directed her aunt's gaze to the front row of the Opposition bench, where a portly, bulbous-featured old fellow sat looking like a dyspeptic bulldog.

"Disgraceful," Hermione agreed, tugging at her bonnet ribbons.

When Sir Jerome rolled to his feet yet again, Hermione groaned audibly and Antonia narrowed her eyes and fingered the chain handle of the handbag in her lap. But the old knight yielded the floor to a hitherto unheard speaker, a young backbencher named Shelburne, who proceeded to take the debate in an alarming new direction.

"One reason put forth in support of this vile bit of legislation," the new speaker intoned, "is that permitting marriage between a man and his deceased wife's sister would be a significant step toward reducing the problem of surplus women."

Surplus women. That hideous term again. Antonia fought an almost irresistible urge to throw her purse over the railing at him.

"But we cannot afford to change our law to suit the whims and caprices of social fortune." He grasped his lapels and inflated his chest as he warmed to his subject. "We cannot abandon our most sacred principles of morality for the sake of providing husbands for a few women, no matter how poor and wretched the creatures may be."

There was a wave of reaction: "here, here's" mingled with hoots of derision and rumbles of consternation. "I cannot speak to the fine theological points of this matter. But I can and must speak to the fact that there are better ways to deal with the unsavory imbalance in the numbers of eligible men and women. Let me read to you the suggestions of one more learned than I in this matter: Lord Remington Carr, Earl of Landon." He lifted a magazine and adopted an oratorical stance.

"Lord Carr writes in *Blackwood's Magazine* this month: 'It has been suggested that one way of dealing with the problem of surplus women is to gather them up and transport them to the colonies, where they would find usefulness as wives and companions of the men on the frontiers of the empire. But there is no evidence that these noble men laboring to enlarge British fortunes abroad are pining for marriage. Indeed, many of them may have fled England's shores to avoid being trapped in that onerous and inequitable union.' "

Antonia's heart began to pound and her eyes burned dryly as she stared at the speaker without blinking. Onerous . . . inequitable . . . how dare he speak about marriage so? Then the name of the author of those words righted in her mind. It was Remington Carr, Earl of Landon —author of that vile, antimarriage piece she had read two months ago in the *Spectator,* and also of a series of articles demanding that women be given the vote, which had appeared in the *Telegraph* over the last three weeks. It was he who had coined that noxious phrase "surplus women." Now even the renowned *Blackwood's* was printing his scurrilous ramblings!

" 'Instead' "—the young MP read on—" 'I venture to offer a modest proposal for dealing with spinsters, widows, and other surplus women. These unfortunates have been duped by the popular, oversentimentalized ideals of Home and Family into believing that they are entitled to the support and status of their own homes—to be provided by men. But most of these women shall never marry, never preside over a home of their own. And even if they could, marriage is no guarantee of security. Nowhere is this more painfully obvious than in the case of *widows*, those pathetic women who have learned firsthand the folly of depending on another for the security and substance of their lives. The false ideal of marriage is as much a trap for these poor, deluded women as it is for the unhappy men who find themselves snared in it.

" 'Revision of the marriage laws is no answer to the problem of our surfeit of women. I propose, instead, that these unattached females who languish about the landscape be reeducated in the realities of life. They could be trained in a trade or craft and put to work at an honorable wage, so that they may be made self-supporting. This would have the effects of enhancing the general productivity, of providing an inexpensive new source of labor, and of reassigning the burden of their care from the male members of society to their own shoulders, where it rightly belongs. These women have most certainly been trained for *dependence* by our societal myths. Why should they not be retrained for *independence* by our societal truths?' "

The young MP went on reading and speaking, but past that point—"trained for dependence"—Antonia heard only one word in three. Marriage and the ideal of the loving family a hoax? Widows called pathetic, dependent, and a burden to others? Women should be forced into shops and factories and mills and offices . . . required to support themselves by all manner of unseemly labor? Dear God, what would happen to the families? the homes? the children?

The loathsome earl was proposing nothing less than an assault upon the institutions of Home and Family! The old wretch would dispense with marriage altogether, if he could—the devil take children, decency, charity, humanity, and all other such worthy products of wedlock and family life!

Through a deepening haze of anger, she watched young Shelburne sit down with a satisfied expression while a storm of controversy erupted around him. The other members of the House jolted to their feet, some outraged, some cheering—both sides spoiling for a fight in the volatile atmosphere.

The shouting and fist shaking accelerated and soon got so out of hand that the Speaker was unable to hammer the chamber back to order. He called for the Doorkeeper and the Serjeant at Arms, and for a moment it looked as if full fisticuffs would break out. Then, abruptly, the Government forces began to make their way to the doors and a number of the Opposition soon followed, effectively tabling the bill.

The turmoil in the gallery penetrated Antonia's shock. She had come here to learn who supported the marriage bill and who opposed it. Well, she certainly had learned. That wretched earl, with his hateful views on women and marriage, was being used as a sort of spokesman for the antireform forces! She was on her feet in a flash, hauling Aunt Hermione up and dragging her across numerous feet and through a dozen apologies on the way to the nearest exit. When they reached the corridor, Hermione pulled back against Antonia's grip and scowled at the sight of the fire in her eyes.

"Merciful heavens, Antonia! What do you think you are doing?"

"I intend to have a word or two with that insufferable young pup," she declared, pulling Hermione toward the stairs once more. "Or perhaps several words."

"Oh, dear."

They hurried down the steps ahead of the spectators pouring out of the gallery. But once on the main floor, they found the entrance to the Commons Lobby blocked by the gentlemen ushers. They hurried along the side corridor toward the Central Lobby and were caught up in a crush of members and lobby correspondents from a number of the leading newspapers emerging from the Commons corridor. Antonia stood on her toes and craned her neck to locate her quarry across the great hall. He was smiling and shaking hands, receiving what appeared to be congratulations from a half-dozen elder members of the House. Frantic that he would get away, she fixed him in her sights and set a course for him, trundling Hermione along with her.

"Quite a maiden speech, Shelburne," a senior-looking MP was saying when she arrived.

"Quite full of inaccuracies and impertinences, you mean," she declared as she halted behind him and hurriedly resettled her tailored, high-crowned hat back to its businesslike angle. Young Shelburne and his fellow party members turned with frowns, which changed to either male interest or male indignation at the sight of her.

"I beg your pardon, madam," Shelburne said, scowling down his nose. "I was neither inaccurate nor impertinent in my speech. The quotations were read verbatim, and with the greatest respect for the tradition of debate and the company of my fellow members."

"Not, however, with any respect for the subjects of that

insulting article," she countered, drawing herself up straight and narrowing her eyes. Hermione, beside her, retreated a half step, knowing what was promised in that fiery look. "By reading such refuse in these hallowed halls, sir, you have affronted all womanhood. This day you have accused women of being stupid, indolent, incapable hangers-on who have no dignity and no rightful place in the home."

In defiance of the male power and prerogative embodied in that wall of serge coat fronts and starched shirts, she took a step closer. To her satisfaction young Shelburne's cocky smile faded, and he glanced at his friends and colleagues.

"According to you, the sacred ideal of hearth and home is nothing but a hoax perpetrated upon pathetic, weakminded females," she continued. "In one fell swoop you have made a mockery of marriage and sneered at the plight of the unfortunate."

The gradual rise of her voice and the sardonic laughter of Shelburne's friends attracted the notice of two men standing nearby, dressed in tasteless plaid wool jackets and large bowler hats, which had paper of some sort stuck in the brim. They scrutinized the young MP, then Antonia's elegantly clad form and state of agitation. Drawing writing pads out of their pockets and pencils from above their ears, they edged closer to hear what was being said.

"You accuse me falsely, madam." Shelburne stiffened and splayed a protective hand over his expensive tucked shirtfront. "I mocked no one. I merely quoted the words of an eminent peer, Lord Remington Carr, regarding—"

"The words of a scandalous radical who holds women in contempt and who assails the moral precepts of marriage and family that are the very foundation of our society." Her expression sharpened with disdain. "A fine sort to model yourself upon, sir. You should go far in politics."

"I assure you, madam, it was never my intent to defame women." Shelburne's tone lost all its condescension. "I strongly believe that this marriage bill is not an acceptable means to right the imbalance in the sexes. And Lord Carr is a most eloquent spokesman. . . ."

"Lord Carr is a callous, unfeeling bore who masquerades as a freethinker," she said, inching forward and tightening her grip on the handle of her purse. "And from the virulence of his diatribes against marriage, he is undoubtedly a *freelover* as well . . . a man morally bankrupt and utterly self-absorbed . . . totally without regard for a higher moral authority!"

Several throats cleared, and gazes that had been riveted on her suddenly flickered to something or someone just out of her range of vision.

"She's absolutely right on that last part, you know," a resonant male voice inserted. "He is totally without regard for any moral authority . . . higher than his own common sense."

Sensing a possible ally, Antonia glanced in the direction of that voice, and her gaze caught on a tall, broad-shouldered man dressed in an impeccable charcoal-gray suit, with an elegant dove-gray vest, silver-striped cravat, and black silk top hat. He was carrying a gold headed walking stick and a pair of kid gloves that perfectly matched his vest. And when her gaze slid upward, he was wearing an expression of cool amusement . . . on the most devastatingly handsome face she had ever seen.

His angular, exquisitely carved features somehow combined unequivocal masculinity with aristocratic elegance. He had broad cheekbones, deep-set eyes, and a boldly curved mouth that made her suddenly, intensely aware of her own.

"As to the balance in his moral bank account, I doubt anyone this side of heaven's gate can truly know it," the gentleman continued, glancing at the others in a way that communicated something inscrutably male. "But I can say with some certainty that he has never found love *free*. Like most men, he has paid handsomely for his pleasures."

As the others chuckled, he smiled, an effortless and assured expression that was somehow both alluring and annoying. Alluring? She stiffened and fought the stubborn fascination of her senses. Clearly this was no ally.

"I am sure that Lord Carr, like most gentlemen of leisure, has *paid* far less than have the women of his acquaintance," she countered, pointedly ignoring his provocative reference to purchasing physical pleasures. "Not content with harassing and misusing the women in his immediate circle, he now seeks to spread his contempt for women and marriage to the rest of his countrymen as well."

"Misuses his women, does he?" the gentleman said, raising an eyebrow in the direction of the others, who were staring at him in abject fascination. "That's one charge I've never heard brought against him. He's a known suffragist . . . favors the vote for women and giving them opportunity to work."

"What he favors is giving them the boot . . . straight into the street," she said, turning to face him squarely and finding her gaze drawn to his eyes, which were fixed intently on her. Dark eyes. Liquid. Absorbing. Her knees felt a little strange, and of their own will her fingers slid to the row of buttons down the front of her jacket. "He would force women to abandon their homes and hearths, and drive them out into grueling labor they are ill suited for. He'd have them digging in coal pits, carrying hod, hauling fish nets, and operating vile machinery of all sorts."

"Ahhh." He raised a long, well-tapered finger, and she couldn't help noticing the evenness of his teeth as he smiled. "But women *already* do all those things—work in Welsh coal pits, carry brickyard hod, work on fishing boats, and operate mechanical marvels in factories. And they work in offices and hospitals and shops, as well."

Antonia stiffened, knowing what he said was true. "Not *ladies,*" was her only rebuttal. "Only those poor women who are not fortunate enough to have a home and family of their own. Or women whose families were left destitute by feckless men and cruel misfortune. A woman's place is in the home, sir. And a man's place is to provide that home."

"Whether he wishes to or not," he stated, clarifying her position.

"We are all born to a duty and a place ordained by a higher power," she retorted. "Few of us get to choose our *lot* in life."

"Then how convenient it is that a woman's *lot* is to be born to security and ease . . . to be waited upon hand and foot and to issue orders to the rest of humanity." He chuckled at the way her chin came up; then he glanced knowingly at young Shelburne and his parliamentary cohorts. "I would dearly love to continue this fascinating debate, madam, but I am seriously overdue for an appointment. If, perchance, a part of your *lot* has been to receive an invitation from Lord and Lady Ellingson for their soiree tomorrow evening, then perhaps we can take it up there."

Without waiting for a response, he touched the brim of his hat—"Madam"—then turned a nod toward the wide-eyed MP's behind her and strode off.

She came to her senses a moment later, staring at his broad back and long, self-assured stride, and feeling irritable at having a ripening debate cut off so precipitously by a handsome, enigmatic stranger. Blushing, and grateful for the hat veil that concealed it, she turned back to Shelburne.

"You see how this idiocy spreads? Because of your airing of those wretched articles, everyone will soon be an expert on Lord Carr's despicable opinions!"

Young Shelburne blinked, then grinned. "That fellow

should be an expert on the earl's opinions." He nodded after the disappearing gentleman. "That was Remington Carr himself."

The Earl of Landon.

Himself.

Antonia drew a sharp breath she couldn't seem to expel, then turned on her heel and bumped into one of the news writers lurking behind her. She gritted out an "Excuse me," seized Aunt Hermione's arm in hers, and sailed for the doors with the sound of muffled male laughter falling at her back.

Lord Remington Carr. The wretch had just sauntered up and made a royal fool of her. Every inch of her skin felt as if it was on fire by the time they reached the street.

They were in the cab and halfway home before she could overcome her embarrassment enough to think clearly about it, and when she did, her humiliation only deepened. From reading the earl's infuriating articles and hearing his hostile views on women and marriage, she had somehow developed a picture in her mind of a stodgy, embittered old man whose suits for ladies' hands had been resoundingly rejected in his youth. Wealthy, educated, and unmarriageable himself, she decided, he had turned his own romantic failures into a vengeful social crusade against both women and marriage. He was a thoroughly dismal human being: miserly, miserable, and warped by a life filled with disappointments.

Nothing she had read or heard had prepared her for *tall, dark, and elegant,* for liquid eyes and an intriguing smile, or for gentlemanly manners and exquisite taste in clothing. And the fact that she was thinking of him in such terms—elegant and gentlemanly—infuriated her.

"He should be a warty old toad," she muttered aloud, glaring at the vision of his memorable half smile, which lingered in her mind.

"What?"

When she looked up, Aunt Hermione was staring at her with that annoyingly perceptive gaze, and it was no use denying where her thoughts had been.

"I said the *out*side should match the *in*," she declared. "It ought to be a law."

"He was handsome, wasn't he?" Hermione said a bit wistfully.

"*Your* word, not mine," she said, feeling a betraying heat creeping back into her cheeks. But "handsome" was the perfect word to describe the insufferable earl, and some unruly part of her was reacting massively to the fact. Alarmed, she took hold of herself and told herself that he was the enemy, no matter what he looked like. As she sorted through the encounter, she came to his last unsettling words just as Aunt Hermione commented on them.

"You're going, of course." It was both a question and a statement.

"Going where?" Antonia asked with a deepening frown that she supposed was probably transparent to the old woman.

"To the Ellingsons' party, where else? You know Constance Ellingson has been after you for the last two years to attend one of their evening dos. Just send her a note and you'll be on the list"—she waved a hand—"as simple as that."

"Why on earth would I want to go to one of her interminable evenings?"

Aunt Hermione smiled, knowing that she had the perfect goad. "Why, to put the wretched earl in his place, of course. He needs to be taught a thing or two about women and marriage, and who better to do it than you?" It was then that Antonia finally realized that Hermione's angelic face hid a devious streak. "And knowing you as I do," the old lady continued sweetly, confirming it, "I know that you simply will not allow such a challenge to go unanswered."

A challenge. Antonia expelled a full breath at last and settled back on the worn leather seat to look out the cab window. That was exactly what the high-handed earl had issued her: a challenge. He had allowed her to rail on humiliatingly against him, then had cut her off and used her own choice of words to toss down a gauntlet that was part invitation, part ultimatum. To continue the debate, she had to comply with his terms: meet him at the Ellingsons' soiree.

She was incensed by his arrogance and was burning to even the score publicly for the humiliation he had just caused her. But was going to the Ellingsons to confront him a courageous or a foolhardy thing to do? If she went, would she find some way to discredit him and his radical views of marriage and the place of women, or would she find herself staring witlessly at his absorbing eyes and handsome mouth again?

Moments later she came to her senses, sitting in the motionless cab and staring at a hand that was extended to her through the sunlit opening of the door. Hermione had already dismounted the cab, and the driver was waiting to help her step down. For one crazy instant, as she looked up, she suffered the impression that the driver's hand belonged to someone else and beckoned to something far riskier than the street outside her doorstep.

A shiver of anticipation ran through her shoulders and left her tingling in two spots that caused her eyes to widen. She looked down at the tightly buttoned front of her bodice, then jerked her face up.

By the time her feet touched the paving bricks beside the steps leading to the broad front doors of her house, her decision was made. And as she paid the driver and mounted the steps, she couldn't say if the unsettling feeling seeping through her was excitement or dread.

As Antonia fled Westminster in high dudgeon, Shelburne and his colleagues had started for the Smoking Room, intent on a round of celebratory drinks. One of the news writers scurried along beside the young MP, who recognized him and quickened his step. The writer matched his haste, mentally measuring the distance to the Smoking-Room door, where he would lose access to the MP. Correspondents were barred from entry into that privileged territory.

"Fine speech, Mr. Shelburne," the writer said in an ingratiating tone.

"As if you would know the difference. Go away, Fitch," Shelburne said, glancing away irritably.

"Who was the ladybird?" Rupert Fitch, correspondent for the sensational and widely read *Gaflinger's Gazette,* asked in breathy, urgent tones. "The one in purple, who near chewed yer ears off?" he prompted. When there was no response, he added, "A fiery little thing, eh? Seems to hate the Ladies' Man, right enough."

The "Ladies' Man" was a title bestowed upon Remington Carr by none other than Rupert Fitch himself. The news writer had long ago decided that a wealthy blue blood who went against both prevailing political winds and royal favor to demand women's political and economic rights might make for interesting reading. In the florid and highly competitive world of Fleet Street journalism, a news writer had to make the most of every opportunity for a juicy byline. Of late he had taken a more intense interest in the radical earl's activities, hoping that he would do something more scandalous than write suffragist magazine articles and work to seat the radical atheist Bradlaugh in the Commons.

When Shelburne glared at him, Fitch apparently took it as a sign of encouragement. He leaned closer and his voice dropped to a wicked ooze. "What's Landon done to 'er? Give 'er the jilt? Give 'er the slip? What?"

Shelburne gave him the shoulder and strode on until he reached the door to the Smoking Room. There he slowed, then paused with a canny look and waved his colleagues through the door ahead of him. Turning to the relentless little muckraker, he looked down his nose at the fellow's ill-fit collar and gin-flushed complexion.

"All right, here's a tidbit for you, Fitch. The ladybird was indeed a lady. Lady Antonia Paxton . . . wealthy widow, do-gooder, and defender of marriage and the sanctity of the home." His expression warmed at the sight of wheels turning in the newsman's mind. On impulse he greased the gears that turned them. "But being a gentleman, I must stop there and leave it to you to discover what they truly are to one another."

Fitch's ferret-quick eyes narrowed and his mouth quirked up at one corner.

"I owe ye one, Mr. Shelburne."

 Night rolled softly over the city. The air had been cleared by a gentle afternoon shower, making it a perfect evening to open the terrace doors and let the perfume of the gardens drift in on the breeze. Men in swallowtail coats and ladies in delicate silk gowns arrived at the Ellingsons' great house on Park Lane in open calashes and stylish barouche coaches. Inside, they moved through the gilt and mahogany splendor of the drawing rooms and into a long glass conservatory, which opened onto ranks of flower-covered terraces.

Into that gathering of wealth and privilege stepped Remington Carr, devastatingly turned out in his best evening dress, and ready for battle. As he made his way through the rooms, heads turned and tongues wagged behind feathered fans and potted palms. He did not appear often at social gatherings, and his presence, even at liberal Lord Ellingson's house, was cause for speculation. He took a hand here and there in greeting, and met an occasional eye, but his attention was trained on the search for what he remembered of the infamous Lady Antonia Paxton.

It had been an unpleasant surprise that afternoon to have Carter Woolworth point out to him a trim, well-dressed figure across the Central Lobby at Westminster. And as he approached her, his surprise had turned to confusion. From the various descriptions her victims had supplied him—a vulture, a charging rhino, a jackal, a fire-breathing dragon—he had expected something more on the order of a zoological specimen than a woman. Something with a few more tusks or talons. At the very least, someone a decade or two older and twenty or thirty stones heavier.

He was unsettled to find her in mere womanly form and dressed in fashionable silk rather than leathery hide or scales. And as he surveyed her attractive figure and heard her pleasant voice—no roar or hiss there—he felt an even stronger rustle of disquiet. She was younger and more feminine than he had anticipated and, as a result, was probably a good bit more dangerous as well.

It was precisely that thought which saved him. Dangerous. She was a diabolical woman, and he knew how to handle them.

He had learned of her interest in the Deceased Wife's Sister Bill from Sir Albert Everstone, who had seen her at parliamentary hearings on the measure and whose wife she had approached for gallery passes. It was a relatively small matter to get young Shelburne to read from his recent piece in *Blackwood's*, and he felt reasonably sure that his inflammatory words would catch her notice and raise her ire. His trap was set.

And she had charged straight into it, seeking out Shelburne right away to deliver him a set-down. All he had needed to do was engage her attention and throw down the gauntlet. Now it remained to be seen if she was proud enough or angry enough to pick it up. A servant approached with a tray of champagne, and as he chose a goblet and sipped, he smiled to himself. She would pick it up; he was sure of it. And the instant she stooped to conquer, she was his.

A quarter of an hour later he looked up from having a word with his host and caught a glimpse of a woman in black-edged purple across the drawing room, speaking with his hostess. As if in response to his intensifying stare, they turned in his direction, and he felt a brief surge of triumph. It was the dragon. It had to be; she was the right size and shape, and dressed in half-mourning colors.

His smile froze. She was also all motion and curves . . . swathed in layers of purple moire that reacted in glorious alchemy with the candlelight to make her seem to shimmer across the floor and set blue-crimson lights in her auburn hair. There was no lace on her gown, no ribbons, no flounces . . . only elegant watered silk trimmed with black velvet at the modest scooped neckline and short puffed sleeves. Her slender arms were covered by long black gloves, and she wore a black velvet ribbon at her throat with a carved ebony cameo dangling from it. Bracing internally, he looked up.

He was not at all prepared for that clear, extravagant heart of a face, with its high cheekbones, straight nose, and full, expressive mouth that, even drawn tight with disapproval, bore the promise of a tantalizing sensual pout.

It was a face more likely to stop a heart than a clock.

Could this possibly be the fabled Dragon of Decency? She didn't look like the type to plant curvy widows in a man's bed, then burst through the door breathing sanctimonious fire. But then—he rescued his reeling thoughts—treachery came in all sizes and shapes. Concentrating on her entrancing blue eyes, he mentally set aside their allure and discovered in them cool, disturbing lights . . . beacons warning of intelligence, strong opinions, and righteous determination . . . a dangerous combination in a woman.

And he felt a curious surge of excitement at the prospect of clipping the wings of this avenging angel of matrimony.

.   .   .

"I was beginning to despair of you, my dear," Lady Constance had said, slipping her arm through Antonia's and pulling her through the drawing room and toward the conservatory, where chairs had been erected for the musical program of the evening. "We're almost ready for Madame DuPont." She raised her gaze above the guests moving around them toward the garden room, to look for a servant bearing refreshments. "Now, what can I get you before we join the others for the musicale?"

"A proper introduction to that gentleman over there," Antonia said after a moment's hesitation. She cast a discreet nod toward a striking male figure in the doorway. "That is the Earl of Landon, is it not?"

She didn't need an answer; his dark hair, angular features, and deep-set eyes were instantly recognizable, as was the insufferable self-assurance of his stance. He wore traditional male evening wear: a black swallowtail coat, white-on-white brocade vest, matching white silk tie, and slim-fitting black trousers with satin piping. But on him the uniform of the upper-crust male seemed somehow different, more imposing.

Scrutinizing him, she realized that it was the fit of his garments that made the difference; his shoulders were just a bit too broad to be purely fashionable, and his exquisitely tailored evening coat had been cut to minimize them, with only partial success. It wasn't the clothes, then, it was the shape of the man inside them that she had found so impressive. And the fact that in her mind she had just separated him from his clothing appalled her.

"Landon? You cannot be serious." Lady Constance stared at her in surprise. Antonia gave her a determined look, and, intrigued by the volatile possibilities in such a meeting, Lady Constance promptly escorted her to the conservatory doors and introduced her.

"A pleasure, Lady Antonia," Remington said, his eyes

lighting as he took her stiffly offered hand a bit too warmly and held it a bit too long.

When he bowed his head over their joined hands, then raised his gaze to her, she felt her heart give an extra thud in her chest. At such close range his clear brown eyes were even more devastating than she remembered; meeting them felt like being immersed in warm chocolate. And his faint, knowing smile said that he was fully aware of their effect on women.

"Then the pleasure is all yours, sir," she said, abruptly withdrawing her hand and scrambling for something to say. "I am here to enjoy the music and then to set you straight on a number of matters concerning the marriage bill before Parliament. I trust you will make yourself available."

He blinked, appearing surprised by her bluntness, then smiled in a way that proclaimed to all watching that he was indulging her. "As you wish, Lady Antonia. I shall make myself available to you . . . anytime you say."

The suggestive tone of his comment raised an alarm in her as she turned away. But it wasn't until she was seated among the other guests on the far side of the conservatory that she realized the full extent of its effects on her. Her heart was pounding so that she could scarcely get her breath, and her hands were icy inside her twenty-button evening gloves.

He was one of those men who had an irritating knack for reducing every normal and necessary interaction to something appallingly intimate. His every word, movement, or expression was borne along on undercurrents of male presumption and sensuality that were meant to smooth the way for his will. She had experienced more than her share of such men while she was still a green young girl, and she knew exactly how to handle them. With devastating candor.

Stealing a look across the room, she glimpsed him sauntering toward a seat on the far side. He charged the very air around him as he moved, and he knew it. Averting her eyes, she snapped open her fan and made brisk use of it.

Before Madame DuPont's second aria ended, word of Antonia's prickly introduction to the earl was slowly passed behind fans and between bent heads, through the Ellingsons' guests. Attention focused covertly on the pair of them, seated on opposite sides of the room but intensely aware of each other. Few of the gossip-hungry guests would remember much about the rest of the ample soprano's musical selections.

Lady Constance rose to lead the applause, then declared that the cold buffet was now being served in the dining room. She hurried to take Antonia's arm and steered her toward the food, intent on knowing what was behind her audacious request for an introduction to the radical earl.

"Come, come, Toni dear," Constance crooned next to her ear. "After years of declining my invitations, yesterday you all but demand one. And in your first minutes under my roof you insist upon an introduction to the most infamous bachelor in London, and demand he make himself available to you. You simply must tell me all or I'll expire of curiosity!"

"It's very simple, Constance," she began, selecting her words carefully. "I have taken an interest in the marriage bill that is before Parliament now. Just yesterday I sat in the Commons gallery while the members debated and then tabled it, and afterward—"

"*Afterward,* I caught her defaming me before a number of House members." A silky baritone poured over their shoulders. They whirled to find Remington Carr standing behind them, adjusting his immaculate cuffs and wearing a knowing look that said he had been closer and heard more of their conversation than was strictly proper.

Antonia stepped back and raised both her chin and her guard. "You seem to have an unsavory habit of eavesdropping, Lord Carr, and of barging into conversations that do not concern you."

"Forgive me, Lady Antonia." He smiled that devilish, polished smile of his. "Damned cheeky of me to think a conversation about me is my concern. But then, I am known for my brass." Then he turned to Lady Constance and proceeded to demonstrate some of it. "Lady Antonia was roundly denouncing both my flagrant hedonism and my views on women and marriage outside the Commons Lobby a day or so ago . . . when I heard my name being bandied about and paused to hear what was being said."

"Your views on marriage *should* be denounced, you rogue," Lady Constance said, giving him a flirtatious rap on the wrist with her closed fan.

"And my hedonism?" he teased, giving Antonia a stroking glance that sent a mild shock rippling through her senses. Alerted, she braced for what came next. "I'm a freelover, you know. A callous, unfeeling bore who abuses his women." He nodded with mock gravity in response to his hostess's shocked expression. "Indeed, I was a bit surprised to hear it myself. But Lady Antonia here is apparently something of an expert on my vices. I was intrigued to learn what other deplorable weaknesses I might possess and suggested we meet here."

Antonia's face flamed. He had just employed the time-honored male strategy of bringing all disagreements with a woman down to an insultingly personal level, and she was not about to let him get away with it. Having uncovered his game and feeling more in control for it, she leveled a scorching glare on him. And she knew the minute she did that it was a mistake.

He caught her fiery gaze in his, absorbing its heat, relishing its intensity, visibly savoring its determination . . . serving notice that he would take pleasure from whatever passion he roused in her, even her anger, indignation, and outrage.

"Your vices—numerous as they undoubtedly are—are of no concern to me, sir," she said as icily as possible. "It is your politics that I find offensive."

"His politics?" Lady Constance said a bit too loudly. Her laughter carried softly around the dining room, giving her other guests an excuse to investigate her mirth. They drew nearer with polite smiles that scarcely cloaked their raging curiosity. "My dear Antonia, politics are far too *dreary* ever to be truly offensive."

It was the perfect womanly retort, one which implied that the world of politics and government was both beyond a lady's comprehension and beneath her proper interests. And Remington Carr's responding smile—with its duality of approval and condescension toward his hostess's view— raked Antonia's nerves like cat's claws. It was more evidence of his contempt for women and their rightful place in the world.

"I would say, Constance, that 'dreary' does not quite capture the essence of Lord Carr's political program." Antonia seized the initiative with fierce pleasantry " 'Absurd' is the term that first comes to mind. 'Alarming' and 'destructive' certainly apply . . . and 'vile,' 'loathsome,' and 'ridiculous' follow quickly on. He doesn't believe in marriage, you see. He proclaims it a relic of our primitive past—an 'onerous and inequitable arrangement' that unfairly burdens the members of his sex." Her voice and manner began to heat. "And he's not too keen on women, either. If he had his way, he'd ship the lot of us to Bora Bora and be done with us . . . indolent creatures that we are."

"Hold on, now . . . that is a bit extreme," he said,

smiling. The way his eyes danced in the candlelight made it clear he was more pleased than perturbed by her vehement characterization of him. "I have never *seriously* advocated Bora Bora. France is plenty far enough. And what's this nonsense about my not being keen on women?" He gave her a raking glance that said he was quite appreciative of certain aspects of femininity. "Why, I'll have you know, my mother was a woman."

A wave of laughter around them alerted Antonia to their growing audience, and she looked around to find at least a dozen wine-warmed faces staring at her, some with disapproval, some with expectation. She hissed privately. She should have known he would make some sort of spectacle of their encounter.

"And what would your mother have thought of your proposal to tear women away from their children and force them to work in coal pits, sweatshops, and woolen mills?" she demanded. "For that is your proposal, is it not? To degrade women . . . to belittle their rightful place in the home . . . to drive them into the streets and make them earn their keep?" She was gratified by the way the satisfaction in his smile faded.

"It has never been my intent to degrade women," he answered in an annoyingly reasonable and sincere tone. "It is my goal to set women on an equal footing with men in every aspect of life—including the vote and the necessity of working for a living."

"And just what makes you think women don't already *work* for their living, Lord Carr?" she demanded.

"Experience, dear lady. Experience," he declared, edging closer. "The women of my acquaintance—indeed, more than half the women of this land—are supported in such a fashion and to such an extent that they need do precious little toward their own maintenance. They have housekeepers for managing their homes, maids for housework, and nurses for child rearing. Seamstresses do their sewing, laundresses clean their clothes, and the public schools educate their children. The men they have sunk matrimonial hooks into both earn their living and do their thinking for them." He paused and cast a wicked look around him, preparing his audience for something outrageous.

"The most strenuous things they have to do are stir their morning chocolate"—he whirled a finger daintily around in an imaginary cup—"and decide whether to wear the yellow bonnet today or the blue."

The laughter, both male and female, that welcomed his summary of women's work outraged Antonia, but she knew that to show her anger here would only play into his hands. He flaunted his contempt for women under the guise of humor, making light of his views in order to make hers seem heavy-handed and puritanical.

What a perfectly devious man he was, she realized. And how delicious it would feel to bring him to his clever male knees!

"Then your *experience,* like the size of your female acquaintance, must be rather limited. Understandably so, considering your hostile attitude toward women and the home." She took a step toward him, outdoing his smile with a fierce one of her own.

"The women of *my* acquaintance work every bit as hard as their husbands," she continued, her eyes flashing. "Or harder. Few have more servants than a maid-of-all-work or an elderly house couple. And even fewer can afford a nurse for more than a few weeks past a lying-in. They manage their homes and their children by themselves, and seldom have to worry about whether their morning chocolate has settled or if their yellow or blue bonnet would suit better . . . for they have neither morning chocolate nor an abundance of hats."

"Females who actually work? It gives one pause to consider just what sort of women you consort with, Lady Antonia." He stepped still closer and looked down his straight, aristocratic nose at her. "No lady of my acquaintance would be caught dead with a mending needle in her hand, wiping a child's nose, or dealing firsthand with sweaty tradesmen. They prefer to languish on their divans, spend money as if pound notes fall from the sky like raindrops, and complain endlessly that their husbands spend too much time at their clubs. To my way of thinking it would do women a world of good to have to learn some of the stern realities of the world outside their pampered nests."

"Pampered nests?" She nearly choked on the words. "I fear, my lord, that you are in dire need of an education where women are concerned. You haven't a clue as to what women's lives and women's work are really like . . . for if you did have, you would never spout such drivel about women and their place in our nation's homes. And you would certainly never air such monumental ignorance in public." There were several gasps, a few titters, and a hearty chuckle or two from the guests around them.

"Oh?" He poured his dark, liquid gaze over her in a way that made her send a trembling hand to cover the buttons that trailed down her waist. "Ignorant and in need of an education, am I? And just who do you propose should educate me in the work and contributions of women?"

She hoped her pleasure wasn't too obvious. He had walked right into her trap!

"Me."

"You?" He glanced around him with widened eyes that elicited suggestive murmurs and chuckles from the men present; then he focused his unsettling attention on her. "An intriguing possibility, I will admit. But I am afraid I must decline, madam. I am long past the schoolroom regimen, and I haven't the slightest desire to apprentice myself to a skirt . . . no matter how fetching it may be." He slid an appreciative glance down the side of her panniered skirt, and there were gasps and titters. Her pulse fluttered disconcertingly, but she pressed on.

"I would never suggest anything quite so rudimentary as a schoolroom for you, my lord. What I propose for your education is more along the lines of . . . a wager."

"A what?" He leaned back on one leg with a surprised but wary look.

"A wager, sir. A bet. A gamble. The risk of something of value upon an uncertain outcome." She glanced archly at the men around them. "Come, come . . . surely you've heard of it. It is my understanding that the gentlemen of London fritter away a majority of their time and money concocting and carrying out wagers of one sort or another."

He frowned. Clearly, he had not expected this. "What sort of wager?"

She smiled, hoping that none of her vengeful urges showed in her expression. "Two weeks of your time, my lord."

His frown deepened. "Against what?"

"Against two weeks of mine."

The rumble of consternation around them gave voice to the confusion in his expression. For a brief moment her heart all but stopped. Everything hinged on his next words. Was he arrogant enough or sufficiently challenged by what had passed between them to consider such an involved undertaking?

"Two weeks of my time?" Interest edged into his scowl. "Doing what?"

She had him!

"*Women's work,* my lord."

All went silent around him while he blinked, stared at her, then dissolved into a surprised laugh. "Women's work?

You wish me to lie around all day, eating chocolates and ordering servants thither and yon?" The tension around them erupted into laughter. Antonia also smiled, though from a very different cause.

"What I propose, my lord, is that you do *an average woman's work* each day for a fortnight. If at the end of that time you have changed your mind about women's place in the home—if you have learned how varied and arduous the average woman's duties truly are—you will say so publicly and give wholehearted support to the Marriage Bill."

"And if I haven't changed my mind?" he asked, folding his arms over his chest and tilting his head to study her.

"Then I will agree to do men's work for a fortnight."

An even more raucous wave of laughter went through their audience, and he grinned as he gave voice to their common thought: "And what makes you think you could *do* a man's work?"

Antonia was prepared. "Oh, I don't think I should have any difficulty doing men's work. After all, what is so difficult about going to an office by ten and quitting it at two, to spend the rest of the afternoon at the races? And if it comes to that, I think I would have no problem spending evenings at the club, swaggering, bragging, and wagering." She lowered her voice to a confidential tone, and when she leaned forward, so did their audience, straining to catch her words. "Though I will admit that smoking cheroots may take a bit of getting used to." She tapped her chin thoughtfully with her closed fan. "And I am willing to admit that hefting a glass of Scotch whiskey and shifting chips back and forth across a playing table may indeed be more taxing than I have imagined."

The laughter her comments generated was almost exclusively feminine. Her tart portrayal of upper-crust men's habits was a bit too close to the mark, and the gentlemen present showed considerably less humor concerning their own peccadilloes than they did concerning women's. Lord Carr was no exception. He stood with his arms crossed over his unfashionably broad chest, glowering as he considered her challenge.

After a taut silence he raised one hand and stroked his generous bottom lip with his thumb and forefinger. Back and forth . . . those long, neatly tapered fingers slid over that velvety surface, drawing her gaze. It was an unconscious thinking gesture on his part, but it caused her own bottom lip to tingle wildly. Back and forth. Those supple fingers . . . rubbing, stroking . . . Her discomfort grew, and after a long, intolerable minute, she raked her teeth over her lip to make it stop.

His expression abruptly changed. It was as if the sun came out in his face, and Antonia felt a hot clutch of embarrassment, as if her instinctive movement and his decision were somehow linked.

"I shall accept your wager, madam," he declared. "I will do your *average woman's work* for a fortnight . . . for no other reason than to prove my own point."

Looming above her, he stared down into her eyes, testing her resolve, plumbing the depths of her resolve. Then his gaze began to wander over her face, and his slow, knowing smile sent a quiver through her. "I fear you have made a difficult bargain. I have been a long time in acquiring my particular views on women and domesticity, and I will not be easily swayed from them."

"I did not expect it would be *easy*, my lord. Only *possible*," she said, barely containing a surge of exultation. "And I will warn you, I am a woman who makes the most of a possibility."

In the pin-drop quiet, they faced each other, their gazes locked, each taking stock of the other's cleverness and determination. The other guests watched between them with bated breath, marking what an incendiary match they made: he the epitome of strident, uncompromising bachelorhood, and she the defender of righteous, all-assuming matrimony. Like air and phosphorus primed, they awaited only a small movement one direction or another to ignite them.

"This is all perfectly scandalous!" Lady Constance inserted herself into the fray, her face flushed with excitement. She seized first Antonia's arm, then Remington Carr's, turning them both toward her buffet table. This titillating challenge, issued under her roof, had just made her reputation as a hostess for the rest of the season, and she was buoyant. "What on earth has gotten into you, Antonia? Wagering like a tar in port! And you, my lord . . . have you given any thought to the consequences of so reckless a course? Whatever will people say?"

Antonia hadn't the faintest idea what people would say; public opinion was the furthest thing from her mind at that moment. She was scrambling to understand the ramifications of getting exactly what she came for: Remington Carr's cooperation in his own comeuppance. When she looked up, her adversary was taking a glass of champagne from a tray and holding it out to her. Glancing around, she found Constance and William Ellingson and a number of their guests with goblets in their hands, waiting for her to accept.

"You may as well begin your education in the ways of men now, Lady Antonia. We men share a drink together to seal a wager. One of our more civilized habits."

"Ummm," she said, considering, then accepting the glass. "And how do men handle the paying off of a wager once it is *lost*?"

"It depends upon the terms of payment. Most meet at a prearranged place and time . . . at the winner's convenience."

"If you're determined to carry through with this madness, you can meet here," Lady Constance said. "I'll have another little evening two weeks from next Saturday, and you can announce the results then."

"Good enough," Antonia said, assuming the victory would be hers and taking the winner's prerogative. "Two weeks from next Saturday." When he did not object, she raised her glass in salute and smiled confidently at him. After the toast she set her glass aside and unfastened the wrist buttons of one of her gloves, drawing out a calling card bearing an engraved address.

"Be there at nine o'clock Monday morning, Lord Carr, ready to assume your new duties," she said, presenting it to him.

He seized her hand and pulled it toward him just as she began to rebutton her glove. She stiffened and tried to pull it away, but he held her securely, then turned her hand palm up to look at the neat little buttons and the pale skin of her wrist, visible through the opening in the leather. She held her breath as she felt his warm, liquid gaze traveling up the long row of buttons on the inside of her arm.

"I cannot help but wonder, Lady Antonia, what else you might have tucked away in that glove." He raised his eyes to hers, searching her in a way that made her tongue seem to stick to the roof of her mouth. Then he raised the card in his other hand. "What is this place you summon me to?"

"My house in Piccadilly," she managed, though with a betraying thickness to her words. When he released her, she lifted her chin and turned to her hostess. "Thank you, Constance, for a most profitable evening. As you might imagine, I have a busy time ahead. I shall bid you a good night."

With a nod to her bemused host, she sailed out the drawing-room doors. As the butler slipped her short cape over her shoulders, she heard the sounds of a delayed reaction breaking out in the dining room. She had just scandalized them beyond words: exchanging thinly veiled insults with a peer of the realm, challenging him to a wager, then pressing him into veritable servitude in her own house for a fortnight. She could scarcely believe she had done it herself!

By the time she settled on the seat of the hansom cab and the door closed behind her, she was weak and trembling with excitement. Her heart pounded as if she had run a footrace, and her mind flew from one detail of her plan to another, savoring the surprises in store for him. But beneath her breathless feeling of triumph emerged the unsettling thought that it had gone perhaps too well. Why on earth had he allowed himself to be maneuvered into such an outrageous situation?

He was not a stupid man; he must know that she intended some powerful and even underhanded persuasions. And though it was true that she had publicly challenged him, he was not a man who allowed the threat of public censure or embarrassment to trouble him. Saving face could not be his motivation. Then he must believe he stood to gain something in such a contest. But what?

Thinking on that, she took a deep, cleansing breath and rubbed her temples. Her eyes fell on the still unbuttoned wrist of her glove, and she paused, staring at that pale slice of revealed skin. In the dim light of the cab she seemed to feel the heat of his hand on hers again. With a slight turn of thought she again saw his dark, velvety eyes trained upon her . . . traveling up her glove buttons . . . fastening on her face with cloaked speculation. She shivered in response. Devilish eyes. Hungry eyes. Her body reacted instinctively to the appetite in them, going taut and expectant.

Instantly she knew. Every penetrating look and each

double-edged comment had held a clue. Taken together, the evidence was irrefutable.

He intended to seduce her.

Like most men of his class, he enjoyed the chase. She had roused his male instincts for combat, she reasoned, and with a man like him, any challenge from a woman must ultimately be brought down to a personal—thus, carnal—level. Set in that logical framework, his seductive banter and his acceptance of her wager made perfect sense. The cad intended to use his wagered fortnight to worm his way into her favors, thinking access to her passions would somehow give him a victory over her and her ideals. How typically male of him.

No doubt he expected that his wickedly good looks and silky manner would prove quite effective. She scowled, recalling her instinctive reaction to him. And well they might . . . if she didn't know who and what he was . . . and if she weren't much too clever to be flattered and beguiled by a bit of male heat.

As the carriage rumbled along the darkened city streets, she burrowed back into the seat and gave a sigh of satisfaction. It was all working out perfectly.

When the cab stopped outside the front door of her house, Hoskins was watching and bustled out with a lamp to help her inside. While he paid the driver, she hurried up the steps, into the hall, and deposited her wrap on the center table. Light was coming from the drawing-room doors, and she headed straight for them.

The large chamber was lit with numerous candles, and a small fire had been laid despite the seasonable warmth of the evening. A half-dozen cats were stretched out on the marble tiles that lined the hearth, and in the quiet their purring mingled with the ticking of the gilt mantel clock and the click of knitting needles. The several divans and upholstered parlor chairs in the room were occupied by women whose hair ranged from gray tinged to completely white. At the sight of her they came to life, calling her name and nudging awake those who had found the waiting too tedious.

"Toni, dear!" Aunt Hermione was on her feet in a wink, hurrying to her side and unleashing a veritable barrage of questions. "What happened? Details—we must have details!"

"Was the earl there?" a tall, slender woman asked, leaning forward eagerly.

"Did you talk with him?" A rotund matron wriggled to the edge of her seat.

"Was there dancing?" a bent old woman with an ear trumpet demanded loudly.

"Did you set him straight on the Sister Bill?" Pollyanna Quimby asked, scowling and crossing her arms.

She looked from one adorably eager face to another, reading in them Remington Carr's downfall. He would have to be made of stone to resist these faces. And her instincts told her he was not exactly made of stone.

"Hoskins!" she called out over her shoulder, and the old butler came shuffling into the doorway. "Champagne, please, and plenty of it!" She turned back to the women who shared her house and her life, with an exultant laugh.

"He will be here at nine o'clock Monday morning. He is ours for the next two weeks!"

Antonia was not the only one savoring the evening's success. Remington Carr had quitted the Ellingsons' for his club not long after Antonia left. As the cab carried him toward St. James Street, he settled back with his hands propped on the head of his walking stick, feeling quite pleased at the way he had managed to turn the Dragon's fire to his advantage.

He couldn't have planned it better himself. He had let her storm and fume and challenge him, accepting it all with infuriating good humor. And she had maneuvered and connived her way straight into his clutches. Astonishing, really. He could never have guessed she would seek him out and demand two long weeks of his undivided attention . . . in her own house, yet! He reached into his pocket for her card and on impulse brought it to his nose. The scent of roses made him smile. The possibilities for seduction in such a situation were endless. And to paraphrase her boast: he was a man who knew how to make the most of a possibility.

He hadn't imagined when he agreed to this scheme that she would prove to be so young or desirable, or that he might find the task of luring her to his bed quite so interesting. There was no use denying it; he had found their first confrontations quite stimulating, and looked forward to future "encounters." He conjured a picture of her in his mind, and his eyes glowed hotly at the thought of persuading those soft lips to yield, of sinking his hands into that mass of fire-kissed hair, of watching those opalescent-blue eyes darken with desire . . .

The drift of his thoughts suddenly alarmed him. Soft lips and alluring blue eyes? Dangerous thinking indeed, he realized, purging a traitorous trickle of heat from his blood and taking his lustful impulses in hand. She might be younger and a bit more interesting than he had expected, but she was still the devious and contriving woman who trapped wealthy bachelors into marriage. And his mission here had nothing to do with enjoying anything.

His plan was to trap her the same way she had trapped her wretched victims. How ironic that by her own conniving and audacity, she had just set the jaws of the trap herself. It added a rather satisfying twist to the situation to know that she would be partly responsible for her own demise.

As they approached St. James Street, that last thought refused to die away. He stroked his chin, letting it circle in his mind. If he was using her own contrived conditions to entrap her, then just what was her original plan? She had come to Lord Ellingson's ostensibly to continue their debate and to teach him about women and their place in the world. She was quick enough with the notion of a wager between them . . . wanted him in her house for some reason.

He scowled, thinking of what devious possibilities might lie behind her attempt to educate him on what she deemed to be women's proper role in life. It struck him like a thunderbolt: *she had undoubtedly marked him as her next matrimonial victim!*

"Good God," he swore, feeling his muscles tighten defensively. Her threat to bachelorhood was no longer an abstraction; his own bachelorhood was at stake this time. She was every bit as dangerous as they had said. Clever, determined, and with more than her share of feminine wiles . . . she was quite possibly the most treacherous female he'd ever encountered. He would have to watch his step with her.

"No more sniffing . . . like some green clod just come to town," he growled, stuffing the calling card back into his pocket. "And no more remembering blue eyes or shapely curves or twenty-button gloves open at the . . . What the hell kind of woman wears twenty-button gloves these days, anyway? They went out with hoops and crinolines. And I ought to know, I've paid enough haberdashery bills for gloves . . . and kerchiefs . . . and purses, petticoats, stockings, and dress improvers. . . ."

The weight of a thousand little outrages, the result of his experiences with women, settled on his shoulders and combined with his conclusions about her to hone his resolve to a razor edge.

By the time he reached White's and entered the bar, his vengeful mood had given way to a sardonic smile. Forewarned was forearmed, he thought. Let her do her diabolical best; it would only make his inevitable victory all the sweeter.

The Dragon's six victims were seated at their former table, at the far end of the room. They didn't wait for him to be seated before they began firing questions at him.

"Was she there?"

"What was it like?"

"Will you see her again?"

"All that and more," he said, beckoning to the barman and settling on the chair they had reserved for him. Before their widening eyes he produced her card from his vest pocket and waved it tantalizingly back and forth.

"Her address, gentlemen. I shall be spending the next fortnight at her house in Piccadilly, as part of a wager between us." His aristocratic features took on a predatory cast. "Within two weeks, my friends, I will slay your dragon and present you with its heart."

Two hours later the front door of White's opened and a half-dozen well-oiled gentlemen spilled onto the damp street. Their voices brought to attention a form lounging against the railing of the nearby service steps. He ducked back against the corner of the building and squinted, searching the dimly lit figures and fastening on one form that was taller than the rest and noticeably steadier on its feet. As some of the men drunkenly hailed cabs, one fellow laughed and threw an arm around the taller figure.

Rupert Fitch crept closer and then pressed back against the building, staying in the shadows as he strained to hear what was being said. He had followed Remington Carr here from Lord Ellingson's party, hoping to learn something more about what had happened between him and Lady Antonia Paxton. Whatever it was, it had sent her home early and had sent him storming off to his club before the champagne had had time to get warm. The tall bloke before him was the Earl of Landon, all right. He'd stake what was left of his sainted mother's virtue on it.

"Brilliant, Landon," Remington Carr's hanger-on declared. "Couldn't be more perfect. A wager . . . and her idea . . . who'd've thought?" A hansom cab clattered up, drowning out much of the rest, but Fitch made out the words "luck," and "Lady something," which sounded very much like "Lady Antonia."

Several of the gents piled into the cab, and the others decided to walk down the street to the nearest cab stand. The earl struck off in the opposite direction, tugging the brim of his top hat lower and raising the collar of his evening cloak against the dampness. Fitch waited until he was a discreet distance away, then slipped out into the street to follow. He did not intend to let his quarry give him the slip after he had spent a long, miserable evening in the wet streets for some clue as to what was happening between the Ladies' Man and the wealthy widow.

A wager of some sort, he thought, as he stole along behind Remington Carr. The gent had been wishing the earl good luck on something with Lady Antonia. A wager on the lady's virtue? Such things were not unknown in the elite and often dissolute world of the gentlemen's clubs. But he discarded that possibility when he recalled hearing something about its being "her idea." There was something brewing, he was sure of it. But to learn what it was, he would have to keep a watch on the earl's posh digs and follow him to learn why he was going to need "luck."

As he slipped from doorway to doorway and skulked

around corners, the news writer's empty stomach growled, and he rubbed it with a grimace. Pulling his coat up about his neck and jamming his hands into his pockets, he hurried along after the unconventional earl, muttering to himself.

"Well, yer lordship, this 'ad better be good."

The sun made a spectacular appearance that Monday morning in Piccadilly, giving a jewel-like luster to Green Park, which lined one side of the broad thoroughfare, and making the windows of the fashionable residences on the other side of the street shine as if they were gilded. The air was filled with the rhyming calls of vendors, the clop of hooves, and the banter between servants and tradesmen, while the avenue itself bustled with traffic: greengrocers' and bakers' pushcarts, milk wagons, and tradesmen of all kinds hurrying to make deliveries to their most lucrative clientele.

Among those making their way down Piccadilly, just before nine o'clock, was Remington Carr. His exquisitely tailored dress—understated charcoal suit, black vest and matching silk tie, and fashionable, square-crowned Cambridge bowler—set him apart from the others in the street. Few of the social elite were ever out and about before ten in the morning, and if it had been up to him, he would not have been out and about either. Beneath his hat his dark hair was still slightly damp, and his freshly shaved face was a bit gray, the result of a late night and of being roused at an ungodly hour to prepare for his first day of "women's work."

Searching the house numbers, he mentally compared them to the one on the card in his vest pocket. It couldn't be much farther, he thought to himself, reaching into his coat to check his pocket watch. He didn't want to be late. Nor did he want to arrive too early or appear too eager— though, quite truthfully, there was little danger of that. In the clear light of day, without the golden glow cast over events by excellent champagne, the wager, and in fact the entire enterprise, was losing some of its allure. Romancing a matrimonially minded dragon, while prowling around her house with a feather duster in his hand, was not an especially inviting prospect.

But before he could slide too deeply into disgruntlement, he found himself staring at a set of polished brass house numbers that looked familiar. His field of vision widened to take in a small iron gate and four stone steps that led to the front doors of Paxton House. Halting, he stepped out into the street to have a look.

It was a large town house, five or six stories, made in the Romantic Gothic tradition: gray stone, pristine white parapets, tall, arched windows, and graceful winglike shutters. The double front doors were painted black and fitted with brass handles and knockers that were kept at high gloss. On either side of the door were stone planters filled with ivy and blossoming geraniums. He scowled.

He wasn't sure exactly what he had expected . . . something with gargoyles and flying buttresses, perhaps. But this house seemed so quietly grand and gracious, right down to its well-tended geraniums, that it somehow unsettled him. He checked the house number on the card and confirmed that it was indeed the place. Squaring his shoulders and fortifying himself with dire images of Antonia Paxton bursting through countless bedroom doors with holy fire in her eyes, he headed through the gate.

A hoary-headed old houseman answered his knock and gave him an insultingly thorough looking-over before shuffling off to announce him. The old fellow returned a moment later with Lady Antonia herself in tow. Remington felt that coil of tension in his middle tighten another notch at the sight of her.

She wore a charcoal-gray skirt and a matching jacket trimmed with rows of small velvet-covered buttons and a prim white collar. Her auburn hair was pulled back in a full chignon that somehow accentuated her large blue eyes, and her face bore a fetching brush of high color. As she came toward him, she smiled, and Remington felt an odd weightless sensation in his stomach . . . which he put down to vengeful anticipation.

"Your lordship." She halted several feet away, clasping her hands at her waist the way school mistresses are wont to do when they are being extremely patient. "You're prompt. That is good to know."

"I have a number of redeeming qualities, Lady Antonia," he said warmly, handing off his hat to the old butler, then dropping his gloves one at a time into its upturned crown. He closed the distance between them, smiling his most charming smile. "Punctuality is only one of them. I would not want you to think I had welshed on our wager . . . not even for a minute."

"Excellent," she said, stepping back. "Then you're ready to begin. If you'll come with me, I'll introduce you to my household and your duties." She led him across a vaulted center hall that was constructed of soaring Gothic arches, and he could have sworn the daft old butler said something very like "poor bastard" as he shuffled away.

She led him into a drawing room and into the midst of a veritable sea of women who were seated on plush divans, fringed settees, and at tea tables. All had some degree of white in their hair, all were clothed in dark colors done up with a white blouse or collar, and all wore tidy lace caps, except one—a rather knotty old woman who wore an extravagantly flounced red dress and a straw bonnet that seemed to be erupting with papier-mâché fruits. His confusion must have shown in his face, for Lady Antonia smiled as if she had expected it.

"Do come in, Lord Carr, and meet my family." She went to stand beside the chair of a dignified elderly woman with a gently aged and beatific countenance. "This is my aunt, Dame Hermione Paxton-Fielding, widow of First Admiral Sir Thomas Edgerton Fielding."

"Also of Sir Dennis Stewart, Mr. Peter Binghampton, and Brigadier Stephen Devere. It's important to remember and give credit where it is due," the old cherub said with an upraised finger. Then she rose and extended her hand with a twinkle in her eye. "It's an honor, your lordship."

"The pleasure is mine, madam," he said, bowing over the old lady's hand with as much dignity as he could muster while trying to make belated sense of what Antonia had said to him. This was her *family*? When he looked up, a tall woman with large, bony features and a severe expression filled his vision.

"May I present Mrs. Pollyanna Quimby, widow of Magistrate Farley Quimby," Antonia said, "and her sister, Mrs. Prudence Quimby, widow of Frederick Quimby, late member of the Board of Trade." The second woman was shorter, rounder and wore a rather engaging smile. "They are sisters," Antonia explained, "who married brothers."

Only the barest resemblance and the fact that they were dressed identically marked the two women as related in any way. He nodded, taking their hands while searching their faces for some trace of familial resemblance to Lady Antonia.

"This is Mrs. Eleanor Booth, widow of Edmond Booth, the inventor of the self-inflating fountain-pen bladder. And Mrs. Molly McFadden, widow of Cecil McFadden, who had a shop in the Farmer's Market for many years."

"A butcher, 'e was," rotund Molly said, beaming.

"Pleased to meet yer lordship." She pumped his hand nervously and blushed. "Who'da thought I'd be shakin' hands wi' a belted earl?"

Bubbly Molly was shortly replaced by a slight, well-dressed woman: "Mrs. Florence Sable, widow of Mr. Jeremy Sable, tailor to the elite of Oxford for many years." Another, somewhat younger woman appeared next: "Mrs. Victoria Bentley, widow of Harold Bentley, carriage maker." When Antonia started to move on, Victoria prodded her with a frown that caused her to recall: "And also of Lieutenant Edgar Jamison, who had a brief but valiant career as an officer in her highness's royal dragoons." Victoria smiled and made a graceful half curtsy.

In short order he met three more women; Gertrude—Mrs. Somebody-or-other, Pansy—Mrs. Whatever-his-name-was, and Maude—Mrs. Dearly-departed. He couldn't be sure later that there hadn't been more, for he was distracted by the thought that this disparate group of females could not possibly be her relatives. But if not, what were they doing here, in her drawing room? He was just recalling that she had also made reference to them as her "household" when the realization came crashing down on him that the place was filled with widows . . . nearly a dozen of them!

Antonia Paxton's household seemed to consist entirely of older women who had each ensnared, exhausted, and then dispatched a husband. Collectively, he realized with mounting horror, they had polished off more than a dozen specimens of English manhood—some had actually worn out two or three good men!

By the time they came to the old lady in the floozy-red dress and the bizarre fruit-motif bonnet, he was bracing internally. When Antonia's voice rose and the old woman nodded and cupped her ear, he was already prepared for the worst.

"This is Mrs. Cleo Royal," she said, bending so that the old lady could pick up her words. "Widow of the renowned actor Fox Atherton Royal. Together they played great halls and theaters all across the continent."

"Pleased to meet you, my lord," the old lady shouted, giving him her blue-veined hand. "Landon . . . Earl of Landon, eh? Then you must have known 'Pinkie' Landon. Took up with him briefly before I met Fox Royal. Now Pinkie was one man who—"

"Yes, yes, very good, Cleo!" Antonia said patting the old lady's hand. "You mustn't tire yourself now. And the earl has things to do." With a smile that seemed to pacify the old lady, she steered Remington Carr back to the middle of the room.

"Well, there you have them." She proudly swept the group with a hand. "Your tutors for the next two weeks."

"My what?" he demanded, his civility evaporating.

"Tutors," she said, savoring both his shock and his attempt to hide it. "These ladies will be teaching you the fundamentals of women's work. Unfortunately, in two weeks we will have time for only the rudiments. The finer points you will just have to acquire on your own."

"But I understood—" He straightened imperially, his face darkening. "It was part of our agreement that *you* would be my tutor."

"Oh, but I will be, in a way. I intend to oversee every detail of your education, my lord. You'll be in most capable hands."

The full depravity of her plan unfolded in his mind. She intended to make him a pupil—a *lackey*—to a dozen elderly females! It was inconceivable . . . intolerable . . . being bossed about by women, truckling after their demands, waiting on them hand and foot. Good Lord, they had already depleted and disposed of more than a dozen men! But most devastating of all, he realized, her devious substitution made a shambles of his plans for her comeuppance.

"This is absurd," he declared with quiet vehemence. "I won't stand for it."

"Of course, if you'd rather, you can just yield the wager to me now," she said in musical tones that hid none of the prickly resolve beneath them. "Just write an article and insert it in *The Times* by the end of the week stating that you recant your previous views and now believe that a woman's rightful place is in the home. A simple statement on the order of 'Men everywhere ought to marry and be grateful for the part women play in their otherwise dissolute, bereft, and aimless lives' would do nicely."

Yield to her? The thought of abasing himself and compromising his heartfelt convictions in writing made his stomach turn. But the only other escape from this horde of man-consuming females would be to walk out on both the wager and his plan to compromise her. The thought of welshing on a bet was appalling. If word got out, he'd be ruined. And this nasty little gambit of hers was the proof that if there ever was a woman who needed humbling, it was Antonia Paxton.

He could no more abandon this cursed wager than he could fly. And he could see, from her cat-that-swallowed-the-canary smile, that she knew it.

He looked around at the Dragon's widows, their graying hair and bespectacled faces, their matronly shapes and probing gazes. In their aged eyes he glimpsed secrets . . . womanly things . . . feminine wiles untold. He squared his shoulders and struck a determined pose, concealing behind an aristocratic sneer the dread those experienced womanly countenances roused in him.

"I wouldn't dream of surrendering this bet, Lady Antonia," he declared fiercely. "Especially when the odds are so heavily in my favor." It rankled him that her superior smile only broadened in response.

"Excellent. Now if you'll follow me into the dining room, I shall explain what plans we have for your education."

Something about the way she said the word "plans" made him tighten internally. He strode after her, relieved to escape the scrutiny of that flock of aging females. His relief was short-lived; soon the hall behind him filled with whispering women, migrating like aged doves toward the dining room, as well.

It was a large, stately room with silk-clad walls and elaborately carved cornices and moldings. The furnishings consisted of a huge walnut table, ranks of high-backed Jacobean chairs, and two elegantly carved sideboards, above which hung elaborate gilt mirrors. At the far end two floor-to-ceiling windows admitted both sunlight and the fragrance of the small garden beyond. The jewellike colors of the walls and upholstery—rich crimson, hunter green, and royal blue—made a princely pallet indeed. He was struck by the harmony of the architecture and furnishings.

Then his gaze dropped from the intricate chandelier medallion on the ceiling and landed on Antonia.

She was standing in a half circle of women, eyeing him . . . holding what appeared to be a very large corset.

Across the street, leaning on the massive iron fence that surrounded Green Park, Rupert Fitch huffed an impatient breath and folded his arms with a jerk. He had waited through the night outside the earl's fancy house in Grovenor Square, then followed him to this address, hoping to uncover a salacious tidbit around which to build a byline that afternoon. A fine house in Piccadilly, he thought, searching his memory for some clue to its owner. His watchfulness was soon rewarded: the driver of an ice wagon exited the alley beside the residence in question. Fitch pulled on his most unctuous and ingratiating smile and strolled over to have a word with him.

"Oh, that there's old Sir Geoffrey's house," the burly fellow answered, giving his nose a sideways swipe. Fitch's heart sank, until the fellow shook his head and continued: "Ol' Paxton's dead now. Just his laidy and a passel o' old cats there now."

"Paxton? Lady Antonia Paxton?" Fitch said, catching fire again. "Thanks, mate." Snugging up his tie and tilting his bowler to a jaunty angle, he shoved his hands into his pant pockets and sauntered down the alley toward what he knew would be the kitchen door of Paxton House. He knew a few things about how gossip flowed in great houses. And he'd always had a way with women who cook.

"What in blazes are you doing with that . . . *thing*?" Remington bit back a profane adjective just in the nick of time. His eyes began to burn as he stared at a rectangular piece of canvas stitched at regular intervals around wicked-looking slats of steel and bone and adorned with pink ribbon rosettes.

"Well, in order to truly appreciate the work women do," Antonia said calmly, "one must understand the conditions under which it is done. Women, you see, perform all their labor under a special burden: their clothing. Did you know that the average woman's day-to-day garments and shoes, totaled together, weigh seventeen pounds?"

He didn't like the direction his answer might take them and refused to respond.

"I thought not. Few people do," she continued, encouraged by murmurs and nods from the other women. "How much do your garments weigh, your lordship?"

He hadn't even the foggiest idea and wouldn't have told her if he had.

"Nine pounds, if you are anywhere near average for a man," she supplied. "Nine versus seventeen. A considerable difference. And women suffer the additional constraint of wearing boned corsets that distort their figures, shorten their breath, and make bending all but impossible. Now if you are to truly experience an average woman's work . . ."

She held up the corset, looking between the contraption and his dapper middle.

His eyes widened in comprehension.

"I *will not* wear that damnable thing!" he declared, making a stand with his feet apart, his shoulders inflating, and his hands curling into fists at his sides.

"Under the terms of our wager, you are to do an average woman's work. And you cannot do that unless you do it the way an average woman would—in a corset."

"I agreed to work, and I will. But I will not permit this wager to be turned into a ridiculous joke, or myself into a fool for your amusement." He stalked toward her with his eyes blazing, and several of the women took a step back.

"None of us are laughing, your lordship," she said, holding her ground and glancing at the others, who shook their heads with serious expressions.

He poured the full, intimidating force of his person into a glare that had at various times brought MP's, fellow peers, and even archbishops to their knees.

"It wasn't part of the bargain," he said angrily. "I won't wear it."

She met his fury without flinching. "Then perhaps you should consider the alternative once again: an article recanting your former views of women and marriage." She paused, tailoring her next words for impact. "For if you do not wear it, I will most certainly send word straight to Constance Ellingson that you have reneged on our wager."

She would do it; he could see it in her eyes. Dangerous eyes. Blue as a midsummer sky and deep as a Scottish loch. Treacherous woman. He could cry foul from now until Doomsday, but the very fact that he had participated willingly in such a preposterous wager in the first place would lend credence to whatever distortions she might decide to weave into the story. He could see it splashed all over the headlines of Fleet Street's oiliest rags: "Nobleman Spurns Corset . . . Loses Bet." His credibility, even among suffragists and reform-minded radicals, would be irretrievably damaged.

He stalked closer, and still closer, his eyes blazing and his features taut with patrician outrage. She was goading him, throwing obstacles in his way. And a moment later, staring deep into those beguiling eyes, he realized that she wasn't *throwing* obstacles, she was erecting them carefully . . . between him and her. She had sensed the direction of his interest in her and made plans so there would always be a human buffer between them.

Antonia watched him stalk closer and wondered belatedly if he was prone to violence of any sort. When he settled before her—his wide shoulders filling her vision, his heat engulfing her—she tightened her fingers around the boned canvas she held. To meet his gaze, she would have to tilt her head up, so she stared at his shirtfront instead. It was a pristine, expensively tailored expanse of white with gold studs instead of buttons. *No buttons.*

She felt a strange sliding sensation in her middle. He was so close, she could smell the warmed wool of his coat, the starch of his shirt, and the subtle spice of his cologne. Sweet sandalwood. Borne on radiated heat, his scent filled her head and seeped down the back of her throat, to fill her lungs. Her heartbeat quickened.

Against her better judgment she raised her chin and looked straight into his eyes. They were a smooth, rich brown, and except for the glow of banked anger in their depths, they were utterly unreadable. She felt them boring into her, testing her resolve and probing for something more. And in spite of the heat of the conflict between them, she shivered.

"Fine!" he snarled abruptly, giving her a start. "I'll wear the damnable thing." He snatched the corset from her hands and stalked back several steps. "How difficult can it be, after all, if *women* do it?"

Before their eyes he ripped off his expensive coat, tossed it onto the dining table, then proceeded to wrap the stern-looking corset around his middle. He shoved the laces through the metal grommets with quick, furious movements, missing a number of holes. Then he yanked the strings with brute force, pulling the binder snug around him. The cloth groaned and stitches popped, but soon he was laced in and whipping the surplus length into a hostile-looking knot at the top edge.

"There!" he declared, bracing with his feet apart and his fists jammed on his hips. "It's on."

It was indeed. Misaligned, ill laced, and improperly tightened . . . it looked a fine mess. But the fire in his eyes dared Antonia, or anyone else for that matter, to correct his use of the thing. And no one did.

"Now, where is this *work* I am supposed to do?" he demanded.

The course of study Antonia had planned for Remington Carr was dictated by the responsibilities that the average woman was required to assume for herself and her family. Foremost among these was providing physical sustenance: the procurement, storage, and preparation of food. Next came tasks relating to raiment and shelter: arranging and cleaning the home, and constructing, cleaning, and maintaining a family's clothing. Beyond a family's more immediate needs, a woman's duties consisted of seeing to the health and education of her children, of enhancing her husband's business or career, and of participating in the Church and charitable works.

Antonia had diagrammed it all on a large slate, which sat on an easel at the side of the dining room.

"We have selected representative duties from each of the areas, which will be overseen by the person who is normally responsible for them in our household. Molly McFadden will instruct you in selecting and purchasing food, for example, and Gertrude Dolly will help you learn what is involved in cooking it. Eleanor Booth will oversee your education in cleaning, and Maude Devine will see to it that you learn the fundamentals of laundry and the care of textiles throughout the house. . . ."

As he listened to her reeling off that list of duties, he stared at the neatly printed words and lines on the slate. How many women of his acquaintance could do such abstract analysis, much less construct lucid diagrams of it? Good God—most had difficulty making change in the coin of the realm!

He stared covertly at Antonia, realizing that for all his foreknowledge of her contriving and treacherous nature, he still had seriously underestimated her.

She had just handed him a slice of his own male pride. But in doing so she had also handed him a challenge of irresistible proportions. As she went on, his concentration drifted from her chart to the intriguing curve of her waist, the natural pout of her lips, and the tendrils of burnished hair lying against the nape of her neck. He watched the sweep of her lashes as she glanced up, discovered him staring at her, and looked quickly back to her precious chart. It was a quick but revealing reaction to his scrutiny.

His mind filled with the way she had stared up into his eyes and with her betraying little shiver.

She was treacherous, true. But she was also a woman, and that shiver had said that she wasn't totally unaware of him as a man. Insight struck, and he flicked a covert glance at the corset he wore, smiling privately. She was, in fact, very aware of him as a man and had attempted to reduce or at least camouflage his manliness . . . to bind him up . . . render him genderless . . . safe.

Ahhh, he thought, there were definite possibilities here, even while wearing a corset and carrying a feather duster.

He came to his senses a moment later to find ruddy-cheeked Gertrude Dolly standing before him with a puzzled look and the others staring at him strangely.

"I said, are ye ready, yer lordship?" Gertrude jerked her head toward the door on the far side. "We got work to do. 'Twill be dinner time afore we know it."

He drew himself up straight and met Antonia's warning look with a pained but defiant smile. "Absolutely, my good woman. Lead on."

Plump, country-bred Gertrude led him along the rear hallway and down a set of steps, straight to the kitchen. It was a large stone-walled room, half underground, with oak beams overhead and two large windows set high on the walls. Iron stoves and a brick-lined oven covered one wall; cupboards and storage bins, and shelves lined with pitchers, platters, and serving dishes, covered the others. In the center sat stout worktables, above which hung racks of kettles, bowls, and utensils. At the far end he could see what appeared to be pantry and cellar doors left ajar.

He stood with his hands clasped, watching Gertrude tying an apron about her middle and snatching utensils from shelves and hooks. A moment later she halted, regarded him with a frown, then came bustling toward him and shoved a large copper bowl in his hands.

"There ye are, yer lordship. Down in the cellar with ye now. I'll need two dozen good-sized potatoes, a shock of dried shallots, and"—she swiveled around, taking instant inventory—"a fresh bag o' flour. An' be quick about it. We have mouths to feed." She flung a finger at one of the doors, then turned back to her work, missing both the look of outrage on his face and the struggle that subdued it. He glowered at the bowl in his hands and let off steam with a quiet hiss. His servitude was indeed beginning.

The stairs down to the cellar were dark; he had to light a kerosene lamp in order to see. Then, once in the cellar, he had to duck and keep his shoulders bent as he searched for flour and potatoes. He found himself oddly short of breath and realized it was the corset; the damnable thing was cutting off his air in this crouched posture. Locating a number of burlap bags of potatoes, he dropped breathlessly to one knee on the pile of bags and counted out twenty-four potatoes. The shallots escaped him until he banged his head on a beam and bashed it with his fist in retaliation. There, hanging nearby in all their pungent splendor, were clutches of the bulbs. He ripped one down and plopped it on top of the potatoes.

The flour, he discovered, came in nothing less than fifty-pound bags. Grimacing, he stooped and tried to haul one of the sacks onto his shoulder. Something gouged him sharply in the ribs, and he gasped and jerked to straighten the offended part of him, realizing it was one of the metal stays. The brief pain, a goad-by-proxy from Antonia, galvanized him. Struggling to breathe and staggering to balance the bag, the bowl, and the lamp, he trudged back up the steps.

Gertrude was waiting with a patient look and a paring knife.

"The flour goes in the barrel," she declared, jerking her head toward several medium-sized barrels against the wall behind her. "Then ye can start partin' them potatoes from their skins." She hurried back to one of the stoves to stoke the fire, then began pumping water into a basin in the sink. When he stood there, scowling, she turned back and planted her reddened hands on her waist. "Somethin' wrong, yer lordship?"

"I can see where this is going," he said, rolling the heavy bag from his shoulder onto the floor, where it made a thud and a cloud of dust. "Where are the rest of the servants, the staff? On holiday, I presume . . . and I'm to fill in for the lot of them."

"Servants?" Gertrude frowned, then her face lit with a broad smile. "We got but two in the kitchen: old Esther, who's abed wi' her lumbago today, an' a girl who comes from the orphanage each afternoon. I'm teachin' 'er to cook. We don't have no servants in this house, 'cept Esther and old Hoskins. Lady Toni mostly keeps him on 'cause he wus old Sir Geoff's man . . . more like a part o' the fam'ly than in service."

"Let me get this straight," Remington said, plopping the potato bowl down on the worktable with a smack. Gertrude had omitted herself from that list; she obviously didn't consider herself to be in service here. "You have no servants in this huge house apart from a lumbago-ridden scullery maid and an aging butler?"

"Nary a one," Gertrude said, eyeing the potatoes.

"Then what, pray, are you?" he demanded, scrutinizing her openly.

"Me?" she laughed, unoffended by his question. "I'm one of the widows Lady Toni took in. She calls us 'er 'ladies.' Invited us in to stay whilst we wus down an' out, an' since we wus too old to remarry, she adopted us. Like 'er aunts, we are. But we're used to work and got to have somethin' to do . . . so we take care o' the house to keep busy. Each o' us 'as got her own bailiwick, here. An' we wouldn't hear of Lady Toni hirin' in strangers whilst we sit on our hands."

She narrowed her eyes at his idle hands, then at the unpeeled potatoes and the bag of flour flopped upon her pristine kitchen floor. "Ever peeled a potato, yer lordship?" When he narrowed his eyes at her, she held the knife out to him and smiled. "It ain't hard. Jus' think of it as"—she tried to think of a male equivalent—"whittlin'."

He snatched the knife from her and grudgingly set to work. Gertrude's well-intentioned analogy was lost on him; he'd never whittled so much as a twig in his life. She looked at the tortured little knots he produced, declared they'd all starve, and sent him back to the cellar for more potatoes. He had just settled back on his stool when the old butler came in, carrying a tray of silver to clean. At the sight of him hacking and gouging away at a huge pile of potatoes, old Hoskins winced, wagged his head, and shuffled out through another door. Remington scowled after him, certain this time that he had heard the old fellow mutter, "Unlucky bastard."

"My man Edgar . . . 'e used to peel potatoes for me," Gertrude mused, pausing in the midst of filleting an enormous flounder intended for the evening's supper. She smiled a bit wistfully and rubbed her nose with the back of her knife hand. "He'd sit on a stool by the table when he come home at night, and jus' peel an' peel."

"Probably shortened his life by a score of years," Remington growled.

By the time he was finished, Gertrude had a mountain of dough for him to mix, which required an astonishing amount of brute force. He set his jaw squarely and ground it into submission, scattering flour over the table, the floor, and his impeccable trousers in the process. Then there was stewed chicken to bone—messy business, that—peas to shell, carrots to clean and chop, fruit sauce to cook and strain. He squashed a number of peas before Gertrude rescued them from him and set him to peeling apples for the sauce. And then *more* apples for the sauce.

Time seemed to stand still as he toted, fetched, lifted, mashed, mixed, melted, and stoked fires, while being treated to a list of dearly departed Edgar's matrimonial virtues. Worse yet, virtually every woman in the house found some pressing errand to bring her through the kitchen. One by one they eyed his progress and his person, then, with sympathetic looks for Gertrude, departed. It gradually occurred to him that the one woman he hadn't seen during his labors was the one he wanted to see.

His features sharpened and his eyes narrowed. His responses to Gertrude's increasingly hurried requests slowed noticeably. And by the time she ordered him to sort the scraps and empty the overflowing slops bucket into the barrel outside the back door, he just stood there, staring at her with a combustible look that made her draw in her chin and frown. It was a standoff for a long, uncomfortable moment. Then she folded her arms over her ample bosom and vehemently pursed one corner of her mouth. He made a noise of disgust, sorted out the scraps, then snatched up the greasy pail.

Conjuring in his mind a few choice words with which to confront Antonia at dinner, he yanked open the alley door and stepped outside. The reek of fermenting food scraps identified the barrel, just outside the door. He took a deep breath, grimaced as he lifted the lid, and began to pour. Turning his face away from the rising aroma, he stopped stock-still.

Standing not ten feet away, leaning against the brick wall across the alley and watching him with unholy glee, was none other than Rupert Fitch, scribbler for one of Fleet Street's most despicable—and successful—scandal sheets. Of late he had appeared with appalling frequency wherever

Remington went, but until now Remington hadn't given it more than the cursory notice such an annoyance deserved.

He felt muscles contracting all over his body as he watched the news writer's ferretlike eyes flit over him, first to the slops he was pouring, then to his rolled shirtsleeves and floury black vest, then down to his grease-smudged trousers and dusty shoes. Fitch's eyes suddenly rebounded to Remington's middle and widened with malicious delight. Remington looked down and felt his face catch fire.

The damned corset! Dirty and bedraggled though it was, there was no mistaking it for anything other than a woman's figure improver—molded bosom holders, pink ribbon rosettes, and all.

He was standing in an alley in a woman's undergarment, awash in slops and looking ashambles, clearly caught in something he'd rather no one would ever know. The gleam in Fitch's eye as he tucked his writing pad into his pocket caused Remington's stomach to sink to somewhere in the vicinity of his knees.

"Fine day, yer lordship." Fitch tugged at the brim of his bowler and strolled off down the alley, whistling.

Remington ducked back inside the kitchen and slammed the door so hard that the frame rattled for seconds afterward. And as he stood there, his fists clenched around the pail handle and his face aflame with humiliation, Antonia swept into the kitchen looking cool and prim and utterly in control.

"How is his lordship doing, Gertrude?" she asked, letting her eyes drift down his rumpled form. He could tell by the tightening of her lips that she was suppressing a smile, and it was all he could do to keep from laying hands on her there and then.

"Well enough," the cook replied. "As long as we got plenty of potatoes."

Antonia laughed softly, seeming to know exactly what Gertrude meant. "Having difficulty with a thin skin, your lordship?" Her eyes twinkled as she leaned across the worktable to pick up a surplus potato and the paring knife he had used. She made quick work of peeling half the potato, then held it up for him to see. "The secret is keeping your thumb at the edge of the blade." She demonstrated despite the fact that he wasn't near enough to see. "Close enough to guide things along and keep the peel thin, but far enough away to keep from getting cut."

Her smile, as she emptied her hands and wiped them on a cloth, said she knew she was doing an excellent job at keeping her thumb on the edge—with both the potato knife and him. He stood mute, not trusting himself to speak. If she were to learn of Fitch's presence in the alley, it would only warm the cockles of her icy little heart.

She went to a set of pegs on the wall by the servants'-hall doors and began to unbutton her jacket. When she looked up and caught him glaring at her, she smiled and addressed the cook again.

"Gertrude, perhaps you should make meringues for supper this evening. That way you could give his lordship some eggs to beat."

Gertrude laughed and shook her head, turning back to the meat pies she was taking from the oven. Antonia continued unfastening her buttons with that annoying little smile on her face, and he began to feel as if time had slowed. She was taking forever to unfasten her jacket. Those seductive hand motions and that broadening expanse of white beneath her opening jacket generated an inexplicable tension in him.

His eyes fixed irritably on the lacy front of her blouse, then her undulating hands and those parting edges of gray. There were at least two dozen small buttons down the front of her jacket, he realized. Then at last she was sliding it from her shoulders and reaching for a long, full-skirted apron to replace it. He watched her slip the ruffled bib over her shoulders and reach behind her to tie it. For one brief moment the silhouette she presented him was a perfect hourglass . . . curves, ripe and womanly . . . small waist . . . shoulders and breasts thrust forward. Heat surged up out of his loins, taking him by surprise and leaving him chagrined.

She said something to the cook, and Gertrude pointed to something. He turned his head and saw that it was the huge bowl of select scraps and fish parts that had accumulated while they worked.

"Time to feed the babies," she said, gesturing to the bowl. "Perhaps you would like to come see them, your lordship."

"Babies? A houseful of old widows . . . and *babies*?" he declared with horror.

"Not *human* babies," she said, watching his reaction with a puzzled smile.

"*Inhuman* babies, then. I see." He dropped the pail he was holding onto the tile floor with a clang. "Charming, I'm sure, but I'll give them a pass. Mrs. Dolly here probably has something urgent for me to do . . . butchering something single-handed, perhaps . . . threshing a bit of grain . . . stomping grapes to make wine for supper . . ."

"Oh, I think Gertrude can do without you for a few minutes before dinner." She was at the doors of the servants' hall when she glanced back over her shoulder and told him: "You can bring the bowl."

He was about to say something satisfyingly profane, when he realized that cooperating might provide an opportunity to further his plan. Brushing the flour from his clothes as best he could, he picked up the scraps bowl and followed her through the swinging doors.

The servants' hall was a long, oak-paneled room furnished with a tressel table and numerous, comfortable old chairs. Antonia was on the other end of the room opening a door that presumably led to some other part of the house. In bounded a small horde of cats: neat little calicos, solid-colored specimens in a variety of shapes and sizes, long-haired aristocrats with their tails up, and big, bruising tabbies pushing their way to the front of the food line.

They sniffed and frisked around Antonia's feet while she talked to them in honeyed tones, asking them if they were hungry. When they caught the scent of the bowl Remington was holding at arm's length, they quickly abandoned her for him. Before he could move, they were upon him, meowing, rubbing against him, climbing onto his shoes, and digging claws into his trouser legs.

"Cats," he said irritably, trying to shoo them away with his feet. "I might have known you'd take in cats as well as old maids."

"Widows," Antonia corrected, watching his nostrils flare and his body tense.

"Where's the difference?" he said, shaking one leg to free it of a set of claws. "Go away—scram!"

"Oh, there's a great deal of difference between a maiden lady and a widow." She watched his predicament with vengeful pleasure. "Widows have experience in the world, while maiden ladies generally do not."

"Experience *with men*," he supplied archly, watching her reaction. There was a hint of heightened color in her cheeks. And for the first time he found himself wondering about *her* experience with men. Sir Geoffrey Paxton. After meeting her the other evening, he had learned that she had been married to a man who by all accounts was old enough to be her grandfather. She didn't seem to think much of men in general, and it gave him cause to wonder what old Geoffrey had done to his young bride to make her dislike men so.

She carried several battered bowls from the stairwell outside the door to the table. "You may do the honors."

He stood for a moment resisting, then decided to save confrontation for another time and portioned out the scraps using the spoon Gertrude had slipped into the bowl. As he lowered the dishes, the cats rushed to eat, and he barely got his hands out in time. Stepping high in order to avoid the creatures, he found one of his feet unusually heavy. When he was safely out of their way, he peered at the back of his leg and found a very young kitten hanging on to his trouser leg for dear life.

"Ye gods—I'm being climbed," he said through a clenched jaw.

When he looked up, Antonia was staring at him.

Her eyes drifted over the layer of flour, the grease spots, and the grimace of disgust he wore. His hair was hanging over his forehead, there was a streak of dirt across one of his cheeks, and his starched collar and silk cravat both were beginning to wilt. The same could not be said, however, of his shoulders. If anything, they seemed to be broader and more powerful than ever—the result, she realized, of wearing a waist cincher that emphasized the contrast between his oversize shoulders and his much smaller waist. The corset might not have been such a brilliant idea after all.

"That's one of the babies. Here—" She detached the kitten from his leg, then stepped back, assessing his snarly mood through the filter of her lashes. "It was born just a month ago." The little beast was all fur and eyes and ears as she lifted it for him to see. "Isn't it adorable?"

"The only thing I detest more than babies is cats." He gave the mewing kitten a wince of disgust. "That means cat babies rank at the very bottom of my list."

"Now, that does surprise me, your lordship," she said, cradling it against her and giving its ears an affectionate scratching. She looked up without raising her head. "I thought *women* occupied that unenviable spot in your esteem."

"Then perhaps you should have read the articles I have written with a less jaundiced eye," he said testily. "I have stated succinctly in each of them that I do not loathe or despise women. I only hate the things women do to men."

"The things women do to men?" she said, feeling a flutter of disquiet in her stomach at the way his eyes intensified and darkened. "And just what do we do to men that you find so objectionable?"

"You lure and beguile and entrap us . . . with our own weaknesses." He set the bowl on the table and brushed his hands together to clear them of debris. Then he took a step closer to her, and she took a step back.

"You trap us into marriages in which we become little more than indentured servants to your unquenchable desires for things and status. You spend our money, our time, and our energy as if all three were limitless." With each complaint his voice lowered a notch, becoming a deep, powerful vibration as he moved still closer. "And you never let us hear the end of it if we try to spend any of the three for ourselves."

She could feel the heat of him reaching for her in some real but intangible way, and stepped backward again, into the edge of a chair.

"You weigh us down with your delicacy, your helplessness, and your coquettish dependency. And you wear us down with your vapors, your silences, and your tears." He loomed over her, leaving her no easy avenue of escape. She was forced to stand her ground and look up into his penetrating eyes.

"You play on our sympathies, our passions, and our sense of decency." Those liquid eyes began an unhurried inventory of her at alarmingly close range. She could scarcely breathe. "In short—you wrap us around your little fingers."

His gaze settled on her lips, and under his scrutiny they became dry and embarrassingly sensitive. She swallowed hard and suppressed the urge to wet them.

"Not all women behave so," she protested, in a voice that had dried to a whisper. "I have never wrapped a man around my little finger."

"Oh? You think not?" He leaned slightly into her, his fascinating mouth curling in a smile that made her knees go weak. "And what about the rest of you?" he said quietly.

"Have you ever wrapped a man around the rest of you, Antonia Paxton?"

She gasped softly, knowing she should push him away and put him in his place. But her outrage was somehow muffled by his nearness; she couldn't summon an ounce of proper indignation. He was so close . . . his mouth so full, so exquisitely mobile. Would his lips feel soft or hard? Cool like his logic or hot like the rest of him?

In her thoughts the space between them closed, his body pressed against hers, and his arms wrapped her. In her mind she melted against him. . . .

He watched her eyes soften and darken with rising emotion, felt them tracing his features, watched them settle with delicious reluctance on his mouth, just the way his were settling on hers. Her lips were ripened by the tension between them into sleek, swollen berries just waiting to be tasted.

On pure impulse he lowered his head and tasted them. Sweet . . . Lord, they were sweet. Just like cherries. And as they parted with surprise, they were so delectably warm . . . soft and yielding, sensuous in their initial hesitation. He seized her shoulders and pulled her toward him. Instinctively, her head tilted and her lush mouth molded to his, accepting, then exploring the changing caress of his lips. One of her arms wound hesitantly around his waist, and his whole body came to life as her body leaned into his. Suddenly he was vibrating with a tension of wanting that was deepening with every responsive motion of her lips. His throat was tightening, his loins were catching fire. . . .

Would you look at that? Gertrude stood with her hands folded, staring through the glass window in the upper half of the servants'-hall doors. She had watched Lady Toni and his lordship come nose to nose, with their eyes bright and faces heated. She sighed wistfully. It was so nice to see a passionate kiss once again, and doubly pleasing to see Lady Toni being kissed to the ends of her toes.

But in the middle of that lovely kiss something caused the earl to jerk his head up, and he glowered at something. Gertrude frowned as she watched, Lady Toni lifted her other hand and the kitten she was holding. Part of his lordship's shirt came up, caught in the little creature's claws, and he scowled and shrank back. Gertrude huffed disappointedly and thrust open the doors as if she had just arrived at them.

"Oh, there ye be, yer lordship. No time to waste . . . we got servin' to do."

Antonia and Remington jolted apart with their faces aflame and their eyes averted. She mumbled something about checking on the table and escaped up the rear stairs, and he snatched up the scrap bowl and stalked back into the kitchen with a countenance like a thundercloud.

They didn't see each other again until Antonia entered the dining room, when Hoskins announced dinner was served. She had recovered and was all the more determined for having surrendered to his licentious intentions. Her behavior, she blushed to think, had been hoydenish, inexcusable. Going all soft and giddy, imagining all manner of scandalous things—the temperature of his lips, for heaven's sake! He was the enemy here, and if there had been any doubt of that, his well-rehearsed diatribe against women should have removed it. But when he kissed her, she allowed it.

Allowed it? She had positively encouraged it. She knew him for a woman-hating cad, not at all the sort of man she could possibly want—if indeed she ever actually *wanted* a man. Why on earth had she kissed him back? He was there to seduce and humble her.

Antonia took herself sternly in hand, patching up the cracks in her resistance to him with bits of his own denunciation of women. By the time they sat down to dinner, she was once again the cool, determined protagonist of women and marriage . . . and once again Remington Carr was her devious and implacable opponent. She made a point of ignoring him through the meal, which was not difficult, since he was seated at the far end of the table.

Remington, however, found ignoring her quite difficult. The details of their encounter kept irrupting unexpectedly into his thoughts: the softness of her skin, the heady feel of her shoulders in his hands, the seductive parting of her lips. He found himself staring covertly down the table, wishing he could trade places with her goblet and hoping she would lick her lip so he could catch a glimpse of her tongue. After a few moments he found himself on the edge of a raging arousal, and he clamped his hands hard on his thighs and took several controlled breaths to combat it.

What in the hell was wrong with him—drooling over a kiss like some schoolboy in short pants? Irritably, he took himself in hand and told himself there was nothing wrong with taking a bit of pleasure from that kiss. It felt good. And better yet—it was a potent confirmation of his instincts about her. He had made that all-important first step on the road to conquest.

But if ignoring her was difficult, he found ignoring the others utterly impossible. Antonia's ladies fussed over him as if he were their long-lost son. Was his chair comfortable? they wanted to know. Did he care for a bit of wine with his meal? Did he want another serving of cottage pie? Did he like the fruit sauce a little sweeter? And what did he learn with Gertrude in the kitchen that morning?

He felt like a schoolboy called to give an accounting of his marks at term's end. Though the women were gracious to a fault and offered tidbits of advice that seemed well-intentioned, he soon found himself aching with tension, poised at the very razor's edge of his defenses. He was not used to being in the exclusive company of women, and older women at that. When it was time to clear away and return to the kitchen with Gertrude, he was actually grateful; it was a chance to escape them.

Once back in the kitchen, he was plunged up to his elbows in a huge pan of soapy water and spent the next half hour scrubbing and rinsing and drying dishes and pans, a duty Gertrude assured him was only temporary and occasioned by old Esther's absence. Once the dishes were put away and the worktables cleaned, Remington learned his first major lesson about women's work: *it never ends.*

"Supper?" he said with genuine horror. "You cannot mean we have to do the entire thing all over again."

"That's th' way it is wi' women's work," Gertrude said, shrugging philosophically. "No sooner done than it begins all over again. Eatin' begets livin', Livin' begets more eatin'. A body's alwus cookin' an' washin' up after."

"Gertrude's right, of course. As soon as a task is finished, preparations for that same task begin again," came Antonia's voice from the doorway. He whirled and found her standing there with a small tea tray in her hands and a thoughtful expression on her face. "And those tasks are repeated endlessly through the days and weeks and years of a woman's life. That is a fundamental principle of 'women's work,' your lordship. And one of the things that makes women's work much harder than it seems." With a little smile at Gertrude, she deposited the tea tray on the table and left.

Remington sat for a minute thinking about that, wondering if it was really true, or if he was somehow being led down the garden path.

He didn't have much time to dwell on it. Gertrude

strode over and plunked a large copper bowl on the table in front of him.

"Potatoes," she ordered. "And plenty of 'em."

Later that night Remington shuffled through the front doors of his house with a gait eerily reminiscent of old Hoskins's. Working in a house full of females apparently rendered a man all but incapable of putting one foot in front of the other. He prayed with everything in him that it wasn't a permanent condition.

Handing the hat and gloves he hadn't had the energy to put on to his butler, Phipps, he issued orders that his valet draw him a bath and prepare his bed. Then he staggered through the house to his study, where he collapsed in his chair. He couldn't remember being this tired. And beneath the exhaustion that flattened his emotions, he couldn't remember being this angry, either . . . both with Antonia Paxton and with himself.

Look at him, he thought, blearing down his slouched body at his rumpled coat, ruined trousers, and badly scuffed shoes. He was a shambles—filthy, dusty, grease-spotted, and covered with cat hair from the waist down. His hands were scalded, his muscles seemed to have turned to butter, and he could scarcely breathe.

Rallying irritably at the realization of what caused that last discomfort, he launched himself out of his chair and ripped open his coat to stare at the vile engine of female fashion that was squeezing him in two. He fell on the knot with both hands, tugging and prying, working frantically to loosen it, all to no avail.

"Good heavens, my boy," came a voice from the doorway. "When did you start wearing one of those cursed things? I didn't even know you had a prolapse."

Remington's head jerked up with eyes ablaze. "I don't

have a bloody *prolapse*," he snarled, jerking at the ties with frustration.

"Then why are you wearing a corset?" Paddington Carr stared quizzically through a thick pair of spectacles at his nephew.

Remington stared at his eccentric old uncle. "It belongs to . . . a friend. I'm wearing it for him."

"Dem peculiar bloke, ain't he?" The old boy crept closer and adjusted his spectacles to study the details. "All them pink posies on it. Downright femmish, I say. But then, a man has a right to a few crotchets here and there. You know you've got the laces all bollixed up, don't you? They're supposed to start down here and work up, hitting every hole—"

"Yes, dammit—I know!" Remington shouted, slipping over the edge. He wheeled and went for the closest cutting edge in sight—a bayonet hanging above the fireplace with two India Corps rifles. He jammed the blade down through the laces, gave several upward rips, and nearly staggered with relief when the thing slid to his feet.

His uncle frowned at him, then wagged his head. "You know, you could avoid all that if you'd just learn to tie a decent bowline. Dem useful knots, bowlines." Having dropped that jewel of wisdom, the old boy sauntered off with his nose once again stuck in his newspaper.

Remington's shoulders began to quake and a moment later he broke out laughing. He laughed so hard, his face began to hurt and his sides began to ache. He laughed until he had purged every bit of angry tension from his body. It was a full minute before he noticed Phipps and Manley standing in the doorway, looking at him as if he'd lost his mind.

Perhaps he had taken leave of his senses. He'd just spent twelve bloody awful hours wearing a suffocating corset and doing slave labor in a kitchen, in hopes of seducing a woman and ruining her matchmaking career—all as a favor to a group of men he was at school with fifteen or twenty years ago! He was exhausted and confused by his own randy impulses and wishing that he'd never laid a hand on his intended victim. All evening he'd suffered the most arousing and inconvenient obsession with her mouth. And to top it all, his dear old uncle now believed he was going "femmish" and developing a yen for wearing women's unmentionables.

It was all Antonia Paxton's fault, he decided, swaying up the long staircase with his arm across his valet's shoulders. Devious female. Her with her indecently pouty lips, come-hither eyes, and dragon's heart. A true daughter of Eve, if there ever was one. And starting tomorrow, he was going to see that she paid handsomely for it.

The next morning Antonia rose early and spent a long while deciding to wear her midnight-blue challis dress with the leg-of-mutton sleeves and covered buttons down the bodice. She pulled her hair back in its familiar chignon, but decided at the last moment to add a small curl at each temple. And on impulse she dabbed a bit of rose water on the lobe of each ear.

She stood before her mirror smoothing the long waist of her dress, viewing it from several angles, and feeling quite pleased with her previous day's work. There had been a few tricky spots, such as his lordship balking at the corset and that wretched encounter in the servants' hall. She would have to see *that* never happened again. But all in all, it had gone rather well. And today he was going to spend time with Eleanor Booth, their resident expert in cleaning and sometime inventor, and by evening he would drag himself out the door, exactly as he had last night, an exhausted but wiser man.

She hurried downstairs to breakfast and discovered her household in a veritable tizzy. Gertrude had brought up another newspaper, besides *The Times,* with the morning scones, boiled eggs, and tea. It was *Gaflinger's Gazette,* one of those vulgar but widely read papers that poured out of Fleet Street in appalling numbers. And on the front page, halfway down, was an article with a bold black header proclaiming:

THE LADIES' MAN TRIES WOMEN'S WORK

Below that, in lesser typeface, was a still more sensational tidbit: "Wager with the Widow Has Him Tied up in Corset Strings!"

Pollyanna, Prudence, and the others were collected around Aunt Hermione's chair with widened eyes, reading the scandalous report over her shoulder, tsking and tutting. When Antonia demanded to know what had them in such a dither, Hermione handed her the paper, pointing to a specific article and saying, "I'm afraid it's all grist for the gossip mill now, dear."

When she looked at the paper, there was her name in bold black print, linked to Remington Carr's in vivid and scorchingly accurate detail. She was portrayed in a sympathetic light, as the lovely and virtuous upholder of the sacred values of home and marriage, while Remington Carr was painted as a rogue noble, the flagrant and hedonistic challenger of society's time-tested and God-ordained order. Detailing the outrageous wager and the writer's glimpse of him on his first day of his compliance with it—corset and all—the article promised the reader future installments and a full report on the outcome.

She lifted her head, and her eyes narrowed in calculation. Then the tension in her frame melted and she turned a smile on the anxious faces around her.

"I think it will be a bonus, at the end of this wager, to have his lordship's change of heart made public . . . as a lesson to others of his radical persuasion." She took a deep, satisfied breath. "I'd say we're doing rather well."

Remington Carr stalked down Piccadilly, his jaw set and his heels raising dust as they pounded the street. When he rounded a curve and glimpsed a knot of men lounging around the front stoop of Antonia Paxton's house, his countenance darkened. There were at least eight or ten of them, some of whom he recognized as writers from reputable papers. The vultures had gathered, he groaned privately.

Fitch and his damnable article. The wretch had already ruined his breakfast by delivering a copy of that scandal sheet to his front door so that he wouldn't miss it. It was bad enough just to see his name in print in that scurrilous rag; now Fitch's inflammatory scratchings had unleashed a whole pack of scandalmongers upon him!

They spotted him coming down the street and descended on him in a rush. "Back for another day of women's work, yer lordship?" they wanted to know. "Do you really intend to scrub floors and empty slops for a whole fortnight?" "What sort of work does the lady make you do? Anything . . . *special*?" "Is it true about the corset?" "How did you like wearing it, your lordship?" And worst of all: "Are you wearing it now?"

His hands clenched at his sides and his face glowed dusky red, but he managed to stride on toward the front door of Paxton House, in patrician silence. During the walk from his house he had steeled himself for this very possibility. The only way to deal with these muckrakers, he knew, was to ignore them. Anything else was not only undignified, it was potentially dangerous; they had an appalling tendency to twist words toward the sensational.

He pounded on the door with his fist and it opened instantly, just wide enough and long enough for him to slip inside. When it was securely closed against the clamor outside, he resettled both his coat and his composure and handed off his hat to old Hoskins, who just stared at him for a moment, then shuffled away mumbling, "Pitiful bastard."

"Well, it appears you made it through the gauntlet outside the door," Antonia greeted him moments later. She paused some distance away, looking fresh and well rested and abominably blue-eyed.

"And why shouldn't I?" he said curtly. "I have nothing to hide. I am doing this to make a point, after all."

"As am I," she said primly. "But making *my* point does not require publicizing our wager all over London."

"Nor does making mine," he said in bristling tones.

In the silence that followed each took stock of the other's determination.

"What's done is done," she said. "This morning you will work with Eleanor Booth, who is in charge of our cleaning and maintenance. She's waiting in the linen room upstairs."

"Lead on, Lady Antonia," he said with a sardonic edge. "I am positively itching to get my hands on a feather duster."

She led him down the upstairs hall toward yet another set of stairs, pointing out the upstairs parlor, the tiled bathroom, and the various bedchambers. When she sailed past a pair of ornate double doors, he paused and asked what was behind them. A hint of pink appeared in her cheeks as she indicated it was her own bedroom and private bath. His smile, which implied a great deal even while appearing

the epitome of politeness, stayed with her all the rest of the
way down the hall.

The linen room was a well-lit chamber on the third
floor, at the back of the house. It smelled strongly of wax
and freshly starched linen, and was lined with shelves that
held a variety of linen and household gadgetry and equipment ranging from warming pans to rug beaters and pillow
fluffers, from shoe trees to darning eggs to candle snuffers.
He strolled around the shelves, trunks, fire screens, and
assorted boxes that littered the floor, wondering if he had a
room like this in his house . . . and if so, why he'd never
seen it.

"Eleanor must have stepped out for a moment," she
said, wrapping her arms around her waist as she watched
him prowl the working heart of her house. He was purely
devastating this morning in his black coat and fawn-
colored trousers with matching vest. He seemed to be made
of one long, smooth piece of timber. With her gaze riveted
on his cloth-covered vest buttons, she felt a rustle of disquiet, and it was a moment before she understood why.
Something was missing.

"Your corset, your lordship," she said, straightening
and confronting him with her most potent stare. "You're
not wearing it."

He leaned back on one leg and gave her an innocent
look. "Am I not?" He glanced down at his middle. "Are you
sure? How can you tell?"

"Well, I cannot . . . ," she began, then halted.

"See it?" he finished for her. He smiled. "Neither can I
see yours. I presume you *are* wearing one." He paused,
waiting for her to respond.

"But I can tell by the way you . . ." She halted again,
sensing the danger in admitting that she had scrutinized
his movements so closely. "You're not wearing it."

"Ahhh . . . you require proof, do you?" His face was

the very picture of male sensual cunning: relaxed, half smiling. "I can see there is only one way to satisfy you." He opened his coat to her and his voice lowered. "Come, feel for yourself."

The subtle purr of suggestion in his voice stroked every nerve in her body, and she reacted with a private shiver. Feel him . . . her cool hands against his warm body . . . searching him, feeling his ribs and rising up the slope of his chest . . . Both her curiosity and her fingers itched to accept that scandalous offer of access to his person. He swayed nearer, and nearer, and the snare of temptation was suddenly within arm's reach. All she had to do was extend her hand . . . touch those vest buttons . . .

Her breath came faster, and in a last burst of confusion she looked up and caught the faint glint of triumph in his eyes. It set off a quiet alarm in her that froze her in place, giving cool reason time to combat his heated allure. A moment later she stepped back with her face aflame. The wretch! To prove him wrong, she'd have to touch him, feel his body. And even if he wasn't wearing it, she sensed he still would have won.

Were they going to touch or weren't they? Eleanor stood watching, just outside the linen-room doorway. Then Antonia stepped back away from him with a scorching look, and the moment was past. Eleanor sighed and charged through the door, seeming breathless and apologetic.

"Here she is, at last. Eleanor will instruct you in the many tasks a woman must perform to keep a house in fine fettle," Antonia said curtly. Then with a nod and a "Good morning," she sailed out the door.

Remington ruefully raised one eyebrow and began to rebutton his coat.

"Oh, you needn't fasten your coat, your lordship," tall, plain-faced Eleanor declared as she lowered her nose to peer at him above her spectacles. "You won't be needing it for a while."

Eleanor knew whereof she spoke. No sooner had he deposited his coat on a peg by the door, than she thrust a slate into his hands and began to tie a long apron around him.

"Each day of the week is given over to a specific task," she explained. "Monday is for sweeping and mopping. Tuesday is turning, beating, and dusting day. Wednesday is for scouring, scrubbing, and washing. Thursday is for polishing . . . Friday for seasonal tasks like window washing, and curtain cleaning, and so on." A twinkle came into her eye as she leaned a bit closer. "This being Tuesday, the first thing we do is dust."

When he turned to the vase full of feather dusters on a cabinet by the door, she stopped him with a tug on the apron. "Oh, no," she said. "Nothing as outmoded as that. We use *this* instead." She threw back a sheet that draped a mechanical contraption that contained elements of what appeared to be a cherry pitter, a fireplace bellows, a rubber hose and funnel, a gear box of some sort, and a canvas laundry bag. She watched him expectantly, waiting for his comment.

"What the devil is it?" was the best he could summon.

"A dusting machine," she announced, glowing with pride.

"A what?"

"A *dusting machine.* I used to call it a 'dust sucker,' because that is precisely what it does: suck up dust. But Lady Toni suggested something a bit more genteel. Just wait until you see it work!" The unwieldy-looking thing was mounted on a barrellike stand on wheels. She rolled it straight for the door, and when he hesitated, she called out, "Well, don't just stand there—come on!"

He helped her roll the machine across the passage and

then carefully nudge it down the narrow steps, one at a time. Once in the broad upstairs hallway, Eleanor set a breakneck pace for the upstairs parlor, leaving him to push it along by himself. In the parlor she threw back the curtains to let in plenty of light, then unwound a long rubber tube, which had a ring of feathers attached to one end, from the body of the machine. She ordered him to turn the crank handle, and the leather bellows heaved, the contraption wheezed, and the canvas bag fluttered, then inflated. Eleanor brushed the feathery end of the hose over the top of a parlor table.

"Crank harder," she said, scowling at the residue of dust left on the wood. And when the machine wheezed louder and pulled harder, her dismay turned to relief. "See there . . . it's working!"

Lo and behold, it was. The machine was inhaling the dust swept up by the feathers and was somehow ingesting it. The table was left as clean as if it had been dusted by a rag. She went from table to desk to lamp, raising dust with her feathers, then whisking it away with her hose. As she worked, she explained the parts and the mechanical principles to Remington, whose chest soon began to heave from the exertion of providing power to the machine.

Before the parlor was dust free, he had to switch hands. And he switched back when they did Aunt Hermione's room, then again when they did the Quimby sisters' rooms. When they reached the hallway and Eleanor bustled along toward yet another room, Remington arched his back, flexed his aching hands, and glowered after her.

"Wouldn't it be a great deal less trouble simply to use a rag or a feather duster?"

She halted and turned back with an expression that branded him as a pure Philistine. "Where would the world be if people all went about doing things the same way they've always done them? How would inventors ever perfect their machines, if they were only looking for the easy way? It takes a great deal of hard work to make something that saves us labor. Someday this machine will make women's work easier by half, and I believe that's worth a bit of sacrifice in the here and now."

It was then that Remington realized it was not just her machine, it was her *invention*. The glow that lit her face as she talked about its potential to save hours of odious labor suddenly made sense—and unsettling sense, at that.

By the time they finished the second floor and trundled the machine down to the ground floor, his shoulders were aching and he was getting blisters on both hands. He was more than willing to rest for a few moments while Eleanor showed him the one room they wouldn't be dusting with her machine, Sir Geoffrey's old study.

They entered a large, paneled room, filled ceiling to floor with porcelain figurines. Every square inch of horizontal surface was covered by a piece of Staffordshire ware portraying some famous person, work of art, or landmark event in British history. Some of the pieces were well-done and artistic, and some were cheap, gaudy—even grotesque —imitations of finer imported pieces. Every one of them, Eleanor informed him, belonged to old Cleo Royal—her sole legacy from thirty years treading the theatrical boards with her famous actor husband. Lady Toni had set aside the room for Cleo's precious things and allowed Cleo to tend and dust them herself, by hand. There was a near reverence in the way Eleanor led him around the room and pointed out specific pieces in hushed tones. And when they left, she closed the door softly, the way she would on a sleeping child.

Remington shoved the pathetic scene from his mind as he returned to work. With genuine relief he accepted Eleanor's offer to let him handle the dusting hose while she turned the crank. But picking up dust with the contraption wasn't as easy as it looked. And when he looked back, he was chagrined to see Eleanor spinning the crank quickly and steadily, with no visible duress.

When the dining room and rear parlor were finished, Eleanor brushed her apron and informed him it was time they went down to the kitchen for a cup of tea.

"Tea?" he said sharply. "At this hour?"

"We aren't as young as we once were, and tea is quite stimulating, you know," Eleanor said, her eyes twinkling. "We take a bit of liberty with the 'usuals and propers,' in this house."

More than a bit of liberty, Remington bit his tongue to keep from saying. Visibly reluctant, he followed her back through the house and down to the kitchen, where they found Gertrude and the aged Esther hard in the throes of dinner preparations. Gertrude smiled broadly when she saw them and took time to brew them a pot of tea. While they waited for it to steep, Eleanor perched on a stool at the end of one of the long worktables and invited him to do the same. He settled stiffly, listening to Gertrude and Eleanor chat about how well he was doing with "cleaning." Then when the tea was poured, Eleanor sighed as she sipped.

"If only I could find a better way to power my machine." She sent him a rueful smile. "It's a beast to turn, I know. I should have warned you. I forget because I'm used to it . . . I always have to turn and dust by myself."

Remington felt an odd sinking in his stomach and sat straighter to compensate. He stole a glance at his stiff, aching hands. She expected him to believe she usually did it all by herself, when he was wilting after just part of a morning's work?

"Someday I'll find a proper way to power it," she went on. "I believe there's a great deal of promise in this 'electricity' business. They say it will run engines someday . . . power all sorts of new inventions. There's talk of electrifying part of London with those French lamps—arc lamps. And there's that American fellow, an inventor named Thomas Edison. He's just made a special glass bulb that will allow them to bring electrical light right inside houses." She looked positively transported at the prospect.

"Imagine flipping a switch and having instant light. No gassy vapors, no hiss, no messy oil or wicks or kerosene. Just clean, beautiful light." Her face softened, and in that moment she was transformed from a plain, spinsterish-looking woman into a creature filled with the light herself, the glow of learning and curiosity and drive.

"I wish my Edmond had lived to see it. He was a brilliant man, you know. An inventor, too. He held a patent on his self-inflating fountain-pen bladder. I used to help in his shop. . . ." Her voice and her gaze trailed away to some former place and time. And she smiled lovingly at whatever —whoever—she saw there.

"I miss him something fierce, my Edmond. You know, whenever I feel too lonely for him, I just go work on my 'dusting machine,' and I feel closer to him."

Remington felt an alarming constriction in his throat and looked about for an escape. He spotted old Esther coming up from the cellar, struggling with a heavy sack of potatoes, and he lurched up. "Here—let me have that—"

"Nah." The gnarled little prune of a woman waved him away and continued to lug the burden herself, saying: "It wouldna do fer yer lor'ship ta get all dirty."

Remington trudged back through the downstairs hall behind Eleanor Booth, red-faced and roundly disturbed by the unsettled feeling the morning's events had produced in him. He shook it off and concentrated on helping his tutor dust the drawing room and center hall, then lug her invention back up two flights of stairs. By the time they reached the top, he was panting and relieved to see his tutor was at least breathing hard herself.

He unrolled his sleeves, doffed his apron, and donned his coat, then trudged back down the stairs to dinner under a thickening cloud of dread. When he set foot through the dining-room doors and Antonia's ladies greeted him with cheery nods and smiles, his stomach tightened into a knot. He groaned silently. They were going to be *nice* to him again.

_____

Remington was Eleanor's for the afternoon as well, and she introduced him to the "turning and beating" part of Tuesday-work. She had constructed a chart that plotted out every cleaning task in every room and scheduled them to be done on a rotating basis. At a glance, she demonstrated proudly, she could tell exactly when a rug was last aired and beaten and when a mattress was turned or a pillow was cleaned or reticked.

In short order he found himself apron clad once more and climbing up onto the ropes at the head of an old tester bed to haul the mattress up and flip it over. Afterward they went from one room to another, stripping beds and turning mattresses, and by the third room Eleanor's nose was red and her eyes were full of tears.

"It's nothing," she said, waving his expression of concern aside and dabbing at her watery eyes with a handkerchief. "This is Cleo's room. She has one of the feather mattresses, and I cannot be around them without my eyes watering up."

He watched her blow her nose, then start to climb back up onto the foot of the bed. "Stay where you are," he ordered. "I'll manage this one myself."

Seizing the unwieldy bag of feathers by the edge, he hauled and twisted and strained. The stuffing kept sliding around inside the ticking, and as he jerked furiously on it, he smacked his head on the bed frame. He would have cursed roundly if he hadn't heard Eleanor gasp, "Are you all right, your lordship?"

"Fine," he said through a clenched jaw. "Excellent. Never better." From that moment his battle with that feather mattress became a matter of male honor; he was going to turn the cursed thing or die trying. After several minutes he succeeded, and while they were resettling and replumping the feathers, he asked Eleanor who usually did such work for her.

"I do it myself," she answered apologetically. "There is a trick to it, you know."

"A trick," he said, running a hand back through his disheveled hair. "Of course. There would be." There was a trick to every bloody thing in this house, he thought. And for the tenth time that day, Antonia waltzed into his thoughts with her blue eyes twinkling at the sight of him all rumpled and sweaty and irritable. He propped his fists on his hips and demanded, "Just what do you have planned for my next torture?"

"Not quite a torture." She smiled and patted him on the arm. "Just a good beating."

In short order they had rolled and trundled three large Persian rugs to the service yard at the back of the house, beside the kitchen. Eleanor handed him a woven cane rug beater, and after a few instructions, he flailed away until the puffs of dust subsided and Eleanor stepped in to rescue the rug. By the time he was through with the second rug, he was tiring, and the third one got a decidedly gentler thrashing.

Antonia stood by the door into the small, high-fenced service yard, watching Remington put his back into every swing of the rug beater. His gentlemanly sleeves were rolled up to his elbows, his tie and starched collar had been removed, and an apron was tied snugly around his narrow midsection. She had lost an argument with herself and had come to see how he was getting along. Now she found herself staring raptly at his broad shoulders and long arms . . . watching his trousers draw taut across his thighs . . . absorbing the singular and intriguing maleness of his movements . . . remembering the heat of his mouth on hers . . .

He halted, straightened, and turned to who he thought was Eleanor. "I think this one's finished. I can't raise so much as a puff of—" He halted at the sight of Antonia, then straightened with a frown.

"Slavery was outlawed long ago, you know," he said. "I could report you."

"Oh?" The impact of his dark eyes shook her free from the trance, and she strolled down the steps and into the yard, giving the rug a thorough inspection. "And who reports it when thousands of women are forced to do this very work—for the very same wage you are receiving?" When his scowl deepened, she smiled. "Women's work is harder than it seems, is it not? It requires a surprising amount of energy and stamina."

"For *serving women*, perhaps," he countered. "That is what you have me doing, servant work."

She laughed softly. "Precisely what most aspiring, middle-class women would have the world believe, that this sort of thing is done entirely by their servants. But in fact, middle-class women, and often ladies as well, must don working clothes and pitch in themselves, managing, directing, and working right alongside whatever servants they can afford. Houses, you see, take a great deal of care. Even the most devoted of housekeepers can accomplish only so much. And good help is hard to find."

"Not, apparently, for you. You seem to have all the help you could possibly need." He propped his arm on the end of the rug beater, scowling as he appraised her. "By the way, just what sort of work do *you* do, Lady Antonia?"

For all his glowering countenance, his words were curiously free of anger.

"I do what most women of substance do: keep the books, pay the bills, meet with financial advisers, oversee the rest of the work, and help wherever it is needed."

She ducked under the clothesline and peered over the rug at him. "I've beaten my share of rugs, your lordship. And turned the crank of Eleanor's dusting machine. And peeled quite a little number of potatoes. A woman in charge of a household has to be able and willing to do whatever is necessary to take care of her family." She found her gaze migrating to his and jerked her head aside, patting the rug with her hand, testing his work.

"Then, of course, there is charity work. I sit on the board of the Parish Council of St. Matthew's diocese and on the board of the Widows' Assistance League, of which the queen herself is a primary patroness. Being a widow herself, she has taken quite an interest in our work. I have had two personal letters from her."

He ducked under the clothesline as she spoke and came up beside her, tugging at her senses the way the slight breeze tugged at her hair.

"Why do you do it?" he asked, looking down at her. There wasn't a trace of condescension in his voice. "Why do you take these women in? There has to be a less drastic way of getting decent help."

"They aren't *help*, they're family," she said, losing her internal battle and looking up into his dark-framed face. "My family. I've taken them in because I like them very much, and I think they've been handed a dismal and unfair lot. They are widows and I'm one, too. I know what they have faced in losing their husbands."

The breeze tugged at the neck of his shirt, and she

couldn't help the way her gaze drifted to it, couldn't help thinking how completely different he looked without his collar and cravat: how male, how . . . accessible. She was fascinated by the way his shoulders seemed to grow as he propped his hands on his waist, the way he canted his head as he looked at her, and the way he spread his long legs as if bracing to take on the world. And just now she was achingly aware of the intensity of his gaze.

"Where is your real family?" he asked.

"If you mean my parents, they both passed away several years ago. My only close relative is my father's brother, the Duke of Wentworth. But I have not seen him since I married Sir Geoffrey." A curl from her temple blew across her cheek, and she pulled it from her eyelashes and flipped it back.

"Your grandfather was Duke of Wentworth, then," he mused, watching her trying to tame that flirtatious lock of hair. He edged closer. She stepped backward, straight into the heavy rug, which stopped her like a wall. He leaned still closer.

"Y-your lordship!" Her hands came up between them, pressing against his ribs as he leaned into her.

"Remington," he corrected.

"You're . . . you're . . ." How could she say what she was thinking? That he was warm and solid in a way she hadn't quite expected? That touching him and kissing him were all she had thought about since that morning? That she found him compelling in a physically arousing way? How could she say that the feel of his ribs against her arms knocked every other thought from— *His ribs.*

"You're not wearing your corset," she charged softly, looking up into his eyes.

"I couldn't breathe," he said, dragging his gaze slowly over her face.

"That was the idea."

"Was it?"

He laughed softly, a low, chest-deep rumble. An instant later his hands slid around her waist, feeling her. She drew in a sharp breath she couldn't seem to expel.

"You aren't wearing one either." His smile broadened as his hands molded to her waist and began to move, exploring and claiming that sensitive curve. "Not entirely proper of you, Antonia. But entirely interesting of you. *No corset.* It gives a man pause to wonder just what other little hypocrisies you practice beneath those proper clothes."

He bent toward her, his eyes sliding over her upturned face as his hands glided down her back, exploring every curve and hollow of her through her clothing, melting her resistance and dissolving her determination. He had wanted to touch her, she could see it in his eyes. Before she quite realized how it happened, she was standing in the circle of his arms, pressed fully against his long frame.

Her hands were caught between them, and to free them, she had to slide them along his stomach. His body felt taut and hard as her fingers splayed, covering as much of him as their span would allow. That firmness, that entrancing male symmetry was made for wielding a sort of raw physical power that was both foreign and forbidden . . . and all the more alluring for it.

His face, lowering slowly toward hers, was all intriguing angles and arresting curves. Prominent cheekbones and strong chin, broad brow and finely sculptured nose; every part fit with every other in perfect balance. His lips were parted, his head tilted, and she instinctively turned her head to a complimentary angle, holding her breath, anticipating that surge of warmth, that first taste of him.

Pleasure, thick and sweet, poured through her from the instant of contact. Oh Lord—it was exactly as she remembered, and more. Her senses opened, her lips parted under his, hungry for the taste of him. He toyed with her lips, licking, teasing her until she moaned softly and slid her arms around his waist, molding herself against him, coaxing from him the deeper, more intimate sensation she craved. She felt his hum of approval resonating through their joined mouths, and then felt his tongue . . . experienced the lush, erotic penetrations that seemed to reach into her passions, her emotion, down into her very—

"Lemonade, your lordship!" Eleanor's voice rang out cheerily over the small fenced yard.

His head snapped up. Hers jerked aside. He stumbled back and she bolted away several steps. Both were red-faced and dark-eyed with embarrassment when Eleanor spotted his head above the rug—"There you are"—and carried her tray of refreshments around. "Oh, Lady Toni! I didn't know you were here or I'd have brought you a glass as well."

"It's just as well you didn't," Antonia said hoarsely, turning her face away from Eleanor, inspecting the rug behind her. Her lips felt hot and conspicuous. "I was just checking on his lordship's progress." She tossed him a turbulent look that she prayed would pass for indignation. "Be sure to keep him busy, Eleanor. Remember: idle hands are the devil's workshop."

And idle lips are the devil's playground, she realized as she sagged against the wall in the stairwell moments later. The proof was the way her lips were on fire this very moment. The wretch had done it again: caught her alone, cozened and tempted and kissed her to the ends of her endurance. Her heart was racing and her whole body was trembling. What was it about Remington Carr that seized her senses and turned her into a witless, libidinous creature bent on possessing his mouth?

Once more, by the barest of margins, she had been saved from his baser impulses. And her own. As she recovered enough to proceed up the stairs to the small downstairs parlor, the thinness of that margin of safety became humiliating. He kissed her and had taken unthinkable liberties with her person. Sweet heaven—she could still feel the heat of his hands on her waist and rising up her back!

She picked up her lap desk and carried it to the window seat, jamming it onto her lap when she was seated, pinning herself in place. A few calming breaths later, she told herself that she was at least making progress. He wasn't as snappish and irritable as he had been at first. Perhaps her ladies were beginning to get to him. If she could just keep her distance and keep her wits about her, there was every reason to believe she might win her wager and change his abominable attitudes toward women. Twelve days . . . they had twelve days yet to go. Suddenly that seemed like forever.

Remington helped carry the rugs back to their respective places, trying to behave as if nothing had happened. But it felt as if a great deal had happened, and he wasn't sure he understood it all. For the second time in as many days, he had had her in his arms and had kissed her within an inch of her soul. And for the second time he felt rattled and hungry and unaccountably disturbed. What in blazes was wrong with him?

Standing there with her in his arms, feeling her softness against him, and tasting her ripe-cherry mouth, he had felt something slipping inside him, something nameless and worrisome. It felt like control and it had nothing to do with mere events. His stomach slid lower, toward the source of that feeling—his loins.

The fact that he was slipping deeper and deeper into lust for the woman who was his sworn enemy alarmed him. But a moment later he was vindicated by the thought that he hadn't been the only one warmed and willing. Her arms around him and her sighs of pleasure had said she too was affected by their kiss. A wave of cool, restoring reason poured through him. He was making definite progress here.

No more of this ridiculous trepidation, he decided as he washed for supper. At the very first opportunity Antonia Paxton was going to find herself on her back, being loved to the very end of her soul. And she was damn well going to like it.

That night Remington dragged himself through his front door in much the same condition he had been in the previous night: frazzled, aching, and weary to the marrow of his bones. Phipps and Manley took one look at him, poured him a killer draft of brandy, and steered him straight into a steaming bath.

When he came out of the tiled bathing room into his ornate Louis XIV bedchamber, Uncle Paddington was sitting on the armless divan, smoking his briarwood pipe and looking grave indeed. In his hand was a folded newspaper, and from the look on the old boy's face, Remington knew it had to be a copy of *Gaflinger's*.

"What's got into you, Remington?" Paddington Carr demanded, removing the pipe from his mouth. "Wearing corsets, and making wagers with women, and doing female labor . . ." He looked indignant in the extreme. "What next? A blistering case of housemaid's knees?"

"It's a wager. A trifle," Remington declared, shrugging and mopping his brow with the towel hanging about his neck. "Nothing for you to be concerned about."

"It is very much my concern." Paddington tossed the paper aside and raised an admonishing finger. "Never said much about your yen for strange politics . . . that female emancipation, and other such nonsense. But things have finally got out of hand. As your father's brother, I feel obliged to step in and do a father's duty by you." Rotund, ruddy-cheeked Uncle Paddington pushed to his feet and stood with his arms crossed over his ample chest.

"See here, my boy, it is your duty to preserve both the family name and the family dignity. It's high time you gave up this wretched shilly-shallying and settled down . . . married and established a nursery." He shook a finger again. "You need an heir, my boy. Nothing like begetting heirs to steady and settle a fellow."

"To *strangle* a fellow," Remington said into his towel as he wiped his face.

"What was that?" his uncle said, scowling.

"I said I'll get around to 'steady and settled' soon enough," Remington declared, louder and more sharply than he intended.

"Better not wait too long," Uncle Paddington said sagely, clamping his pipe back between his teeth and letting his gaze and thoughts drift. "All the good women will be snapped up. I should know, my boy. Happened to me. While I was dillydallying, the one true love of my life up and married another. Never found a woman half so pretty or clever or sweet-natured, ever again." His voice and attention trailed off, as they often did, into events long stored in his mind.

Remington watched the old boy's shoulders round and felt a painful surge of protectiveness toward him. Disappointed in love and living a life overshadowed by regret, the Carr men seemed to have an exceptionally bad time of it with women. His father had had too many, his uncle too few. And *he* had had—

"A nursery." Uncle Paddington roused enough to look at Remington with a smile that bore traces of transitory bewilderment and sadness. "Always liked babies. Never had any offshoots myself . . . you were the closest to it. Dem frisky little thing. Keen as a whip-crack. Used to make me your hobbledy horse, y'know." He crossed that narrow boundary into reason's twilight again. "Little blighter . . . you wrecked several of my best cravats. Never could stay angry with you, though. Still always tiptoed into the nursery at night . . . to hear your prayers. . . ."

Remington's jaw clamped fiercely against the hot tide of feeling surging into his chest. In those precarious days Uncle Paddington had been far more of a father to him than his own self-absorbed and pleasure-seeking sire. He had no intention of spoiling the old boy's dreams with the nasty jolt of his loathing for marriage. But shortly, Paddington himself roused to burst that fragile bubble of memory. He straightened, focused both his gaze and his mind once more, and leveled a firm look at Remington.

"Babies require women. What we need to do, my boy, is get you a wife."

Remington groaned.

The story of Remington and Antonia's wager appeared in no less than nine newspapers the next morning, including *The Times.* Fully two thirds of London awakened to accounts of the wager, which were grandly embellished and embroidered—not the least of which was an imaginative description of Remington's newly discovered aptitude for swinging a rug beater. One enterprising news writer had apparently scaled a neighboring fence to look down into the service yard for that scoop.

From peers to shopkeepers, from household domestics to Liberal Party leaders, London tongues were awag with the juicy details of the earl's latest outrage. And since *The Times* was one of two papers the queen permitted in her personal residence, the tale was soon rattling boxes there as well.

Anyone who knew the aging Victoria knew that the years had not dulled the sharpness of her ears any more than it had her tongue or her stubborn will. When she saw her daughters whispering over the paper that morning in her Buckingham House sitting room, she demanded to know what had them in a tither. Under her formidable gaze they read the article aloud.

As the wager and its noteworthy participants were unfolded before her, she stilled, scowled, and reddened ominously. She sat for a moment after the reading was finished, smoothing the black silk of her gown with a methodical hand.

"Landon . . . that hideous scapegrace," she announced her opinion with a billow of royal and righteous ire. "The man has no sense of decency, morality, or duty. He's a perfect example of what comes of too much education. We have always said all that intense brain work is unhealthy. It turns a man inward, makes him amoral and selfish." She pushed up from her chair and began to pace.

"Worse yet, he's giving the old and honorable title of 'Landon' a royal drubbing. It's unconscionable, unpardonable." She paused halfway back from the window. "What was the name of the lady again?"

Princess Beatrice glanced back at the newspaper. "Lady Antonia Paxton, Mama."

"Paxton? Yes, we remember it. A most honorable name. It was Sir John Paxton who built our Crystal Palace for the Great Exhibition."

"It says here she is the widow of Sir *Geoffrey* Paxton," Beatrice offered.

"Widow?" The queen's plump face knotted briefly with concentration, then eased. "Ah, yes. The late Sir Geoffrey's wife. We thought the name sounded familiar. She is on the board of the Widows' Assistance League. A fine woman, we are given to think." She straightened her rounded shoulders and drew herself up to her full height. "If anyone can teach him the value of hearth and home, she can. Let us lend her our good thoughts and the sustenance of our own personal high regard." Her eyes narrowed and her chin raised regally. "And let us pray she shows the wretch no mercy."

"What's happened? What's the matter, Auntie?" Antonia rushed into Hermione's darkened room that same morning, and straight to the armless settee on which the old lady reclined. She turned with a questioning look to Prudence Quimby, who sat nearby. "Is she all right?"

"I'm fine, Toni dear," Hermione answered for herself. "Or at least I will be when I rid myself of this merciless headache." She looked up with eyes that seemed frightfully worn and delicate.

Anxiety washed through Antonia. "Are you certain?" she said, reaching for the old lady's cool, dry hand and settling onto the edge of the fainting couch beside her. "I could send for Dr. Bigelow."

"That silly man?" Hermione harumphed softly. "He'd just give me one of his pacifying herbals and tell me to loosen my stays. No, my dear, you needn't fret. I shall be fine." She patted Antonia's hand as it rested on her own, then recalled something. "Oh, but his lordship—I was to tutor him in menu planning this afternoon!" The thought clearly distressed her as much as her malady did.

"Don't worry, Auntie, I'll see to it. I'll—" She bit her lip and thought of whom she could get to replace Aunt Hermione. There was no one else. "I'll just have to do it myself." She tucked a knitted coverlet around Hermione and then tiptoed out.

As the door clicked shut, Hermione's eyes popped open and she raised up onto one elbow. "Well," she said, meeting Prudence's conspiratorial smile with one of her own, "that wasn't too difficult."

Silence fell over the sunlit dining room as old Hoskins shuffled out, carrying the last tray of breakfast dishes back to the kitchen. Antonia straightened a small stack of papers on the dining table, then picked them up and arranged and rearranged them, waiting for Remington to arrive.

She had not counted on having to deal with him at close range. All evening and well into the night she had been haunted by the memory of their kiss yesterday in the service yard, and by her unprecedented paralysis in the face of his size and potent male heat. She had just stood there, letting him kiss her, unable either to rebuff him or to retreat, suffering all sorts of wild and pleasurable physical sensations and thinking all manner of dangerous thoughts. About kisses and intimate touches . . . and about what other pleasures they could lead to.

She hadn't thought about kisses and caresses in a very long time, and had *never* spent time thinking about the deeper and more intimate pleasures they sometimes preceded. She had kissed and been caressed before. She was a widow, after all. But she had never actually anticipated it, *longed* for it!

"Here I am, as instructed," he declared, startling her. She whirled and found him standing in the doorway with his arms crossed and his head tilted at a provocative angle.

"I didn't hear the front door," she said, blushing and pressing a hand delicately across her pounding heart.

"That's because I didn't use it. There was a ravening pack of newshounds outside again, so I came down the alley and in through the kitchen door."

"Very enterprising of you."

"I have always been a rather enterprising fellow," he said, glancing at the papers on the table. "And just what is it I am supposed to learn this morning?"

"The rudiments of menu planning," she said, lifting her

chin and fixing her gaze on the door frame beside him. She intended to claim and retain control here. "If you'll recall, we felt it important that you understand something of the effort and skill required in planning meals. So this morning I will endeavor to show you—"

"You? I thought someone else was to tutor me, that you only oversaw the process," he said, invading her vision as he leaned a shoulder against the doorjamb. When she glanced up at his face, he was giving her that insinuating smile that always generated such annoyance in her.

"My aunt Hermione is not feeling well. I am merely taking her place." She pointed to a chair at the end of the table. "Please be seated and we'll begin."

He strolled slowly forward, spurning the chair she had assigned him, and came to stand face-to-face with her. "I prefer not to sit, thank you. I always think better on my feet."

Precisely what she was afraid of, she thought as he loomed beside her. "Suit yourself," she said, snatching up her stack of papers and spreading them across the tabletop as a pretext for putting distance between her and him.

"It must be noted," she began, when she had finished both arranging papers and retreating a discreet step or two, "that the way we do things at Paxton House is not entirely regular. We have a rather unusual household."

"A prodigious understatement," he muttered, just loud enough for her to hear.

"But virtually every woman in charge of a home is faced with the same task we face: planning meals to meet the needs of her family and household. Firstly, it is important to note that there are certain principles of proper nutrition that are vital to the welfare of body and mind. As you can see, I have outlined for you the foods that medical science has shown should be consumed in order to maintain health and vigor."

When he didn't follow her pointing finger, she lifted a sheet of paper and held it up in his line of sight. "You can see . . . dairy goods, breads and grains, fruits and vegetables, and meats, fowl, and fish are all required."

"Are they indeed?" he said, letting his attention wander past the edge of the paper to her breasts.

"They are," she said irritably, feeling as much as seeing the drift of his concentration, watching him pondering whether or not she was wearing a corset today. She raised her list, using it to block his view. "A good part of women's work deals with seeing to the needs of family members. While making selections from these necessary foods, there are additional considerations. There may be health requirements to take into account . . . and, of course, personal preferences."

"Personal preferences?"

"Obviously, not everyone likes the same kinds of food. Some people have refined and particular tastes, while others have more accommodating palates," she said in her most authoritative tone, directing her gaze and her words into his cravat.

"And what about you, Lady Antonia?" he asked, studying her with an intensity that made her feel all-too-familiar prickles along her shoulders. "Are you known to be particular? Or are you more the *accommodating* type?"

He was at it again, she realized, feeling her heartbeat quicken in spite of her. He was turning every statement, every exchange into a personal and provocative encounter, and she couldn't allow him to get by with it. She took a deep, fortifying breath and made herself look him square in the eye.

"Particular. Most particular," she declared, answering his multilayered question on every devious and suggestive level on which he intended it. "And I make no apologies for it. I am of that school of thought which says there is a wisdom contained within each person's own physical constitution . . . which is expressed in preferences for certain foods. The body knows what it needs." The instant she said it, she knew it was a mistake.

"It does, does it?" he said, looking her over with a smile that contained an indecent amount of pleasure. "And what does *your* body need, Lady Antonia?"

She felt her face heating. The wretch. How dare he stand there, with his insolent eyes and presuming smirk, and torture her with her own verbal indiscretions? She quickly looked out over the table to find a sheet with her name printed on it and held it up beside the other list.

"Roast fowl, steamed fish, and an occasional bit of lamb at Easter."

"That's all?" He peered around that curtain of paper, looking quizzically down her elegantly rounded body and then back up. "Surely you eat more than that."

"Well . . . of course . . . I also require grains and vegetables and dairy foods."

"But no red meat? No red wine?"

"Never." She reddened, knowing what he insinuated. Such foods were widely known to incite the passions. "They don't agree with me. They're much too . . ."

"Stimulating?" he offered, watching pink blooming in her cheeks.

"Stultifying," she countered, goaded to find the right word by his use of the wrong one. "They dull the palate and the senses."

"Ummm . . . but they also warm and enrich the blood." His gaze slid over her. "And it appears to me your blood could use a bit of warming."

She felt him taking hold of the papers, pulling them down, down, to look at her and make her look at him. Abruptly, she surrendered them to his hands and sat down on the chair behind her, turning to face the table. She expelled a relieved breath, but stopped halfway through when she realized that he was dragging a chair down the table and settling on it beside her.

"Cleo, for instance, can eat nothing but sops, and soft, bland dishes. Her stomach is very delicate." She saw his hand moving toward her from the corner of her eye, and quickly stuffed the listing of Cleo's dietary requirements in it.

"And Eleanor will eat only dairy foods, vegetables, beans, and legumes . . . things like peas and beans and mustard greens. She has very strong convictions against killing warm-blooded creatures for food." She located Eleanor's sheet and thrust it into his handful of papers. "Whereas Molly—having lived all those years with a butcher—is very fond of ham, chops, and sausage. And then there is Aunt Hermione, who will eat most forms of fowl and fish, and Pollyanna, who has a taste for pickled foods . . ."

As she called each woman's name, she snatched up a sheet of paper listing her dietary requirements and preferences, read from it, and stuffed it into his hands. She refused to look at him, but some extra sense told her exactly how far he was from her shoulder—*two inches*—and exactly what he was doing—*staring hotly at her*. When she picked up a sheet, he pulled it from her hands before she had a chance to read it. She picked up another and he took it the same way . . . then another, and another.

In that slow, inexorable slide of paper, she felt control of the situation passing from her hands to his. He was pulling it from her, little by little, and in the process gently stealing her attention. For some reason she couldn't summon any outrage or even any resistance. She turned her head slowly and found him leaning close, his eyes clear and compelling, his features polished with an irresistible half smile.

"I will not need your lists and charts, Antonia," he said, tossing the lot of them onto the tabletop. "I am of that school of thought which says one can tell what a woman eats just by looking at her. Gertrude, for instance, has a passion for potatoes . . . and she looks like a dumpling. Old Esther, from your scullery, eats so many prunes she has turned into one, and Pollyanna's pickled fare has soured her, from the inside out." His head tilted and his gaze flowed appreciatively over her.

"And you, Antonia," his voice lowered to an intimate rumble, "I can tell you exactly what you eat."

She sat entranced, unable to move.

"You love milk and cream."

"Gertrude told you that," she said, her voice a dry whisper.

"No." One side of his mouth curled in a lazy, heart-stopping grin. "It is here, in your skin." He trailed a finger down the side of her face and around her jaw. "It looks and feels like sumptuous cream."

She shivered at his touch, feeling the thick, tantalizing vibrations of his voice pouring through her with a warm, clinging richness . . . like cream themselves. When his hand withdrew, she released the breath she had been holding and felt those liquid sensations trickling down through her to pool in her middle.

"And cherries. I can tell you love cherries." His hand came back, gently tracing her lips with its fingertips, back and forth, with lingering and seductive strokes, coaxing them to part. "They are here in your lips . . . so red . . . and soft . . . and ripe. Sweet and tart all at once."

It felt as if the underside of her skin were being stroked. Her whole body reacted by tightening: her throat, her clenched hands in her lap, her knees gripping the edge of the chair. That relentlessly gentle touch drifted down her chin and throat, teasing, rousing, caressing, then reversed, rising up her neck and broadening so that he cradled her face in his hand. She felt herself swaying on her seat.

"But I admit that one thing does puzzle me, Antonia. Your eyes. What can you eat that makes them so blue? Robin's eggs? Sapphires? Bits of morning sky? It must be something strange and exotic indeed, for I've never seen eyes like yours."

He was so close that his breath bathed her lips in a stream of warmth as he spoke. Then his face softened into the most heart-stopping expression she could imagine: part expectation, part pleasure.

"Ahhh, you won't tell." He sent anticipation curling through her on a shared breath. "Then perhaps I can still taste it on your lips."

It took an eternity for his mouth to reach hers, but in the wait she never once thought of avoiding it. Warm—his lips were lavishly warm, and their heat quickly melted her, tilting her head, molding her mouth to his. It was like sinking naked into a hot tub of water on a cool autumn night; her skin tingled with a sharpness that was somehow both shocking and pleasurable. Her hand came up to brace against him, touching both the warm skin of his neck and the cool surface of his collar.

Impressions crowded into her senses: scents of sandal-wood and male heat, firm flesh beneath her hand, lips that tasted faintly of peppermint. His arms slid around her, pulling her hard against him, and her hands slid around his neck, pulling his mouth tighter against hers. The yearning that had simmered in her through the long night just past rose to the surface. She arched into him, seeking the feel of him against her. Every part of her came alive; her skin flushed, her limbs tingled.

He drew back partway, raking her swollen, sensitive lips with his, and tracing slow, delicate circles over them with his tongue. The sensations were tender, adoring—

shattering to her. She had never imagined such fineness and subtlety of sensation in a kiss; it was like being stroked by butterfly wings. Then he took the next kiss deeper . . . claimed her lips firmly, coaxing a response with the soft velvet rasp of his tongue against the sleek inner borders of her mouth. Then, exploring the range of the possibilities between them, he crushed her lips beneath his, plundering her mouth, demanding her passion, devouring her response.

Icy-hot shivers of pleasure racked her as she felt him pulling her across his lap, pressing her tight against the hardening ridge in his lap. She felt his hands on her sides, her back, roaming her breasts, reaching for her through the stiff constraint of her garments, and suffered a wild and compelling urge to shed those barriers, to peel every stitch of her clothes away and feel his hot hands on her cool, bare flesh. The core of her grew strangely taut and molten . . . hungry in a way she'd never experienced. She wanted to touch him, too, to feel his body on hers . . . inside hers . . .

"Beg pardon, ma'am," came an age-brittled voice from the doorway.

Antonia jolted back so hard that she nearly toppled from his lap, and as she lurched back onto her own chair, Remington whirled around in an instinctive crouch. Old Hoskins stood there with his shoulders bunched and his mouth drawn into a thin, disapproving line.

"A female visitor, ma'am"—he gestured to Remington with an impatient hand—"calling for his earlship, there."

Antonia was frozen with horror; her heart was pounding, her eyes had trouble focusing, and her lips felt humiliatingly thick and wet. Remington quickly shuttered the need in his eyes and shoved to his feet, adjusting his coat front and cuffs and scowling. It took a moment for him to make sense of what the old butler had said. When it hit him, he blanched and the heat of his desire was channeled into the service of anger.

"A female?" he choked out.

"A tall, bossy female . . . hat like a pile of cowpats and bustle from here to Belgravia," Hoskins snorted, waving his hand irritably in demonstration. "Lace and feathers everywhere"—his mumble trailed off—"looks like the floor of a damned haberdasher's workroom. . . ."

Chapter

8

Remington strode from the dining room in high dudgeon. There was only one woman in his personal acquaintance who fit old Hoskins's irreverent description. When he emerged from the passage into the entry hall, his suspicion was confirmed. There stood a tall, willowy woman in a figured silk dress, extravagantly piled velvet hat, and prodigious feather boa. In one hand she held a folded newspaper and in the other a delicate Parisian parasol, raised as if she intended to use it on someone.

"So there you are," she declared, shaking the newspaper at him.

"What in—creation—are you doing here?" he demanded, heading straight for her, his countenance dark and his voice thunderous.

"The same might be asked of you, Remington Carr!" she said in a voice that with a little more volume might have curdled the paint on the walls.

He glanced furiously around the entry hall and caught sight of Prudence and Pollyanna Quimby at the bottom of the stairs, staring at him and his visitor. Catching a glimpse of the open drawing-room doors, he seized the woman by the arm and, over her piercing protest, ushered her forcibly into the drawing room.

"Sit!" he commanded, propelling her toward one of the

settees, then swinging both of the drawing-room doors closed. When they were alone, he turned back to find her standing beside the settee with her mouth in a petulant line that was dramatized by the lip rouge she wore.

"How dare you come here—barge into this house, demanding to see me!"

"I have sent you notes and messengers for three days," she said with a tremor of outrage in her voice, "and you have coldly and callously ignored me. Then this morning I opened the newspaper to find you have been cavorting about the city with this—this *Paxton* woman—wearing female unmentionables and making laughingstock of yourself. Doing a menial's work when you won't even—"

"Hillary—" he said with a warning growl. "This is none of your—"

"It's abominable and I won't have it, do you hear?" She stomped her foot. "I won't allow you to wash your hands of me just so you can carry on with your hideously selfish life. You have time to cook and to scrub this wretched woman's floors, but you cannot bother to pay me a civil quarter-of-an-hour call to see if I'm fully recovered . . . when you *know* how ill I was!" She pressed her gloved hand to her temple and sniffed artfully. "And I've been waiting for more than a fortnight for you to order my banker to release my quarterly funds early . . . when you know I need to take the waters at Brighton. You owe it to me. You're responsible—"

"Hell, yes, I am responsible!" he snarled, advancing on her so that she started back. "I've been responsible for four bloody long years and you haven't let me forget it for a minute! But I told you after that debacle at White's that one more such outrage and I'd wash my hands of you altogether. And so help me, you've done it again!" He shoved his face into hers, and she shrank to avoid him and dropped onto the settee with an unceremonious plop.

"Charging in here like some wounded harpy, scolding and demanding. Well, by God, enough is enough!"

She stared up at him, her kohl-enhanced eyes widening with the realization that she had pushed him too far. His fists were white at his sides, a vein in his neck bulged, and a new, implacable fire burned in the depths of his eyes. Instantly her strident persona crumbled, and with it she seemed to change physically. Her haughty form deflated over the settee cushions, her shoulders slumped, and her chin shrank as it lowered to her chest.

Remington saw it happening and braced internally. He knew from experience what came next, and this phase infuriated him even more than her strident demands.

"Why are you doing this to me, Remington? abandoning me, casting me off? You know your father wouldn't—"

"Don't you dare bring him up to me!" he bit out, lashing a finger at her. The fury that flared in him caused her to sink even lower into the settee cushions. Out of nowhere a lace-rimmed handkerchief appeared. No, not that, he groaned. Not now, not here!

Her eyes crinkled at the edges, betraying the delicate web of lines that veils and cosmetics usually hid. Tears welled and she lowered her lashes, releasing the tears down powdered cheeks that were beginning to show the crepe of age, past rouged lips that had lost some of their alluring fullness. Bending her head to shield her face from him with her hat, she dabbed at her tears and sobbed enough that her shoulders trembled.

Oh, God . . . the tears. How he hated this part. Her tears were real, he knew, but he couldn't escape the knowledge that she used them against him. He could almost feel the tugs as each sob pulled the strings of duty and protectiveness that bound his male pride. He hated that most of all.

"Enough, Hillary," he said, the anger in his voice dampened. He paced to the door and back, then fished in his coat pocket for his unused handkerchief and thrust it into her hands. "For God's sake, dry it up. I haven't abandoned you . . . I *can't* abandon you. But as God is my witness: from this day on you'll have to find someone else to truckle after your endless needs and appetite for attention." His voice hardened around a core of steel. "I have come to the very end of my patience."

Moments later he pulled open the drawing-room doors and ushered her through the entry hall at an undignified pace. Her hat wobbled and her feather boa dragged forlornly behind her. She stiffened and tried to halt, looking up at him with one last wounded-doe look. "Please, Remington, I promise—"

"No!" he ground out, with a look that said he would not suffer another single appeal. Without waiting for Hoskins he jerked open the front doors and trundled her down the front steps and into her waiting carriage. And as she drove off, glaring through the carriage window at him like an angry child, he shuddered and stalked back up the steps and into the hall.

Hoskins, Eleanor Booth, and the Quimby sisters were standing in the hallway, staring at him as if he had suddenly sprouted another head. But the one that concerned him most was at the far end of the hall, near the dining-room doors. Antonia stood with her arms crossed over her waist, looking at him, then turned on her heel and reentered the dining room.

Setting his jaw, he strode back through the hall and found her gathering up the papers scattered over the table.

"In future," she said, without looking up, "I would prefer you receive your *friends* elsewhere."

"She is hardly a friend," he said, and instantly wished he could take it back.

Her head came up, with eyes shining. "I don't really care to know what she is, your lordship. How you label your *acquaintances* is your affair. Just keep them out of my house."

It did not take a genius to discern what sort of woman his visitor was; one look at Hillary's showy dress and artfully painted face was all that was needed to know her profession. But it would have taken a closer look to see that she had aged beyond her prime in the world of the demimondaine, and to guess that her days as a wealthy earl's mistress were well behind her. And Antonia had not been close enough for that.

Deep in her eyes he could see the traces of unspent passion colliding with outrage at having her home invaded by a member of the demimonde. As he watched, he could see her consigning to the moral trash heap every pleasurable sensation she had just experienced with him.

Damn and blast his father's old mistress for charging in and wrecking his plans!

"Very well. Shall we continue where we left off, Antonia?" he said, stifling his anger beneath a layer of aristocratic control. Her head snapped up, and if he had been any closer, the fire in her eyes would have scorched him.

"Continue where we left off?" She nearly choked. The colossal male conceit! One minute he was seducing her, reducing her to puddles in his arms, and the next he was closeted in her drawing room with his overdressed lightskirt, who had the gall to invade her home! And now he expected to take it up with her again?

"Not on your life, your lordship," she declared, snatching up the lists and charts and thrusting them into his hands as she sailed out the door.

She stormed through the hall toward the stairs, not knowing why she was so angry. Was it because he had plied his devious charm with such devastating effect? Or was it because he had the nerve to suggest they just go on as if nothing had happened, when a great deal had happened, at least in her?

It had felt to her as if she were being turned inside out, body and soul, so that every nerve, every desire, every longing was utterly exposed. As humiliating as her participation in that kiss was, the feelings that erupted in her were far more shattering. Elation, hunger, pleasure, and wonder . . . she had all but come unstrung from that wretched kiss. And the worst part of it all was that it had been but a transitory bit of pleasure to him. Or less.

Shall we continue where we left off? he had suggested coolly.

A moment later her face flamed. It hadn't occurred to her until that moment that he might have been talking about the menu planning.

The man was a menace. And she was seven kinds of a fool to take him into her own house, knowing what a devious and carnal beast he was. Striding furiously into the upstairs parlor, she paced across the room and back, before the presence of Aunt Hermione and Prudence on the settee brought her up short.

"Auntie . . . Prudence." She glanced between the startled women. "What are you doing in here? Auntie, shouldn't you be in bed?"

"N-no, my dear," Hermione answered for the pair, her cheeks suddenly Cupid-pink. "I'm feeling much better now."

Aunt Hermione provided Remington's instruction for the rest of the morning. She arrived in the dining room to find him in a toweringly surly mood. She gave him an understanding smile, which became even more beatific as his glower deepened.

"I'm afraid you're now saddled with me, your lord-ship," she said, looking over the papers littering the table. "How far did you get with Antonia?"

Remington stilled and stared at her. The question had a number of possible interpretations, but her angelic smile made it seem obvious and innocent.

"Not too bloody far," he said with a growl, unsure just which question he was answering.

"Ummm." The white-haired cherub nodded thought-fully. "Then it appears you still have a good bit of work to do. Where did you leave off?"

He had the strangest feeling they were carrying on two conversations at once. But when she just smiled sweetly and focused her attention on the papers strewn about the table, he told himself he was imagining things.

"She had just laid out the dietary demands of the mem-bers of your household when I was called away. If I re-member properly: one will eat nothing uncooked, and another nothing that isn't raw. One will eat no meat, an-other no vegetables. One will eat no fat and another will eat no lean." The sense of it suddenly struck him. "Ye gods—it's Jack Sprat and wife, twelve times over!"

Hermione took no offense. "We are a bit like that, we finicky old cats," she said with a laugh. "And poor Toni lets us get by with it." She shook her head fondly and beck-oned him to a seat beside her at the table. As he held the chair for her, then settled stiffly into one across the table from her, she looked up at him with a decidedly mischie-vous twinkle in her eye. "Ridiculously softhearted, that girl. But her head . . . now, that is another matter altogether."

Midafternoon that same day, Remington found himself burdened with a large willow basket and trailing Molly McFadden along through the vast and bustling Farmer's

Market—under Antonia's watchful eyes. It had taken most of the morning, even with Dame Hermione's able tutelage, for him to wade through that morass of competing nutritional demands and develop a menu plan for the Paxton household. At the end of it he learned that his work was just beginning, for he would be required to do the shopping for it, then to help with the cooking as well.

Buying food didn't sound like a particularly formidable task, until he learned the constraints under which it had to be accomplished: a strict budget. He had to acquire a considerable amount of food with what appeared to be a miserly amount of money.

"It cannot be done," he declared, standing in a busy butcher shop amid hams and hanging strings of sausages, eyeing the numbers on the price board. He turned to Antonia, who had been pressed into accompanying him and Molly McFadden. "What's the point of taking in all these extra mouths to feed," he demanded, "if you cannot afford to feed them?"

"What I can and cannot afford is beside the question, your lordship," she said curtly. She wasn't pleased about being here with his imperial lordship. She wouldn't have come at all if Maude Devine, who usually helped Molly with the shopping, hadn't suddenly come down with a bout of her recurring back ailment. "It is always sound practice to keep expenses—especially food costs—as low as possible. And when it comes to getting the best price on food, our Molly has no peer."

He glanced doubtfully at the figure on his list and back at the price board, then scowled at Molly. "So you think it can be done."

"You bet yer rosy arse it can," plainspoken Molly said with a determined tug at her bonnet strings and a rather indelicate adjustment of the corset straining at her ample waist. She looked for all the world like a bare-knuckles fighter getting ready to step into a ring. "Just watch, yer lor'ship. An' take a lesson."

She stepped up to the counter, peering down her nose at the cuts of meats stacked behind smudged glass cases. With regal disdain she passed over one pile of chops, loins, and cutlets after another. Then she turned that eloquently discerning gaze on the sides of meat hanging behind the counter, near the butcher's worktables. When she was asked what she would like, she threw her first punch:

"I want a solid piece of good English beef wot ain't rouged up nor shot full o' brine nor short-weighted." Then she fixed the butcher with a narrow-eyed look. "So far, I ain't seen a thing wot measures up."

What followed was the baldest and wiliest bit of bargaining Remington had ever seen in his life. Molly shamelessly berated the fellow's meats and poultry, and he just as energetically defamed her judgment, the acuity of her senses, and her knowledge of what constituted good meats. She charged behind the counter and invaded his hanging stock to select the pieces she wanted, then proceeded to question every cut the fellow made for her. She wouldn't pay a pound and six for that joint of ham, she declared, when it wasn't worth more than eleven and ninepence. She finally agreed to take it off his hands for one pound even. The huge capon seemed a bit gray, would have to be cooked that night to keep it from going "off," and she reduced the price by a third.

In a short while she had contracted for their meats and poultry for the week ahead, all within the allotted budget. When they stepped outside into the street, Remington's jaw was set and his nostrils flared with indignation.

"That was the most outrageous display of pound-flogging and penny-pinching I have ever witnessed in my life," he gritted out. The words were intended for Antonia's ears, but they carried to Molly's as well. The butcher's widow lapped one hand over the other around the handle of her market basket and fixed him with a canny look.

"Ain't never had to watch yer pennies, eh, yer lor'ship? Many's the woman who would envy ye. But many more would think ye a fool to pay more than goin' rate for decent food."

"And you. You actually condone this sort of thing in your house?" he demanded of Antonia. Molly spoke for her.

"Ever house must practice some economies, yer lor'ship. It ain't no disgrace. I be Laidy Toni's buyer, and them shopmen would think she run a slack house if I didn't bargain proper." Then with a devious smile she picked up his hand and deposited her bag of coins in it. "Hope ye were watchin' close, m'lord, 'cause it's yer turn next."

He stiffened and gave her his fiercest and most aristocratic glare. "I will not haggle over ha'pennies like some deprived fishwife."

"Afraid you cannot do it, your lordship?" Antonia challenged with a smile that wouldn't have melted butter.

What she couldn't make him do by reason or wheedling, she intended to lever him into by goading his pride, he realized. But recognizing her tactic didn't make it any easier for him to resist, especially when she removed several coins from the household purse and genteelly bargained for a number of spices in the neighboring grocer's shop. He was boxed neatly into a corner of his own male pride. She could do it without apparent loss of dignity, her smug little smile said, but could he?

With a growl of protest he snatched the list from her hands, stuffed the purse into his pocket, and strode into the nearest greengrocer's to do battle for peas, carrots, leeks, and turnips. He felt conspicuous in the extreme among the housekeepers, cooks, and matrons prowling the bins and stands. Worse yet, he had no idea what faults one could decry in a leek or a turnip that would make a shop-keeper reduce its price.

As his frustration mounted, he retreated further and further into hard-nosed aristocratic hauteur. In desperation he inquired after the price of the turnips, declared it "too bloody high," and demanded to know if the local constabulary knew of the shopkeeper's thieving prices. He held his breath as the grocer quickly sized up his mien, his garments, and his superior air, and began—in long-standing English tradition—to defer to his better.

As Remington watched the little man scrambling to refigure his prices, it occurred to him that when all else failed, a pigheaded and insufferable air of nobility had been known to carry the day. And armed with that bit of insight, he was soon bargaining for the rest of his list as well.

Antonia and Molly watched from the front of the shop, biting their lips to keep their laughter from reaching his ears. His manner and countenance were a rather outrageous and self-conscious parody of his own upper-crust assumption and superiority. Seeing him behaving with such inflated condescension, Antonia could not help contrasting that insufferable aristocrat to the man who sat at her kitchen table in a corset, whittling potatoes into nubbins, and the tender, larcenous rogue who poured heated words into her ear and kissed her within an inch of her soul.

Remington Carr seemed to be several men inside, she suddenly understood. Her anger from that morning was dealt a fatal blow. In its place she felt an odd warmth growing for the prideful but sporting man she usually saw. How many noblemen would have braved a whole houseful of women, or donned a ladies' corset, or taken on the work of a scullery maid even to make good a bet? And how many men of any breeding would have braved having their name bandied about in Fleet Street scandal sheets to return for a second dose of women's work?

Dangerous musings, she realized as he stepped out of the shop with his basket filled with vegetables and early fruits, and his eyes filled with satisfied light. Dangerous light. Mesmerizing light.

"Your change, madam," he said, sifting coins through his fingers into Molly's outstretched hand. He turned to Antonia with a triumphant sniff. "And I managed to get some fresh strawberries thrown into the bargain. I love strawberries." He cast her a devastatingly tactile look from the corner of his eye as he started off.

"Not, however, as much as I love cherries and cream."

Antonia managed to stall her reaction until his back was fully turned, then let the shiver come. The handsome wretch. He had just served notice that he wasn't giving up his pursuit of her. To her everlasting shame she flushed hot with pleasure from the top of her head to the ends of her toes.

There were more lessons in store for Remington that afternoon. They entered several plain grocers, baker's stalls, and tea and coffee shops where he watched Molly, and sometimes Antonia, taste, smell, or otherwise test the foodstuffs, then leave without purchasing anything. After the second or third of these fruitless missions, he stopped in the street outside and shifted his heavy shopping basket from one aching hand to the other, demanding to know why they hadn't just made their purchases and gotten on with it.

Molly sidled closer, looking up at him from under the rim of her bonnet, and beckoned him down and into whisper range. "A body has to be wary these days," she said confidentially. "Not all foodstuffs is good food. Even in decent shops ye get food wot's cut wi' tuck an' filler. That coffee . . . he already ground it an' added roast beans an' chicory to stretch th' poundage. Ye cannot buy anythin' but whole, roasted beans and be sure of proper coffee, these days. A body must watch all the time. They'll put potato flour in yer lard, water yer milk, shake barley rubble in yer oats, and put pea flour in yer pepper. Wheat flour gets cut with sulfur, lime, or alum, and yer tea is some part syca-more leaves if yer not careful. Then yer pickles an' yer marmalades—well, ye wouldn' want to know." She shook her head at his expression of disbelief. "Come, I'll show ye."

They led him into a lower-end shop and let him sniff and sample a few ripe offenders. On holding a jar or joint into the sunlight, he could see the blue copper salts in the pickles and that some of the meats looked oddly red. His eyes widened, then narrowed as he began to see the sharp trafficking around him. And when they steered back to the better shops, they found several examples even among the more reputable merchants.

"Food is dear enough," Antonia said to him as she saw him looking at working-class women doling out hard-won pennies for flour and salt that he had only minutes before discovered were badly adulterated. "They can scarcely af-ford it. And when they can buy, it may be as apt to do them harm from some noxious additive as it is to nourish them and their growing families. A woman must know how to tell what is good and what isn't to safeguard her family's health."

"But aren't there acts to stop such things?"

"Look around you, your lordship." Antonia nodded around them, her mien quietly fierce. "Do you see anyone enforcing any 'acts'?"

It was a lesson that followed Remington all through the evening. When he sat down to eat at Antonia's table, he found himself looking at the deliciously crusty bread, tender poached halibut, and savory roast capon with new eyes. When the ladies inquired as to what he had learned while shopping that day, he felt an odd tightness in his throat and glanced at Antonia. She was watching him with an unreadable expression.

He lifted the glass of wine Antonia's abstemious ladies had provided for him and with a bit of effort produced a strained smile.

"I learned that spending money can be exhausting . . . that one should never buy a fish with milky eyes . . . and that I must never make a wager with Molly McFadden. She drives a mean bargain, indeed."

The women laughed and nodded approvingly.

And in spite of himself, his smile began to broaden.

For the next two days Remington was kept busy at a number of tasks; inventorying linen, scrubbing bathing-room porcelain fixtures, polishing floors and furniture, and separating and preparing laundry to be sent out to be cleaned. He learned what constituted a worn bedsheet, how to keep gravy and wine stains from setting in table linen, how to bleach and sanitize a sink, how to scrub down a floor for waxing and then mix a proper beeswax and turpentine mixture, then wax it.

He also learned that women love nothing better than to talk while they work.

It occurred to him that here was a perfect chance to learn things about Antonia that might give him an advantage with her. He began with a simple question or two about them at first: "Where did you live before coming here?" or "How did you meet Lady Antonia?" They generally paused and glanced away into remembered vistas.

They spoke of parents: old and young, well-fixed and penurious, indulgent and stern. And they spoke of their husbands: a young officer, a butcher, a watchmaker, a sailor, a farmer, a petty magistrate, a vice admiral, and a tailor . . . always with heartrending traces of longing.

As he watched Dame Hermione, the most oft-married of the lot, recounting the pleasures of her various husbands' company, he found himself imagining them and envisioning them with a younger version of her. Her girlish smile was contagious as she recounted their exploits, some bordering on the wicked, some on the sublime. All her husbands were held and remembered with great affection. When a mist rose into her eyes, the smile still played at the corners of her mouth. Remington cleared whatever seemed to have gotten stuck in his throat and went back to counting table napkins, trying to think what it was he had intended to ask.

Each woman had a story to tell about how she met Antonia. Some had placed ads in papers or magazines, some had bundled up their possessions and come to scour the streets of London in the desperate hope of finding employment, and some had found her when they stumbled into the settlement house operated by the Assistance League.

"There she stood . . . with the saddest, sweetest eyes," Maude Devine said, dabbing at the corners of her own eyes.

Remington shifted uncomfortably; he knew all about those beguiling blue eyes.

"Like a pure angel, she was," Gertrude said, wagging her head. "A smile so sweet and kind . . . an' me so desperate as to do whatever flesh allowed just to line my belly wi' food."

He adjusted his collar, remembering the alluring little smile that could seem so proper and so wicked at the same time.

"Not a word of rebuke or shaming. Naught but words

of comfort and consolation," Victoria Bentley remembered with disarming candor, lowering her eyes. "Not even when she learned where I had . . . slept . . . the week before."

He fidgeted, thinking of just how sweet Antonia's tongue could be.

Antonia hadn't judged or blamed or coerced these women, he understood. She had merely offered them a place to live, a place where they were needed and wanted. The warmth and admiration in the way they spoke of her unsettled him. He didn't like all this goodness and virtue; he could feel it chipping away at his righteous male indignation. Just as he was about to abandon this potentially dangerous tact, her aunt Hermione came up with a bit of information that piqued his interest.

"She brought a breath of fresh air into Geoffrey's life," Hermione said, pausing in the midst of her stitchery. "He was considerably older and a bit set in his ways. Not a very romantic husband for a young girl. But she didn't seem to mind. Humored him, she did, indulged all his crotchets . . . like candles of an evening. Geoffrey was forward thinking in many ways, but he hated gaslight. Preferred candles at night." She smiled fondly. "And we still use them. Antonia does it out of respect for his memory. That" —the old lady laughed—"and I suspect she loves the candlelight herself."

A woman who loved candlelight and stray cats, but coldly trapped men into marriages. A woman who looked and sounded like an angel but held a devil of a grudge against men, bachelors in particular. One minute she was breathing fire at him, the next she was melting in his arms. He couldn't seem to get a grip on her. And that didn't seem likely to change anytime soon; she seemed to have completely forgotten him.

He looked down at the parlor table he was waxing and saw his scowl reflected to him. What in hell was he doing here?

Contrary to Remington's conclusion, Antonia was far from abandoning or ignoring him. She knew from hour to hour and minute to minute exactly where he was and what he was doing, including the fact that he had begun to talk to her ladies. She made rounds periodically and watched him from a distance as he listened, watched, and bent his efforts—however reluctantly—to the tasks they set for him.

His guarded manner was still there; he still didn't trust them. But as they talked, over the course of two days, Antonia could see additional signs of change in him. His tightly coiled frame had begun to relax, and the hard angles of his face had begun to soften in her ladies' presence. He wasn't as easily startled, and at meals he no longer braced in his chair as if he were ready to bolt for the door at any moment. She was going to win their wager; she could just feel it.

On that first Saturday he finished helping restock and rearrange the larder in the kitchen, then found himself at loose ends for the first time in quite a while. It was a perfect opportunity for a "chance" encounter with Antonia, he thought, prowling the first floor, looking for her.

Most of the ladies had gone out for the morning to pay charitable calls, shop, or simply take the air in the park across Piccadilly. The house was quiet, and as Remington passed the study, he heard a noise and ducked through the doorway, thinking he might have found Antonia. It was only old Cleo Royal with her feather duster and chamois cloth, dusting off both her figurines and her memories. Remington paused, watching her tawdry theatrical finery and birdlike movements from the doorway, then turned to go.

"No," she declared, but not as loudly as he was used to hearing her speak. "Stay, your lordship, and keep me company awhile."

He turned and found her facing him, wearing a garish purple satin with tattered sprigs of silk violets drooping here and there. In her frizzled silver hair was a grand Spanish comb made of carved tortoiseshell inlaid with mother-of-pearl, and she wore ropes of tawdry glass beads.

"Better yet," she said in her papery voice, tottering closer to him and thrusting the handle of the feather duster into his palm. "Come and help me."

"Help you?" He scowled at the feather duster, then at the room full of figurines.

Taking hold of his sleeve with a thin, blue-veined hand, she pulled him toward a graceful set of porcelain miniatures. "You can start there." She pointed to a group on a sideboard nearby. "I've already done these over here."

When she stared expectantly at him, he tucked his chin and looked uncomfortably around him. This would take the better part of the day to finish, he grumbled to himself with a trace of annoyance. But the trust he glimpsed in the old woman's expression tempered his response. He heaved a disgusted breath, picked up a figurine of a milkmaid and her cows, and began to dust it.

"Why don't you just sell them?" he said aloud after a few minutes. As he watched her pick up a figurine of a waltzing couple and clasp it to her breast, he thought better of that and amended it. "Or at least a part of them?"

"Sell them? What for?"

"For money, of course," he said, stepping back a pace.

She laughed. "And what would an old girl like me do with money, eh?" Looking down at the porcelain couple she held in her hand, caught forever in blissful youth and festivity, she sighed. "I have all I need here." After a moment she looked up with an otherworldly glow in her face. "And I do so like to pet them. They make me think of the old days, you know. Each is like a frozen memory.

"This one makes me think of Vienna, where we waltzed until the sun came up, Fox Royal and me." Her faded brown eyes focused on some other time and place. "I wore my most scandalous red gown—actresses always wear indecent red dresses—it's traditional. The archduke wanted me to waltz fast and loose with him, but I declined. When he insisted, Fox called him out. There was such a scandal.

"And this one." She picked up another, the figure of a goosegirl and a country swain adoring her over a split-rail fence. "We played a pastorale together in Geneva. Fox wooed and won me in verse and song, seven nights a week and twice more on Sundays." She caught Remington's eye with what on a younger person would have been called a lascivious grin. On her it seemed oddly gnomelike and endearing.

"I always said yes to that man, both onstage and off. But then, very few people—male or female, high or low, rich or poor—ever said no to Fox Royal. He was a man of a thousand persuasions." Her eyes fluttered closed and she just stood there for a moment.

The sliding sensation in his middle had something to do with defenses, he knew. But he couldn't stop it; she seemed so small and frail. When she swayed, he didn't understand that she was falling at first. He barely had time to catch both her and her figurine before they crashed to the floor.

Setting the statuette aside, he gathered her up gently in his arms. She weighed next to nothing and felt dry and reedy, like a crumpled bird, against him. Calling her name urgently, he looked about for a place to lay her down. He spotted an overstuffed leather sofa along the side wall beneath the windows and carried her there.

"Don't put me down just yet." She threaded her arms around his neck and refused to let go. "I am so cold. Just hold me."

For a brief moment he wondered if he should go for help. But she patted his shoulder and looked up at him, seeming more lucid than he expected.

"It's just one of my spells." She managed a weak smile. "You know, it's been a long time since a handsome young gallant held me in his arms."

Something in that time-weathered countenance and those faded brown eyes that had seen so much of life tugged at him. It was the same full-chest sort of feeling he got when dealing with Uncle Paddington's less rational moments—a sense that he was responsible, a feeling that something timeless and precious had been entrusted to him.

With effort he managed to lower himself to a seat on the sofa, still holding her. She sighed and settled against him wearing that faint, angelic smile. Neither spoke for a few moments; then she lifted her head from his shoulder to look up at him.

"Toni says you don't like us very much."

"She does, does she?" he said defensively.

"Women, I mean. You don't like women. Says you don't like marriage much, either." She looked him over. "What happened? Some skirt give you the jilt?"

"You certainly get points for bluntness, madam," he said rigidly.

"Cleo," she insisted. "I'm too old to put a fancy skirt of manners on my yens and curiosities. I speak my mind. And right now I want to know what it is about us you don't like." She frowned. "Aren't of the 'Greek' persuasion, are you?"

It took him a moment to react to what she'd said. "I . . . am not." She had caught him totally off guard, and in reaction he slipped easily into phrases he had written and spoken numerous times:

"I have nothing against women in general, just against women who expect to be married and kept and cosseted by men. I suppose it's marriage I object to most. All that nonsense about home and family and love . . . it's a house of cards, an illusion. Marriage is primarily an economic arrangement, hideously one-sided." His voice thickened. "To make us go into it more willingly, society dresses it up in respectable or romantic terms. But all their talk of love and happiness is nothing more than a cynical deception at worst, and at best, a socially useful myth."

He felt her moving against his chest and looked down to find her grinning and wagging her head. "Don't believe in love, eh? Poor boy." She patted his chest gently, and he glanced away, roundly annoyed by the way she seemed to be patronizing him.

"That's the greatest fairy tale of all," he said with a growl. "That *love* business."

She reached up and stroked his cheek, comforting him. After a moment she laid her head against his chest again and sighed.

"You know, my boy, I'm an actress, bred to the drama, the paint, the applause. I know a great deal about illusions . . . I've lived my whole life making believe." Her voice lowered as she descended once again into the halls of memory. "With all that, my love with Fox Royal was the only *real* thing I ever had."

Remington felt something in his chest begin to sink, leaving a hollow space.

She nestled closer to him. "I can tell you've never been

in love, my boy, and I'm sorry for that. It's the only thing that makes life really worth living . . . two hearts beating as one. My Fox had a hundred ways to say it. But it all came down to that: just two hearts beating as one. When I lost my Fox, half of my heart died, too."

Something seemed to be stuck in his throat; he couldn't speak. But it was just as well, for he had no response to make. In a few short statements she had penetrated his finely honed defenses and made him admit for the first time that it was possible. Perhaps on rare occasions, for a special and ordained few, there was such a thing as lifelong and soul-binding love, unions of man and woman that transcended the bondage of matrimony to a higher plane. Love. It was exactly what Uncle Paddington carried on about. Perhaps belief in it was something people settled into as they aged.

Her eyes closed and shortly he felt her grip on his neck loosen. From the rhythm of her breathing, he could tell she had fallen asleep. He drew a deep breath, and for the first time felt the years creeping up his spine.

Antonia had stood in the doorway, hidden by the partially closed door, watching the exchange between Remington and Cleo. Cleo's compensatingly loud voice had carried in the quiet house, and Antonia had arrived just in time to hear the last part of their conversation. Now she stood, transfixed by the sight of him holding old Cleo against him as she slept. She felt a sliding sensation in her middle as he shifted and freed one hand, then gently tucked wisps of white hair back into Cleo's bedraggled lace cap. Swallowing hard, she stepped out from behind the door and into his vision.

He reddened at the sight of her, and she could see his shoulders straightening as he scrambled for an explanation of his compromising position.

"She . . . ummm . . . fainted, and I caught her," he declared in a defensive whisper. "Then when I made to lay her down, she wouldn't let go of me . . . demanded I hold her a while."

"She did, did she?" Antonia said softly, gliding forward. She could read his embarrassment, could feel it as if it were her own. It was boyish and sincere, disarming in the extreme.

"You don't believe me," he charged.

"Oh, I believe you," she said with a laugh that was dangerously warm, even in her own ears. "Cleo always has had an eye for a handsome man, and she's perfectly shameless about taking advantage of an opportunity with one." Halting beside the sofa, she bent and pressed the back of her hand against the old lady's pale, downy cheek. She seemed warm enough, and Antonia straightened, searching his unexpected and utterly appealing chagrin.

"What I have trouble believing is that you honored her request." She couldn't help the bit of wonder that crept into her voice as she trained her eyes on his elegantly clad chest. "There must be a heart in there, after all."

Their eyes met, and in the stillness of the library, seconds, minutes, or whole eons might have passed; she had no way of telling. The ache in her chest spread downward through her, weakening her knees. His expression was turbulent, but through that she glimpsed a calmer center, a hidden softer aspect to his keen-edged character. It was all she could do to keep from reaching out to try to take hold of that inner man.

A distant noise, the closing of a door, set reality rustling around them. His eyes darkened and lowered to Cleo, and the moment was past.

"Would you be willing to carry her upstairs and lay her on her bed?" she asked, struggling to keep her voice from betraying the turmoil inside her.

He nodded and slid to the edge of the sofa. Shifting the old lady in his arms, he thrust to his feet and carried her toward the door. Antonia led the way to Cleo's room and they deposited her gently on her bed. For a moment they stood side by side, looking at her.

"She's not well," Antonia said quietly. "Of late she spends more and more time with her memories and less time with us." She glanced up and found a surprising bit of understanding in his expression. "We're worried about her."

He nodded, and from his concerned expression she had the strangest feeling that he really did know what she meant. She turned for the door, and he kept pace with her. When she closed the door behind them, he was so close she could feel his warmth, could catch his dusky, sandal-wood scent. Her heartbeat quickened. Against her better judgment she looked up. His eyes were again that warm-chocolate color.

"Thank you for being so kind to her."

The air seemed to sweeten and thicken around them.

He was so close, she thought . . . with a whole world of warmth unexplored inside him.

She was so tempting, he thought . . . with those clear, bright eyes that seemed to shine their beguiling feminine light into his rawest and most tender emotions.

He was trembling, and the thought that she would see it was all that kept him from reaching for her there and then. After a moment she lowered her lashes and turned away.

He watched her walking down the hall toward the stairs and felt as if she had just unlocked the door of his heart and left it standing wide open. He turned in the opposite direction.

Minutes later he found himself breathing hard, standing in the linen room on the third floor. He ripped off his coat and seized a rag and a sooty lamp globe—anything to take his mind off the disturbing sense of connection he had just felt with Antonia Paxton, and off the rebellion occurring in his passion-starved loins.

Chapter

9

That night, after Remington left, the ladies gathered in the main drawing room, as they usually did of an evening. Most knitted or worked on stitchery, though some wrote letters or played cards while they listened to Victoria play the pianoforte.

"You know what his lordship needs?" Prudence said, loudly enough to carry above the music. Every head in the room came up, including Antonia's. *"A wife."*

The words and the music died together on the air as Victoria ceased playing to stare at her. Several pairs of eyes darted Antonia's way, then back to Prudence. "I think he needs a wife," she repeated. "There he is—handsome, well-to-do, unattached. Perfect husband material. I'm surprised you didn't think of it yourself, Lady Toni."

"Perfect h-husband material?" Antonia said on a rising note.

"Truly, a wife might be just the thing for him," Eleanor agreed earnestly.

"He can be quite a gen'lmun," Gertrude offered. "All them nice manners, an' that handsome smile o' his. Now that we got him peelin' a proper potato, he'd make some widow-woman a right sweet fellow to have around."

A wave of consensus swelled around Antonia, forcing her to her feet in order to keep her head above it. "How could you even think such a thing, knowing his vile views on women?"

"Oh, I ain't seen no vile stuff. Been right respec'ful, he 'as," Maude put in.

"And you were saying only two weeks ago that it was time to choose another matrimonial project," Prudence Quimby reminded her. "I know you usually choose the widow first, but since you already have a prime bachelor under your own roof, why not start with him?"

"Why not? I-I'll tell you why not," Antonia said hotly, then had to scramble to come up with a plausible reason. "The man is a sworn enemy of women and marriage."

"Oh, that. Every man talks big when he's a bachelor," Pollyanna responded, with an authoritative nod that was echoed by others about the drawing room.

Antonia backed away from her chair to face them with her hands clenched at her sides and her stomach contracting into a knot. "Who on earth could I possibly hate enough to sentence to a lifetime of wedlock with Lord Carr?"

"She has a point there," Prudence put in, taking that point in her own direction. "Who would we get for his lordship? What sort of woman would he like?"

Antonia felt whatever had such a grip on her stomach squeezing tighter. What sort of woman would Remington Carr want?

"More to the point," she countered frantically, "what sort of woman would put up with him? He is arrogant, argumentative, amoral, and utterly without . . ." She was going to say decency and compassion, but after seeing him with Cleo that afternoon, her conscience rebelled furiously at such a lie. "Without . . ."

Apparently she couldn't think of a thing he was utterly *without;* his flaws came exclusively from *excesses.* Too much determination, opinion, wit, experience, passion, and sensuality. Rampant, overwhelming sensuality. And nerve. The thought made her face catch fire as she stammered to a halt.

"He would need someone wellborn, gently reared."

"And lovely, too. She should be young like him, and pretty as a picture."

"And she should know about running a house—all the work involved. And how to deal with servants—his lordship undoubtedly has a whole raft of servants."

The list they reeled off made Antonia unaccountably furious.

"She should have a bit of music in her," Victoria put in from the piano bench.

"Smart dressing, too—she would need a sense of style and taste," Florence Sable added. "As a countess, she would have to carry herself with grace and dignity."

"As *his* countess she would have to carry a club!" Antonia snapped, coming out of her embarrassment. "This is absurd. Listen to you." He had condescended and patronized and somehow managed to charm the socks off the lot of them. The realization produced a sense of betrayal in her. She strode toward the door, but turned back briefly. "I won't hear of saddling some poor, unsuspecting woman with his wretched attitudes and excesses. There will be no more talk of marrying him off!"

"Sorry, my dear," Aunt Hermione said, tucking her chin. "We had no idea you would feel so strongly about it. He seems to be softening up nicely, and we thought it might be good to think about his future."

"His future, auntie, is *his* problem. All I want is his present."

They sat a moment in silence after she sailed out the door. Hermione turned to the others and let a wicked little smile bloom on her face. It was quickly matched by others. "That went well enough. Did you see how flushed and irritable she was at the thought of marrying him off?" She glanced at the door, then back at them, beaming.

"Excellent. Just excellent. I believe our Toni may have finally met her last bachelor."

An hour later, lying in her bedchamber, swathed in silk and cocooned between cool linen sheets, Antonia felt the heat of her own remarks setting her conscience aflame. All she wanted was Remington Carr's present, she had said; just enough of his time to teach him some respect for women and perhaps a grain of humility in the bargain. And it was a lie.

The heat of her burning conscience spread to her naked lips, then trickled down her body to warm her breasts and womanly core. She turned onto her side, then to her stomach, punching down the bolsters and searching for a position that could relieve the arousal she was feeling as memories of their encounters shuddered through her. Full, hot kisses . . . openmouthed and searingly sweet. Warm, masterful touches . . . deliciously penetrating and endlessly desirable. Those tactile remembrances were bad enough, but now she had another, more potent memory to contend with: the sight of him cradling old Cleo in his arms, stroking her hair, and the bared-soul look he had given her afterward. There was indeed a heart in him, and her ladies had managed to reach and to breach it.

The sheets and her nightgown tangled around her legs as she turned again and again, trying to squirm away from her own longings. Tonight there was no refuge from them, or from the fact that she couldn't bear the thought of him spending his life and his passion with another woman. And the only possible reason for her deep, visceral reaction was that she wanted him herself. And the strength of that desire shook her to the marrow of her bones.

Her blood simmered in her veins, her skin felt naked and hungry, and her limbs ached with years of unspent embraces. As she tossed and turned, her garments rasped softly against her body. The sensitive tips of her breasts began to tingle, then to burn. Soon her loins were aching to feel the burden of his driving male weight.

It had been nearly five years since she had given herself to a man. Sir Geoffrey had ceased to visit her bed after the second year of their marriage, owing partly to his health and partly to his self-deprecating sensibility. He was an old man, he had told her, and she deserved better. He was a wonderful man, she had responded, and there *was* none better. He had smiled sadly, touched her face with heart-breaking tenderness, and turned away. And she had slept alone from that day to this.

Now Remington Carr was interrupting her sleep and making her want what she had consigned to the darkest, most forbidden regions of her being. She hadn't thought of physical pleasures in a very long time. But since the other day, when he kissed her and boldly ran his hands over her body, pleasure was all she could think about. And tonight, in the fragrant darkness, in the rising warmth of the spring night, it was twice as bad. His presence, in her house and in her mind, was opening doors to desires that she sensed she might not be able to close again.

Untangling her legs from the covers, she threw back the sheets and squeezed her eyes shut against the ache growing in the core of her body.

She couldn't wait to get him out of her house. But the darkness around her whispered that when he was gone, she would never be quite the same.

By the end of the first week, the number of news writers waiting outside Paxton House had dwindled by more than half. But those who were left were a tenacious lot indeed. They were there when he arrived in the morning and there when he departed of an evening. They began shinnying up streetlamps and climbing atop fences to peer into Paxton House for a glimpse of the earl in action.

Antonia and her ladies had been forced to draw the front curtains and keep them closed, for even the smallest detail made for juicy reading at their crassly inventive hands. One story reported that he was kept on his knees and forced to scrub floors, another told of him prancing around on beds wearing only an apron and a smile, and a third recounted his shopping trip, faithfully detailing every item he bought but speculating nastily on the quantity of prunes in his purchases.

With grist for their scandal mill so meager, their minds quickly turned from the reporting to the conjuring of events. The earl was closeted in a house, day after day, with a dozen women. Something had to be going on. Just what, they led all London to wonder, was the earl learning from all those females? Had women's work begun to change his mind about women? Had the Bastion of Bachelorhood finally met his match in the Paxton household?

Remington had steadfastly refused to read the several papers that were dropped on his doorstep each morning. However, it was growing more and more difficult to ignore the news writers collected outside Antonia's house. They quickly had learned of his backdoor arrivals and now both entries to Paxton House were haunted by scandal-hungry correspondents.

How did it feel to be the only cock in the hen house? they demanded. What was the big attraction at Paxton House? Surely he wasn't coming there just to scrub floors and carry the ladies' shopping baskets. Had he suddenly developed a taste for mutton dressed as lamb?

Low and disgusting as such insinuations were, he ignored them and continued on toward the house . . . until the odious Rupert Fitch heaved into his sights, hot-eyed and determined to get a rise from his imperturbable quarry.

"Or maybe that Lady Antonia's been teachin' you a few new twists on the ol' crinkum-crankum, eh? She's a mighty fine piece of—"

Fury erupted through Remington's facade of indifference, and he went for Fitch with both hands, seizing him by the coat and collar and slamming him back against the gatepost.

"You putrid little slug—you print that filth and I'll see you flayed alive—" When Fitch's eyes bulged and he gasped for breath, Remington released him abruptly and strode for the front doors with his chest heaving.

He stood inside the door collecting himself and purging the crimson from his gaze, while Hoskins waited with outstretched hands for his hat and walking stick. The speed and violence of his reaction stunned him. He had acted out of raw passion and instinct, and it baffled him that he had allowed Fitch's badgering to affect him so profoundly. What was happening to him? The sound of the butler muttering "Poor bastard" brought him back to his senses. He looked down to find Hoskins's time-weathered face scowling up at him.

"You don't like me very much, do you, Hoskins?" he said curtly, handing over his hat and gloves. The old boy tossed him a rueful look as he turned away.

"You ain't got a snowball's chance in hell, your earlship."

Remington's jaw set as he watched the irreverent old retainer shuffle toward the kitchen. Hoskins obviously believed he was doomed to lose his wager with Antonia. Such skepticism from the only member of his own sex who shared the experience of working within this womanly conclave was unsettling.

He squared his shoulders and strode into the drawing room, then stopped dead at the sight that greeted him. Antonia was standing by Aunt Hermione's chair, helping to pin a day cap in place over the old lady's spun-silver hair. She turned to greet him with a womanly smile, and he felt a sudden, powerful contraction in his chest.

"I am here," he declared, hoping his distress wasn't evident in his face. "To begin week two." He stiffened as his eyes slid down her fawn-colored silk dress, noting the way it hugged her waist and draped gently around her hips. Her auburn hair was curled around her face and was swept up at the back into a mass of curls, high on her head. She looked so different—like rare, translucent porcelain set in sunlight—that he was momentarily undone. It took a moment for him to reassemble his wits and mark the reason for the difference in her; this was the first time he had seen her in anything besides mourning colors. She was radiant.

And he was in trouble.

"Eleanor will teach you about floors this morning," she said, smiling as she approached. "And this afternoon Florence and Victoria will give you lessons in mending and sewing. You have a busy week ahead of you, your lordship. I hope you made wise use of your Sabbath."

Remington hurried up the stairs to the linen room, tore off his coat, and slapped an apron around his gentlemanly vest and trousers. Shortly he was wielding a broom and mop as if they were the oars of a boat and he was hurtling downstream toward a roaring waterfall.

By afternoon he had regained his equilibrium and was able to report to the upstairs parlor for his sewing lesson with a modicum of male skepticism. Florence Sable and Victoria Bentley, he soon learned, were accomplished seamstresses who not only did mending, but designed and stitched garments for the ladies of Paxton House, even Antonia.

"She doesn't have a modiste or dressmaker of her own?" Remington said, watching them laying out an assortment of sewing paraphernalia around him and thinking that all those sharp metal edges and points looked vaguely menacing.

"Of course she does," petite, dark-eyed Florence said sweetly. "She has us. Now, if you'll direct your attention to the items needed in a woman's sewing basket."

There were tapes, pins, shears, and curve setters; seam rippers, stitching gauges, thimbles, gathering hooks, grommet punches, and darning eggs. Remington felt his jaw tightening as the list lengthened, and he began to understand that this was going to be a tedious business indeed. With strained courtesy he nodded as they demonstrated a number of pieces of the sewing equipment, then introduced him to a treadle sewing machine. When he saw the ominous way the needle jabbed and the machine's foot clawed at the fabric, he declined their offer to give it a try.

Just as he was on the verge of sinking into surliness, they trundled out one last bit of equipment from behind a screen: a dressmaker's form. It was a startlingly detailed female figure, and when they announced that it was set to Antonia's measurements, his gaze fixed raptly on that padded shell.

There were her breasts, her narrow waist, her nicely rounded hips—by proxy, but tantalizing to the imagination all the same. He was staring at it so intently that he missed the knowing exchange of looks between Florence and Victoria.

"We have discussed it, your lordship," Victoria announced. "One week is not much time. The most we can do is have you observe our work and learn a few basic mending stitches and how to sew on buttons."

"A grave disappointment, of course. But I shall try to bear up," he said dryly.

With indulgent wags of head they put him to work learning to thread a needle. The work was every bit as tedious as he had expected, and his fingers seemed to possess all the dexterity of boiled sausages. The ladies couldn't find a proper thimble in his size, so he was reduced to puncturing his thumbs several times before he mastered the technique of spearing the fabric and not the flesh beneath it.

The gashes of thread he made through the fabric were wildly uneven, and they puckered the material or left it too loose. Florence and Victoria smiled patiently and corrected his grip on the cloth, the angle of his needle, and his assumption that sewing was simple, mindless work. He was just showing some promise at making an even stitch when they added a significant complication: a button.

"Buttons are so important to good clothing," Florence said earnestly, leaning over the edge of his chair as he struggled to hold the button in place while he jabbed the needle through the holes again and again. "We're forever having to set or replace buttons in this house." She looked to Victoria, who nodded and took it up.

"Because of Lady Toni, of course. She has a perfect passion for buttons."

"She does?" He tried not to sound too interested.

"Oh, yes," Florence agreed, nodding and peering through her spectacles at the bollix he was making of the thread. She put her own work down to help him untangle it. "You probably haven't noticed, but she wears a million buttons. She doesn't own a single bodice that has less than thirty of them. Most of them are small and delicate. She wears whole rows of them to close up her seams."

Ah, but he had noticed.

"Even her gloves. She wears five-button length most days, but a full twenty buttons for dress," Victoria added.

He smiled with what he hoped passed for polite attention, while his mind flew back to the sight of her at the Ellingsons', with her arms lined with rows of delicate kid-covered buttons. Twenty-button gloves. What kind of woman wore twenty-button gloves and thirty or more buttons on every bodice? A woman who was deathly afraid of . . . what? *Coming unbuttoned?*

"Well, I see they have you hard at work."

Antonia's voice startled him and he jabbed himself with the needle.

"Owww—damm—" He stuck his wounded finger in his mouth and turned to glare at her. But his eyes quickly slid from her cool smile down to the rows of buttons slanting downward over each breast. There had to be at least thirty silken spheres caught in loops that formed a V-shaped panel down the front of her fawn silk bodice. In spite of himself, he smiled.

"He's doing rather well, we think," Victoria said, holding up his work for Antonia's inspection. She swayed closer and looked it over.

"Very good, your lordship. We may convert you to something useful yet," she said with a teasing smile.

"Don't depend on it," he said easily.

"You find needlework not to your taste?" Her eyes sparkled. "Well, I must confess: neither do I. But it is a duty virtually all women must contend with, willingly or not." She pushed a parlor chair toward their circle, picked up a needle and a bodice in need of some work, and seated herself.

"It is only one of many women's tasks that men find tedious and taxing of the patience and fine skills." She engaged his eyes briefly, then began to thread her needle. "Another characteristic of women's work is that it comprises a thousand tiny details, each task made up of smaller, more intricate steps that must be mastered and executed in close succession. You have spent an hour learning to execute the simplest mending stitch and beginning to sew on a button. Just imagine the work involved in constructing an entire dress, a child's smock, or a man's coat."

She looked up at Florence. "While his lordship wrestles with that button, why don't you show him the steps required in making a dress and tell him how much it would cost to hire the work done?"

Florence obligingly launched into a lecture on the process of dressmaking, beginning with constructing and altering a pattern, then laying out the fabric, cutting, basting, lining, stiffening, sewing. Then came fitting and seam binding and altering and trimming and hemming . . .

Remington listened with half an ear and watched with half an eye. His attention wavered between the dressmaker's form and Antonia's neatly imprisoned curves. Then as Florence and Victoria chattered on, his attention settled on those tantalizing little fastenings stretched in pert rows across the tips of Antonia's breasts.

Antonia felt the heat of his stare, shifted distractedly, and tried to bury her interest in the garment she was mending. Neither realized at first that the lecture had stopped. The silence finally registered, and Antonia looked up to find Florence leaning on the table and holding her head with an anguished expression.

"What is it, Florence?" she said with concern, snapping forward on her chair.

"One of my headaches, I fear. Ohhh—" Florence stiffened, reacting to a sharp pain, and Victoria hurried to put an arm around her.

"It's all this fine work again. You need a lie-down,"

Victoria said determinedly, turning to Antonia. "I'll see she gets her powders and a cool cloth."

Antonia nodded gratefully; Florence was in capable hands. When the door closed behind them, she sat a moment, then turned to Remington with the dawning realization that she was left to carry on the lesson. The challenge in the lidded look he gave her made it impossible to call it off without feeling like a coward.

"Well," she said, sliding to the edge of her chair and setting her own mending aside, "at least now you have some idea of how it is done."

"Indeed I do. But then, I have known how it is done for some time."

Clearly, he wasn't referring to stitchery or mending. She swallowed hard and pushed to her feet, willing herself to ignore his wretched double entendres. But the rule of her will did not quite extend to the beating of her own heart or the sudden sensitivity of her lips. She rose and put the fabric-strewn table between them.

"Now, after only one lesson, you're an expert in sewing and dressmaking?" she said, dismayed to hear the breathiness in her voice.

In a moment he was on his feet and standing beside her, alarmingly close. It took every bit of control she possessed to keep from looking up.

"Not in dressmaking." His voice poured down over her like warm honey. "Only in how I would dress you, Antonia, if you were mine."

The shock of his words freed her gaze and it floated up. There he stood, with his dark, tempting look that melted her knees and made her skin hunger for contact with his. She braced, both anticipating his touch and dreading it. But he backed away and reached instead for the dressmaker's form, pulling it in front of him and placing his hands on its shoulders.

"I would dress you in soft tea gowns—sheer, embroidered surah or whisper-soft tussore silk, with no stays." As his gaze melted her defenses, his hands slid down the sides of the form to what would be her waist and splayed possessively over the ticking that stood as proxy for her ribs. "Your waist needs no improving, and I would be able to feel the warmth and the softness of you through your garments."

She quivered as she remembered the feel of his hands on her waist.

"I would toss out all your bustles . . . dress you in skirts that hug your hips." His hands drifted downward over the form. "Skirts that flare and swirl softly around you with each step, draping and wrapping around your legs. Such lovely curves. And I do love the way you make them sway as you walk."

Her gaze fastened helplessly on his supple, long-fingered hands. As they cupped and slid down the abdomen of that form, she somehow felt every stroke, knew the intensity of each touch. She couldn't protest; could only feel the promise of his hands on her belly, firm and possessive, caressing her. Longing settled, hot and growing, into her deepest core.

"Your bodices would always be low and clinging, ready to slide down your shoulder at the slightest inducement, baring the lovely skin you hide." His hands slid up the form to draw a deep circle around its chest, across the tops of its molded breasts. His fingers slid with tantalizing hesitation across those unresponsive mounds, carrying her gaze with them, making her body respond the way that carved and padded wood could not.

A low, sweet flame ignited in the tips of her breasts, and she stiffened visibly. Her eyes darkened as she visually measured the distance to his hands, wanting to pull that lifeless form from them and replace it with her own yearning flesh.

But the steps that would have required yawned like miles between them, stretching farther and farther . . . until they snapped something in her consciousness. She surfaced from that sensual immersion, and gasped quietly as she stumbled back.

"Well then, I must be thankful I am not at your mercy. I would be the laughingstock of polite society . . . dressed as a . . . as a *gypsy*." She picked up his sewing and held it out with a glower. "Enough talk. You have work to do."

He hesitated a moment, then rounded the table and took the cloth from her. Snatching up her scissors and mending, she hurried to the settee on the far side of the room. He watched her flee, noting the high color in her cheeks and the tremble of her hands as she had held out the fabric to him. He had gotten to her.

Smiling lazily, he crossed the room and settled on the end of the settee beside her. "The light is much better here," he said without an ounce of sincerity.

She huffed irritably and withdrew to the far end of the settee. Undaunted, he moved closer and craned his neck to peer at what she was working on. Buttons. He bit his lip thoughtfully and let his gaze wander from her sewing project to her person.

She had a passion for buttons.

Suddenly so did he. He was seized by the most irrational urge to grab her and pull her beneath him and undo all those saucy little buttons—one delicious flick of the thumb at a time. He edged still closer and began to count.

"Sixteen, seventeen, eighteen, nineteen," he finished aloud. Examining her lowered lashes and fiercely set jaw, he leaned close enough for his shirtfront to crush the puff of her sleeve. "I assume there are the same number on each side."

"I beg your pardon?" she said hoarsely, lowering her needle and communicating her outrage by her refusal to look at him.

"Your buttons . . . nineteen on a side. That makes a total of thirty-eight. Florence and Victoria said you have a penchant for them. But even so, thirty-eight on one dress . . . it's enough to make a man wonder." He paused and watched her fighting the urge to look at him. She needed a bit more incentive.

"What are you afraid of?" he asked with a low, husky laugh. "That something will get out?"

"What?" She whirled on him, her eyes flashing.

"Or perhaps you're afraid something else will get in." He lowered his head, breathing her roselike scent, feeling her allure curling through his blood. Then he boldly engaged her eyes.

"Ah, Antonia. Buttons aren't much of a barrier if a man is truly determined."

And his expression said he was a most determined man. Tilting her backward as she strained to avoid contact with him, he impulsively picked up the scissors in her lap. She gasped as he opened them and slid them around her top button on one side, shearing it off. A heartbeat later he slid them around a second . . . a third . . . and a fourth.

He cut off button after button. It was an outrage, an assault upon her person, but she couldn't bring herself to stop it or even to protest it . . . not when he was so near and her blood was surging against her skin in eagerness for his touch. She couldn't move, could only watch as her buttons rolled and the top of her bodice began to slide.

"I want in, Antonia," he said in low, penetrating tones that set her every nerve vibrating. "I want to see you . . . to touch you."

Suddenly those scissors were at the tip of her breast,

separated from that exquisitely sensitive flesh by a mere layer or two of cloth. *Snip. Snip.* Every muscle in her body contracted in response. Then those cool, dispassionate blades slid down the underside of her burning breast, severing threads that seemed to be connected to her sense of control. In turmoil she looked up into his face and found there, unshuttered, the same desire she was feeling.

This was no teasing, no contrivance on his part, she realized dimly. He truly wanted her. A dizzying surge of joy washed through her, and the release of tension made her feel oddly weak and air starved.

Then the entire row was gone, and with a nudge from his hand, the soft fabric rolled back, baring one fashionably imprisoned breast. His eyes slid from hers to her pink-blushed skin and she held her breath as he lowered his head and pressed a passionate kiss just above the rim of her corset.

He coiled his arms around her and drew her hard against him, raining kisses over her chest, up her throat, and across her cheek. When he covered her mouth with his, her arms wrapped his neck, and a moment later neither could say where the moan that resonated between them originated.

This was what she had been waiting for . . . this tempest in her blood, this storm of desire. She opened to his kisses, welcoming that sultry and erotic penetration. She arched against him, hungry for the feel and the motion of him, aching for the realization of every sensation promised in her night-spawned dreams.

They sank back onto the pillows, parting briefly as he braced above, allowing her to turn beneath him. Then he settled over her once again, molding tightly against her narrow skirts. As his mouth poured over hers again, she coaxed his tongue with hers, enticing him to resume his exquisite oral caresses. That invitation melted the last barriers of propriety between them, and his hands began to move over her, caressing, claiming, invading her bodice, touching her as no one ever had.

His kisses drifted down her throat to her breast, leaving a trail of liquid fire behind. She gasped and shivered beneath him as he slid a finger under the edge of her corset and gently pried her tightly budded nipple above the edge of it. With agonizing tenderness, he kissed and tantalized that aching point with his tongue. Whimpering with pleasure, she arched toward his mouth, instinctively seeking a firmer possession, a deeper pleasure. Eager to oblige, he took her taut nipple into his mouth, suckling, conjuring erotic undulations in her body as it lay beneath his.

Half of her was on fire and the other half ached to be consumed by that same exquisite flame. Her fingers fumbled hopelessly with the buttons on the other side of her bodice before he raised above her and brushed her hand away. An instant later the scissors reappeared and more buttons began dropping like her inhibitions, scattering on the floor around them. With eyes like burning coals, he finally seized the front panel of her bodice and yanked. Cloth groaned, stitches popped, and she groaned with soft satisfaction as his mouth closed over the tip of her other breast.

Heat welled within her, responding to the weight of his body on hers, and her hands began to move, seeking the shapes and textures of him. His hair was silky, his cheeks raspy, and his neck was corded beneath his starched collar. Beneath his coat, inside his vest, beyond the cool barrier of his shirt, he was firm and sleek against her hands. His back was layered with bands of muscles that shifted and bulged as he molded himself against her.

Each kiss, each motion, pushed her higher along a broadening plane of excitation. Of its own will her body began to gather and tighten, bracing for an approaching storm. She parted her legs as much as her restrictive skirt would allow and felt him pressing down through her clothes. Unerringly he found that singular burning point around which her desires were somehow gathered. Her hips angled and rocked slowly against his, finding his weight now focused behind the swollen ridge that was the counterpart of the heat and pressure building in her loins. She strained closer as once, twice, that luscious hardness raked her.

More, she wanted more. His body flexed and thrust, providing it, pushing the tension wildly, precipitously higher within her. She gasped for breath as turbulent waves of pleasure crashed over her, one after another, wrenching all sense of control from her. One instant she was floating, exultant, the next she was drowning under those powerful deluges of sensation. Her heart beat erratically, and her body seemed to be turning molten.

Then a sharp flash of panic erupted through her feverish excitement.

It was too much! One last desperate flare of reason illuminated the dim corners of her awareness, and she understood what was happening . . . sensed the approaching limit of excitation . . . realized where this wild, impulsive pleasure was pushing her. It was a forbidden limit, a shattering apocalypse of self.

She stilled abruptly, drew a tortured breath, and began to push back from that sensual boundary with everything in her, desperately battling the seduction of her senses.

As her head cleared, she found herself on her back on the settee with Remington wedged intimately against her body. The front of her bodice was gone and her damp nipples tingled decadently above the edge of her corset. He braced above her, staring down at her with eyes like burning coals, his passion unslaked and raging visibly.

The sense of it shocked her to the ends of her soul. She

was lying with him, entwined, exposed, and aching with unspent pleasure. A chilling draft of horror began to invade the steamy expectation that suffused her body and limbs. When he reached for her mouth with his, she turned her head and squeezed her eyes shut.

Denied her mouth, he kissed the edge of her jaw instead, then bent to aim his kisses toward more appreciative targets.

Frantic to escape, she gave him a shove that caught him off guard and sent him rolling off the settee. She scrambled up and staggered back with her knees trembling, her skin on fire, and a humiliating wet heat in her woman's core. Wrapping her arms over her exposed breasts, she searched frantically for the missing placket of her bodice.

"Antonia, wait—" he ordered as she located the missing part of her dress and started for the door. She wouldn't look at him, but whatever self-possession she had just managed to salvage fled as her heel struck one of the round buttons littering the floor. She slid with a cry of surprise and barely kept herself from hitting the floor. That delay gave him time to reach her.

"Antonia, I—" He seized her shoulders and stared in frustration at her anguished eyes and kiss-swollen lips. "Look at me," was all he could say, sensing that looks might reach an understanding that would elude mere words.

Her head came up with a snap and he caught a sharp breath. Her eyes were deep wells of emotion, open, vulnerable. In them he could read every shred of confusion, every impulse of longing and self-loathing she was suffering. The impact hit him like a fist in the gut.

When she wrenched from his hands and slipped out the door, he didn't try to stop her. Wobbling back to the settee, he sank down on it and rubbed his face. His body was overheated, his blood was pounding viciously in his head, and his loins felt as if they were going to burst. He gave the aching ridge in his trousers a pacifying stroke that only sent a wild rush of heat through his loins and made him writhe with unexpected misery. With no immediate relief to be had, he shot to his feet, threw open the window, and gulped breath after breath of fresh air.

Several moments later he was marginally in control again, and he forced himself to think about what had happened.

Antonia. She astonished him. He leaned a shoulder against the window frame and closed his eyes, seeing her as she had lain beneath him: her bodice cut away, her long, velvety nipples peeping over the erotic constraint of her corset, her expressive eyes glistening pools of desire, her passion-stung lips parted invitingly. And he felt again the way she had moved: hesitant at first, then yielding and fluid beneath him, around him. She was sensuality personified. He'd never had a woman respond to him the way she did . . . fully, genuinely, with every part of her.

Then reality descended; the distress in her face, her shock at her own response. What did she know of such things? Had she ever felt pleasure before? She was a widow; she had known a man's passion. But had any man ever known hers? The sight of her as she stood by the door rose in his mind: her eyes were luminous with desire and confusion. Antonia Paxton without defenses. Antonia Paxton as a woman, a lover.

Suddenly his body was vibrating, his chest was tight, and his breath was coming hard and fast. Pressure surged in his loins. He wanted her . . . God, how he wanted her.

He started for the door, but his heel also struck a stray button, which threw him off stride. Recovering, he snatched up the offending sphere. As he stared at it, his irritation slowly transformed into a smile. He closed his fingers around it, and when he stepped out of the room later, there was a handful of buttons in his pocket and a hum of expectation in his blood.

Down the hall, at that very moment, Antonia sat on the bench before her dressing table, staring at her mussed hair, swollen lips, and guilt-darkened eyes. She rounded her shoulders and clasped her hands together between her knees. Her wild and uncontrolled response to his lovemaking shocked her to the very ends of her being.

Maybe he hadn't noticed. Maybe he couldn't tell how close she had come to . . .

How would she ever face him again? How could she possibly sit at the supper table with him that evening and hold her head up? She glanced at the mirror, and it seemed to her that the illicit pleasure she had taken in their encounter was written all over her face. He would see it and take loathsome satisfaction in it and . . .

And what? Shame her?

Good Lord, wouldn't he love that? To seduce her and then torment her with her surrender . . . to reduce her to a shamefaced little shrinking violet before his awesome male prowess and potency. Wouldn't he love to claim her response as his victory?

That was what he had come to do, after all: seduce her. And on one level he had just succeeded—*with her help*. But, she made herself think more rationally, there was still a vast difference between what had happened and a full sexual encounter. The joining of bodies, of course. And completion. Technically it couldn't be considered intercourse if he didn't . . . *finish* . . . could it?

A cool draft of relief wafted through her as she recalled the unslaked need visible in his face and body, and realized that he couldn't have taken the satisfaction he probably expected from that licentious encounter. Close on the heels of that thought came another rather surprising one: just as he couldn't seduce her without her cooperation, he could not shame her unless she allowed him to do it.

It was nothing short of a revelation to her. *Shame was an internal thing . . . a punishment a person inflicted upon herself.* She thought about it for a moment, then relief poured through her like a cool, cleansing balm. He might smirk and wink and make tawdry, suggestive remarks, but she hadn't done anything truly dishonorable or immoral. She didn't have to feel dirtied or disgraced. She didn't have to let him win that way.

Her shoulders squared, her chin rose, and when she met her eyes in the mirror this time, they were bright with fresh insight and resolve. In her mind she conjured an image of him strutting into the dining room, full of triumph and condescension. If his devious lordship expected her to be cowed and contrite, he was in for a rather nasty surprise.

But apparently even the memory of his aristocratic features had the power to send a shiver through her. The tips of her breasts tingled and drew taut, and she looked down at the rosy edges of her nipples, still visible above her corset. With a huff of disgust she began stuffing them back into place.

"That will be quite enough of that."

Chapter

10

That evening Antonia sailed into the dining room like a naval frigate, bristling with visible defenses. She smoothed and adjusted her severe charcoal-gray jacket, checking every one of its thirty-four buttons, and tugged upward on her lace-rimmed standing collar, the stiffness of which was a continual reminder to keep her head up. But all the sartorial and emotional armor in the world couldn't have prepared her for what happened when Remington strode into the room.

She watched in mounting confusion as he went straight to Aunt Hermione, who was already seated, greeted her, and kissed her hand. Her disbelief turned to dismay as he personally escorted to the table Eleanor, Pollyanna, and Florence, and every other lady still standing. When he finally turned to her and extended his hand, it was impossible to refuse without being inexplicably rude.

"You look lovely this evening, as usual, Lady Antonia," he said with a smile that was irresistibly polite. Before he released her hand, he brushed it with his lips.

She stiffened and clasped her hands in her lap as he pushed her chair in, feeling the spot he had kissed glowing in heated contrast to the chill of her fingers. For the rest of the meal he was the most gracious and entertaining table guest she could have imagined. He made it a point to speak to each woman present and to tease and flirt within the bounds of good taste . . . until it came to her.

For her he reserved looks and comments carrying an understated warmth that made a shambles of her hostile expectations of him. Smirks and leers and smug male arrogance she had expected, and was prepared to handle with cool, vengeful grace. But this warmth, this genuineness, this wretched charm of his—she didn't know what to make of that, or how to deal with it.

Why wasn't he gloating and preening?

He was either far more decent than she had given him credit for, or far more devious. And she hadn't a clue which.

By the end of supper, when she escorted him to the front doors, she was reeling inside from vacillating between those two extremes. He took his hat and cane from Hoskins and stood a moment, looking at her with an intimacy that disarmed and unsettled her. When he reached for her hand, she couldn't bring herself to deny him.

"It's been a most educational day, Antonia," he said, cradling her hand in his and using it to draw her closer. "And most enjoyable." Then in forgivable violation of his new courtly manner, he bent his head and brushed a kiss lightly across her palm. And with an openly desirous glance at her tightly buttoned bodice, he strode out.

Antonia stared at the closed door, feeling as if every bone in her body had just melted.

This, she thought helplessly, *this* was being seduced.

Dreading a repeat of what happened between them, Antonia absented herself from Paxton House the next day, leaving Remington to spend the day with Gertrude in the kitchen, implementing the menus he had planned the week before. She spent the day at Walther Place, the settlement house for destitute widows that was operated by the Widows' Assistance League, and arrived late for supper.

"How good that you could clear your busy schedule to join us," Remington said with a caustic edge that caught her back for a moment. Strained silence ensued as she hurried to the table, saw the unused china, and realized they had waited for her. Lifting her chin, she allowed Hoskins to hold her chair, then gave him the nod to proceed with the serving. When she looked up, Remington was giving her a dark look indeed.

"Gertrude has had his lordship working hard all day to lay on this supper," Hermione explained, catching Antonia's eye with a mildly accusatory look.

"The lettuce will be wilted," Remington said in a scathingly patrician tone. "And my peas will have turned to mush."

Antonia chewed the inside of her lip to keep from smiling at the irony of the high-handed Remington Carr sounding for all the world like a neglected housewife. Collecting herself, she looked straight at him and smiled.

"Sorry I'm late. We had several new arrivals at Walther House and I lost track of time." She allowed some of her humor to warm her expression. "But I've always liked wilted lettuce salad. And I've always been a bit suspicious of peas that are too . . . round."

Early the next afternoon Remington found himself being tutored on the finer points of making and preserving marmalade and jam, a lesson in patience if there ever was one. And patience was one thing he was running precariously short of just then. He slogged his way through peeling and cleaning and squeezing, washing glass jars and straining pulp through colanders, all the while growing more and more annoyed. He hadn't seen Antonia alone since their encounter in the upstairs parlor nearly two days ago.

He was beginning to regret his decision to take the high road in dealing with her, expecting that his gallantry would lull her into another delicious indiscretion. Somewhere at the bottom of his strategy was the assumption that her own intensely sensual nature would help create the appropriate opportunity. He paused in the midst of chopping a mountain of orange peel and scowled at his recent memory.

Cocky bastard, he thought, expecting that her desire for him would prove so overwhelming that she would make it easy for him to seduce her again. In her actions and demeanor he could see no trace of the passionate and vulnerable creature who had taken such pleasure in his arms. When she had given him a cool, civil smile down the dinner table two hours earlier, it had taken every bit of his self-control to keep from snatching her out of her chair, throwing her down between the salt cellars and the sauce bernaise—and kissing her until she melted into a searing hot—

He came abruptly to his senses as Gertrude gave his arm a shake.

"I said ye've got a caller, yer lordship," she repeated with a quizzical look.

"A caller?" He straightened, put his knife down, and began to wipe his hands. "Who could possibly be—"

His brow smoothed and his eyes narrowed. Would Hillary dare intrude on him again? Ripping off his apron, he donned his coat, and in a moment was bounding up the stairs with fire in his eyes.

He stopped dead in the middle of the hallway, staring at an ample woman wearing a flame-red dress and a hat with the dimensions of a beach umbrella. She was fidgeting with silk flowers on the shoulder of her dress until she caught sight of him from the corner of her eye.

"Remmy . . . darling!" She extended a fashionably gloved hand and floated toward him as if propelled along by something other than human limbs. "So *this* is where you've been keeping yourself!" She cast an appraising gaze around her at the understated elegance of the hallway. "I just had to see, darling. You're in all the papers, you know. Such a naughty boy. Such outrages . . ."

"Carlotta?" he growled, reddening. "You?"

"But then you always were headstrong and full of surprises," she carried on, ignoring the warning signs of his temper as she swayed voluptuously to his side and threaded her arm through his. "Tell me, Remmy dear . . . I'm dying to know . . ." She lowered her voice and winked seductively. "Does she make you wash out her unmentionables?" Halfway through her next cooing laugh, she choked. "Ohhh! Remmy, w-what's gotten into you?"

He had grabbed her by the arm and was hauling her at breakneck speed toward the drawing-room doors, where he thrust her ahead of him into the empty salon and turned to slam the doors behind them. When he turned on her, she was adjusting her hat with a coquettish wriggle of her overblown curves.

"My, my. We are in a temper, aren't we?" she crooned.

"What in bloody hell are you doing here, Carlotta?" he demanded, jamming his fists on his hips in a way that thrust his shoulders forward ominously.

"But I just said, Remmy." She smiled up at him. "I simply couldn't stay away. I've read every article they've written about you and your little *arrangement*."

"Now that does surprise me," he replied. "I didn't know that reading was among your . . . *accomplishments*."

"Oooh, we are testy," she declared in a husky voice, swaying closer and giving his body a thoroughly insulting examination with her kohl-rimmed eyes. "All overheated and sweaty. Goodness, doesn't she know to give a thoroughbred a rubdown after a good hard ride?"

He seized her by the arm, his eyes narrowing to burning slits. "Enough, Carlotta. How dare you come here?"

"Well, if I didn't, I wouldn't get to see my Remmy, would I?" she said with exaggerated petulance, pressing the arm that he held against her breast so that his hand was trapped against her pillowy softness. "Spank me purple if it hasn't been more than a month since you came by. And you know how lonely I get." She wriggled suggestively against his hand and sent him a through-the-lashes look.

Her daring eyes and hennaed hair, her avid, rouged lips and excessive cleavage, were caricatures of what had once been sexually mesmerizing attributes. In former days her exquisitely sensual face had commanded male passions, her scandalously ribald talk had titillated the most jaded of male sensibilities, and the sultry sway of her opulent curves had set proper society on its ear. She was a woman who loved carnal sport as much as men did, and who didn't mind playing by their rules—hot and consensual sex, no holds barred, and no grudges or obligations. To a number of London's elite she had been a ravishingly good ride, the carnal adventure of a lifetime.

But to Remington she was merely a ravishingly huge pain in the neck.

"I'm not your 'Remmy'!" he ground out, ripping his hand from her and jolting back a step. Rising fury temporarily choked off his speech.

"Oh, but you are," she said, scowling resentfully at him. "And in one way or another you always will be mine. You can't escape it, Remmy dear. And it strips the drawers off my rosy bottom why you would even want to. I mean, it's not as if you have a wife or a reputation at stake." Beneath her playful and seductive manner the glint of determination showed through. "You've already abandoned all that—"

"Don't say another damned word," he ordered. "How I live and who I see is my affair. I want you out of here"—he pointed toward the door—"now!"

"Well, now that you've brought it up," she said, slipping back into her provocative teasing. "I want something, too."

His countenance turned to granite and his hands curled into fists at his sides.

"Madame Pernaud's bill was returned unpaid, and Galtier Brothers actually tried to reclaim those cases of Perrier-Jouet champagne I ordered." She oozed coquettishness. "They said your offices refused payment, and I just knew it had to be a mistake. So I thought I'd come and have you straighten it all out for me, Remmy."

"It is no mistake," he declared tersely. "I sent back the bills myself. You get a stipend—a damned generous one, at that. Learn to live within it, Carlotta." He seized her upper arm and propelled her toward the door. "If you cannot, then find some other poor wretch to badger and stick with your bills." He halted with his hand on the door handle and glared at her wriggling, sputtering form. "From now on you will contact me only through my solicitors. Harass me again and I swear I'll have you in the courts before you can say 'Spank me purple'!"

"B-but Remmy . . . darling!" she cried with genuine alarm as he threw open the doors and escorted her forcefully toward the exit.

"Don't you 'darling' me," he shot back, refusing to watch her theatrical protests. Hurrying her down the steps and into a waiting cab, he bounded back up and through the door, then strode furiously back into the drawing room, where he slammed the doors shut behind him.

How dare she come here, importuning, demanding,

crassly bartering her "services" for a raise in benefits? He stood staring at the doors, panting for air, roiling with unspent anger. Then he strode to the window overlooking the street and heaved a sigh of relief that both the cab and the wheedling female in it were gone. Closing his eyes to regain his internal bearings, he leaned a shoulder against the window frame.

When he felt his sense of balance returning, he turned to go and was startled by the sight of Antonia coming toward him from the far side of the room. Her eyes were dark and the train of her skirt brushed the floor, back and forth, like an angry cat's tail.

"W-what are you doing here?" he said, looking at the door and realizing with a sinking feeling that he hadn't heard it open or close. A glance at the corner behind her revealed a sewing basket and a number of pieces of stitchery spread over a table. Good God—had she been there the whole time?

"May I remind you that this is *my* house," she said with strained calm as she wrapped her fingers around the back of a parlor chair. "You might think of that the next time one of your 'lightskirts' charges in to *negotiate* for better terms."

It was a credit to Antonia's upbringing that she managed to appear cool and controlled, for inside she was in turmoil. She had been finishing some needlework for stretching when they burst into the room, and unable to leave, she had been forced to witness the entire scene. The sight of the woman hanging on Remington, the demands she made, and the contemptuous way he treated her—everything about the ugly encounter had stunned Antonia. Loss, hurt, and anger had mounted in her as she watched Remington's disregard for women being focused and trained on a woman whose claim on him was appallingly obvious.

In recent days, under the benign influence of her ladies,

he had seemed to be softening his harsh attitudes toward women. And her attitude toward him had warmed and gentled in response. She had begun to see him as a person, to see positive aspects in his nature, to glimpse the warmth that lay in his well-guarded heart. Now she felt betrayed by both his deceptive charm and her own vulnerable response to him. Underneath, despite his moments of need and tenderness, he was a treacherous and self-seeking *bachelor* after all. The thought was somehow devastating to her.

"I had no control over her coming here, Antonia," he said in ragged tones.

"Obviously," she said with more heat than she had intended. In spite of her determination to remain cool and ladylike, each word thereafter grew more impassioned. "But then, perhaps you would have more control if you paid either a better wage or better attention to your 'lights of love.' You do surprise me, your lordship; I wouldn't have taken you for a stingy man"—she swallowed hard against the humiliating tightening in her throat—"or a cruel one."

"Dammit, Antonia," he said, stalking toward her, his eyes hot with frustration.

She had no idea what he intended; she only knew that she couldn't bear the thought of his touching her, not after seeing his callousness and disdain for women in its fullness —not after seeing him with his mistress. As she veered around him and started for the door, the thought bloomed in her head: *another of his mistresses*. This was the *second* such visit he'd had from a member of the disreputable demimonde. And who knew how many more were yet to come? Good Lord—he might have an entire harem of castoff paramours languishing around the city!

He lunged, snagged her by the arm, and hauled her back toward him.

"Take your hands off me." She dug in her heels and just managed to keep from being pulled hard against him.

"How dare you treat me like one of your . . . *women!*"
The words halted him momentarily.

"One of my—"

"I won't be manhandled the way you did that poor
wretched creature."

"That 'poor wretched creature' doesn't object to being
manhandled in the least," he retorted, refusing to release
her. "In fact she's been *handled* quite thoroughly by virtually every *man* in London." When she slowed her struggles
to spear him a contemptuous glare, he absorbed that visual
thrust in his gaze. *"Except me."*

Several heartbeats passed as his dark eyes and heated
declaration penetrated the volatile haze in her senses. He
hadn't bedded the woman? A flash of longing that it was
true streaked through her, replaced quickly by a more
worldly bit of disdain for so obvious a lie. And she traded
him lie for lie.

"It doesn't matter to me whom you *handle,* your lordship. As long as you keep it out of my sight and out of my
house. Now, if you would be so good as to release me."

"You don't believe me." He searched her pained and
angry gaze, and pulled her closer. "She is *not* my mistress.
And she never has been."

"And I suppose you provide her an income out of the
goodness of your heart," she countered furiously.

"No, I do it because I cannot avoid it—I am bound to it
as a part of my father's will. She was *his* mistress, and he
saddled me with an entailment that requires me to provide
for and take care of her for the rest of her appallingly
hedonistic life." The heat and righteous anger of his declaration drove the words past her scalded pride and into the
very core of her reason. He was deadly serious.

"She is not your mistress?" Her resistance died as she
struggled to take it in. He released her and withdrew, giving her a heated, distancing look.

"Knowing my attitude on the support and maintenance of women, can you honestly believe I would voluntarily support a woman, even for the most immoral of purposes?" His laugh had a bitter edge. "I would not keep a mistress, Antonia Paxton, any more than I would keep a wife."

She lowered her eyes, caught between relief and distress by the surety in his logic. She had known from the start that he disliked women. But it still somehow shocked her that he detested and distrusted her sex so much that he would not even ally himself with a woman in pleasure.

In a bizarre and sudden reversal of feeling, she began to regret that the much-handled Carlotta was nothing more to him than an irksome financial drain. Perhaps if he had wanted a woman in that way, if he had been deeply and passionately involved with a woman, he wouldn't hold her entire sex in such contempt.

"And if you are wondering about my other visitor," he said, his face now hard and polished with male indignation, "I can assure you that the story is the same. My father, it seems, had a broad taste in feminine companionship and a lamentable streak of both male protectivism and noblesse oblige. He didn't abandon his old mistresses; he kept them in the style to which he had accustomed them—and gallantly wrote them into his will. In the end he saddled me with them. Hillary and Carlotta are a part of my legacy: I inherited them along with my title. And they never let me forget it for a moment."

Antonia was speechless. His bitterness, his antipathy for women, his adamant stand against marriage—had they been spawned by his father's peculiar generosity toward women who were unworthy of the care and protection he had lavished on them?

"They run up accounts all over town," he declared, pacing away. "They hound my solicitors and haunt my business offices. They cannot deal reasonably with tradesmen or physicians or even their own household staffs. They lurch from one catastrophe to another, hysterical one minute, scheming the next. And when they've bollixed things up royally, they simper and whine and drop it all in *my* lap." He halted and glared indignantly at her. 'Remington will handle it,' they say."

Against her better sense her gaze migrated to his. In its depths there was a flintiness she hadn't seen before. Even when he had spouted his absurd ideology of equality, there had always been a roguish gleam in his eyes. And of late she had seen his gaze warming and softening as it rested on her ladies and, she fancied, on herself. The sudden loss of that warmth and its accompanying possibilities now made her feel strangely desolate.

"And so you tar all women with the brush they have handed you," she said in a voice compressed by hard emotions. "Because of those two, all women are weak, dependent, contriving, and greedy."

He turned away, visibly angered by her accusation of unfairness. "Oh, if it were only *two*," he said caustically. "Pray give me *some* credit, Antonia. My experience with scheming, dependent females is broader than that. Paired with my father's clinging paramours are my own long-standing observations of women, both wedded and not. Together they have soundly ratified my conclusions."

"So we women are clinging, demanding creatures with no integrity, no character, no decency, and no initiative of our own," she said, fighting the hurt in her voice as she felt at last the full impact of his disdain for women. "We exist solely to satisfy our own acquisitive urges and make men's lives barren and miserable."

She took a step closer, her eyes darkening.

"Have you ever thought that perhaps the fault might not lie with women at all, your lordship? Have you never once met a thinking, competent, capable woman who had ideas, convictions, and interests outside her own comfort? Would you even recognize one if you did?"

The choked intensity of her voice penetrated his self-absorbed haze, and he turned to her with a scowl. Moisture sprang to her eyes.

"What have you been doing here at Paxton House, your lordship? Have you seen nothing? Heard nothing? Learned nothing?"

She searched him for a moment as her questions faded into his silence; then she headed for the door. Pausing with her hand on the handle, she looked back with a controlled expression that only emphasized the distress visible in her eyes.

The sight of her face as she turned away lingered in his vision well after she was gone. It was not anger, not righteous indignation on behalf of her sex, nor even disgust that haunted him, though he had seen all that and more in her expression in those last moments. No, it was something else. It was the personal hurt he glimpsed in her face that had taken hold of his feelings and wouldn't let go.

His discomfort grew, intensifying so that he had to escape. He headed for the front doors and quickly found himself standing in the sun-drenched street, hatless, glove-less, and directionless. When he began to walk, his feet carried him across the carriage lane and through the gate of the huge iron fence that surrounded Green Park.

The greens and paths were busy with fashionable gentlemen and ladies strolling, nurses pushing prams, and well-dressed children rolling hoops and playing ring games while governesses gossiped nearby. The activity stayed on the periphery of his vision and his thoughts as he stalked along the cobbled walkways.

What had he been doing at Paxton House? she asked. What had he heard, seen, and learned? The questions echoed louder with each step. Soon they were all he could hear.

"Lord Carr—"

Something loomed up before him and brought him jolting rudely back to the present. He narrowly stopped in time to keep himself from bowling over someone in his path. Instinctively reaching out to steady his victim, he found himself holding Eleanor Booth by the shoulders.

"I beg your pardon, Eleanor," he said, releasing her when he determined he had done no damage.

"Where were ye going in such a frightful hurry, yer lor'ship?" Molly McFadden's voice brought his head up.

There were Aunt Hermione, Maude, Molly, Pollyanna, Prudence, Victoria, and Eleanor, sitting on benches, standing, and strolling nearby. What a sight they made . . . some in sunbonnets, some carrying parasols, and some simply past the restrictions of vanity and letting the sun shine on their bare faces. They were like delicate old roses in glorious late-summer bloom. And they were looking at him with what could only be called affectionate concern.

"I . . . um . . ." He had to clear the odd catch in his throat before going on. "I decided to take a bit of air and sunshine."

"Ahhh." Hermione nodded, smiling. "Excellent weather, indeed. Will you join us, your lordship? We were just having a good gossip about some of the styles we see parading up and down the promenade." The others chuckled and she lowered her voice to a loud whisper. "I think I can promise you a juicy scandal or two."

She looked like a worldly cherub: cheeks pink, eyes twinkling. Remington stood for a moment staring at her, unable to speak. Then he looked around at the others and found them smiling at him, too. He shook his head with what he hoped passed for an apologetic smile.

"Another time perhaps. I feel the need of a walk just now."

He reeled off down the path, and with each step he felt his long-cherished prejudices colliding head-on with his feelings about the ladies of Paxton House.

Heaven help him, he liked them. Liked them? Hell—he was crazy about them. They had worked and winked and nodded and cosseted their way right into his impervious male heart. How could he have allowed such a thing to happen?

More to the point, how could he have kept it from happening? He groaned. Nothing in his experience with women had prepared him to deal with a houseful of beguiling old ladies with irresistible smiles, endless patience, and absolutely nothing to gain by being nice to him. They were nothing at all like the wide-eyed debs, grasping mamas, haughty doyens, and clinging courtesans that he had become inured to over the years. He had no defenses against women with white hair and cheery dispositions and forgetful spells that reminded him uncannily of his Uncle Paddington.

Intentionally or not, Antonia couldn't have found more perfect agents to undermine his cynical beliefs about women.

He thought of Eleanor . . . bright, curious, practical yet visionary, an inventor in skirts. Then there was Gertrude . . . homey, sage, hardworking, and fiercely independent. Scrappy and resourceful Molly met the less-than-perfect-world on its terms, staring it in the eye until it blinked. Aunt Hermione managed and persuaded and compromised to see that everyone got what they needed and wanted. Florence and Victoria plied their needles with equal enthusiasm for a butcher's wife or a duke's granddaughter. And Cleo, wizened and wise, blunt and garish, even long past feminine, she somehow still seemed the very soul of womanliness.

The world they had introduced him to was vastly more textured and complex than he could ever have imagined. Their society was full and productive and pleasurable. And their work was far more demanding and multifaceted than he had guessed; it required the patience of a saint, the timing of a circus juggler, and the strategic skill of a field marshal mounting an offensive.

With Antonia's help these women had made a place for themselves, a life independent of men, doing their own work, thinking their own thoughts, sharing their own concerns. Yet each had once been intimately linked to a man, shared her bed and her days and the vicissitudes of life with him. And when they spoke of their husbands, it was with respect and affection, and not a little longing. They seemed genuinely to like men. They seemed genuinely to like him. And in spite of his prejudices and suspicions, he had come to know and understand and respect them.

That was what he had learned at Paxton House: that he could *like* a woman.

Striding along with his thumbs shoved into his vest pockets and his eyes trained unseeingly on the ground, he hadn't paid much attention to where he was going. But his own contrary instincts had led him back to the very place he started.

When he looked up, he was standing in front of Paxton House. Gazing raptly at its elegant winglike shutters and well-tended geraniums, the insight struck him with such force that he almost staggered.

Antonia Paxton had just won their wager.

The house seemed to purr in the late-afternoon sun, the result of the fact that every available sunbeam streaming through every available window had a cat at the bottom of it making contented noise. Remington strolled through the downstairs on his way back to the kitchens, looking for Antonia and trying to think of what he would say when he found her.

As he passed the study, he paused. Antonia wasn't there, but he was drawn inside for a moment. In the stillness he stared at Cleo's visible memories, thinking about the stories she told and the life she had lived. He couldn't help wondering what memories he would have when he was her age. Stories of grand passion and life fully lived, like hers, or a single story of missed opportunity and regret, like his Uncle Paddington's?

"You look just like Pinkie when you frown like that!"

Cleo's loud voice startled him, and he turned to find her tottering into the study with her feather duster. He took a steadying breath and dragged a chair from the figurine-laden table for her.

"Pinkie Landon?" He recalled she had mentioned that name before.

"I called him that because he had a fondness for pink. I was wearing pink the night we met." She scowled at him, trying to remember. "Young fella . . . some years younger than me. He was an earl, too, like you."

Remington stopped in the middle of reaching for her arm. "An earl? You mean Landon as in the *Earl of Landon*?" It couldn't have been. "What was his given name?" he asked anyway, trying once again to steer her toward the chair.

"Rupert . . . Reginald . . . Rutabaga . . ." She scratched her head. "Maybe Rutland? Rutland sounds about right. He's here somewhere." She weaved back and forth among the tables and shelves, searching for a certain figurine.

Remington stood watching her numbly. Rutland Carr,

eighth earl of Landon, was his father. Had he also been "Pinkie" Landon? His father had an infamous yen for actresses. Had old Cleo been among them?

"There it is." She pulled out a figurine made like an ornate birdcage. Cobwebs trailed along with it; she obviously hadn't dusted off that memory in quite some time. As she stared at it, her frown turned into a rueful smile. "I remember now. He was in Paris on his grand tour . . . takin' in the high sights and the low life. Loved me madly. Wanted me to quit the stage and go back to London with him. Wanted to set me up in a fancy house. Even talked of marriage." Her gaze drifted far away. "But I couldn't."

Remington managed two words. "Why not?"

"That's why not," Cleo said, thrusting the figurine into his hands. He looked down at the birdcage and saw inside a bird with plumage a faded shade of pink. "He would have locked me up. I couldn't live like that. Soon after, I met Fox Royal." Her gnomelike grin softened into a heartbreaking smile of longing.

"My Fox gave me a nest, not a cage. And when I wanted to fly, he flew with me."

She patted his arm and rambled off among her other memories, leaving him to stare at that dusty bit of porcelain in turmoil. He thought of his father's penchant for choosing disastrous women and wondered what would have happened if old Cleo had said yes to Rutland's first proposal and he had made her another, more permanent one. Rutland wouldn't have been the first young nobleman to embarrass his family by bringing home an actress-bride. If it had been so, then perhaps Cleo would have been his mother. And his life, as well as his father's, would have been vastly different.

The insight struck: there were two different kinds of women in the world. Some women were Hermione's and some were Hillary's; some were Carlotta's and some were

Cleo's. And how a man chose among them had a great deal to do with whether his life was broad and fulfilling or cramped and miserable.

The question roiled up inside him with alarming urgency: just which kind of woman was Antonia Paxton? Try as he might, he couldn't seem to fit her into his new classification scheme, and her defiance of his neat new categorization unsettled him.

Antonia Paxton was the kind of woman who took on impossible challenges and somehow managed to come out on top. She was clever, determined, passionate about her causes, and entirely capable of employing deviousness and subterfuge in the service of her heartfelt convictions. Under duress she was cool and controlled and virtually never at a loss for words. She was a woman with a point of view and a plan of action to back it up. Aunt Hermione certainly had the right of it when she said Antonia had a very hard head.

He felt an odd crowding in his chest as he remembered that in the same statement Hermione had also declared that Antonia had a very soft heart. One after another, his recent experiences with her played through his memory: the fond smile she reserved for her ladies, the gentleness of her touch on Cleo's sleeping face, and the way her eyes lingered on him when she thought he couldn't see. With a bend of thought he experienced a vivid recall of her lush passion and responsiveness as she lay beneath him . . . of the passion, wonder, and confusion that had swirled in her luminous eyes when he kissed her . . . and of the tender sense of discovery in her erotic touch. Hermione, he realized, was right again. She did have a remarkably tender side.

She was a little bit Carlotta, a little bit Cleo . . . and a great deal more that was uniquely Antonia. She had a most desirable set of curves, a dry wit, and a wicked tongue that chose the most tantalizing times to turn sweet. She fascinated him. She annoyed him. She aroused him as no woman he had ever known. And now she had managed, with a bit of help, to make him see women in a different way.

The fact that he was thinking of her in such terms—remarkable, passionate, desirable—jolted him. Apparently she had made him see *her* in a different light, too. He shook his head in disbelief. She had gotten exactly what she wanted.

Now it was his turn. And what he wanted was Antonia Paxton—breathing her dragon's fire into his blood.

He wanted to reach into her very sinews and claim her responses. He wanted to bury himself in her softness and her strength, to rouse and luxuriate in the passionate and vulnerable woman at the core of her . . . the woman he had glimpsed so briefly and memorably that day in the upstairs parlor. He wanted to get under her skin the way she had gotten under his.

As he strode through the servants' hall, a thought occurred to him in a flash of male cunning. *It was time to let Antonia know she had won.*

Chapter

11

The next morning Antonia waited impatiently in the drawing room for Remington to arrive. Her face was pale and strained from her sleepless night, and her hands were icy in spite of the warmth of the room. More than once she had thought of fortifying herself for this meeting with a glass of sherry. Only the possibility that he might smell it on her breath and take credit for driving her to drink kept her from it.

She intended to confront him and concede that their wager was pointless. It was painfully obvious that his dislike of women was too deeply rooted to reform in a mere fortnight, no matter how wonderful her ladies were. And in light of her wretched experiences with him, she was not likely to change her opinions of men in the near future. Therefore, the only result they could reasonably expect was that the wager would end in an acrimonious draw. And where was the point in prolonging that?

But even as her head told her it was the right thing to do, the rest of her felt increasingly desolate at the thought that in an hour or two he would walk out of her house and out of her life forever.

Remington appeared well rested and abominably alert when he arrived an hour late, at ten o'clock. Through the drawing-room door she could see him handing off his dapper hat and walking stick to old Hoskins, who confined his opinion this morning to a silent wag of the head. When Remington stepped into the drawing room, Antonia pinned her gaze on his left shoulder and forged ahead.

"You're late, your lordship," she said with the air of a displeased governess.

"So I am." He made a show of checking his pocket watch. "Not of my choosing, however. I do have business concerns: land and tenants, an office to direct, investments to tend, and a fortune to manage. Difficult work, I assure you." He paused and let his gaze slide over her pale face and black-trimmed purple silk. "Not as grueling as cranking a dusting machine, beating rugs, or hand-waxing floors, perhaps."

He caught her gaze in his. "And it cannot compare with spending all day in a stifling kitchen tending fires, chopping, grinding, and peeling. Or with bargaining nose to nose with a twenty-stone Yorkshire-bred butcher. Or with bending over a thimble all day, going half-blind while stitching garments for a household. But in its own way, my work is taxing."

"I beg your pardon?" Antonia stared blankly at him, trying unsuccessfully to reconcile his manner this morning with his attitude of yesterday afternoon.

He sauntered closer, crowding her senses. "Yesterday you asked what I have learned here at Paxton House. I am doing my best to answer you, Antonia." Taking in her disbelief, he gave her a dangerously appealing smile. "Your ladies are most effective tutors."

"They are?" She stepped back, feeling unsteady on her feet and unable to trust her ears.

"You know they are," he charged quietly, cutting straight to the core of her confusion. "That is precisely why you insisted I work with them. You're a diabolical woman, Antonia Paxton. The PM ought to give you a seat in the Cabinet. You'd have The Opposition on its knees inside of a fortnight." His laugh had a husky, intimate quality. "Or perhaps even less. You certainly didn't need that long with me."

Silence descended as she searched his face for some clue as to what was happening between them. His smile settled into a warm, thoughtful expression. His eyes were so clear that she felt she could see to the very center of him. And the fact that he didn't flinch at so intimate an examination told her more than she wanted to know. She stepped back, breaking that disturbing contact and blushing furiously at what seemed to be a genuine compliment.

"What do you have planned for my education today, Antonia?" His voice was low and caressing. Her skin responded for her—with gooseflesh.

She hadn't planned anything, since she had assumed he wouldn't be staying, or returning to Paxton House. Desperately, she made herself think.

"Eleanor has things for you to do." Eleanor always had more work than three people could do, she reasoned. "I believe she and Pollyanna are airing beds today."

"Good enough," he said in those same affecting tones. "I suppose I'll see you at dinner, if not before?"

She nodded and he was gone before she could blink.

What in heaven's name had gotten into him? As she stared at the door where he had disappeared, she was gradually overcome by a powerful urge to kick something—anything—but preferably *him*. Vibrating with jumbled and confusing emotion, she snatched up two needlepoint pillows and hurled them at the door. How dare he just waltz into her drawing room as if nothing had happened yesterday, announce she had all but won their wager, and then look at her as if he wanted— She staunched that last dangerous thought before it was fully formed.

The gall of him! Calling her ladies effective and herself diabolical, and declaring that she'd brought him to his—

Knees. His clever male knees. He had just told her the very thing she had planned and schemed and longed to hear: her ladies had made such an impression on him that he was reevaluating his attitudes toward women's work and just possibly toward women themselves!

Excitement crowded into her chest, shortening her breath. She had won! Wrapping herself with her arms, she whirled around the room in delirious spirals, laughing and giddy and light-headed. Staggering, she realized she had to share the good news with Aunt Hermione and the others. But she halted halfway to the door as her elation drained and caution born of woman's intuition rose in its place.

Had she really won? Had his attitudes really changed, or was this just a ruse to lull her into lowering her guard with him?

She expelled a ragged breath and leaned her shoulder against the door frame, feeling drained by the wild swings of emotions he produced in her. This cursed wager could be over, he could declare his conversion to all of London, and she still would not be certain what was going on inside the man. Was he sincere about his change of heart or not? And how would she ever be sure?

That was the problem with being clever and contriving, she thought, making her way to the kitchen stairs. You always expected the same thing of other people.

The clock in the small parlor seemed infuriatingly slow as Antonia paced and waited, unable to concentrate on anything but the fact that Remington was somewhere on the floors above, working with her ladies and, by his own admission, undergoing a change of heart.

Rubbing the back of her neck, she closed her eyes and saw again the speaking look he had given her as he left the drawing room. With the slightest surrender to her unruly impulses, she could imagine his long legs striding and bracing, his arms stretching and flexing as he worked. Her skin flushed and her body grew irritable with sensitivity. She wanted to see him, to talk with him, to satisfy her unresolved questions and anxieties. But she had no pretext for charging upstairs to confront him, except her distrust or her desire to see him. And she was not eager to admit either in his presence.

When Eleanor's and Pollyanna's voices drifted through the open sitting-room door, she hurried into the hallway, expecting to see him as well and feeling embarrassed by her excitement. "Are you finished already?" The two women looked up from their conversation with surprise-pinked cheeks.

"Oh, not yet. His lordship remembered how the feathers always give me sniffles and watery eyes." Eleanor smiled affectionately. "He positively insisted on finishing your rooms by himself."

"My rooms?"

"And a good thing, too," Pollyanna added. "Dusty bed hangings, musty mattress and bolsters . . . your bed was very much in need of attention, Lady Toni."

"We were just going down to the kitchen for a cup of tea," Eleanor said as they started off. "Care to join us?"

"What?" Antonia started out of her swirling thoughts. "No, thank you. You go ahead." She picked up her skirts and headed for the stairs.

He was in her room this very minute, she thought, rushing up the steps. He was beating the dust from her bed curtains, stripping her linens, overturning her mattress . . . plumping her feathers, for heaven's sake. Crimson crept into her cheeks at the thought of him lurking about in her most personal and private domain, the place where she slept and dressed . . . and lay awake at night thinking of him. He had something indecent in mind, she was sure of it.

"She's headed straight for him, of course," Pollyanna said, watching her go.

Eleanor chuckled. "What I wouldn't give to be a mouse in the corner."

Antonia's bedroom was a masterpiece of Louis XIV opulence, in shades of teal and seafoam and ecru, with touches of gilt, burnt umber, and apricot. Sir Geoffrey had spared no expense to see to her pleasure and her comfort: from the hand-tinted freizes on the ceilings, to the ornate floor-to-ceiling bed, to the thick Aubusson carpets, to the exquisite tile stove, hand-painted with spring flowers, that he had imported from Sweden to ensure the room would be evenly warm all winter. Every shape, every texture, was lush and feminine, meant to delight her eye and satisfy her touch—the way her youth and beauty and energy had delighted her aging husband. It was her personal retreat, a balm for her spirits, her sanctuary away from the world.

And Remington Carr had invaded it.

When she arrived breathless at her chamber door, she could see that the heavy brocades at the windows had been gathered back and the south-facing windows had been thrown open to catch the sultry breeze. Her hand-painted and gilded bed was mounded with bare ticking, and her linens, comforters, and counterpane were piled in heaps on the floor around the foot of the bed. It took a moment to locate Remington.

He stood by her dressing table with his back to her, his shirtsleeves rolled up and his vest, cravat, and collar missing. The sight of his long black-clad legs and his wide wedge-shaped back sent a distracting shiver through her.

When his head bent and his shoulder flexed, she leaned to one side to see what he was doing.

He was holding one of her short black gloves, and as she watched, he brought it to his nose, closed his eyes, and breathed in. A moment later he strolled to the nearby bench, where her shot-silk petticoat and French-cut corset —the purple satin one, covered with black Cluny lace—lay exactly as she had left them the evening before. She looked on, horrified, as he lifted and wiggled the frilly hem of her petticoat, watching the delicate flounces wrap around his wrist. Abandoning that, he ran a speculative hand over the molded cups at the top of her most elegant stays, then dragged his fingers down the front of them to toy with the suspenders that held up her stockings. She could see his smile in profile.

"No garters," he murmured, just loud enough to hear in the quiet.

"Just what do you think you are doing?" she demanded, lurching forward a step before catching herself.

He turned sharply, then relaxed into a heart-stopping smile at the sight of her.

"Women's work . . . what else?" he said in insufferably pleasant tones. "I've just given your featherbeds a sound thrashing, and I am waiting for the dust to clear so I can get on with turning your mattresses."

"My mattresses don't need turning, thank you," she charged, her face reddening. "No more than my most personal belongings need plundering. How dare you invade my bedchamber and handle my things?" She was halfway across the room before she realized he wasn't retreating, and that, in fact, the gleam in his eyes intensified as she approached, making it seem that he had been waiting for her. Warnings sounded in her better sense, and she halted in the middle of the thick carpet.

"Put those back"—she pointed to the gloves in his hand—"and leave at once."

He raised one eyebrow, then glanced at the dainty black seven-button glove he held. "Only the best Swedish kid, I see. One can always tell Swedish glove leather by the musk that blends so nicely with a woman's own scent. Your scent is roses, isn't it?" He inhaled the glove's scent again and gave her a desirous look. "I do love roses."

He was teasing, flirting with her again—the handsome wretch. It was no good appealing to his sense of shame; where women were concerned, he didn't seem to have one. Her only hope, she realized, was to maintain her distance and her composure and use deflating candor to put him in his place. And his place, she told her racing heart, was anywhere *except* the middle of her bedroom.

"You rush headlong from one outrage into another, don't you, your lordship?" she declared, crossing her arms and resisting the hum of excitement rising in her blood. "You haven't the slightest regard for decency or propriety—"

"I do wish you would call me Remington," he said with exaggerated sincerity. "I don't think a first-name basis would be considered too much familiarity with a man who is about to climb into your bed and turn it upside down." Trailing that flagrant double entendre behind him, he tossed her glove aside and started for the bed.

"Into my . . . ?" Before she could protest, he was indeed climbing into the middle of her bed, pushing the featherbed to the foot of the bed and seizing the corners of the mattress. As the ropes shifted and groaned and the thick mattress began to roll, she felt a weightless sensation in the pit of her stomach and understood that he was moving more than just a cotton-stuffed ticking. The sight of him in those vulnerable confines was turning *her* inside out, as well.

"Come down out of there this instant, Remington Carr!" She hurried to the edge of the bed, frantic to get him out of it.

"I have a better idea," he said, shoving to his feet and bracing his legs to remain stable on the springy ropes. "Why don't you come up here? There's plenty of room." He flicked a suggestive look around him, then pinned it on her. "You know, this is a very large bed for a woman who sleeps by herself. How long has it been, Antonia, since you've had your ticking turned?"

"The state of my . . . *ticking* . . . is no concern of yours," she declared, feeling her resistance thinning. He was an incorrigible rogue, a professional bachelor who was insufferably sure of his sensual attraction. And he was still trying to seduce her. She jerked her gaze from the skin at the open neck of his shirt, only to have it catch on the way his trousers stretched taut over his thighs. And if she didn't get him out of here soon, she realized, he stood a very good chance of succeeding.

"Well, well. What's this?" He paused in the midst of his work and leaned over the mattress to pluck something from under the edge of the featherbed. With one finger he raised a garment that made her eyes widen. "Yours, I presume."

"My nightdress." She snatched at the tail of it, grabbing only air as he jerked it out of her reach.

"So this is what you sleep in," he said smoothly, examining the rosette-rimmed neck, the long, flowing sleeves, and the play of light through the fabric. "Foulard, I believe. You do have interesting taste in nightclothes, Antonia. Most respectable matrons consider foulard too thin, too provocative for decent nightwear." His eyes glowed as they settled on the row of mother-of-pearl fastenings down the front of the garment.

"And would you look at all those buttons?" He cocked

a rakish look at her and chuckled. "Trust me, Antonia, if a man ever gets his hands on you in this nightgown, a *million* buttons won't keep it closed."

Embarrassment burst through her control, drenching her with crimson and heat. "Give me that!" She lunged at the gown and this time succeeded in grabbing the hem. In a flash she had both hands on it and was pulling for all she was worth.

Caught off balance, he toppled onto his knees, but he managed to keep his grip on the gown. Each pulled with determination, but their tug-of-war soon settled into a seesawing stalemate. She ordered him to let go. He refused, claiming finder's rights under the Common Law. After a lulling moment she gave a heroic tug, which he countered by sinking onto his rear and then using her grip on the gown to drag her onto the bed with him.

"Why, you—" She gasped as she fell on her front across a mound of feather ticking. And a moment later she found herself staring breathlessly into his eyes.

"I do love teasing you, Antonia Paxton," he said, slackening his hold and giving her a warm chocolate look that made her suddenly crave a taste of him. "I've never seen a female out of schoolroom smocks who blushes the way you do."

"I'm not responsible for my wretched skin," she said, scrambling to hang on to her indignation as she wrestled up onto her arms.

"I know. That's what makes it so appealing. It always tells the truth about what is happening inside you, whether you like it or not. And do you know what your skin is telling me now?" He inched closer and relinquished half of his grip on the nightgown, now that he held her by something more powerful. Trailing a finger down the side of her heated face, he felt her involuntary shiver.

"It's saying that you like this. It's saying you haven't

forgotten what it felt like, skin against bare skin." His finger drifted from her chin to the top of her bodice. "And it's saying that you're wearing far too many buttons."

She was buffeted by waves of perception. His heat, his male scent, the promise in his eyes, the irresistible tenderness of his hand on her face . . . she was drowning in sensation. Her beleaguered better sense gave one last gasp, which produced a corresponding breath in the physical plane. That half-voluntary reaction was enough to raise her wits above the flood engulfing her senses.

"You have no right to do this." She abandoned the nightgown to his hands and pulled back to the edge of the bed.

"To do what, Antonia?" He sobered instantly. "To make good my part of the wager? To do an average woman's work and learn something from it? To change my mind about women?" His face filled with breathtaking intensity. "To want you . . . to make you want me?"

The playful, teasing rogue was gone. In his place was a forceful and penetrating man used to going against the "givens" of his world, a man who in a few short words had distilled the essence of their conflicts and poured it out between them: the wager, his opinion of women, and what lay unresolved between them as a man and a woman.

To want you. To make you want me. The words echoed in her heart.

Everything that had gone before had prepared the way for this moment. She was afraid to seize it and yet terrified to lose it. Her mouth dried and her frame tensed as she felt him reaching for her without hands, without words, with only his desire. Temptation mounted as she searched his eyes, seeking in them the answers that could free her longing for him. She had to know.

"You say my ladies have taught you," she whispered dryly. "Then what have you learned?" She held her breath, not knowing exactly what she needed to hear. Some of the tension in his face drained as he searched her intensity and realized that his answers were important to her.

"I've learned I'm no match for a dozen charming old ladies," he confessed, edging closer, watching her, ready to halt at the first sign of her withdrawal. "Or for one beautiful and devious younger one."

"And?" she said, blushing, her pulse drumming faster.

"Lord, you are a bloodthirsty wench. You want the gory details, I see. You want to hear how Gertrude faced me down that first day and reduced me to something in short pants. And I suppose you won't be content until I've confessed that Eleanor is one of the brightest and most inventive persons I've ever met, regardless of sex. She and your Molly have the constitution of a pair of prize Belgians . . . they worked me to the bone. And Molly has my vote for chancellor of the exchequer any day; the French wouldn't stand a chance in tariff negotiations. Then there's your aunt Hermione. I'm not convinced she's quite mortal; I expect her to sprout wings and start sprinkling fairy dust about at any moment. It's no wonder at all to me that she managed to snare four husbands." He raised one brow. "Need I go on?"

"Yes," she said softly, her eyes luminous. "Do."

He expelled a long-suffering breath. "Well, Prudence isn't the least bit prudent, and Pollyanna is practical to the point of either the ridiculous or the sublime . . . I haven't yet decided which. But by far the worst of the lot is old Cleo. All that wizened charm and wisdom—and she reads minds, you know. It's nothing short of terrifying."

She bit her lip, watching him reveal a seldom-seen part of himself in his descriptions of them. They had indeed wormed their way past his smug male defenses, and from the deepening tenderness in his expression, she sensed that the lessons had reached all the way to the core of him. She had never seen him quite like this: warm and open, honest and engaging. She could scarcely draw breath around the joy expanding in her heart.

"And women's work?" she asked. "Do you still think women are all devoted to feathering their 'pampered nests'?"

"We run whole government bureaus with less logic and organization than your ladies employ in your linen room," he declared a bit sheepishly. "I've always believed women are more capable than they are credited with being, that with time and training they would be able to do most things men can do. It never occurred to me that they might already be doing it . . . only in a different venue." He smiled wryly. "It's disconcerting to learn you've been so right, and yet so wrong."

He couldn't have chosen more perfect words to answer the half-formed questions in her mind. She could only stare in wonder at him as he leaned forward and took her face between his hands. His angular face, his dark, caressing eyes, and his full, mobile mouth were suddenly all she could see.

"You know what this means," she whispered softly, and he nodded.

"It means you've won, Antonia Paxton."

His lips met hers and the warmth of his kiss billowed through her, thick and sweet, like applewood smoke. It filled her head, her lungs, and seeped into her blood, freeing her responses as it poured through her body. Its source was a now familiar flame in the very core of her, and the fuel of that flame was his touch.

She felt his body jerk and opened her eyes to find that he had kicked the mattress so that it unrolled beside him. In a moment she was wrapped in his arms and sinking back onto that soft expanse. She slid her arms around his neck, luxuriating in the feel of him against her, and threading her fingers into his hair.

They were suddenly in the same position, feeling the same heady rise of passion as they had the other day in the upstairs parlor. It was as if the three intervening days, filled with doubts and conflicts and confrontations, hadn't existed. Within moments her long-reined desires were straining at the bounds of her experience, hungry for every bit of sensation he could provide.

Hindered by the tiny buttons of her bodice, he impatiently pressed a kiss on the skin just revealed at the base of her throat. As the fastenings slowly yielded and her bodice parted, baring her chest, he trailed steamy kisses down her breast to the edge of her corset. Then either a stubborn button or perhaps the tremble of his hands halted his progress, and he raised his head with a laugh.

"Is this why you wear so many of the wretched things? To deter would-be ravishers? What I wouldn't give for a good pair of scissors."

The darkened-jewel glow of her eyes and the delectable reddening of her lips snared his gaze. Lying beneath him, she was the embodiment of womanliness in a way he had never experienced it—open, warm, and vulnerable. For the first time in his life he knew what it was to truly want a woman. With growing wonder he realized that the wanting involved every part of him, from the depths of his passions to the very heights of his pride. He wanted to touch every part of her with every part of him.

For one heart-stopping moment his evolving desire met the awakening need in her eyes, and the power of that convergence shook him to the core of his being.

"I was wrong about Cleo," he murmured, when he could free his desire-seized throat. "She's not the worst."

"Oh?" she said in a whisper, closing her eyes to hold

that breathtaking moment of intimacy a bit longer before letting it go.

"You are."

It was a stunningly sweet accusation. To be the worst thing he could imagine: a woman who defied his prejudices and charmed his fears and coaxed him out of his closely guarded resentments. To be the woman that he couldn't help looking at with all the tenderness and longing he was capable of feeling. To be the most irresistible woman in Paxton House. She absorbed that charge into her heart, where it freed her feelings and unleashed her responses.

Breathless with excitement, she surprised them both by dragging his mouth back to hers and brazenly capturing the tip of his tongue between her lips, demanding he make full use of it. He complied eagerly with her demands, laving her lips, teasing her tongue, exploring the silken depths of her mouth even as his hands explored her body. Her skirts began a gradual slide up her legs, then bunched and caught somewhere around her knees. He groaned in frustration.

"If it isn't those wretched 'crinoline' cages, it's these stovepipe skirts. Whoever designs these things must despise both men and lovemaking." When he raised his head, she could see his aggrieved expression and laughed softly.

Then she took her lip between her teeth, giving him a frankly provocative look that challenged him to do the same thing. With a quiet groan he abandoned all talk in a long, voracious kiss that left them feverish and straining together.

He drew back to watch her response as he released her nipple from her corset and teased it rhythmically. She caught her breath and undulated, pressing against his fingers, seeking a deeper touch, wanting more. He released her other nipple and lavished succulent, drawing kisses on it, then took it into his mouth, commanding her response, wringing shudders of pleasure from her that produced corresponding tremors in his own loins.

A familiar pressure settled in her woman's core as his mouth caressed and tantalized her breasts and his hands slid over her bared knees. She somehow understood that this desire had resided, dormant, in every part of her body until the stroke of his hand awakened it. His supple fingers slid between her knees and under the lacy edge of her drawers, rising along the bare skin of her inner thigh, and pleasure trickled from his fingers in quicksilver rivulets up her limbs, pooling in her woman's flesh.

The stroking went on and on, rising ever so slowly up her thigh until his hand reached the limits of the access her skirts would allow. Digging her fingers into his shoulders, she urged his body on top of hers. Her hips were caught between the thick pad of her bustle and the tantalizing force of his body bearing down on hers behind a hard ridge of flesh. The weight and heat of him drove out the last of her inhibitions, so that when he flexed against her, she responded by tilting her hips to direct that divine pressure downward and inward.

Suddenly there it was—that rasp of sensation that seared through her nerves and flung her aloft on a rising draft of excitement. His kisses deepened, his hands grew more urgent at her breasts, and she could feel the pulse of his desire in the swollen ridge thrust hard against the barrier of her garments. She wanted him to salve this burning ache inside her, to fill the taut, expectant hollow of her body. With a soft groan she rocked her hips, seeking that part of him that she knew lay hot and ready against her.

"Remington." She whispered the deepest longing of her heart: "Love me."

For one moment he paused, then raised his head from her mouth to look at her. She was glowing with heat and her body was fluid with passion beneath him. The sight of her and the feel of her coaxing motions unleashed his reined desires. "I will, sweetheart."

He captured her lush, swollen lips and bore down, thrusting against her, finding her center, making her shudder deliciously with each stroke. Again and again he raked against her, carrying her higher, pushing her beyond the bounds of control and reason, into realms of pure sensation.

She gave herself up to it, waiting, expectant, suspended on wild rising waves of pleasure. Abruptly, she stilled, and the collected tension exploded in her loins.

Searing bolts of pleasure shot outward from her woman's center, burning along her nerves, contracting her muscles, driving her against him with a choked cry of pleasure. Her arms convulsed around him as she arched, shuddered, and surrendered. After a long, blinding moment of white-hot intensity, the feeling began to slowly fade, retreating like a wave, lowering her gently back into reality, leaving her limp and trembling against him.

He held her tightly as he felt her tension draining. He was panting, trembling, aroused to the very edge of his being, but he was still lucid enough to understand what had just happened. She had taken her full woman's pleasure, he was sure of it. Never, in his entire carnal career, had he encountered a woman whose response was so volatile and near the surface that she could find paradise in just the caresses of his body. After a moment he shifted back to look at her.

The soft fringe of her lashes lay against her moist and glowing cheeks. Her lips were parted and the skin of her throat and breast was rosy with the blush of climax. She was sensuality incarnate: female, desire, completion. And when she opened her eyes, the dark mystery, the wonder of the ages was there in their depths.

"Madam?" A querulous voice burst through the heat. "Are you there, madam?"

Antonia squeezed her eyes tight, wishing she could shut her ears as well. But the voice came again, closer this time, and she felt Remington stiffen against her, listening. Over the surge of her blood in her head, she recognized Hoskins's voice. Annoyance was her first reaction: billowing irritation that someone should interfere with her impulsive pleasure. But then horror was her second.

Hoskins stood just inside the door, scowling as he searched the room for his mistress. The bolsters and feather mattress that were mounded up on the end of the bed prevented him from seeing them, and the old fellow grumbled and shuffled out.

It was a long, prickly moment before Remington pushed up onto his arms and peered over the mountain of feather ticking beside them. The room was empty.

"He's gone. I don't think he could see us behind the featherbeds." He managed a wry, somewhat confused smile. "Why is it whenever I have you in my clutches, he barges in? Do you plan these things? Or does he just have an exceptional nose for sniffing out roused passions—like a moral bloodhound of some sort?"

His words slammed through her senses, driving the embarrassment she felt into her very marrow. *Did she plan this?* Did she plan to lose all control? To take the ultimate pleasure from him? To disgrace herself yet again with her rebellious passions? Her heart and her body both contracted with humiliation.

"I did *not* plan this—" she said in a choked voice, pushing him off her and fumbling with her garments as she sat up and scrambled toward the edge of the bed. Her panicky reaction caught him off guard, and it took a moment for him to reach her. Caught in his grip, she strained to escape, turning her face as far from him as possible. "Let me go—"

"Antonia— Toni—" Confusion gave way to understanding as he watched her shrinking, trying to escape both him and the fact of what had just happened to her. "Look at me," he said, his voice husky with both need and compassion. "No, you don't plan these things," he said softly. "*I* do. I'm the one who plots and schemes to get you into a compromising position. And I'm not the least bit sorry for it." He slid to the edge of the bed, beside her, and pressed a soft, evocative kiss on her cheek. "And you mustn't be sorry for it either."

Something in his tone, the unexpected softness of his words, reached through her shame. When he reached for her chin this time, she let him turn her face back to him. Her heart gave a painful, arrhythmic thud as she faced the soft glow in his eyes. It wasn't what she would have expected of him in his moment of conquest. It was a mercy when tears welled in her eyes and blurred the sight of him.

Her shame pulled strings in him that he hadn't realized had wound around his heart. He dragged her against him and wrapped her in his arms, holding her tightly. She was stiff and resistant to his warmth, but he wouldn't let her go.

"Was that the first time?" he murmured into her hair. After a moment she pushed back as far as his arms would allow. "It was, wasn't it?" he prompted.

She shook her head and lowered her eyes, sinking under the humiliation, but clinging to the hope that, this once, the painful truth might protect her from his smug claim of victory over her. "No."

"No?" He said, his arms loosening around her. "But how could . . . ?"

"I was *married*," she said with a flare of anger, trying to break free, holding back the shameful fact that her passionate response had disturbed her old husband so much that he had ceased, from that day, to visit her bed.

"Toni, please—listen to me." Wrestling her into the featherbeds, pinning her there on her back, he took her face in his hand and made her look at him. "I don't know what happened in your marriage—I don't want to know. But I do know I want you, Antonia Paxton. I want your sultry blue eyes and your kiss-me-quick lips, and every squirm and wriggle and moan of pleasure that comes with them." He feathered his knuckles down the side of her face and along her jaw. "I love the way you kiss, the way you touch me, and the way your eyes go dark and sultry. I love the way your body moves with mine, the way you feel beneath me, and the way you shiver when I touch you." He drew a ragged breath and confessed from the bottom of his soul: "God, Toni—I've never wanted a woman the way I want you."

She stared up at him, feeling a strange wrenching, shearing sensation in her chest. Then as she held her breath, searching the depths of his eyes, it seemed that a dark husk fell away from her heart. He wanted her. He wanted her response, wanted her passion . . . wanted *her.*

"I want to make love to you, Toni. I want to feel all the things you make me feel. And I believe you want me the same way."

Where was the point in denying it? she thought. Her eyes, her lips, and her body had just confessed her passion for him in spectacular detail.

"Heaven help me, I do want you," she said in a thick whisper, making herself look deep into his chocolate eyes and praying she wouldn't get irretrievably lost in them. "You make me feel alive and full of wonderful new feelings and possibilities. But I don't know if I *should* want you. I never know what to expect of you, or of myself when I'm with you. You make me do and feel such things . . . I can't wait to see you each day, and yet I dread the way you steal my self-control and take over my senses."

"I don't want your control, Toni." He smiled softly and pressed small, butterflylike kisses on her face. "And I don't want your pride or your self-respect or your integrity. I don't want to take anything from you." He straightened and met her darkened gaze with his. "This is no game, no part of our wager."

He saw her search his face, yearning and tempted, but uncertain, and he realized he meant what he had just said, with all his heart. He didn't want to take anything from her. He didn't want to hurt or embarrass or cause her loss in any way. He only wanted—

The realization struck with the impact of a fist: *hurting and embarrassing her were the very reasons he came here!* Frantically, he fought that thought down inside him and concentrated on Antonia.

"This is not the time or place." He couldn't resist one last kiss; then he pulled her up with him. He watched as she tugged her bodice together and shoved her skirts down into place. Her face was crimson as she slid to the edge of the bed and fumbled with her buttons. He smiled, feeling a sweet fullness in his chest, and brushed her trembling hands away to do them for her.

Chagrin and pleasure battled in her as she allowed him to refasten her bodice. She couldn't bring herself to meet his gaze until he paused and made her look at him. His face was dusky, his chocolate eyes sweet and compelling. Gathering her hands in his, he dropped a kiss on them. More of her defenses crumbled. She had never imagined him like this: so honorable, so tender, so considerate in intimacy.

"I would not force you, Toni. I want you to be sure, to decide of your own free will." He glanced around her bed-chamber. "I think that this place might hold too many memories." He smiled. "It certainly holds too many inter-ruptions."

He helped her to her feet, then pulled her against him, circling her with his arms. "There is my house. It is private and quiet. My staff retire early, all but my butler, Phipps. Will you come tonight, Toni?"

"I—I—" She wanted to say yes, to cast all caution to the wind and follow the yearnings of her body and heart. But the enormity of it all came crashing in on her; the strength of her desires, the storminess of their relationship, the un-certain future. Consequences, there were always conse-quences—and she hadn't even begun to think of them. How could she say yes? She trembled in his arms, absorb-ing his heat, hungry for his strength and certainty. How could she not say yes?

"Please, Remington, I have to be sure."

He drew her tighter against him, running his hands over her waist and up her back. The softening of her body against him said that he had the power to persuade her. But as he searched her face, he understood that her heart was divided, and that to exert pressure now might be to push her further away. After a moment he nodded, bowing to her need for time and knowing that he had issues of his own to settle.

"Take the time you need," he said, releasing her with a final squeeze of her hand. When he reached the door, he turned back with a tender but confident smile. "I don't know how it happened, but I'm crazy about you, Antonia Paxton. I'll wait . . . tonight . . . every night . . . for as long as it takes."

A storm of conflict rose in her as she stood looking at the empty doorway, then wobbled to her dressing-table bench on weakened legs. Several minutes passed before she looked up into her mirror and was jolted by what she saw. In the glass, staring back at her, was a woman with mussed hair, kiss-swollen lips, and a dark, sensual luminosity to her eyes. Who was this brazen creature, this woman with desire simmering in every inch of her body? Was this how Remington saw her? Was this what his loving made her into?

Her hands flew to the half-finished buttons of her bodice and frantically began to undo them. A moment later she pulled her bodice apart, staring at her half-bared breasts. Her gaze fastened on one rosy crescent peering over the top of her corset and she again felt the wet heat of his mouth on her there. Desire hit her with gale force and she swayed on the bench.

What was she going to do?

Remington held turmoil at bay long enough to exit her room, retrieve his vest and coat, and leave the house. But as soon as he reached the street, it descended with a vengeance, causing his heart to pound, his chest to heave, and the muscles in his gut to contract into a rock-hard knot. It felt as if he'd burst if he didn't move, so he began to walk the streets, arguing with himself and battling both his best and his worst impulses. Up the Piccadilly, through Mayfair and on to Hyde Park he went, with his hands shoved into his coat pockets and his gaze all but melting holes in the paving bricks. More than once he jostled a fellow pedestrian and tipped his hat in irritable apology. He was nearly run down by a high-wheeled phaeton in the hands of a reckless young whelp. But the prospect of being flattened by a team of runaway horses wasn't half so daunting as the quandary he now found himself in.

His agreement with Woolworth and the rest of Antonia's Whites' Club victims was that he would lure Antonia to his bed and let them catch her there, just as she had once caught them. But after all that had passed between him and Antonia, he could never carry through that degrading scheme.

He had told Antonia the stark, undeniable truth of the matter: he was crazy about her. Twelve irresistible old coquettes had blown a hole in his heart the size of Nelson's flagship, and Antonia, with her cool beauty and fiery passions, had sailed right in through it. She had roused and toyed with his affections, and despite all the preparation and determination in the world, despite being "forewarned" and even "forearmed," she had still gotten to him.

She was no longer the cold, calculating arbiter of morality who trapped indiscreet bachelors into marriage. She was a woman, with pride and vulnerability and irresistible passion. Today she had almost become his lover, and with any luck, that "almost" would be revised to "certainly" tonight.

He had come to Paxton House with bitterness in his heart, intending to match and best her, to seduce and subject her to the same humiliation she had inflicted on his fellow bachelors. Now every sinew, every thought, every impulse of his being rebelled at the thought of causing her pain. God, he groaned, what was he going to do?

The faces of his coconspirators appeared in his mind's eye. Angry, resentful, and bemoaning their common matrimonial demise, they had enlisted him to work out their revenge. If he backed out now, after so much publicity and expectation, they would be irate, furious, implacable. His personal standing, never sterling in polite society, would be ruined in the last place where it had any meaning: the exclusive and honor-bound world of a gentleman among gentlemen.

But then, as a gentleman of honor, how could he live with himself if he sacrificed Antonia's honor in the service of his own? More important, as a man of flesh and blood, how could he forfeit his desire for Antonia, and hers for him, to appease the vengeful urges of a few old school-mates?

Somewhere between Grovenor Square and his Hyde Park mansion his decision was made. When he stepped through the front doors of his house and handed his hat, walking stick, and gloves to Phipps, he ordered the butler to send for two messengers.

"Two, sir?" Phipps said, raising an eyebrow.

"I have several messages to send," he declared, heading for his study. "And I want them to arrive in plenty of time."

Chapter

12

The bar of White's was busy that evening; there was scarcely a place to sit or stand. Remington managed to secure the table in the corner, where the noise was not so loud and where there wasn't room enough for anyone to take a swing at him, should it come to that.

Remington's fellow conspirators arrived in pairs, well before the appointed hour. Their faces were flushed and they were in jocular spirits as they hurriedly pulled chairs from nearby and seated themselves around the table.

"We've followed you in the papers, Landon," Searle declared, perching on the edge of his seat. "God—corsets and scrubbing floors and scullery work—"

"Read every word. Especially the articles from that Fitch bloke, in *Gaflinger's*. Great stuff!" Sir Albert Everstone added gleefully.

"Made you sound like a godless heathen, though," Peckenpaugh said, outraged.

The knot in Remington's stomach wrenched tighter as he looked around the circle. Their eyes were glowing, their bodies were taut with tension and excitement. They were all but salivating at the prospect of a taste of long-awaited revenge.

"Well, don't keep us in suspense, Landon," Woolworth declared nervously, jerking the tray out of the waiter's hands, waving him off, and serving the drinks himself. "You've got news, obviously."

"Come on, man, tell us!" Bertrand Howard demanded. "Is it tonight?"

"No," Remington said, steeling himself.

"Well, then . . . when?" Basil Trueblood demanded breathlessly. "Tomorrow? Saturday?"

The clock over the bar seemed to labor over every second as Remington searched their faces. Tension condensed on his skin, making it feel moist and prickly.

"I'm afraid the answer is never. The plan, gentlemen, is *off*."

Despite the noise all around them, it seemed as if the room went pin-drop quiet. As the sense of it sank in, their eyes widened and their jaws loosened. Woolworth glanced at Searle, Searle looked to Trueblood, and Trueblood turned to Sir Albert, who sputtered to life.

"Off?" he echoed. "You're joking. And a damn poor jest it is, Landon."

"I assure you, Everstone, I am completely serious." He lifted his head and narrowed his eyes with the same patrician disdain that had served him well with greengrocers. "The plan is off. It was a cockeyed scheme at best, doomed to failure. Quite frankly, I am fed up with washing, scrubbing, and mending . . . sick to death of being held a hostage of my own poor judgment in a house filled with crusty old women who watch my every move. It's off, and that's all there is to it."

Shock quickly melted into distress as the six stared at him, unable to believe their ears. Something had gone terribly wrong. Their stares of horror turned slowly to fierce scrutiny. They detected a new bit of tension and a reserve that spoke of a great deal left unsaid. It didn't take them long to put one and one together and to come up with . . .

"It's *her*!" Trueblood declared in a choked voice.

The others snapped to attention, staring at Remington, expecting a hot denial. All they got was a telling bit of red creeping up his neck, above his collar.

He knew they could read in his embarrassment a capitulation to their declared enemy, and it took every bit of his manly self-control to sit there and endure the horror and disillusionment dawning in their faces.

"Good God—look at him. It's true!" Everstone croaked, groping the table for his glass of Scotch.

"But it can't be true," Woolworth declared, looking as if he'd been gut-punched.

"Not you—not our Last Bachelor—not the Bastion of Bachelorhood!" Peckenpaugh insisted in a rising whine.

Remington lifted his chin, resurrecting his most imperious manner. "I have stated my reasons. I will say only that the situation was far more *complicated* than I was led to believe." He scowled accusingly, in an attempt to turn their disapproval back upon themselves. It failed.

"She learned why he accepted the wager and booted him out!" Searle proposed.

"Or caught him in one of her nooses—set him up with one of her widows and compromised him," Peckenpaugh declared. "It's blackmail, most likely—"

"Ye gods—she's shackled him to one of her crepe-hangers!" Everstone gasped.

Remington listened to their wild suppositions in shock. All evening he had prepared himself to withstand the fury of their disappointment in him, only to have them cast the entire blame for the failure on Antonia. They honestly believed she had plotted and schemed to marry him off!

He was appalled by their bias and ignorance, until he suddenly recalled that he had expected the very same of her. He, too, had fully expected her to cast some needy female into his arms and then demand that he do the right thing by her. But she hadn't done it, or anything else they were charging her with. Her only plots had been against his opinions and affections, and the only woman she had caught in his arms was old enough to be his grandmother.

Through the thick, smoke-laden air he regarded his fellow conspirators with new eyes. They looked like petulant schoolboys whose sporting privileges had been taken away, or whining adolescents caught smoking and forced to finish a stolen cigar.

In the back of his mind the image of Antonia appeared as she had been that afternoon: her blue eyes filled with passion and uncertainty, her body trembling, vulnerable. She wasn't what they had made her out to be, and if not, then perhaps neither were their forced marriages nor the circumstances under which they were arranged. Suddenly he knew his decision was the right one.

"That is all I have to say, gentlemen. The plan is over and done. I'd advise you to go home and take a good long look at your wives and your lives. Someday, with a bit of luck, you'll understand that what I am doing is the right thing." He tossed back his drink and with a grave nod headed for the door.

They stared after him in disbelief, then turned to one another.

"I wouldn't have believed it if I hadn't heard it with my own ears," Trueblood said, ashen and gripping his glass with a trembling hand.

"Beet-faced, he was. And wouldn't hardly look at us," Searle added.

"He avoided our eyes the way a man does when he meets the husband of a woman he's just bedded," Woolworth said, scowling toward the door. The others halted, middrink, glanced at one another, then looked at him in dawning horror.

"Good God," Everstone choked out. "He hasn't fallen into her trap . . . he's fallen under her spell!"

A moment later he turned from his stunned, slack-jawed companions and motioned frantically to the barman. "Scotch, man—bottles! And be quick about it!"

The cab sped through the darkened streets, wheels clattering over bricks and cobblestones. Antonia had told the driver to hurry, fearing that in the darkness and quiet of the ride she would lose her nerve and turn around before she reached Remington's Hyde Park address. But the ride was mercifully short, through the mostly deserted streets, and soon she was being handed down onto the sweeping front steps of Remington's house.

Drawing her cloak tighter and her hood lower, she mounted the steps and stood before the massive front door with her hand poised at the knocker. This was her last chance to turn back from this mad, impulsive course. But, she chided herself, it could scarcely be called impulsive if she had spent several hours weighing, deciding, planning, and anticipating it. And she had.

Every argument and line of reason she had pursued, throughout that endless evening, had ended in the same confusing tangle of fear and longing. In all her life she had never encountered a man like Remington Carr, never experienced feelings like the ones he produced in her . . . never expected to fulfill the romantic dreams of her girlhood. All the sober and logical arguments in the world couldn't outweigh the combination of Remington's desire for her and the unexpected seduction of her own girlish hopes, resurrected.

Married at barely eighteen, to a man more than thirty years her senior and a lifelong bachelor, she had quickly buried all adolescent notions of love and romance. "Better to be an old man's darling than a young man's slave," her uncle had quoted with cruel candor, assessing her upcoming nuptials. Sir Geoffrey had proved to be a kind and understanding husband, and she had quickly learned the more durable and comforting side of love: respect, concern, and even mild affection. But passion and excitement and the sweet agonies of romance—she had been denied all that. And she had not understood how much she had missed until Remington Carr awakened those desires and feelings in her again.

Now she wanted to experience all that could be between a man and a woman. She wanted to understand what was behind those far-off looks of longing and fulfillment that Cleo, Aunt Hermione, Eleanor, and the others sometimes wore. She wanted to taste life the way Aunt Hermione had, wanted to know what it was like to be a part of "two hearts beating as one" as Cleo had been. And she couldn't imagine wanting those powerful and intimate experiences with any man but Remington Carr.

The door swung open with a clunk and a scrape, and she jerked her hand back with a gasp. A balding houseman in crisp black and white appeared in the opening with an air of having expected her. "Welcome, madam," he said, stepping back to admit her.

She hesitated, glanced toward the empty street, then swallowed her trepidation and stepped inside. The large center hall was dimly lit by brass and crystal gas sconces, burning low as the late hour dictated. The butler closed the door behind her, then asked if she would prefer to have him take her cloak or to keep it. As she followed him toward the stairs, still wearing it, she wondered if it was the sort of question butlers asked of women who visited by night—implying they might need a cloak at hand, in the event they had to make a less than dignified exit. The thought produced a sinking feeling in her stomach, and she almost turned back halfway up the stairs.

"His lordship had to step out for a short while." The butler chose that moment to speak, and his respectful tone arrested her flight. "He begs you to wait in his apartments and has instructed me to welcome you warmly in his stead." When they reached the top of the stairs, he smiled and gestured gracefully along the ornate gallery. "I fear I am a poor substitute for his lordship's hospitality, but I shall try to make you comfortable. I am Phipps, the earl's butler."

Antonia nodded, thinking that no amount of courtesy could have made her feel comfortable at that moment.

Phipps installed her in an ornate sitting room, done in grand Louis XIV style, where a bottle of wine and a tray of succulent cheeses, fruits, and chocolates had been laid out. He removed her cloak, asked her to ring if she needed anything further, then departed, closing the doors behind him.

Antonia wandered about the chamber, absorbing with her fingers the richness of the silk brocade upholstery and the polished mahogany and gilt-edged wood. The comforting golden light came from candles, not gas jets. Nervously, she investigated the books on his writing table and the portraits and paintings on the walls. She came to a door and, after a slight hesitation, opened it to discover a rich bedchamber dominated by a massive estate bed that was richly draped and laden with bolsters and pillows.

She jerked back into the sitting room, found her hands trembling, and in desperation hurried to pour herself a glass of the wine. Rich vapors filled her head and comforting heat seeped into her blood, thawing her icy hands and frozen limbs. By the time she finished her wine, her circuit of the room had taken her back to the bedroom door. She set her glass aside, took a deep breath, and stepped into his bedchamber.

It was breathtaking: brocades and velvet plush, gold cording and gilt edging on upholstered chairs and divan, with thick carpets underfoot. But the bed was what captured her attention. The crest of the house of Landon was carved above the headboard, tucked between the massive posts, and there were layered drapes on each side—graceful swags held by heavy, fringed cords and translucent inner curtains. Pillows made of shimmering satins, rich tapestry, and downy velvets formed a backdrop for the pristine linen of the sleeping pillows.

Her gaze trailed over the bed and her eyes widened on the expanse of white linen, invitingly turned back. A wave of longing swept her, and she swayed against the foot of the bed, resting her cheek against the drapes as she imagined the feel of the cool linens against her heated skin.

"You came." Remington's voice startled her. She whirled and found him standing in the doorway, watching her with a look of pleasure. She backed away from his bed, mortified that he'd caught her in the midst of anticipating the pleasures she would discover in it. Before her embarrassment could raise an obstacle between them, he was at her side.

"Do you know, this has been the longest evening of my life," he said in intimate tones that set her skin tingling. "Longer than the dance with the chaperon at my first cotillion. Longer than any Christmas Eve on record. Longer than the first thirty years of my wretched life." He took her hands in his and raised them to his lips, pressing a soft kiss on each. Then he dropped a caressing look down the front of her dark satin dress. "You look wonderful, Antonia."

She looked away, feeling suddenly all nerves. "Your house is beautiful."

"Thank you. Of late, I've thought it seems rather

empty." He chuckled softly. "Though there are times that an empty house can be an advantage. Like now."

Before she could protest, he wrapped her in his arms and kissed her with all the joy, tenderness, and hunger he possessed. By the time he lifted his head, she was warm and pliant against him, and all embarrassment between them had been dispelled.

"Ahhh, Toni," he said, breathing in the scent of her hair, "do you have any idea what it does to me? Having you in my house, seeing you here by my bed?"

The heat and hardness of his body against hers produced a thickening in her blood, and she instinctively understood the same thing was happening to him.

"I have a fair idea," she murmured.

He scooped her up into his arms, carrying her to the bed. After depositing her against the bank of pillows, he dropped a kiss on her forehead and disappeared into the sitting room. He returned moments later with the tray of wine and glasses.

"Would you like something to drink?" he said, pausing to consider the label of the bottle with a wry smile before pouring. "My best Bordeaux." When he looked up, she was sinking into a sea of elegant down pillows and looking a bit overwhelmed. He laughed and held out a glass to her.

"Are you having some?" she asked, struggling up out of the pillows to accept it with a trembling hand.

"Of course I am." He smiled and tilted her glass to her lips. When she had sipped, he removed the glass and replaced it with his lips, savoring the mingled sweetness of her mouth and the wine.

"Ummm," he murmured. "Phipps and I had a rather lengthy discussion about what sort of wine was appropriate for the occasion. He said champagne. I said red wine." He planted a knee on the bed and dropped to his hands to prowl across the linen toward her. "I believe red wine goes best with voluptuous widows. Shall we test my theory?"

He tilted his head and captured her lips, sending warm spirals of pleasure winding luxuriantly through her body. Only the feel of wine dripping on the bed linen, as the glass tipped, caused her to pull away. She meant to react to the spill, to see how bad it was, but he held her gaze with lidded eyes.

"I was right. Bordeaux is perfect. And red wine is always better when served at body temperature," he whispered, pulling the goblet from her fingers and setting it aside. Then he raised himself onto his knees above her, ripped his coat from his shoulders, and flung it past the edge of the bed. His vest was next, then his stiff collar and neatly wound tie.

He stretched out over her, bending her back onto the cushions, and lowered himself onto her, blanketing her senses, rousing her responses as he pressed soft, clinging kisses over her face and throat. After several tantalizing moments she felt him pull back and realized his fingers were fumbling to work her buttons from their loops. Laughing raggedly, he shifted to one side and propped himself up on his arm, looking at her. "I think I'd better let you undo them this time."

"Me?" she said, gazing up at him.

"I'll watch." He grinned and settled back on the pillows with his arms crossed behind his head. When she frowned, he added: "Unless you'd prefer that I ring Phipps for a pair of scissors. If I do, you may find it difficult getting dressed in the morning." When she hesitated, he popped open the single stud of his shirt. "There—I've undone mine. Now it's your turn."

She had come this far, she thought desperately. But the idea of undoing her own buttons was unsettling on several levels. He was asking her to open more than just a few fastenings, she sensed. He was asking her to open herself to him, of her own will. It underscored the fact that she was giving herself to him, not being seduced. And on a still deeper level, it stirred memories in her.

As her hands worked the buttons, she lowered her eyes and glanced away. Her attention caught on the open door and she hesitated, feeling vulnerable and unsettled as her past boiled up inside her.

"Could you . . . close the door?" she whispered.

"No one will disturb us, Antonia," he said with a lazy smile. "This is my *empty* house, remember?" But when she caught her lower lip between her teeth and gave him a beseeching look, he gave an exaggerated groan and rolled from the bed to do as she asked. When he turned back, she was standing by the bed, clutching her bodice together with one hand. Her hair was escaping her upswept coif, and she looked tantalizingly rumpled.

"Take it off, sweetheart," he urged softly, leaning his back against the door.

The endearment caressed her like a reassuring hand.

Sweetheart. Never in her life had she been anyone's *sweetheart.*

She peeled her bodice back and let it slide down her arms, revealing that she wore no corset, only a thin French chemise. In both her choice of garments and her furious blush, he read her desire to please him, and he smiled, pushing off from the door to gather her in his arms.

"You're trembling," he murmured into the edge of her hair.

"It's just that I'm not used to . . . My husband was not . . ."

She seemed so troubled by thoughts of her past that he caught her face between his hands and stared deep into her eyes, willing her to forget everything but the moment. "Whatever he was or was not does not matter. We have each other now, and what we will do is only a step beyond what we have done before. Pleasure, sweetheart, has no commandments. We will make this night our own."

He kissed her lips, her shoulder, and the hollow at the base of her throat, each touch from his lips a promise of security. Her tense frame relaxed. His hands ringed her waist and found the buttons of her skirt, then the ties of her petticoats. Soon they were sliding down her hips, and he helped her step out of them.

She saw the need collecting in the depths of his eyes as he stood gazing down at her in her thin chemise and frilly drawers and gartered stockings. With feminine instinct she realized that the power to fulfill his need lay solely within her. The delicious arousal of the senses, the sumptuous and enthralling banquet of sensation, and the sweet release that restored balance and reason—they would be his only by her giving. And she began to understand that in the giving, her own deepening needs would be satisfied.

That was the way of it. The giving and the receiving were part of the whole, like sides of a coin. One was not possible without the other. The wanting and the yielding were one. Inseparable. And at the base of it all was desire. Desire for the other. Desire for the intimacy, the joining, the love.

When he reached for her, she let him take her . . . let him open those parts of her that had been locked away . . . let him rouse the tenderness and giving that lay unexplored in the long-sealed chambers of her heart. He pulled her up into the bed and she responded to his desire with a need of her own.

They lay together, their bodies pressed close, unhindered by layers and bones and stays. Kiss by kiss she accepted and then sought his hands on her. When he made to remove her remaining garments, she redirected his hands beneath them instead, and closed her eyes, savoring the deepening pleasure of those hidden caresses.

He nibbled and nuzzled and caressed her, freeing her hair and exploring the erotic curves she withheld from his sight. His arousal was enhanced wildly by the way he had to seek her inside the constraints of those soft, clinging silks.

As his fingers edged toward the sleek heat of her woman's center, she gasped. He touched her in a way no man had, making slow, erotic circles around the burning focus of her arousal. The heat of her embarrassment was quickly absorbed into the desire intensifying in the deepest hollow of her. She arched sinuously and twined her legs with his, urging him onto her, seeking his weight.

"Is this what you want?" he whispered hoarsely against her neck, fitting himself snugly within the wedge formed by her parting thighs.

"Yes," she said on an indrawn breath. "Well . . . almost."

He laughed softly. "We'll get to *almost,* soon enough." And he flexed his body, rubbing his hardened shaft along the sensitive groove of her woman's mound.

She reacted with a spasm of pleasure and, after a stunned pause, undulated against him, entreating another. Each movement thrust her higher along a bright, swirling vortex of pleasure. This time she would not run from it. He was taking her into realms she had never known, not even in the depths of her passionate response. She prayed that he would see her safely through, for she was long past the point of stopping.

Tension mounted in her like waves, pushing her higher, faster, further. Then a swelling, heart-stopping crest of pleasure broke within her, flinging her through fragile barriers of perception. She clung fiercely to him as that flood of sensation rumbled through her again and again, and slowly subsided. When she could focus her gaze, his face filled it . . . so warm, so loving.

And she finally understood the longing in her ladies' wistful smiles.

Outside, Rupert Fitch shifted uncomfortably against the brick wall that surrounded the carriage court of Remington's house. His shoulders ached with tension and his eyes burned from the strain of unblinking scrutiny. He had followed Antonia Paxton here almost an hour before and watched her disappear behind that formidable door. Every predatory nerve in his body was vibrating with the conviction that all his snooping and skulking was about to be rewarded with the juiciest of scandals. The lady's late call on the Ladies' Man was certain to prove a lover's tryst.

Over the last two weeks he had cultivated something of an acquaintance with the cook of Paxton House, who had unwittingly supplied him with the hint of a developing attachment between the lord and the lady. This evening when he called at the kitchen door, he found Gertrude distressed, and he learned that something had happened between Lady Antonia and the earl that had sent the nobleman flying from the house that afternoon. And he hadn't returned . . . not even for supper, which he was scheduled to help prepare. Fitch had pacified the anxious Gertrude with a wink and a flirtatious pat, then slipped away himself, wondering what it meant and where the earl might have gone. Then, as he emerged from the alley, he spotted Lady Antonia in a long cloak, hurrying stealthily toward the local cab stand.

Galvanized, he had given chase. And she had led him straight to the earl's posh residence.

Some time later the earl himself arrived home in a rush, and Fitch now waited and watched, writing headlines in his mind for the next edition, trying to decide how best to word it. He wanted to be the first thing Lady Antonia saw when she opened Remington Carr's door the next morning. And he intended to be the one to break the scandalous news story that the stakes had just become intensely personal in the notorious Woman Wager.

Just as he was settling in for the long night ahead, a pair of cabs came rumbling down the dimly lit street. Something about them drew him upright on his seat. It was a moment before he realized what had tweaked his sense of expectation: they were slowing . . . stopping . . . at the earl's house. Scrambling off the wall, he hurried toward the circular steps and crouched by the side, in the shadows.

The coach doors banged open and several figures tumbled out—men that Fitch recognized. Sir Albert Everstone, Lord Carter Woolworth, Lord Richard Searle, and Basil Trueblood were there, along with two others Fitch couldn't place at first. As they staggered and lurched up the steps to the earl's front door, he realized they had all been drinking heavily; some were positively stewed.

"Come on, Landon—open up!" Everstone demanded, pounding the side of a brawny fist against the door repeatedly.

"Come out an' face us, you . . . dir-rty welsh-sher!" Trueblood yelled, shaking a fist.

"We come to s-settle th' s-score, Landon! You owe us-s!" Woolworth yelled, adding his fist to Everstone's, battering the door.

It was a veritable lynch mob, Fitch realized with shock that quickly turned to delight. Whatever it was about, it was a disastrous turn for the earl, and manna from heaven for a newshound like him! He instinctively snatched his pad from his pocket and began to scribble as he worked his way around the bottom of the steps to get closer.

The huge door opened and a blanched butler appeared

in the slice of interior light, protesting that the earl had retired for the evening and was not receiving visitors.

"Bloody hell 'e ain't! He better s-see us-s, the bounder!" Everstone growled, shoving and strong-arming his way past the helpless houseman. The others surged into the entry hall after him, staggering to a halt and ignoring the butler's outrage and his threats to call the constables if they didn't leave at once.

"Where is 'e?" Woolworth shoved his face into the butler's. "Where is the lous-sy cad?" Then he staggered back and called out, "La-andon—where are ya?"

"He's abed, remember?" Searle said. "Retired a'ready."

"Then, by gawd—we'll wake 'im up!" Peckenpaugh declared, waving a fist.

Things were happening too fast to call for help. The invaders were suddenly headed for the staircase, and the butler rushed ahead of them to plant himself bodily on the bottom steps. Undaunted, they charged right into him and nearly bowled him over. He struggled to hold them back, pleading for them to stop, to consider the infamy of their actions. As a last resort he made an appeal to their gentlemanly code: "I beg you to cease, gentlemen—his lordship is not—*alone*!"

The shock of that news froze the lot of them in place for a moment. They gaped at each other, jaws slack and eyes widening. Then Sir Albert roared to life:

"Good God—he's wi' th' Dragon, right now!"

In the warm, luxurious cocoon of Remington's bed, Antonia lay in his arms, savoring the feeling of release that permeated her warm and glowing body. Her senses seemed cleansed and awakened, so that every color, every sound, every stroke of his hand seemed heightened. She had never felt so right, so at peace, in her life.

He raised onto one elbow beside her, looking down at her flushed breasts and tousled hair. Running his hand through her thick tresses, he smiled. "I can't imagine that I ever thought of you as a fire-breathing dragon."

"Ummm." She reacted with a shiver, as if he'd stroked her physically, and responded by tightening her arms around him. "Is that why you waited so long to kiss me?"

He chuckled. "Undoubtedly. Every time I came near you, I could feel heat. I think I was afraid of getting burned."

She laughed and pulled his head down to tease his lips, then joined their mouths, with her hunger rising in an open and possessive way she had never experienced before.

He read in her demanding kiss that the time had come, and he shifted his weight, settling the swollen ridge of his desire against her liquid heat. They moved together, exploring the rhythm of their bodies, the natural resonance of their movements. She scarcely felt it when he slipped a hand between them to unbutton his trousers and push them aside.

The first sound from outside went unnoticed. It was his house, his bed; nothing would disturb them here. But even as he fitted his body against hers and began the first, tentative motions of loving, the sound grew and soon was recognizable as voices. Neither Remington nor Antonia wanted to hear it. Neither wanted to return to reason and responsibility in order to deal with the world outside the circle of their arms.

When the door to the sitting room slammed open, Remington's head snapped up, and he glanced toward the bedroom door in confusion. It was men's voices, and as he listened, he realized that he recognized some of them. In one horrible instant he knew what was happening and met Antonia's widened eyes with a look of compressed longing, dread, and searing regret.

He rolled from her and from the bed, fumbling with the buttons of his trousers. But before he reached the door, it burst open, and in a flash he was grappling with two men. Desperately, he fought to shove them back toward others who filled the doorway.

"What in bloody hell are you doing here?" he shouted furiously.

"Who's that in yer bed, yer lordship?" one of the invaders snarled, craning his neck to get a look at her. "Look—he's bedded down wi' the Dragon, all right!"

"So that's why you were so eager to be off—s-so you could be *on,* you traitor!"

"Get your stinking carcasses out of my bedchamber—out of my house!" Remington roared, wrestling them back, trying to get them away from her.

Antonia lurched up, clutching a sheet to her half-naked breasts, watching in horror as Remington battled several men back through the doorway. Beyond his straining form she glimpsed leering male faces that were drink-reddened and ugly.

"It's her all right!" came a high, reedy voice that was terrifyingly familiar. "So—Lady Matrimonia—where's your high an' mighty airs now, eh?"

"Look at 'er—caught with her drawers down, in a man's bed!" came another voice that she recalled but in her panicky state could not quite put a name to.

"Vicious bit of skirt—paradin' around all holy and righteous, forcin' men into marriage while she spreads her knees whenever she likes!"

"How does it feel, bein' on the *receivin'* end for a change, eh, milady?"

"You did a fine job of helpin' us get our revenge, after all, Landon!"

Remington sent a fist plowing straight into the closest face, and the man fell back with a shocked cry of pain.

"You can't do that!" another of them howled, and a scuffle broke out as he battered them back into the hall. Their drunken reactions were no match for his anger-fueled assault. He shoved one and gut-punched another, and with the belated help of Phipps and his valet Manley, sent the pack of rum-hounds reeling back along the gallery and down the main stairs.

Even after those vile, bloated faces were gone from the door, they remained in Antonia's mind, scored deeply into her passion-stripped and vulnerable senses. She trembled as her recovering wits matched identities to the faces. Sir Albert Everstone. Margaret's husband. Then she recognized Lord Richard Searle, whom she had matched with Daphne Elderston. And that thin, annoying voice—that was Alice Butterfield's Mr. Trueblood. And the one Remington punched—Lord Carter Woolworth—was the husband of Elizabeth Audley, one of her more recent protégées.

They were all men she had caught—*How does it feel to be on the receivin' end?*—in the very same situation she was in now! She swayed from the force of the impact. They had each sat where she now did: in a bed, half-naked, burning with shame—*Caught with your drawers down in a man's bed*—facing the same humiliation, feeling the same sickness inside. And it was *she* who had stood over their cowering forms and demanded that they pay for their pleasures for the rest of their lives. Now, craving vengeance, they had burst in on her and—*You did a fine job of helping us get our revenge, Landon*—

Her heart stopped. She couldn't draw breath.

Revenge. It was as if she had just fallen down a well; every part of her felt numbed and broken, crushed by the mounting realization that Remington had had a part in it. He had pursued, tempted, and seduced her . . . beguiled her into his house and into his bed. And then he had betrayed her into their hands. In the name of revenge.

Dearest God, it couldn't be! She gasped at the pain that crushed through her chest, and clasped her heart with trembling hands. But it was. Every teasing look, every provocative remark, every sweet, incidental touch had been luring her to her ruin. Every smile, every caress, every kiss had been bait for his trap. And she had walked straight into it, knowing his contempt for women, knowing that he was trying to seduce her, and even knowing that he considered her the enemy.

He had betrayed her, but it was her own fault: for believing him . . . for trusting him.

For wanting him.

Remington raced back upstairs to find her sitting in the middle of his bed, holding her heart, her face desolate, her blue eyes filled with prisms of tears. As he stood there with his chest heaving, his first impulse was to murder half-a-dozen utterly spoiled and worthless excuses of British manhood. But his second, and more powerful, one was to pull her into his arms and comfort her, to take her shame onto his shoulders, to somehow right the wrong they—and he —had done her.

"Toni?" When her face turned to him, the impact of her misery took his breath. "God, Toni, I'm sorry—" He rounded the bedpost and climbed onto the bed, reaching for her.

She jolted to life and skittered back out of his reach, dislodging the tears. "Don't touch me."

"Antonia—" He climbed across the single imprint their joined bodies had left in the feather mattress, and she jerked back and slid from the bed.

"No!" Snatching up her petticoats, she fumbled blindly to step into them. "S-stay away from me." All she could think was that she had to get away from this house and away from *him*. Her whole body trembled as she managed to blink away enough of the tears to see where to put her feet. She jerked up one layer, then another, scarcely able to manage the simple ties and buttons.

"Antonia, please, it's not what you think, I swear—"

"How would you know what I think?" she choked out, trying to right her skirt while searching frantically for her slippers. He tried to take her arm to make her look at him, but she gave his hands a panicky shove—*"No!"*—and grabbed her bodice from the floor, uncovering her slippers.

"You have every right to be angry, but at least let me try to explain. I had no idea they would come here tonight."

She halted and looked at him with all the pain she was feeling compressed into one devastating word.

"Liar."

Humiliating tears burned down her cheeks, and she bit her lip hard, concentrating on the pain to keep from breaking down. Shoving her feet into her shoes, she groped for the opening of her bodice with icy, unresponsive hands, then thrust her arms blindly into the bodice.

"Antonia—Toni—"

Something in his voice caused her to halt and look at him with all the devastation in her heart visible in her face.

"They *thanked* you." It was part statement, part question . . . so full of pain and disbelief that it came out a hoarse whisper. "How could you?"

He bounded from the bed and she shrank back as if she expected him to strike her. That telling movement stopped him in his tracks. His hands curled into impotent fists and his face darkened as he stared at her anguished eyes.

"I never want to see you again . . . as long as I live," she said, feeling the words turning like a knife in her own heart.

She located her cloak in the sitting room and managed to pull it around her shoulders. Fearing that he might come after her, she cast a glance over her shoulder and caught a glimpse of him standing near the bed, glowering. Her battered heart felt as if it were collapsing inside her. It was all she could do to hold herself together as she rushed down the stairs.

Focusing frantically on what she had to do to get home, she didn't hear him coming after her until it was too late. As she pulled open the heavy front door, he grabbed her by the shoulders and spun her around.

"Antonia, you can't go out there," he ordered thickly. "You're in no state to be out in the streets alone."

"Take your hands off me." Anger finally billowed into the emptiness in her savaged heart, giving her the strength she needed to jerk free. "I couldn't possibly meet with more harm out there than I just did in here."

Remington stood on the landing, watching the outline of her dark cloak fading into the shadows of the street as she fled him. His chest was heaving, but he couldn't seem to get enough air. And for a long, harrowing moment afterward, all he saw was the anguish in her face.

When he finally turned back to the house, he did manage to see one more thing: Rupert Fitch, standing at the bottom of the steps with an obscene grin, scribbling on a pad that glowed a vile yellow in the dim light. The little wretch tugged the brim of his bowler mockingly, then turned to swagger down the carriage turn to the street.

It was the final calamity. It took every bit of his self-control to keep from going after the nasty little cockroach and pounding him into the cracks between the paving bricks. After a moment he stormed back into the house and through the drawing room, past the liquor cabinet and then on to his study, with his hand wrapped around a bottle.

He poured a drink and looked up to find Phipps and Manley in the doorway, looking distraught. "If you would be so good as to close the door," he said with quiet ferocity. "This won't be a pretty sight."

They closed the door, and Remington poured and downed a large, fiery draught of brandy. He intended to get roaring, furniture-smashing drunk and make himself forget everything that had happened that night. But as he gulped a second shot of liquor, he found he couldn't get it past a sudden constriction in his throat. He tried again and again to swallow, but finally had to spit it out. Bloody hell—he couldn't even drown his guilt and misery in liquor!

Antonia rose in his mind as she had looked sitting in his bed: warmed and stripped of her defenses by his loving —then devoured like a lamb by a pack of wolves. She was hurting, and there was absolutely nothing he could do about it.

Antonia. Fiery, spirited Antonia. Vulnerable, girlish Antonia, whose exploratory touch made him feel a kind of bone-deep pleasure he hadn't known existed. It had felt so right to hold her, so perfect to be with her, that he had conveniently dismissed the fact that it had all begun as a callous plan for revenge, a favor done by one gentleman for others. It was meant to be a demonstration of male solidarity and cunning, but it had become a demonstration of male cruelty.

He saw again her blue eyes, dark with passion one moment and glazed with pain the next, and realized with sickening clarity that her anguish had only just begun. Originally, the conspirators had agreed to keep their revenge quiet, to savor it privately and use it as leverage to see that she ceased her matchmaking forever. But now, out of spite, they might spread the story from pillar to post. And the bulk of the blame, he knew, would fall on Antonia. The woman always lost more than the man in such a situation; men's *indiscretions* were allowed to fade, but women's *sins* were not. Antonia would be labeled and ostracized by decent society—ruined.

His blood began to roil, his hands clenched, and his

arms tensed with a violently protective impulse toward her. If only there was someone he could challenge or something he could do to see she didn't get hurt more.

Out of an unguarded chamber of his heart came a thought that both shocked and disturbed him: *he could marry her.*

Every muscle in his body contracted in response, but he made himself face it squarely: marriage was the traditional remedy for such a moral transgression. Once a compromised couple was married and produced a child or two in acceptable order, a layer of respectability generally descended over their past, and the woman was reaccepted into society. He vibrated with tension. *Marriage.*

Then he thought of Antonia's reaction to such a solution. Right now she would probably rather wear sackcloth and lash herself all the way to Canterbury Cathedral on her knees than even talk to him again. He could just imagine how she would take a proposal of marriage.

In spite of his nobler impulses, his whole body wilted with relief.

Calmer now, he stared off into the shadows of his darkened study, thinking of her and feeling a return of the emptiness he had felt as he watched her run away from him. If she had her way, he would probably never see her again. He lifted his glass and took a small sip, realizing that no amount of brandy could deaden the pain that caused him.

Gaflinger's hottest correspondent rushed back to his newspaper office to file a story on the scandal of the month—perhaps the year—and convince the editor to give it space on the front page of the next day's edition.

Fitch had seen and heard it all: the men crashing through Remington Carr's front door, their drunken taunts, and the way they charged up to the earl's bedchamber. He had made it halfway up the center-hall stairs himself, before the butler and footman found him there and tossed him out on his ear. But he had heard enough, and shortly he saw the drunken crowd retreating—nursing bloodied noses and aching eyes and ribs—before an enraged earl. And if that wasn't enough to get him a frontpage headline, he had the good fortune to see Lady Antonia fleeing the house in tears and dishabille . . . pursued by the earl, clad only in a pair of trousers.

It didn't take much to put two and two together, even for Rupert Fitch. The Ladies' Man and Lady Antonia . . . caught in a love nest by a bunch of drunken aristocrats. It was a steamy scandal punctuated by flying fists and seasoned with womanly tears of disgrace. Fitch rubbed his hands together in anticipation. It all sounded like a fat raise in pay to him.

Chapter 13

The sun came up at the usual time that next morning. The tea was hot, the scones were buttery, and the marmalade was sweet and golden, as always. But the ladies of Paxton House glanced up at the sky in confusion and stared forlornly at each other around the breakfast table, knowing that all was far from normal in their world.

Last night Antonia had come rushing through the front doors just before midnight and had gone straight to her rooms and slammed the door. She wouldn't admit anyone or talk to anyone, not even Hermione. And as they collected in the hall outside her rooms, they heard her weeping as if her heart was breaking. It had been a long night indeed, and they knew without being told that it had to do with Remington Carr.

Then a copy of *Gaflinger's* had been delivered to the doorstep, proving their conjectures and confirming their deepest fears. A front-page header proclaimed:

WIDOW AND NOBLEMAN CAUGHT IN LOVE NEST!

The writer of the piece, Rupert Fitch, declined to supply the names of the unhappy couple, but provided enough details about their adversarial relationship, including the mention that the lady and gentleman were prone to "public wagering," that it took little effort to deduce the identities of the lovers. The pair had been discovered in a compromising situation by a number of "leading gentlemen" paying a late call on the nobleman. And the details of the encounter were recounted with prurient accuracy: bare chest, unpinned hair, and all.

With heavy hearts the ladies realized that Antonia and his lordship had finally succumbed to the attraction growing between them. And instead of the start of a deep and enduring love, it had proved to be the disaster of a lifetime!

It was well on toward noon when Antonia emerged from her bedroom with puffy eyes and a pale, drawn face. She was dressed in unrelieved black, buttoned all the way from chin to waist, and her manner was every bit as grave as her retreat into full mourning colors suggested. Hermione and Eleanor hurried to her side the moment she set foot in the hushed drawing room.

"Are you all right, my dear?" Hermione asked, putting an arm through hers and directing her into their midst. The others gathered around, and she looked at their concerned faces and felt the dread that gripped her stomach loosen.

"You probably already know that . . . that for days now . . . that last night . . ." She paused and lowered her eyes, feeling her courage wane.

"We know all about it, Toni dear." When she looked up, Aunt Hermione was holding a newspaper. "And by this evening I'm afraid the rest of London will, too," she said gently, placing the paper in Antonia's hands.

Antonia glimpsed the headline, swayed, and stumbled to the closest chair. In deepening shock she read the article that recounted in ghastly detail the humiliation she had suffered only hours before. The links to her and Remington Carr were unmistakable; what other nobleman and widow were involved in an ongoing and notorious wager? There was her humiliation, in pitiless black and white, for all to read.

"It was that Rupert Fitch," Eleanor said, watching her distress. "He has been snooping around the house for days—"

"Th' miserable little sod," Gertrude added with a fierce expression.

Antonia looked up and found them gathered around her chair, some scowling, others smiling sadly, but all clearly offering her their love and support. "I'm so sorry," she whispered. "I knew it was wrong to go, but I believed him when he said he had changed his mind about women, about us. And I believed he really cared—" Her voice caught on a ragged emotion and she had to pause to free it. "I don't care what people say of me. But I know that my indiscretion will reflect upon Sir Geoffrey's memory and on you. I only hope you can find it in your hearts to forgive. . . ."

"There ain't no need to apolly-gize, Lady Toni," Molly said, patting her shoulder and looking to the others to support her words. "You ain't never held a single wrong against one o' us. How could we blame ye fer falling into th' same sin all women been caught in, one time or other . . . havin' too soft a heart?" As the others nodded and gave her warm hugs, the few remaining worried expressions melted into rueful smiles.

Antonia didn't think she had enough water or salt left in her to make two good tears, but she did. Then as she absorbed their touches and reassurances, the warmth of their affection transformed those tears into a grateful smile. In that moment she felt a bond with them that went far beyond good works or friendship or even ties of blood. It was an attachment made of love. She had once given help and comfort to them, and now found it returning to her, twelvefold.

"Poor Lady Toni," Prudence said mistily, breaking the sweet, emotion-filled silence. "Just when you and his lordship were coming to an understanding. No doubt he is fit to be tied."

Antonia froze as the shock of his betrayal descended with unexpected violence on her again. Remington. As she sat in his bed, savaged and humiliated by their taunts, they had congratulated him on doing a fine job of helping them with their revenge.

How could he have done such a thing to her?

How could she have trusted him?

"Fit to be tied?" she said, struggling to contain the pain inside her. "Fit to be *hanged* is more like it." She met their confusion and dismay with anger that had fermented in the heat of the long night just past. "He knew all about it. In point of fact, he *planned* it."

Paxton House was not the only place where the article was having an impact. Over the last two weeks *Gaflinger's Gazette* had found its way into Buckingham Palace on a regular basis and had been circulated both below stairs and above—out of the queen's sight, but not entirely out of her hearing.

When Victoria entered her private sitting room that same morning and glimpsed Beatrice and her daughter-in-law Alexandra whispering animatedly over a newspaper, she called them to account. They jerked the paper beneath the sewing table, stalling until she demanded to see what they were reading. As they produced the publication, she took note of the florid masthead and chastised them.

"Imagine. Princesses of the realm patronizing such a vulgar and sensational bit of ink-blotting as that *Garflunker's*." No one corrected her pronunciation. "What can you have seen in that scandal-rag that has you in such a dither?" She folded her thick hands at her middle and waited for them to speak. When they hesitated, knowing how it would enrage her, she extended a much-beringed hand for the paper and was soon reading of the scandal herself.

Her face reddened, the way it did when someone referred to Gladstone as "GOM" in her presence. Her eyes narrowed, as they did when someone mentioned marriages or betrothals in the hearing of her unwed daughter Beatrice. And her mouth pursed in the very same manner it did when she learned her profligate son and heir, Bertie, had taken up with yet another red-haired actress.

She stiffened to her full, diminutive height and summoned the royal wrath she reserved for those she considered to be under the grave and God-given obligation imposed by noble rank and fortune.

"A 'nameless nobleman involved in a public wager with a lady'?"—she erupted—"Troth! It could only be that scapegrace Landon!"

"Now, Mama, you know how these newsmongers are. If there is no news to be had, they brew some themselves so they can stir it," mild-mannered Beatrice said.

"It matters not who did the brewing—we know full well who will do the *stewing*. Whether or not any part of this monstrous report is founded in fact, Lady Antonia Paxton has been grievously compromised. We cannot believe she would stoop to an assignation with the wretch; she is too good and decent a woman—a widow, herself, who has lived quietly, in extended mourning for her dear husband." And the queen could give no higher praise to a woman than to link her mourning to the profound and ongoing grief she felt for her dear Albert.

"She has devoted herself to helping those less fortunate. Her work for the settlement house of our Widows' Assistance League has been exemplary. No, Landon is the one to blame; that much is clear. He should be horsewhipped from here to Canterbury for embroiling her in such a deba-cle." She paced back and forth, rapping the folded paper against her palm as she grasped the ramifications of the earl's perfidy.

"Him and his nonsense about women's equality and women's rights—he's carried on a veritable crusade against marriage these last two years. The Almighty alone knows how many seeds of discord and malcontent he has sewn across our realm." She turned to them with her mind work-ing visibly and her jaw set at a particularly Saxe-Coburg-ian angle.

"The situation must be rectified and the lady's good name restored. What better way to do that than to make the accursed earl actually *reap* the crop he has sewn?" She turned to her daughter-in-law with a fiercely compelling smile. "Alix, dear, find John Brown and have him send us a palace messenger."

When the queen had seated herself at her writing table, Beatrice rose and hurried to her mother's side. "What will you do, Mama?"

The queen looked up with her pen poised above a sheet of her black-edged vellum. "We will send for the Earl of Landon . . . and congratulate him upon his upcoming marriage."

The next morning, exactly upon the stroke of eleven, Rem-ington Carr was being escorted up the stairs to the queen's receiving room at Buckingham Palace. He was dressed im-peccably, in his best gray morning coat and pin-striped trousers, and as he strode along the corridors, his carriage and manner were the very essence of noble assurance.

But his air of confidence hid a wealth of dread. He knew the moment the black-edged envelope bearing the royal seal was placed in his hands that he was in trouble. For a nobleman involved in a scandal, receiving a summons from the dour and reclusive queen was like being sent an engraved invitation to the guillotine.

The footman delivered him to a chair-lined antechamber, where he remained, cooling his heels and simmering in his own expectations. At length he was admitted to the main receiving room, a long, ornately appointed chamber. The queen, dressed in her customary black dress and white cap, sat at the far end on a regal-looking chair supplied with a footstool. She was attended by her private secretary, her Scottish gillie, John Brown, and two of her ladies-in-waiting.

Protocol dictated that he wait at the far end of the room until he was given permission to approach her. So he waited, standing uncomfortably at attention while she perused him from afar. She murmured to her secretary, then glanced at Remington. She spoke for some moments with her gillie and tossed a narrow look in Remington's direction. Then she rose from her chair and began to pace, setting her heels down sharply and folding her hands before her as if to constrain them. For several minutes she paced, lashing him with a contemptuous glance each time she turned—delivering him a scathing lecture without uttering a word.

At long last, when she was worked into a fine temper, she returned to her chair and raised two queenly fingers, giving them a faint twist that ordered him to approach.

With a sick feeling in the pit of his stomach, he came forward and made a restrained bow. She did not extend her hand to him, and from that he understood that he was to maintain a distance of several paces.

"We have taken note of your activities, Landon," she said, speaking to him directly. "And we have been appalled. You have made it a point to challenge decency and

morality and to try the patience of society, the Church
. . . and the Crown. You have at last succeeded in tres-
passing the good graces of all three. Do we make ourselves
perfectly clear?"

"Yes, ma'am." He was relieved to find that the cotton in
his mouth didn't prevent him from forming intelligible
words.

"In the matter before us"—she considered it indelicate
to mention the exact nature of his offense, but her meaning
was never in doubt—"you are to make full restitution to
the injured party." Sitting straighter, she announced with
steely pleasantry: "We are pleased to be the first to congratulate you on your coming marriage."

Remington felt his face reddening and clenched his jaw
briefly before loosening it to speak. "My *marriage,* ma'am?"

She met his reaction with a cool smile.

"A drastic remedy, perhaps, but a fitting one. We are
given to understand that you have declared marriage an
onerous and hateful burden, a veritable shackle to be borne
through life." Her dark eyes snapped as she leaned forward
in her chair. "It is our sincere hope that you find marriage
to be *exactly* what you expect. For it is through suffering
that mankind learns repentance." She sat back with an air
of vengeful satisfaction. "We shall save our compassion for
your bride."

He opened his mouth to speak, but she sat back and
raised those imperious two fingers, giving them a dismissive twist. She turned her face from him, declaring that the
interview was over. Swallowing back his protest, he bowed
and started toward the door. The sound of his name halted
him in his tracks. He turned back and braced.

"We expect we shall see your marriage notice in *The
Times,*" the queen said, without looking up from the document she was reading, *"within the fortnight."*

Remington strode from the palace in turmoil. He had

just been given a royal raking, along with the promise of much worse if he did not marry Antonia within a fortnight. Though she lacked the power to throw him into prison or confiscate his lands as monarchs in former days were wont to do when displeased by a noble, the queen certainly had the power to ruin him politically and financially if he refused to comply with her wishes.

He stepped into his carriage and sat for a moment under the driver's expectant gaze, stunned by his unexpected sense of relief. For a day and a half he had prowled his house and offices, antagonizing his staff and servants, feeling angry and guilty and impotent to do anything to resolve the situation. Drastic though it seemed, the queen's ultimatum had given him the excuse he needed to see Antonia and set things right.

"Where to, yer lordship?" his driver asked when he looked up.

"Paxton House," he answered, squaring his shoulders. "And be quick about it."

"M'lady isn't at home," Hoskins said with a glare as he peered out from the narrow opening of the door. "Not now. Not ever."

The door closed with a slam that Remington felt like a slap in the face. Red crept up his neck as he seized the knocker and gave it several forceful raps, determined to make the old fellow admit him. But the door remained shut, and the deafening silence from the other side roused both anxiety and irritation in him. He knocked repeatedly, without success, then added the side of his fist on the door, and finally called out to old Hoskins and to whoever else might be listening that he intended to stay and pound until they admitted him.

After several minutes, just as his hand was throbbing

and his blood had come to a low boil, the door opened a small crack . . . then wider . . . and wider. Hoskins stood in the way for a moment, staring daggers at him, then stepped aside to reveal Aunt Hermione. She looked uncharacteristically solemn as her gaze drifted over him.

"Please, Mrs. Fielding, it is imperative that I speak with Antonia," he said, rubbing the battered side of his hand. She engaged his eyes, searching his intentions, then with a heavy sigh gestured to Hoskins to admit him.

When he stepped inside, he found himself facing Eleanor, Victoria, Florence, Molly, and Pollyanna as well. The looks they wore ranged from outrage to accusation, to wrenching hurt, expressions that said he had betrayed and disappointed them even as he had Antonia. He shifted awkwardly, from foot to foot, until Hermione instructed Hoskins to take his hat.

The old butler resisted, blazing with indignation, but finally snatched the hat from Remington's hands. Then, with a blistering look of defiance, he dropped the elegant hat on the floor and set his heel down savagely in the middle of it, splitting the brim and squashing the crown flat. As the old boy shuffled back through the hall, Remington blanched, unmanned by his virulent reaction.

"Forgive us, your lordship." Hermione's gentle tones were an island of civility among hostile currents. "It has been a most trying time for all of us, especially for—" She sighed and led him into the drawing room. "I cannot promise she will see you."

"I must talk to her, if only briefly," Remington said, lowering his guard enough to let her see that it did indeed matter to him. "I need to explain and set things right."

Hermione appraised him with a look that said that might not be possible, then left the room. When she returned, she asked him to stand out of the way, by the window, then positioned herself by the door. When Antonia entered, calling, "Auntie? What is it? What is so urgent?"—Hermione darted back out the opening behind her without being seen, and the doors closed with a bang, sealing them in.

Antonia whirled to look at the doors, confused, and Remington stepped out of the shadows of the window curtains, calling her name. She started and turned back. The sight of him caused a rush of hurt and longing deep inside her, and she panicked briefly, retreating as he advanced.

"Antonia, you must allow me to explain," he said tightly.

"I must?" she said with a catch in her voice. Then the first, painful shock of seeing him passed and she came to life. "I cannot believe you have the nerve to show your face here. Remove yourself from my house"—she flung a trembling finger toward the doors—"before I call for the constables and have you removed."

"I know you're furious," he declared, stalking closer. "But you must believe that I never intended . . . what happened."

"You can stand there and pretend you never intended to charm and seduce me? To make me a laughingstock all over London? To take revenge on me?"

"Yes. I mean *no*. I mean—I never meant—"

"Liar," she charged, starting for the doors.

He caught her by one arm, then the other, and pulled her to a halt. "All right—I admit it. At first I did come here to slay the dreaded Dragon of Decency . . . to see to it that she never again trapped a man into marriage." She looked up at him with shimmering heat in her eyes as that word—*dragon*—dredged up the painful memory of something he had said in the lulling and treacherous confines of his bed.

"The Dragon of Decency?" she said in an indrawn breath.

"That's what they called you . . . among other things." He glanced away, pained by the admission. "And I believed them. There were six of them, all with the same story—how could I not? I came here to slay a dragon . . . and instead I found you." His eyes darkened and his hands tightened on her arms. "That afternoon, in your room, I knew I could never go through with it. I went to them and told them the whole idea was off. They were furious, and after I left, they started drinking. That night they came to my house to confront me, not knowing you would be there.

"I had no idea they would break in on us, Antonia." The tension in his face and frame were compelling. "Please believe me, I didn't want to hurt you."

The tenuous bit of hope that crept into the recesses of her heart almost undid her. Against her better judgment she looked up, searching him, needing to know that at least something of what had passed between them had been genuine.

She found herself staring into his chocolate eyes, longing for the sweetness she had glimpsed in them, hungry for the passion they had offered her. She was still susceptible to his touch, his smile, his desire. She still wanted some part of his heart.

The depth and intensity of that wanting suddenly terrified her. She had lowered her defenses and forsaken hard-won wisdom about the nature of men, to follow silly, girlish dreams of love and romance. She had believed it was possible for him to have a change of heart, because she believed he had a heart to change. Now she knew better.

He might have actually desired her. He might have taken pleasure in the banter, the chase, or the challenge of seducing her. And he might honestly regret forfeiting the pleasures he had taken in her arms. But those losses had to do with his pride and his loins, not with her. And they certainly had nothing to do with things that came from the heart, like compassion or affection—or love.

The knowledge hurt, but it also stayed and settled her. She couldn't allow those old, adolescent dreams or newly awakened hungers to betray her, ever again. She was a woman, not a green girl. There was no turning back the clock, no second chance.

"What do you want of me, your lordship?" she demanded with a bitter edge. "Absolution? Forgiveness?"

He hesitated, searching her eyes even as she had his.

"I want to make it up to you." He swallowed hard and braced himself. "I've come to offer you . . . marriage."

Surprise melted some of the rigidity of her shoulders. She stared at him, sensing that he was serious and completely at a loss for how to deal with so unexpected a development. It was the very last thing she would have expected of him. The Ladies' Man. The Suffragist. The Freethinker. The Ultimate Bachelor.

Marriage. It rumbled through her. She jerked her arms free and stumbled back.

"I was right all along. You are deranged," she said tightly. "And I think this odious interview is at an end." He lurched into her path as she headed for the door.

"Listen to me, Antonia." He tried to touch her again, but she jerked back out of reach. "I've never been more serious in my life. I accept full responsibility for your present difficulty—"

"Difficulty?" she demanded, drawing herself up tautly, vibrating with rising emotion. "I am in no difficulty."

"You think not? By now word that you were caught in my bed has spread all over London. In every borough, lane, boulevard, and market stall, your name is being whispered, tittered, and slandered." Sensing that to reveal the queen's marriage edict at this point might be unwise, he omitted just how high the scandal had flown. "You're a woman compromised, and I am the man responsible. I feel obliged to make it right . . . compelled by all that is honorable to offer you what protection I can. After all, what better protection can a woman have than *marriage*?"

His mouth twisted slightly as he said it, as if the words left a sour taste on his tongue. Something in that unconscious tic of distaste made her feel desolate and cavernously empty. Obliged. Compelled. He didn't want to marry, he loathed the very notion of marriage. But he would marry her to satisfy the needs of conscience, or perhaps to forestall society's censure—certainly to salve his precious male honor.

She recoiled inside. Somehow that proposal of marriage seemed as indecent and self-seeking as those made years ago by her father's opportunistic business acquaintances and her uncle's lustful cronies. Both made a means of her in achieving their ends, both reduced her to a commodity that could be acquired and disposed of to suit a man's urges, for pleasure or for honor. Fresh pain unleashed a wave of raw anger in her.

"Damned generous of you, your lordship, offering to *salvage* me." She advanced on him, charged with emotion and generating sparks with every step she took. "But I'll have to decline your noble offer to sacrifice yourself on my behalf. You see, I don't feel ruined or disgraced or sullied— or anything else dirty little minds and still dirtier tongues care to call me. I made a grave error, allowing myself to be seduced by a dishonorable wretch. But the pain and humiliation I have already suffered on that account is quite enough. I refuse to be punished for the rest of my life by being shackled to you in marriage!"

"Shack-led?" He nearly choked on his own tongue. He hadn't expected her to be exactly overjoyed, but he certainly hadn't expected her to think of marriage to him as being *shackled*. "See here, Antonia," he said irritably, "you cannot ignore the problems this ugly bit of notoriety will cause. You need a husband, and I am offering to marry you."

"A husband?" She made a sound that was part laugh and part sob as she glimpsed the absurdity of it. The destroyer of her reputation now proposed to make himself the rescuer of her reputation by yoking her to his exemplary self. How outrageously, insufferably *male* of him!

"Unlike most women, your high-and-mightyship, I have no need of a husband—especially one as treacherous as yourself. I have my own incomes and investments, I manage my own household, and I already live my life contentedly outside what you term 'polite' society. I do not feel the least bit ruined, and I certainly do not need to marry to hold up my head in the streets."

"Don't be ridiculous, Antonia. You must marry me," he demanded, his face and manner heating precipitously. She crossed her arms and looked him square in the eye.

"I'll do no such thing."

"You don't mean that," he declared, his shoulders swelling and fists clenching.

"Oh, but I do." She lifted her chin and refused to be intimidated by his display of brute male power. "You see, our encounter has reminded me of a very valuable lesson I once learned about the nature and character of men. I wouldn't marry you, your lordship, if you were *the last bachelor on earth*!"

She meant it. It struck him like a dousing of icy water; she was actually turning him down. This was not coquetry or feminine pique or even petty womanly retribution for the hurt she had suffered. She honestly refused to marry him!

How could that be? In all his mental grappling and coming to terms with the idea of marrying her, he hadn't even considered that she could possibly refuse him. He was a belted earl, a man of considerable wealth, and the man in whose arms she had found pleasure. And she was the Defender of Domesticity, the Maven of Matrimony—a woman passionately devoted to the idea of marriage. How could she *not* want to marry him?

In a sudden and inexplicable reversal of intention, what had begun as a distasteful but noble duty was somehow transformed into a massive and intensely personal compulsion. He not only had to marry her, he felt a new and compelling urgency to marry her!

"Don't be absurd, Antonia," he growled, running his hands back through his hair, pacing away, then back. "You have to marry now. It might as well be me."

"Absurd?" she said, letting the hurt and anger flow freely inside her. "On the contrary, according to your vaunted social theories, I am being utterly logical and completely responsible." Her mind raced, propelled by her raging emotions. "In fact, I have decided to follow your advice that we widows—we *surplus women*—take up our own lives and make ourselves both independent and useful. I am well educated, sound of constitution, and free of the social constraints and obligations that bind a *decent* woman to her home and hearth. As a *ruined* woman, I can hardly be expected to conform to society's womanly ideal. Thus I am free to pursue whatever I wish."

Even as she said it, she recognized a curious and defiant sense of freedom rising in her. It was new and a little frightening. But it energized her form and set her countenance alight.

"It is quite liberating, your lordship, not having to worry about a husband, a home, or a reputation. Who knows? Perhaps I'll start a business or take up a trade," she said, gesturing toward the horizons opening before her. "I may decide to join the suffragettes and work for the vote, or write magazine articles or novels, or even organize an all-woman labor union. I may invent something . . . or manufacture something . . . or go to Barbados and paint pictures of flowers and naked people. And I may even take up drinking whiskey and smoking cigars! In fact, the one thing I know I will *not* do, your lordship, is *marry you!*"

Before he could close his gaping jaw, she was already across the room and throwing back the door—which sent a number of ladies who had their ears pressed to the panels scrambling back to avoid being hit.

"Hoskins!" she roared with exultant fury. "Show his lordship to the door!"

Remington slammed back into the velvet seat of his carriage, outraged and frustrated and more than a little desperate. How dare Antonia refuse to marry him? Had the strain of what had happened completely unhinged her? Starting a business, joining the suffragettes, painting pictures of naked people in Barbados, and smoking cigars—damn-it-all!—she was talking pure nonsense!

She didn't seem to realize that her name would be bandied about, that people would refuse to include her on guest lists or speak to her in the streets, and that even the people she did business with—her brokers, investment bankers, and property managers—would be forced to retreat from contact with her in order to avoid suspicion and comment. Didn't she understand that she would be asked to resign quietly from her charities, and that because of the smirch on her name, her time and efforts probably wouldn't even be welcome at the women's settlement house anymore? Didn't she know that "reputation," for a woman alone in the world, was everything?

He felt a little sick at the dawning realization that he was the agent responsible for destroying her most precious asset—her good name. Perhaps it was merciful that she didn't understand the full extent of the damage he'd done her. He groaned and dropped his head back against the seat, closing his eyes.

That proved a dangerous move, for into the darkness of his mind crept glimpses of her as she had been that night: soft, yielding, vulnerable to the passions and feelings he roused inside her. He felt again the gentle exploration of her hands, and tasted again the sweetness of her mouth. He watched her disrobing, saw her opening her feelings even as she opened her bodice, and heard her whimpers of pleasure as he brought her to the fullness of a woman's response. He was caught unprepared by a towering wave of need.

His head snapped up. His fists clenched and his body went taut with the need to pull her against him, to cradle her in his arms, to protect her. He wasn't sure where this primal and overwhelming impulse came from; he only knew he was ready to put his still-aching fist through a thousand more leering, smirking faces if that was what it took to make her safe. A moment later he expelled a breath he hadn't realized he was holding.

He wanted Antonia Paxton more than anything he had wanted in his life. He wanted her safe and secure, in his house, in his bed, and under his name. He wanted her across the breakfast table each morning, and in his bed each night. He wanted to know she was his to enjoy and pleasure and make memories with. He wanted to take possession of her the way she had taken possession of him. And in order to have her the way he wanted, he would have to marry her.

And just how the hell was he going to do that?

He sat straighter, his eyes lidded, and his lips drawn tight in concentration. There had to be a way to make her marry him. He had schemed his way into this mess; he would just have to scheme his way out of it. Summoning every shred of his instinctive male cunning, he began to think. His eyes darted over the scenery passing outside the coach window, and something briefly caught his eye. No, it was someone. As he frowned at the memory of that fleeting image, the identity of the person came together in his mind. Lady Constance Ellingson.

He scowled . . . gradually came alert . . . and broke into a beaming smile.

"Ahhh, Antonia, you were so right," he said wickedly. "I am deranged."

That evening, when Antonia entered the drawing room, all conversation became stilted and self-conscious. The temperature of the room seemed to rise as she picked up her sewing basket and settled in her chair. Looking up, she found every eye in the room fastened on Hermione, who set her stitching aside and edged forward on her seat.

"Forgive us, Toni dear. We're not ones to pry, you know that." She paused, evaluating Antonia's mood and quizzical frown. "But would you just clarify for us . . . did his lordship ask you to marry him, or not?"

She glanced around at their folded hands and intent expressions.

"He did not," she declared.

"No?" Hermione drew back into a flurry of confused whispers and murmurs. They had been listening outside the door, Antonia realized, and had heard the word "marry" bandied about that afternoon. "But we understood that he—"

"He did not ask it," she clarified, "he demanded it. And I declined."

Another round of whispers and murmurs produced frowns and shakes of heads, where she was used to seeing smiles and nods. "But *marriage,* Toni," Hermione went on, speaking for the group. "It's what you've always believed in and worked to uphold. And now, with this fearful scandal raging, you will need protection. And you have always said that marriage is a woman's best protection . . . that marriage and home are a woman's rightful place."

Antonia gripped the edge of her chair with cold hands. "That may be true, marriage may be most women's place. But it's not *my* place, that much is clear."

The sound of those words coming from her mouth shocked not only her aunt and her ladies, it shocked her as well. She who had always championed marriage and believed it was the only real locus of power and protection a woman could have in this world, now found the thought of marriage for herself—especially to a man who had betrayed and hurt her—intolerable.

"But, Toni, you have to marry his lordship." Hermione looked to the others, reading their agreement in their eyes.

"You've been . . . compromised," Prudence said, looking genuinely disturbed.

"You have to think of your good name," Eleanor added anxiously.

"You have to think of the future," Florence contributed.

"An' of the baby," Gertrude put in, raising eyebrows. "If there be one."

"You see? It's the only decent thing to do," Pollyanna proclaimed, crossing her arms emphatically.

"No, I don't see," Antonia said in disbelief, pushing to her feet. "After what Remington Carr did to me, how can you even suggest that I submit to a marriage with him? He's ruthless and callous, treacherous, devious, and unpredictable. He cares for nothing but his bachelor cronies and his precious gentlemanly 'honor.' He's the worst of the lot— the archbachelor of all times. I was wrong to go to him, it's true, but I won't be forced into a disastrous marriage to pay for it."

"I don't believe you have a choice, Toni," Hermione

said, with genuine alarm at the apparent depth of Antonia's conviction.

"No choice? But of course I have a choice. No one can force me to suffer a lifetime of bondage in a hateful marriage because of one night's indiscre—"

She halted and her color drained. She looked from face to alarmed face, feeling the devastating insight dawning: *other people had been forced.* The truth rained down on her long-denied conscience like hot coals: *she was the one who had forced them!*

She rushed from the drawing room and then from the house into the lamplit street, desperate to escape her thoughts and the responsibility she bore for sentencing numbers of bachelors and widows to a lifetime of marriage —for the real or apparent sin of just one night together. But their faces and the memory of their compromising situations raced with her, flashing before her eyes, one after another, after another.

There they sat, half-naked, shocked, humiliated, desperate . . . trapped. And heaven help her, she had taken a vengeful pleasure in watching those men squirm and wheedle and ultimately concede to her righteous demands. With stunning clarity she now understood that what had happened to her had sprung from seeds she herself had sown. Her "victims" had turned her own strategy on her, with devastating results.

She now knew what it was like to sit naked in a bed, under the sneers and judgmental stares of strangers—vulnerable and drenched with shame. And she knew one additional horror: what it was like to be betrayed into that humiliation by the one to whom she had opened her most private self, by the one she wanted with all her heart.

For the first time she thought of what the marriages she had "arranged" were like now. On the surface—in the streets, over dinner tables, and in the eyes of society—they seemed to be normal, respectable, even amicable couples. But in the privacy of their homes, in the darkness of their beds at night, were their marriages anything more than cold, face-saving contracts? Was there any caring left between them? Any trust or affection?

Were the women she had matched still grateful, or were they now bitter at having been levered into marriage with an unwilling groom? If marriage wasn't right for her, then what about her protégées? She stumbled over a loose brick and almost fell as the possibility descended on her: *what if she had sentenced them to lives of misery?*

Marriage, which had always seemed to offer women security and protection, now seemed like a trap—one she had vengefully sprung on both men and women.

After a time she looked up to discover she was on St. James Street, mere steps from the Bentick Hotel, the scene of a number of her marriage traps. She stood on the walkway outside, staring up at the windows of the room, thinking of Daphne Elderston, Rosamund Garvey, Margaret Stevenson, Alice Butterfield, Elizabeth Audley, and Camille Adams—her Bentick Hotel brides. The sight of their faces on their wedding days rose into her mind: bright, nervous, and filled with expectation. What expressions did they wear now? Contentment or bitterness? Serenity or anger?

She had to know.

The doorman of the Bentick was good enough to summon her a cab. The minute she returned home, she went straight to her rooms and closeted herself with pen and paper. And before the last candles had been snuffed for the night at Paxton House, there were thirteen letters lying on the entry-hall table, awaiting the morning post.

The last thing Antonia might have expected the next morning was to receive a call from Lady Constance Ellingson.

But when she responded to Hoskins's announcement, there Constance stood, in the drawing room, dressed in impeccable morning-call attire: white gloves, a stylish, figured-silk dress, and a perky tilt-brimmed hat trimmed in peacock feathers. Grateful for a diversion from the tension in the house, Antonia greeted her warmly and would have rung for coffee, but Constance prevented her.

"No, truly. This is not quite a social call. Is there someplace we may speak candidly?" She glanced around the empty drawing room and settled a frown on the open doors.

"Why, yes." Antonia closed the doors to the entry hall and instantly found herself being pulled to the settee. "What is it? What has happened?"

"That, my dear, is something I should be asking you. You've touched off quite a storm." Constance lowered her voice to a whisper. "There are ruts in my doorstep from foot traffic—everyone seems to think I have all the particulars since you made that unthinkable wager at *my* soiree. Half of London has paid me a call in these last two days"— she fixed a passionately expectant look on Antonia and announced—"including the Earl of Landon."

"The earl?" Antonia found herself edging back as her guest leaned forward.

"Remington Carr presented himself on my doorstep yesterday evening. And you'll never guess what he wanted."

Antonia didn't trust herself to speak and shook her head to indicate she hadn't a clue.

"He called on me about the party I was to give Saturday. You remember—the soiree where you were to report the results of the Woman Wager? He suggested—and I quite agreed—that after the other night, carrying on with the soiree is out of the question. Then he asked me to function as his 'second' and call upon you."

"His *second*? Good Lord—he's challenging me to a duel?" she said.

"No." Constance winced. "He is insisting that you make good your half of the wager."

"What?" Antonia blinked, unable to take it in.

"You do remember, surely," Constance prompted, then repeated it for her. "You agreed that if you didn't change his mind about women's work in a fortnight, that you would do men's work for the same length of time."

"The scurrilous wretch," Antonia said in a disbelieving whisper. Her eyes widened. "The unthinkable deceit of that man! I *did* change his mind—he told me so. He ceded me that cursed wager!"

"He did?" Constance looked puzzled. "When? Where? I thought you agreed you would announce the results at my party."

"Here, in my house, not three days ago," she declared furiously. "We were upstairs, in—" She jerked her pointing finger down, hiding that hand in the other, and wishing she could hide the rest of her, as well, from Constance's avid stare.

"Did anyone else hear him say it?" Constance asked, hanging on her every word. "Do you have witnesses?"

Antonia turned slightly on the settee to avoid Constance's curiosity. "No. I didn't think witnesses would be necessary—I assumed that the earl was a man of honor and decency. But then, this is not the first time I've been proved wrong on that account." She struggled internally for a moment. "It's nothing short of blackmail. God knows what he intends, but if he thinks he can force me to—" She glanced at Constance's tense and eager form and left the settee to pace. "I'll not do it. You may go straight back to him and tell him so."

Constance pursed her lips, seeming momentarily at a loss. "Well, he anticipated some resistance. He instructed me to tell you that he is prepared to go to the papers with the story, if you refuse to honor your part of the wager."

The story? Which story? Antonia's head reeled. About her matchmaking? The revenge plot gone awry? What happened and didn't happen in his bed? Or the fact that he had gallantly offered her his name as "protection" and she refused it? Dearest heaven, she had never guessed he could be so ruthless.

"So the beast finally shows his fangs," she said, visibly shaken. She closed her eyes briefly to compose herself, then took a deep breath. "I refuse to give in to such coercion. I won't do it."

"Antonia, dear." Constance hurried to her chair and knelt beside it, taking hold of her hands. "I don't think you have a choice. If you refuse and he goes to the newspapers— You've narrowly escaped a fatal blow to your reputation, as it is. Only the fact that the story was printed in that scurrilous *Gaflinger's* gives you any hope at all. Prolonging the scandal by allowing him to resurrect this wager and publicly declare you've defaulted on it could have devastating consequences."

It was the second time in as many days that Antonia had been told she had no choice, and the opinion did not sit any better with her now than it had the night before. It wasn't enough for Remington that he had romanced and seduced and betrayed her, she realized. Now he was determined to bend her to his male pride and "honor," regardless of the consequences.

"Despicable man," she said through gritted teeth. "I've held my head up this far. I'll just go on doing it. Besides, who is to say that wretched *Gaflinger's* didn't just make it all up?"

"Antonia, please." Constance appraised the stubbornness in her face and began to worry. "*Gaflinger's* may be a vile, sensational rag—but a lot of people read it, all the same. And if Remington Carr begins giving interviews, the rest of London's newspapers will be gouging and elbowing each other for the chance to print whatever he says. You saw what they did with the idea of an earl doing women's work. You can bet they're all green with envy at *Gaflinger's* over this last story and are itching for an exclusive themselves. And none of them are above embellishing a bit, here and there. You could find yourself without a decent social acquaintance or financial contact in all of London." She squeezed Antonia's hands and engaged her eyes.

"Antonia, I have only your interests at heart when I say *go* . . . get it over with. Settle whatever has to be settled between you and the earl, once and for all." With a look of genuine concern she held out a card bearing the earl's business address.

Antonia felt her stomach contract. Settle it? She had been foolish enough to think she had already done that. She took the card and stared at it as if trying to set both it and its sender aflame. She would go and settle it, all right. And when she was done, Remington Carr would know he had indeed tangled with a *dragon*.

The City, London's financial district, was bustling the next morning. The massive stone columns and soaring brick and granite walls of the banks, exchanges, and brokerages loomed over the narrow streets and cast long shadows over the less pretentious blocks of homes, shops, markets, and pubs squeezed between them. The streets were thick with carriages and cabs picking their way along through the hordes of clerks, brokers, and civil servants hurrying to and from their offices. Vendor calls, newsies crying out stock prices on street corners, the creaks of lorries, and the droning thuds of building construction filled the air. All around were the sights and sounds of the lifeblood of the nation: commerce.

Antonia watched it all from the window of her cab, feeling some part wonder, some part anxiety. She had never visited the financial district before; her banker, broker, and solicitors always called on her at home to conduct business, as they were wont to do for their more genteel or lucrative clientele. As she studied the pedestrians hurrying along, she was struck by the number of top hats and similarly cut dark suit coats in the crowd—an angularity and colorlessness unrelieved by bright silks, lively patterns, and curved lines. This was a world of men, those stark lines and somber tones said. And that visual declaration brought Antonia to the edge of her nerves.

"Not exactly neutral ground," she muttered. "It will be like walking right into the lion's den."

Aunt Hermione, seated beside her, reached over to squeeze her hand reassuringly. "You will do fine, Toni dear."

"I intend to give him a sizable piece of my mind," she said irritably.

"Of course you do."

"I'll show him that I won't be intimidated or coerced."

"Absolutely."

"And you're not to let me out of your sight," Antonia said, betraying the dread she felt at the prospect of seeing him again.

She had scarcely slept the night before, thinking of what she would say to him and trying hard not to think of or remember anything else about him. It simply hurt too much. When she told her ladies about Remington's demands, they were shocked that he was behaving in so reprehensible a manner. When she mentioned taking a chaperon, they thought it seemed prudent and suggested Aunt Hermione accompany her.

Antonia and Hermione alighted from the cab before the south entrance to the ornate Mappin and Webb Building, the location Remington had designated on the card he sent with Constance. Soon they had climbed the stairs to the third floor and located the suite of offices bearing the name "Carr Enterprises, Ltd." in gold letters on the door.

The large outer office was plainly but prestigiously appointed, furnished with several handsome chairs, a large mahogany desk, a set of cubbyholes filled with packages and documents, and a small cloakroom. Three doors opened onto the outer office, and a hallway extended to the left, along which several doors leading to inner offices and workrooms stood ajar. A drone of voices and the sound of a mechanical clicking drifted back through the waiting area. When Antonia identified herself and stated she was there to see the earl, faces appeared in the doorways, and there was a noticeable drop in the noise level.

"Yes, madam." The clerkish, middle-aged man at the front desk shot up. "We've been expecting you. This way, please." He escorted them down the short hallway, through a gauntlet of curious stares and a pair of massive doors.

Remington greeted them from behind a huge mahogany desk, in the midst of paneled walls, thick Persian rugs, and leather-upholstered furnishings, looking every bit as elegant and self-possessed as his surroundings. Seeing him like this, face-to-face and on his ground, was even more intimidating than she had imagined. She suffered a craven impulse to run, not walk, to the nearest exit.

"Welcome, Antonia, Mrs. Fielding." He nodded to her, then to Aunt Hermione, a smile unrolling across his too-handsome mouth. "I hope the ride into the City—"

"Please do not insult us by pretending you are concerned for our comfort, Lord Carr," Antonia said, with all the force she could summon. "If my well-being truly meant anything to you, I would not be here at all."

"Not so, Antonia." His smile dimmed. "I am intensely concerned for your welfare. So concerned, in fact, that I am willing to brave your anger and—"

"And threaten me with God-knows-what exactions if I refuse to give you your pound of flesh," she declared, her emotions rising at an alarming rate. "I would think you had taken enough revenge on me to last a lifetime."

"This has nothing to do with revenge, Antonia," he said, rounding the desk and sending her back a step, where she bumped into Aunt Hermione.

"Oh, dear, I can see I'm in the way." Aunt Hermione was out the door before Antonia could stop her.

"If it isn't revenge, then it's your accursed pride at work," she declared, holding her parasol defensively in both hands. "I won our wretched wager and you know it. You admitted it to me not three days ago. But apparently you cannot bear to see a woman win fairly and honorably. How *typically* male of you. If a man sees he cannot win, he changes the rules or tilts the playing field . . . does whatever it takes to secure victory, no matter how low-minded or loathsome it is."

He grabbed her arm as she turned to go, then caught her parasol in his other hand as she brought it up between them. He searched her veiled face as the full impact of her charge struck him. *Typically male. Low-minded and loathsome.* The anger that vibrated in her words was not for him alone.

"God above—you're angry. And not just at me," he said, studying her with new perspective. "You were furious at those poor bastards you trapped into marriages, weren't you? Why? What is it that makes you despise men so?"

"I did not come here to discuss my feelings about your sex, Remington Carr." She tried to pull away, but he wouldn't release her. "I came to tell you I will have nothing more to do with you or with a wager I have already won.

And if you feel compelled to go running to the papers, you would do well to recall that there are *two* sides to every story."

"Was it your husband?" he demanded, reeling her closer, refusing to let it go. "What did he do to you, to make you detest every man you meet?"

"You still don't understand, do you?" she said furiously.

"Something is responsible for your anger. . . ."

"*You* are responsible for my anger!" she shouted, then took advantage of his momentary shock to pull away from him. "You and every other arrogant, insufferable man in the world. You want to know why I detest men? It is because of what you do to us women!

"You belittle and dismiss and demean us," she charged, halting in the middle of the floor. "You command and control and constrain us as if we are troublesome children with no sense of decency or responsibility of our own. You mistake our emotions for a lack of logic, our patience for passivity, and our softness of heart for weakness of character."

She watched him approach, focusing fiercely on her every word. Taking a step backward, then another, she willed herself not to look at his eyes. Little by little, bruised feeling crept into her heated words.

"You treat us as if we are commodities—goods that must be disposed of before we go bad on the shelf . . . as things that may be ruined or soiled or cheapened by even the suggestion of use . . . as objects that must prove both decorative and useful to you, in order to have any worth." Her voice caught as she bumped into the desk behind her. "And you refer to us as *surplus,* when you don't consider us decorative enough or useful enough to enhance your lives. Surplus women."

Remington stopped an arm's length from her as her words—*his* words, spoken from her hurt—went straight to the core of him. She was no longer speaking of *men*, she was speaking of Remington Carr, bachelor, social observer, detractor of women. For the first time he glimpsed the full, personal meaning of the caustic term he had coined. Surplus. Women of no intrinsic worth. Expendable females.

"The women of my household are surplus, just as I am. Women without men—whether fathers or husbands—are surplus in your wretched scheme of things. And that is exactly what I have always been . . . surplus." She watched the troubling of his eyes, and felt powerful, conflicting urges both to wound and to comfort him.

"Worst of all, you make us the quarry in your games of conquest. You seduce and cosset and tempt us, then blame us and brand us as 'ruined' if we succumb to you." Her voice dropped to a pained whisper. "And even when you decide to 'rescue' us, you do it on your own terms . . . to satisfy your needs, not ours."

Seduction, duplicity, selfishness, betrayal—he was guilty of all that and more toward her. He stood for a moment with his ears burning, being tried and convicted by his own conscience. Her experiences with him had only confirmed her opinion that men were opportunistic, arrogant, and callous. Worse—they had forged a link between her feelings toward him and the rest of the male gender. Unless her views of men changed, he stood little chance of making her see him in a positive light, much less agree to marry him.

There was now a gulf between them that would not be spanned by a few soft words or stolen caresses. It was the kind of chasm that required a bridge. And bridges took time to construct. He had to keep her near him and let her experiences, her passions, and whatever feeling she might still have for him change her mind about him.

"You sound exactly as I did when I came to your house, Antonia—angry, suspicious, and resentful of a whole sex.

And it serves only to point up the wisdom of my course of action." The straightening of her spine warned that his next words had better be well chosen. In desperation he seized ones she couldn't help but welcome.

"You won your part of the wager. I was and still am perfectly willing to concede that." He paused, delaying his next breath to gauge her reaction. She came alert, listening with open suspicion. "But you have yet to fulfill your part of the bargain."

"My part?"

"I did your 'women's work' and it did change my thoughts and feelings about women. As a result, I am preparing a letter to the PM and the Liberal party, registering my support for the Sister Bill, as we agreed. Now it is time for you to make good your pledge to do 'men's work' for two weeks."

"That is absurd!" she declared, her eyes widening as she scrambled to make sense of his concession and his unexpected demand. "I was to do men's work only if I failed to change your attitude toward women and their work."

"You did your work well, Antonia." He forged ahead, adamantly ignoring her protest. "You taught me there was more to women than dependence, emotionalism, and vanity. Thus it is only right that I be given the chance to show you there is a good bit more to men than the callous, brutal, and self-centered behavior you have just described."

"D-don't be ridiculous," she stammered, trying to sort out what he had in mind. Two weeks of men's work meant . . . good Lord . . . two weeks of being at his mercy, two weeks of having to see him and deal with him and her feelings for him each day!

"It's not ridiculous, Antonia. It's reasonable. You've gone to great lengths to convince me of women's honor, decency, and fairness. Now show some of it. Do a man's work for a while and learn something from it. Spend time with real men, outside your narrow, all-female world."

"My nar—? My world is anything but narrow, and you know it," she ground out, scarcely able to believe he was turning the charges she had made against him to his own treacherous purpose.

"Oh? Then perhaps you can tell me what sort of backing is required to keep a financial enterprise thriving, or what the Bank of London requires as collateral when making a loan, or what it feels like to have the livelihood of hundreds of families riding on each decision you make. If you intend to start your own business concern someday, you certainly must know all that and more." He could see her outrage rising and plunged ahead.

"Or perhaps you would rather start with something simpler—like what happens to your money when you put it in a bank, how goods are imported to this country, or the latest advances in woolen knitting mills." She was caught flat-footed, unable to respond. He produced a superior smile. "No? Then at very least you can show me how to operate a typewriter machine or how to balance a five-column ledger—"

"For your information, I *can* balance a five-column ledger!" she declared hotly.

"Well, well. Can you indeed?" He looked inordinately pleased with himself. "We shall just have to see about that."

Seizing her by the hand, he pulled her out the door and down the hall. Shortly, she found herself being hauled up before a tall clerk's desk, in a large room filled with other desks and lined with bookshelves and paper cabinets.

"This is my head clerk, Aldous Bexley." Remington introduced a short, wiry man with hunched shoulders, long, nimble fingers, and a very heavy pair of spectacles. "Bexley," he addressed the fellow with a proprietary tone, "Lady Antonia, here, has just informed me that she has more than a passing acquaintance with ledgers. And I would like to give her a chance to prove it."

Before Antonia could think how to extricate herself from his bullying, she was plunged, wholesale, into receipts and debits and credits and endless, exhausting columns of numbers.

Remington gradually worked his way out of her immediate awareness and back to the door, where he stood watching her wrestle determinedly with an accounting scheme that had sent more than one clerk staggering from the room with ink blots swirling before his eyes. She was here, in his territory, in his world, and he was going to see that she stayed. He took in the stubborn angle of her jaw, the rigid set of her shoulders, and the curve of her waist and felt himself going taut with possessiveness. He was going to rescue her whether she bloody well liked it or—

He halted, hearing her words in his mind: "When you 'rescue' us, you do it . . . to satisfy your own needs, not ours." Surplus. She said she had always been surplus. Her anger at men wasn't just about social convictions, abstractions about gender and place, or even the plight of destitute women. It was about *her*.

Grappling with those unsettling thoughts, he withdrew to his outer office. There he encountered Aunt Hermione, perched daintily on the edge of a chair.

"Where is Antonia?" She rose and peered past him with a wary look.

"Having her first taste of 'men's work,' " he announced, and braced as if expecting a protest. She softened and gave him a cherubic smile that bore a hint of complicity, instead. The surprise of her goodwill disarmed him.

"I was just about to have a bit of coffee, Mrs. Fielding. Would you join me?"

They settled on the sofa in his office, sipping coffee and talking amicably for a time. There was no delicate way to broach the subject of Antonia's past, and so, trusting to Hermione's good graces, he came straight out with it. "Mrs. Fielding, would you be willing to tell me how Antonia came to marry Sir Geoffrey?" As he had hoped, Hermione was forthcoming with her impressions. But he was not quite prepared for the first words out of her mouth.

"I suppose it's no secret. Geoffrey rescued her."

"R-rescued her?" He set his cup down and reached for his handkerchief to dab at the coffee he'd spilled on his trousers. "What do you mean?"

"Her parents died when she was a young thing, you know. And she went to live with her uncle, Wentworth, who took no interest in her." She paused and looked a bit uncertain, deciding how much to tell him. "Some of the duke's friends, however, took a very particular interest in her . . . if you know what I mean. And the duke"—her usually smiling eyes tightened briefly with a deep and fermented anger that startled Remington—"conveniently looked the other way."

He knew exactly what Hermione meant and it made him tighten inside. The clubs were full of the callous and cavalier boasts of men in their cups . . . about helpless young girls who were forced to submit to an uncle's "care" and were expected to be properly grateful.

"Geoffrey had been in business with her father. When he got wind of what was happening, he went to see her and offered her a home with him—which, of course, necessitated marriage."

"He *rescued* her," Remington said, chagrined that he hadn't realized it before now. Young girls married aging men only out of avarice or necessity. And Antonia didn't have a greedy bone in her body.

"He was a dear and generous man." Hermione's dark mood faded. "A bit of a dry stick at times, and full of crotchets. But he adored Antonia, doted on her. He had given up all thoughts of marriage long before he offered for her, you see. And he certainly never expected to have a wife as bright and lovely as Toni."

But how had Antonia felt about him? He thought of the anger in her voice when she spoke of being rescued, and wondered if some of it was for old Sir Geoffrey as well as for him. There was no polite way of asking what he needed to know, and at the risk of affronting her, he finally said: "Was it a marriage in every way?"

Hermione put her cup back on the tray and stared at him, deciding how much to reveal. "It was." She sighed. "Though I believe it took Geoffrey quite a while to get around to it. At the base of it, I believe he was embarrassed by the difference in their ages. He felt old and knotty and—" She lowered her lashes and her voice. "I believe the dear boy always insisted on nightshirts—if you know what I mean."

Remington nodded.

"Funny old thing, he was. But Toni always—" She frowned and set her cup on the table. "Well, she will tell you herself, in her own good time."

Remington's disappointment was softened by the fact that Hermione seemed to think Antonia's "own good time" would actually come. He drew a cleansing breath, feeling both encouraged by his new understanding and daunted by the magnitude of the task ahead of him.

"Remington, come quick!" Paddington Carr's voice burst through the partly open doors before he did. "Bexley's gone right over the edge—taken to wearing skirts, high-buttons, and bonnets—" He barreled through the doors and jerked to a halt, staring back over his shoulder in bewilderment. "Either that, or"—he scowled as he thought belatedly of a more plausible explanation—"there's a female planted on top of his stool." He scratched his head. He apparently found the two possibilities equally alarming.

"It's a woman, Uncle Paddington," Remington said, shooting to his feet. "And it's all right. I know all about her."

"You do? Oh. Well, then." That simple declaration seemed to reassure Paddington. His braced shoulders relaxed and he swung around to look at his nephew. Then his eyes fell on Hermione and he blinked, squinted, and went utterly still.

"Mrs. Fielding," Remington said with a wry smile, "allow me to present my uncle, Paddington Carr. Uncle Paddington, this is Mrs. Hermione Fielding, the aunt of the lady occupying Bexley's stool."

"How do you do, sir?" Aunt Hermione flushed with pleasure and extended her hand to him, taking in at a glance his elegant charcoal suit, tastefully embroidered vest, and dapper spats. His barrel-chested form and silver hair seemed dashing indeed in a man fast approaching seventy. She gave her best midnight-blue silk an arranging stroke and perked her lace-rimmed collar with a subtle finger. After a somewhat awkward moment Paddington came out of his trance and approached her.

"Ch-charmed," he stammered, accepting her hand with widened eyes. After staring at her hand for an unseemly time and bestowing a reverent kiss upon it, he continued to hold it, fixing his gaze on her as if seeing a memory aged and materialized before him.

She was nothing short of beautiful . . . silvery hair, saucy blue eyes, rosy-apple cheeks, and a tilt to her head that was somehow both demure and spirited at the same time. Another minute passed before he realized she seemed to be waiting for a response.

"Beg, pardon, ma'am." He released her and fidgeted with his hands until he tucked his thumbs in his vest. "Got quite distracted by your . . . by the way you . . ."

"I asked if you would care for coffee," she said, blushing prettily and sitting straighter. "His lordship asked me to pour and there is plenty left."

"Coffee? Oh, yes. God, yes. Coffee. Absolutely." He realized he was staring like a red-eared schoolboy. "Love coffee, don't you know. Have it every morning. And after dinner some days. With a cigar. Love cigars, too." Then she extended a cup to him, and he looked as if she'd handed him the keys to Camelot. "Excellent things, cigars and coffee. And prunes."

Remington watched his flustered uncle with amazement, which turned to embarrassment when he remembered Hermione couldn't know about his less than lucid spells. He dragged a chair over for his uncle, hoping to catch Hermione's eye and give her a look that might help explain. But she was looking at Paddington with a feminine twinkle in her eye.

"Well, how utterly refreshing to meet a handsome and refined gentleman who . . . appreciates a good prune," she said. And she laughed. It was the kind of sound that came with a blush, in women of all ages.

Paddington realized what he'd done and looked embarrassed. But something in Hermione's teasing, absolving laughter reached through his chagrin, and after a moment he was chuckling, too. "Sink me!" he said with bluff good humor. "Don't know what's got into me, Mrs. . . . Mrs. . . ."

"Fielding," she supplied, sending a subtle hand to be sure her perky hat was tilted to the proper angle and settling a smile on him that could only have been called flirtatious. "Hermione Fielding."

"Mrs. Fielding." He nodded. "It's just that you put me so in mind of someone. I got a bit flummoxed."

"Your wife, perhaps," she suggested, in a tone that said she hoped it wasn't so. She lowered her chin to look at him from under her lashes.

"Oh, no, ma'am. Not married. Never made that blissful trip to the altar. I say, Mrs. Fielding, do I know your husband? Perhaps that is why you look so familiar."

"It is possible you *knew* him. I am a widow, you see. For some years now."

"Sorry to hear that, ma'am," Paddington said, staring at her with an outrageously inappropriate smile. "Dashed bad luck . . . losing a husband and all."

"Oh, I didn't lose him, Sir Paddington. I know exactly where I put him last." She laughed coquettishly, behind a discreet hand.

Uncle Paddington caught the humor in it and chuckled, his eyes bright in a way Remington couldn't remember ever seeing before. Remington sat dumbfounded, watching his elders flirt like giddy adolescents. A short while later he asked his uncle to entertain Aunt Hermione for a while and slipped out. Standing just outside the door, he watched his uncle glowing with robust good humor and, unless his senses had completely betrayed him, with an unmistakable spark of amorous interest.

Lord. Who would have thought the old boy had it in him, at his age? At any age? It caused a strange fullness in his chest to think of his lonely and sometimes bewildered uncle finding a bit of happiness and companionship at this time of life.

He stood watching the pair a moment longer, realizing that whatever was happening between them, it was a stroke of luck for him. For with Antonia's chaperon out of the way, he had more room to maneuver her into his arms. For it was in his arms, he sensed, that she would finally be persuaded to marry him.

Four hours later Antonia was still sitting on Bexley's tall stool, listening to him drone on about his method of reverse checking, and wrestling with credits and debits, in such large numbers that just keeping the columns straight was a monumental task. Her eyes were burning from the glare, her fingers were cramped and ink stained, and her back felt as if it were going to snap in two. When Bexley checked her balances and declared there had to be a transposition somewhere, she frowned at him and demanded to know just how he could know that without re-adding the lot.

"The rule of nine, madam," he said evenly, in tones that made her sense he had given this same lecture to junior clerks again and again. "You divide the balance by nine, and if it comes out even, you know there's been a transposition."

"And how do you know it's not just divisible by nine?" she insisted testily, straightening her protesting spine. He shook his head in a way that said he had expected that very question.

"Because it never is unless there is a transposition. I don't claim to know all the number theory. I'm not a mathematician. I only know it is the usual practice for us, because it works."

"That's one of the things about men's work," came Remington's voice from the door behind her. "We discover sound rules and practices and we employ them without wasting a lot of time asking why. Time is of the essence here. Many of the things we do have strict time requirements, for when a doorway of opportunity closes, it is gone. And it almost never comes around again. In the world of trade and commerce, we seldom have time for the luxuries of 'why.'" He turned to his head clerk. "What do you think, Bexley? Does she know something about bookkeeping?"

The wiry head clerk raised one eyebrow. "She would do . . . in a pinch."

Antonia's first reaction was indignation at that bit of male condescension. Then, over his shoulder, she could see several of the junior clerks suppressing smiles. Her reaction must have shown in her face, for Remington laughed and lifted her down.

"You may not realize it, but you've just been given a mighty compliment. Now, come with me and let these poor overworked wretches get on with their dinner."

She paused by the door and looked back around the clerk's room, realizing that she'd spent the entire morning there, doing exactly what Remington had planned for her to do: men's work. It annoyed her that she had found it more rigorous and complicated than she might have expected. The clerks were brisk and efficient and, oddly enough, they didn't seem to mind Bexley's sharp comments and corrections. They concentrated on the work and didn't take mistakes and admonishments quite so personally as she would have expected. And if she thought her ladies had to deal with petty details . . .

Once outside the door, she shrank from Remington's guiding hand and looked up and down the hallway. "It's time we were going. Where is Aunt Hermione?"

"She is occupied at the moment." He took her elbow and steered her toward a nearby door and the encounter he'd been planning for the last two hours. "I thought, since you've worked so hard on my books, the least I could do was offer you something to eat." He pushed the door back, and there, in the middle of a comfortably furnished office, sat a small linen-draped table, supplied with china, crystal, and fresh flowers. As she watched, a black-clad waiter lit a pair of candles and reached for a bottle of wine chilling in a silver bucket.

Her knees went weak at the sight; it was a pure seduction for her aching senses. And it was that very thought that saved her. Seduction. She whirled and was halfway down the hall before he caught up with her.

"You haven't a drop of shame in your blood, do you?" she said, making straight for Remington's office to find Aunt Hermione. "You never quit scheming."

"What? A bit of luncheon?" he said, gritting his teeth at his stupidity.

Antonia burst through the door of the office and stopped dead. Aunt Hermione and a silver-haired gentleman with oddly familiar features were snuggled together on the sofa, hands entwined, foreheads together, gazing into each other's eyes. They didn't bother to break apart, but turned together to face the interruption.

"Toni dear!" Hermione flushed becomingly. "You simply must meet Paddington—Sir Paddington Carr—his lordship's uncle. Ever since his lordship introduced us, we've been having such a lovely time."

Antonia stared at the ruddy, beaming face of the gentleman holding her aunt's hands, then at Remington. The resemblance was unmistakable. Fury erupted in the middle of her. Remington had gone behind her back to introduce her aunt and his uncle! And Aunt Hermione, who was supposed to be helping her avoid Remington's scheming, had apparently succumbed to it herself. She felt doubly betrayed.

Whirling, she rushed back down the hall and snatched her hat from the coatrack. Remington was close behind and followed her out into the wide upper hallway. There he startled several people passing in the hall by demanding: "Where do you think you're going?"

"Anywhere, as long as it is away from you!" she insisted, plopping her hat on her head and fumbling to pin it in place, while walking briskly for the stairs.

"Don't be absurd, Antonia. Come back with me and

have something to eat, and we'll discuss this as two responsible, sensible people."

"You're not responsible and I'm obviously not sensible —otherwise I would never have come here in the first place!" she said, halting in the middle of the main stairs to glare at him. "Do you think I don't know exactly why you brought me here?"

"Why did I?" he demanded, adding, "I'm beginning to wonder myself."

"You obviously intended to . . . White linen, flowers, wine in the afternoon . . . Lord—you're as transparent as glass. And you must think I'm as thick as lead!"

He pulled his aristocratic chin back as if she had smacked it. He watched her hurrying down the stairs and jolted after her, red-eared with chagrin at being so easily understood and dismissed. When he caught up with her in the lobby of the building, there were people all around— men who recognized him, then quickly guessed who she must be and nudged each other. He vibrated with the urge to snatch her back, but dared not put a hand on her in so public a place.

"Antonia, listen to me—" he said in a loud whisper as he reached her side.

She ignored him and quickened her pace, blending into the stream of pedestrians when she stepped out onto Queen Victoria Street. He had to dodge and weave and excuse his way through the flow of foot traffic to keep up with her. Then he ran into a knot of elder gentlemen taking up the middle of the sidewalk, and his frustration erupted. "Antonia—come back!" he yelled across them.

But she kept going, and when he disentangled himself he caught sight of the feathers of her hat bobbing along between the top hats well ahead of him. Then she seemed to pause, and he thought she might be changing her mind, until he glimpsed the sign of a cab stand on a lamppost above her head. The sight spurred him to a near run.

He arrived just in time to see her lifting her skirts to mount the steps of a cab. He felt a terrifying sense that if she got into that carriage and left, she would somehow be exiting his life forever. Only mild panic could have made him behave so rashly. He grabbed her by the waist and snatched her back from those steps.

"Ohhh! What are you doing? You're mad—let me go!" Antonia tried to squirm away from him, but he held her firmly by the waist. The cab driver jumped off his box to intervene, but Remington was already hauling her out of his reach.

"Just a bit of a tiff with the wife," he growled at the confused cabbie. "Nothing for you to get involved in."

"Wife? You lying bully—" she snapped, straining to peel his arms from her.

He wrestled her as discreetly as he could along the side of the buildings, feeling his grip on her gradually loosening. Then he spotted the alley behind the Mappin and Webb Building, and it seemed the closest place both to get her alone and to make her listen to him. He pulled her into the shadowy lane and, after a short scuffle, had her imprisoned between his arms and pinned against a brick wall with his body.

"I'll scream—" She panted and shoved at him.

"No, you won't," he countered, breathing hard himself as he scrambled for equilibrium. And as that simmering silence lengthened, she proved him right.

The turmoil in her senses slowly settled. Antonia found herself standing in an alley, pressed against a wall, with Remington finding every sensitive spot on her body with every hungry and demanding part of his own. Worse yet, the fire of her moral outrage was being redirected, translated into a very different kind of heat. Suddenly, all she could see was the roused sensuality in his face. All she could feel was the rush of her blood in her veins and the heat of his body, melting her outer surface and her inner resistance. All she could taste was the desire rising up the back of her throat.

"Antonia." He lowered a hand and dragged his finger-tips down the side of her face. Again and again he stroked her, tracing her lips, caressing her skin, absorbing the nuances of her body's softening. She could feel him watching the hurt and desire swirling in her core; could feel him reaching into her chaotic emotions. And she was powerless to stop it. Then he cradled her chin in his hand and brought his lips down on hers.

His mouth was warm and firm and soft and exquisitely mobile as it caressed hers in gentle, changing patterns. She tilted her head, wanting him, seeking him, and, with a helpless sense of wonder, finding him.

It felt exactly the same as it had the first and the last time he had kissed her, and all the times in between . . . that initial, breathtaking drench of pleasure, then the low, responsive resonance in her head and heart, and finally the inner calm that settled over her—the feeling that she was exactly where she belonged. When his arms slid around her, she couldn't help sending hers around his neck and couldn't stop her body from arching into his.

He groaned softly and leaned into her, pressing her back against the bricks. He was so intent on reminding her of the fact that she wanted him, that he completely forgot the dingy alley, the traffic rushing by a few yards away, and the unfortunate fact that dozens of people had witnessed him dragging her into the service lane.

In the middle of the financial district, emotional outbursts and the sight of women being set upon in the streets were emphatically not "business as usual." Worse yet, it was just past two o'clock, the dinner hour, a time when many of the offices released their inhabitants into the streets. The cabbie had no difficulty finding gentlemen to verify his story to the local constable: a well-dressed lady snatched right out of his cab and dragged, kicking and flailing, into a nearby alley. With the backing of a pair of dedicated civil servants, an MP, and an assistant director of the Bank of London, the stick-wielding constable went charging into the alley after the pair.

Running footsteps and shouts of "There they are!" and "That's the bastard—get 'im!" broke in on Remington and Antonia. Several men rushed down the alley at them, and the sound and motion finally penetrated their passion-drugged wits. He wheeled belatedly and spread himself protectively across her cringing form, only to find himself seized roughly and wrestled back against the far wall of the alley. Antonia's scream died halfway through as the sight of a black-clad constable and several men in business suits registered in her head.

"Wait!" one of her rescuers yelled, just as Remington took a fist in the solar plexus. The blow knocked the wind from him and doubled him over. "Good God, man—that's Landon!" said the same voice. "It's the Earl of Landon!"

"You sure?" The constable, who had just given Remington a punch to subdue him, blanched and drew back in horror. "A belted earl draggin' women into alleys?"

The MP bent to look at Remington's face and came up wide-eyed. "Good Lord—it *is* Landon." Then the fellow turned to look at Antonia, who stood paralyzed with horror, in the grip of two solicitous gentlemen. As the others turned to stare at her, the MP took in her half-mourning purple and announced: "Ye gods—then this must be the widow! You know—from the papers!"

The murmurs of the onlookers grew to include such alarming phrases as "the bounder," "a menace," and "horsewhipped." The constable, caught in the untenable position of having both apprehended and assaulted a peer of the realm, panicked and decided to drag him off to the station and let his sergeant sort it out. Remington recovered his breath just in time to protest.

"Release me at once!" he gasped out, planting his feet and resisting with every ounce of physical strength he possessed. "I've done nothing wrong—"

The cabbie stepped out of the crowd filling the alley, with a fierce scowl. "An' wot do ye call draggin' a woman right outta a coach, eh? An' haulin' her down a alley?"

Antonia's reeling wits finally righted. One minute she was melting in Remington's arms, and the next a constable and an angry mob were carrying him away. Good Lord— they were arresting him for assaulting her! Much as he deserved to be thrashed for his wrongs against her, she couldn't stand by and watch them arrest him for the crime of . . . a kiss. But, in truth, it was the sudden thought of this scandal breaking atop another one not yet laid to rest that spurred her to action.

"Stop! Wait!" she called out, twisting free of the hands restraining her. "This is all a hideous misunderstanding." But now that she had their attention, she realized that she had to come up with some sort of explanation. "It's not what you think!

"I was in the area and stopped by the earl's business offices . . . to inquire about the outcome of some investments. But I found he wasn't in . . . and I left, intending to take a cab home. But he arrived just after I left . . . and thought to catch me before I got into the cab. But he startled me, coming up from behind, so I cried out. He asked me to have a word with him and there was no place else as private. . . ."

She could see from the looks on their faces that they didn't believe a word of it. And she could see from the narrowing of their eyes and the direction of their gazes—

aimed at her kiss-swollen mouth—what they thought of her as a result of her weedy explanation. She stood simmering in the heat of her own lie as the constable weighed the merits of her story and seized upon it as the excuse he needed to wash his hands of a potentially messy situation.

"Then you ain't willin' to bring charges?"

"Charges? Of course not." She gave what she hoped passed for an innocent smile. "It would be a miscarriage of justice for his lordship to be inconvenienced on my account."

"Very good, ma'am." The constable ordered the fellows restraining Remington to release him. Apologizing profusely, he ordered the crowd to disperse.

Remington straightened his coat and tie and offered Antonia his arm. She accepted his escort, and he led her back to the street at a quick but dignified pace.

She was so busy keeping both her head and "appearances" up, that she didn't notice the scrawny little fellow with the oversize brown bowler and ferretlike eyes at the edge of the crowd. Remington saw him, but so briefly that the name and face didn't register until they were halfway to the doors of his office building. Belatedly, the fellow's identity hit him like the constable's fist, and he stopped and looked back over his shoulder. All he saw behind them was the constable, speaking to one of the gentlemen who had apprehended him and dispersing the gawkers who stopped to see what had drawn a crowd.

He expelled an uneasy breath, praying that he had just imagined Rupert Fitch.

Antonia jerked her hand from Remington's arm the instant they were out of view of the street. "You are without a doubt the most loathsome man who ever walked."

"Which raises the interesting question of why you spoke up for me, wretch that I am," he said, keeping pace with her as she started up the stairs.

She was in no mood to have to explain why she had interceded for him. She wasn't even sure herself, though she feared it had something to do with that wretched kiss and with the peculiar ache she had felt, watching them haul him away. She still had feelings for him . . . perilously near the surface. And if she didn't get away from him soon, they could make her do something she would regret.

"Don't take it personally, your lordship. I simply could not abide the idea of seeing my name linked infamously to yours again, in the newspapers. I've quite enough to live down already."

"A sensible conclusion," he said, trying not to sound as desperate as he felt. "And all the more reason for you to make good your part of the wager."

She stopped in the middle of the hallway and stared at him. "You cannot be serious."

"I assure you I am. I intend to hold you to every syllable of our bargain."

She closed her mouth and hurried down the hallway to the open door of his offices, intent on finding Aunt Hermione, then finding the first available cab to take her home. But when she demanded to know where her aunt was, the fellow at the desk looked a bit unsettled. Hurrying down the hallway with Remington on her heels, she found his office empty and reversed course to search the other offices. But he prevented her from leaving by closing the door and leaning his back against it.

"You're not through here, Antonia."

The intimate tone of his voice raised her defenses. Spotting her parasol on a chair, she snatched it up and held it threateningly.

"Why are you doing this?" she demanded.

"I thought you said I was painfully obvious."

"You are obvious. You're also devious. And I've learned the hard way that 'the obvious' is not your only motive. You want to seduce me again. What I want to know is why? What is it you really want from me?"

"I thought that was the obvious part," he said earnestly. "I want to marry you."

She was braced for something low and underhanded; she thought she was prepared for it. But hearing him say it still took her breath.

"Well, I don't want to marry you." She managed a fair counterfeit of disdain, until he came toward her with a wry, self-mocking smile.

"Why won't you marry me?"

She backed a step. There were at least a thousand good reasons, but at the moment she could think of only two or three.

"I—I don't like you. I don't need you. And most important, I don't trust you. You've lied to me and about me, and deceived me in every way possible. You've treated me like a troublesome child and a commodity to be acquired and disposed of at your whim." Her voice thickened. "I don't need rescuing, thank you. And I will not spend the rest of my life shackled to a man I don't like, don't need, and don't trust."

"What about one you *want*?" he said. "Can you imagine spending your life with someone who makes your blood burn and your bones melt?"

He moved forward slowly, and she felt an irresistible tension rising beneath her skin; a desire for touch, a hunger for pleasure of the sort she knew only he could supply. It was confirmation of his claim on her sensual responses, and it infuriated her. She retreated again and found herself trapped in a corner near a window.

"I have always told you the truth, Antonia. You may not believe it now, but I meant every word I said about your ladies and about you. I wasn't responsible for Woolworth and the others breaking into my house—I wouldn't have hurt you like that for the world. And as to the rest . . . you know my faults and flaws all too well. I think it only fair that you give me, and men in general, a chance to redeem ourselves in your estimate. Two weeks, Antonia. For you to learn to like me, to trust me again."

By the time he touched her hand, she was incapable of more than a token resistance. But he merely pressed something into her palm and curled her fingers around it. It felt small and cool and hard. She found a tiny sphere covered with fawn-colored silk lying in her palm. It was a moment before she recognized it as one of her buttons—one he had cut from her dress that day in the upstairs parlor.

Tenderness and anger and longing surged through her at once, clashing, leaving her defenseless. Feeling panicky, she pushed him aside and headed for the door.

Aunt Hermione was in the very office where Remington had laid his romantic trap. She and Paddington Carr had made use of the luncheon Antonia had spurned, and now sat drinking wine and staring warmly at each other across the linen-clad table.

"Oh! Toni!" Aunt Hermione said, flushing at being caught indulging in a bit of romance. "We are just having the nicest luncheon."

"Didn't think Remington would mind . . . since you didn't seem quite on your feed," Paddington said, rocking back in his chair. He looked a bit embarrassed, but not so much so that he would release Hermione's hand, which lay under his on the tabletop.

Antonia glowered at her aunt. "It's time to go Auntie, if you're *quite* finished."

As they quitted the offices, Remington accompanied them downstairs, where he had the doorman hail them a cab. He helped Hermione into the coach, then casually mentioned that he would send his own carriage around to Paxton House the next morning to collect her at nine o'clock.

"There is no need," Antonia protested irritably, "I won't be coming back."

He smiled as he handed her up the steps as well.

"Oh, yes, you will."

His knowing look lingered in her mind, the way that small silken orb stayed in her hand, both fueling her irritation on the ride home. Her annoyance gradually focused on Hermione, who sat huddled on the far end of the seat with a petulant look. It was some time before Antonia could bring herself to say anything to her aunt on the subject uppermost in both their minds.

"You surprised me, that's all," she said, trying to explain her irritation at something that obviously gave Hermione pleasure. "Remington's uncle, of all people."

"I cannot understand what you find so horrible about my having a bit of luncheon with him," Hermione said with an air of injury. "I've always liked gentlemen, you know that. And he's a perfectly charming man. And handsome. And so droll. He makes me laugh, Antonia, and no one has done that in a very long time."

Antonia was hard put to come up with a reason to dislike the man, except his connection to Remington and her suspicion that this was another vile bit of maneuvering on Remington's part.

"He fairly raised Remington, you know," Hermione said, glancing furtively at her, then back out the window. "Remington's mother died when he was young, and his father was . . . well, interested in other things. Paddington stepped in to take care of him. He's so hopeful that Remington will marry and give him a grandniece or -nephew before he passes on. He just loves babies. He didn't get to have any of his own, and I must say: I know how that feels. You're the closest thing I've ever had to a daughter." She gave Antonia another sidelong glance. "You know, he thinks you're very pretty."

"That's very . . . gallant of him," Antonia responded, a bit embarrassed by her truculent attitude. She looked out the window. "I think he's quite . . . dignified."

Hermione relaxed and breathed a sigh, but a moment later she was back at it.

"You know, Remington's not had many lady friends," she volunteered. "Paddington worries about him a great deal . . . thinks he should have someone to . . . ummm . . ."

"Play *footsie* with," Antonia supplied, leveling a disgusted look at her.

"Well, yes. And make babies with. And you know I have thought for some time that it would be good for you to . . . ummm . . ."

"Play footsie, too," Antonia finished for her, understanding now why she had been so suspicious of this liaison. Hermione was now solidly in Remington's camp.

"Well, yes. It's clear that his lordship is still very much taken with you, and eager to make amends for what happened."

"Aunt Hermione," Antonia said tightly, narrowing her eyes.

"Yes, dear?"

"Hush."

Because of the long spring days, the candles were not lit in the drawing room until nine o'clock that evening. Aunt Hermione was deep in the midst of telling the others about her adventure of the day, when Hoskins arrived to announce a caller.

"At this hour?" Antonia said, rising from her chair by the window.

"A man or a woman?" Aunt Hermione demanded of the butler.

"It is Mrs. Howard, ma'am," Hoskins intoned.

"Mrs. Howard? Do we know a Mrs. Howard?" Eleanor asked, looking at the others' equally blank faces.

"Mrs. *Camille* Howard, madam." He addressed Antonia.

"Camille? Our Camille?" Antonia's heart nearly stopped. "By all means, show her in, Hoskins."

Everyone hurried to greet Camille as she entered, but most stopped just short of embracing her. She stood there in her best frock and bonnet, her blond, girlish beauty marred by blotched skin and dark smudges under puffy eyes. Antonia paused, then held out her hands to the young woman, whose chin quivered as she took them.

"Camille, dear . . . are you all right?" Antonia said softly, searching the signs of distress in the young woman's countenance with mounting dread.

Camille opened her mouth to speak, but instead of a greeting, out came a sob.

"What is it? What's happened?" Antonia enfolded the young woman with a hug, knowing already, in her heart of hearts, what must have brought the young woman there. The others hurried to join her, speaking words of comfort as they helped her to the settee in the middle of the room. Wedged between Antonia and Aunt Hermione, in a circle of sympathetic faces she had grown to know and trust, she cried for a while before she was able to answer Antonia's questions.

"It's Bertrand," she said, dabbing at her tears. "He's a beast."

"He ain't taken a hand to you, has he?" Molly demanded furiously. Camille looked a bit shocked and shook her head.

"Does he holler an' cuss an' pitch a fit if 'n the meat ain't right or his drawers is scratchy?" Gertrude asked. Again Camille shook her head.

"Then what is it, Camille? What does he do?" Antonia asked, clenching her teeth and steeling herself for whatever would follow.

"He doesn't *do* anything, Lady Toni," she said plaintively. "He won't hardly speak to me, except to ask me to pass a dish at supper—that is, when he's actually home for supper. Most nights he eats at his club and then stays to do whatever it is men do at those hideous places. And he only comes home well after I've gone to bed. He will hardly look at me or talk to me, and he has yet to introduce me to his friends and their wives. He pretends I don't even exist . . . except when . . ."

She dissolved into sobs again, but every woman present knew exactly when a man like Bertrand Howard acknowledged his wife's existence: late at night, in the dark, in his bed.

"Then when I got your letter, Lady Toni, asking if I was happy and . . . I just couldn't bear it anymore. I know you said you'd call on me in a few days, but I just had to talk to someone now."

Antonia held Camille while she cried it out. All around them her ladies exchanged sad looks and sighs. A few dabbed at tears.

"Well, you don't have to suffer his coldness anymore, Camille," Antonia said with a tightness in her throat. "If that's the way he behaves, he doesn't deserve you. You can just come back here and stay with us. Your old room is still empty, and to be honest, we've missed you terribly."

Camille raised her tear-streaked face to Antonia. "Really?" she whispered.

"Really," Antonia said with a definitive nod, which was repeated around the group. "And if Mr. Bertrand Howard doesn't like it, he can just go hang."

"I doubt he'll do that," Camille said miserably. "I don't think he'll even notice I'm gone."

"Fine." Antonia rose and pulled Camille up with her. "That will give us time to retrieve your things from your house. Hoskins! Go for a cab—"

"That won't be necessary, Lady Toni," Camille said, lowering her eyes. "My bag is outside on the steps."

Antonia laughed. "Welcome home, Camille."

Near midnight, in a set of small but tidy town houses behind Regent's Park, Bertrand Howard fumbled to insert his key into the lock of his front door, swayed, and made a second, more successful try. He let himself into his house, hung his hat on the hall tree, and launched himself up the stairs in the dark. He had to grope his way through the bedroom door by the wisps of light coming through a set of lace curtains *she* had put up recently. Moving stealthily, he undid his tie and removed his coat and collar. Soon his shoes sat side by side, stuffed with his stockings, and his trousers and shirt lay on the chair near the window. He felt for his nightshirt—on the seat of the chair, where *she* always left it for him—and drew it over his head.

The darkness and the quantity of whiskey he had consumed at White's kept him from noticing that her dressing gown wasn't hanging over the end of the bed. And it kept him from reaching for *her* as he usually did when he came home late. Tonight, his heavy eyes and limbs told him, it was just too late.

It was the next morning before Bertrand Howard squinted at the other side of the bed and saw it was smoothed and tucked as if it hadn't been slept in. He glowered and padded into the hallway in his bare feet and nightshirt, thinking of calling to her but deciding against it. It was something of a relief to be able to dress and make it downstairs without encountering her and her doleful morning-after looks.

But when he reached the dining room, there was no pot of coffee, no morning paper, no scones or griddle cakes or fluffy eggs, and none of that marmalade he loved so well. In the kitchen he found their maid-of-all-work lolling about beside a cold stove. "Where the hell is my breakfast?" he snapped.

"Wot?" The maid looked up at him with a disagreeable expression. "Ye be wantin' somethin' to eat, after all?"

"Of course I want something to eat!" he snapped. "Where is she?" When the girl looked a bit puzzled, he clarified: "My wife . . . Mrs. Howard . . ."

The girl shrugged and pushed to her feet, annoyed. "I ain't seen 'er. Figured you wasn't to home, either. I cain't read minds, y'know." She reached for an iron skillet and smacked it down on the stove. "It'll be a spell a'fore the stove gets hot. Ye'll just have to wait."

He snorted. "Don't bother—I won't have time." Irritably, he stalked through the house, looking for *her,* calling her name. There was no answer. And as the silence loomed and reverberated around him, it finally registered: she wasn't there . . . probably hadn't been there last night when he came home. He straightened, alarmed.

Rushing upstairs, he discovered that the little table where she kept her hairbrush, mirror, creme pots, and jewelry was empty. With mounting disbelief he went to the bureau and opened a drawer. Bare wood. He threw open the wardrobe they shared and found her things gone, except for two hatboxes tucked away on top. He looked around in shock. There was hardly a trace of her left in the place.

Rushing downstairs, he searched the parlor and dining room and came to a lurching halt in the entryway. Caught between anger and guilt over having wished for this very thing—that he would wake up one morning and she would be gone—he missed seeing the envelope bearing her handwriting on the hall tree. It fluttered to the floor when he grabbed his hat, and he snatched it up and tore into it. There was her girlish script—neat little rows and rounded letters—telling him she couldn't bear his coldness and silent censure anymore. The truth slowly sank in. She had left him.

He read and reread the part of the letter stating that she had gone to stay with a friend and that he needn't trouble about her ever again. And each time he read it, he felt a wrenching and unexpected sense of loss deepening inside him.

Promptly at nine o'clock the next morning, the Earl of Landon's stylish black carriage rolled up before Paxton House and sat waiting, while Antonia stared down at it from the window of Aunt Hermione's bedroom, and everyone else in the house clustered by the front windows to have a look. At length she sent Hoskins out to tell the driver to move on. The driver shrugged and said he was under orders to wait for the mistress of the house. She sent Hoskins out a second time, instructing the driver to carry a message to the earl that she wouldn't be going to his offices —not today, not ever. But the fellow just shrugged and said that he had all day. The carriage didn't move.

By ten o'clock Antonia was pacing and wringing her hands. She asked Hermione to go for her and deliver her message. Hermione politely declined, then offered to accompany her if she decided to go herself.

By eleven o'clock the house was full of whispers, some of which were aimed at Antonia. Her ladies had clearly taken sides in the matter, and hers was not the side they had taken. But the final blow to her determination came when several men in checkered wool coats and tasteless bowler hats appeared and began quizzing the driver. His answers to their questions caused them to grin at each other, whip out their notepads, and stare expectantly at her front door.

News writers, she realized with no small alarm. What on earth were they doing at her door again? She had no way of knowing what might have brought them down on her this time, but she did know that the longer she delayed the inevitable, the more vultures would gather. This was all Remington's fault, curse his hide.

She sent for Aunt Hermione, went for her hat and gloves, and strode furiously out the front door. The driver hurried them into the carriage, then climbed onto the box and set off for the City at a fast clip, leaving several newshounds running down the street after them, shouting questions.

"I'm going to give him a royal piece of my mind," she informed Hermione.

"Of course you are," Hermione said with an ubiquitous smile.

"And then I'm coming straight back home."

"Absolutely."

"And his carriage can rot in the street the next time," she declared, giving the soft velvet upholstery and gilded trim of the carriage a glare of warning.

When they entered the lobby of Remington's building, Antonia immediately noticed a number of strange men milling around, and it took a moment to realize why they seemed so out of place. They were wearing wool coats with eye-popping checks, and cheap bowlers that would have been much more at home on the rough East Side. They were not a part of the financial world, she was certain. They looked more like—

"There she is—that's her!" one of them yelled, pointing at her.

In a heartbeat she was besieged by a dozen men with stubbled faces and hungry eyes. They crowded around her, assaulting her with smells of sen-sen and cheap cigars, and questions.

"Is it true the earl attacked you on the street yesterday?" She grabbed Hermione's arm and tried to pull her along, but whatever direction she moved, the newshounds scrambled to block her path. "Is it true he's making you keep your half of the Woman Wager, after all?" "Does that mean you lost?" "What kind of men's work does he make you do?" "Do you deny that it was you and the earl who were caught together last week by a pack of gents?" "How do you feel about giving women the vote?"

She tried to make her way through them, but they squeezed together, shoulder to shoulder, and refused to let her pass, still hammering away at her with their questions. When she pushed, they pushed right back! She had never been treated with so little respect in her life! Just as panic was setting in, a black-clad arm broke through that pack to take hold of her wrist. She looked up to find Remington snarling at them to clear the premises before he had them removed. When they began firing insulting questions at him instead, he turned to several men on the stairs and motioned for them to intervene. A brief shoving and shouting match ensued that sent the pernicious newshounds into a hasty retreat.

The gratitude Antonia felt as Remington pulled her and Aunt Hermione up the stairs and out of the writers' reach was humiliating to her moments later, when she faced him in the upstairs corridor. He was, after all, the cause of the entire mess.

"What are they doing here?" she demanded, flinging a finger toward the stairs. "And how did they learn about your requiring me to fulfill the wager?"

"Someone may have heard us speaking in the hall. Or it could have been that nasty little article in *Gaflinger's* this morning about the contretemps in the alley yesterday, or the fact that you were seen in my offices—but it doesn't matter. I won't let them near you again."

"It doesn't matter?" Then the rest of what he had said struck her. "What nasty little article?"

"There was a story on the front page of that scandal-rag, *Gaflinger's*. Apparently someone witnessed my little misunderstanding with the constable yesterday and decided to turn it into a headline." He eyed her accusingly. "This sort of upset could be avoided entirely if you'd just accept my offer of protection."

"What you have offered me is a form of eternal servitude, not protection. And for your information, your lordship, I am quite capable of fending for myself," she snapped, reddening a moment later as she realized how ridiculous that sounded in the wake of what had just happened. He smiled.

"Good day, Mrs. Fielding," he said, turning to Aunt Hermione. "I believe Uncle Paddington is eagerly awaiting your arrival. And you, Antonia"—he narrowed his eyes—"are late for work. One of the things men prize in their employees is punctuality, you know."

"Late for work?" Only the prospect of being arrested and carted off to jail kept Antonia from committing mayhem just then. The effort of stifling her violent urges momentarily robbed her of words, and he seized the moment.

Ushering her into his offices, he took her straight to a conference room containing a large table ringed with chairs. He introduced her to a number of men in dark suits, some of whom had helped to clear the news writers from the lobby. She quickly learned that they were all employed by him in one or another of Carr Enterprises' various financial or commercial concerns.

Remington pushed her gently down onto a chair, and one by one his managers and directors began to lay out charts and diagrams detailing his financial empire. They quoted prices and government policies and tossed out numbers, categories, and percentages until they began to run together in her head.

"All this is fascinating, to be sure," she said finally, with a thinning air of civility. "But it has nothing to do with me."

"Oh, but it does, Antonia," Remington said confidently, stepping around the table to meet her as she rose. "You see, I've decided to give you not only a taste of commerce, but a taste of power as well. These gentlemen will not only explain my commercial interests to you, they will also help you make decisions on various matters. Just the sort of thing *men* are required to do every day."

"I—I'll do no such thing," she protested, sensing a trap of some sort like a small animal senses a snare. "I don't know anything about sheep farming, or knitting mills, or import-export regulations, or the mercantile trades—it's ludicrous to expect that I would. And I have never been in a 'departmental store,' as you call it, in my life."

"No?" He seemed ungodly pleased by her admission. "Not prepared to start at the top, eh? Then I take it you prefer to work your way up, instead. For that is how it is with men's work, you know. If you don't inherit, marry, or buy into the upper ranks of a concern, then you have to start with a modest position and improve yourself as you go. Something of a burden, wouldn't you say . . . having to prove yourself constantly?" His gaze connected with hers, letting her know he was speaking of more than just men and their work.

"But I believe it can be done," he continued, gesturing to the men around the room. "Every one of my managers, directors, and heads has come up that very way." As she looked around, she saw them nod and glimpsed the pride in their eyes.

"His lordship has a policy about making opportunities for self-improvement available," Hallowford, the director of the central offices, put in. "A number of the younger men take advantage of the program. And then there are the reading and typewriting classes for the wom—"

"Yes, thank you," Remington interrupted, "but we'll not burden Mrs. Paxton with details. What we need is a place where she can start—at the bottom."

He sighed and rubbed his lip as he was wont to do when thinking. Then one of the others, a bookish, tidy-looking fellow spoke up. "The mercantile has always been a good starting place for those with little experience of the business world."

"Excellent! Thank you, Markham," Remington declared. He took her by the hand and headed for the door. "Come with me. I have just the place for you."

Over her protests he led her out a little-used rear door tucked away behind a series of cabinets and cartons. She found herself on a rickety set of wooden steps that zig-zagged down the outside of the building and lowered toward a dark service lane.

"You're putting me to work in an alley?" she demanded, straining against his grip as she stared anxiously at the ground far below.

"A shortcut to avoid prying eyes," he said, looking up at her pale face. "Unless you would rather face another gauntlet of news writers."

She couldn't argue with that and reluctantly allowed him to guide her down those steps, then out of the alley and to a cab stand.

Three hours later Antonia found herself standing atop a ladder in the departmental store, Carr's Emporium, wearing a bib apron and an ugly dust cap, and wielding a feather duster. Spreading before her were what seemed like miles of shelves stocked with every form of dry goods imaginable: fabric, sewing notions and trims, flat irons, lamp wicks, linen sheeting, ready-made pillows, machine-knitted socks, children's knickers, and manufactured shoes, to name a few. Looking out over the huge store, across the bustling walkways and past racks of ready-made clothes and displays of housewares that were touted as the latest conveniences, she felt a bit bewildered by her presence there. What on earth was Remington trying to prove, installing her as some sort of menial and then disappearing for hours on end?

What sort of seduction was this? She glared at the feather duster in her hand, wondering just how this was supposed to convince her to marry him.

Before she completed the dusting of the upper shelves, the department head, a fusty old fellow named Hanks, appeared, scowling at the way her ankles were revealed by her position on the ladder.

"Mrs. Paxton, would you please step down from there," he commanded shortly. When she was safely on the floor, he gave her a dour look. "In future you will confine yourself to work on the floor. It is most unseemly to have you dangling about in customers' faces with your . . . *footwear* . . . showing. Go help Davidson tidy displays instead."

As she surrendered her feather duster and walked away, she could feel the department head's glare boring into her back. He hadn't been told who she was or why she was there, only that she would be working in his department. And he clearly resented having her added to his staff without his consent.

Davidson proved to be one of the junior clerks, a lanky young fellow with a generally pleasant face—which just now was drawn taut. With terse efficiency he showed her how to tidy and reposition displays to show the goods to advantage. When they finished, they were set to restocking shelves and dusting lamp globes, and Antonia watched him turning frequently to stare across the other departments to where the other young clerks were busy with customers. When she dropped a lamp globe, he managed to catch it before it reached the floor, and glanced up with a scowl.

"I'm sorry you're saddled with me," she said. "I hate this as much as you do."

He set the globe back on its shelf and turned to her with a severe look that melted when he saw the distress in her face. "I don't hate the work . . . or you," he said. As he relaxed his guard, a tired but boyish smile tugged briefly at the corner of his mouth. "It's just that I'd rather be waiting on customers. We're paid on commission, and the more I sell, the better my wages. And if I want to advance and someday make a marrying wage, I have to keep on my toes and make every sale I can."

"A marrying wage?" she said, reaching for another lamp globe.

He frowned. "You know . . . enough money to get married and support a wife."

"Oh." She didn't know, had never heard the term.

"If Hanks sticks me with too many other duties, like cleaning, my pay suffers."

"It does? You mean they don't pay you to do this work?"

"No. Didn't they explain all this to you when you started?" he asked with genuine concern. When she shook her head, he made a noise of disgust. Then he eyed her and her tailored silk dress. "You're new to working, aren't you?"

"Not really," she said with a defensive edge.

"Those are mourning colors. You must be a widow." She nodded and he smiled sympathetically. "I thought so. Those are mighty fine clothes for a shop clerk."

His consoling look made Antonia realize that he believed her bereavement was recent. She sensed that to correct that impression could open a number of other questions about her being there. As they progressed to rearranging a display of bed linens, she ventured a few questions of him and was surprised to learn he was the son of a knitting-mill foreman from New Market and had come to London hoping to find an entry into the world of business. He worked at the Emporium by day, attended classes by night, and had a fondness for a girl named Meg, which made the need for a marrying wage more urgent every day.

"What sort of classes? From what sort of a school?" Antonia asked, warming to this good-hearted young man who seemed to think marriage a desirable state.

"It's a company-sponsored school, with classes taught by leading men from banks and companies and firms in the

City. It's the best part of working here. We learn bookkeeping, the laws of commerce, and the principles of good business. If my commissions are good and I study hard, I can work my way up . . . someday have my own department, or even my own store."

Antonia watched the light in his eyes and recalled that the men in Remington's employ spoke proudly of having worked their way up to positions of trust and authority. Young Davidson seemed to have pinned his hopes for the future on just such a possibility. A sweet ache developed in her chest at the thought that Remington's liberal policies might give Davidson the chance to marry his Meg and fulfill his dream.

The young clerk had a sudden thought and leaned eagerly across a stack of pillow covers. "Say . . . play your cards right, and maybe they'll let you into the classes. The store's owner is known to favor giving females a hand."

"He is?" Her suspicions came alive as she realized how her thoughts were softening. "Well, any man would give a woman a hand," she said primly, "for a price."

Davidson frowned, puzzled, then took her meaning and reddened. "Well, I know what they say about Lord Carr in the papers, but I don't believe it. He's a good man. He'd never attack a woman on the street."

"Attack a woman?" Her shock was genuine.

Davidson glanced around to see that no one was looking, then slipped around a counter and snagged a copy of a newspaper hidden beneath it. Holding it low, he showed her a front page bearing *Gaflinger*'s gaudy masthead and a story title on the lower half that declared:

NOBLEMAN ASSAULTS WOMAN ON STREET!

Below that hideous accusation was a subtitle that only muddled the issue further: "Landon Forces the Lady to Do

Men's Work!" Antonia's heart stopped as she read the rather bizarre account, in which Remington was supposed to have seized her in the street, dragged her back to his offices, and forced her to perform "degrading male labor."

The story, like the ink and paper used to print it, presented everything in stark black and white. Once again she was the courageous woman and Remington was the jaded, world-weary beast who was determined to ruin her good name and virtuous spirit. The sensational way they described his actions struck her with unexpected impact, and she reddened and gripped the paper tighter. How could they print such obviously false things?

"It's a lot of bunkum, is what it is," young Davidson said, bringing her back to the present. "His lordship's a fair man and a good employer. He's given me a chance to better myself, and I can't believe he would do such a thing to a decent woman—"

"Here, here—what's going on?" A harsh voice demanded their attention, and they stuffed the paper behind them as they whirled to find Mr. Hanks glowering at them. "I'll not have you standing about idle, gossiping like old women. I want an accounting of every runner, tablecloth, and napkin on the shelves," he ordered. Antonia did an admirable job of constraining her irritable impulses, until she turned to follow Davidson, and Hanks put out an arm to block her way. "Not you." He thrust a broom in her hands instead. "You . . . sweep."

"I think it would be much more efficient if one of us counted and the other kept the tally," she said emphatically.

"You think? You're not paid to think." He reddened ominously. "I'll not have women handling numbers in my department. I want an *accurate* count."

Hanks strode away, leaving Antonia hot-faced and sputtering. She would have gone after him, but Davidson pulled her back and shook his head in warning. "Don't get on the wrong side of him," he whispered. "He'd sack you in a wink."

"What—does he think women can't count?" she demanded, matching his whisper, though with extra force.

"He thinks women should be at home, not in shops doing men's work." He shrugged apologetically and advised: "Better start pushing that broom."

Men's work. She frowned and looked down at the broom handle in her hand. Sweeping, dusting shelves, cleaning lamp globes, counting linen . . . this was *men's work*? It was called *women's* work when it was done in the home. What made it so different out here, in the almighty world of trade and commerce? She looked up at the male clerks going about their tidying, tending, and assisting customers. The answer was: *nothing*. There wasn't any difference, except the location in which it was done. Women's work. Men's work. How dare the old cod tell her she wasn't capable of simple counting, just because he believed all women belonged at home! What if she actually *wanted* to work here?

The thought struck: what if she *needed* to work here? What if she had to make her own way in the world, like so many unmarried and widowed women did? What if she had children to feed and no husband to provide for them? What must it be like for such women to be told they belonged at home because all they were capable of was "women's work"?

The incident lingered in her mind through the rest of the afternoon as she was shifted from department to department in the store. Admittedly, the display shelves at the front of the store needed cleaning, the brass fittings on the glass cases needed polishing, and the display shoes needed to be shined. But the narrow looks she received from the various department heads hinted that their choice of work for her had to do with the fact that they were eager to have her off their hands.

The coveted task of waiting on customers and the reward of earning commissions were reserved for the senior clerks and those juniors fortunate enough to escape lesser duties. She watched the clerks in each department vie for the chance to assist customers. And on two occasions, when she was approached by a woman customer desiring help, the department manager quickly intervened and steered the customer toward one of the senior clerks. Davidson, she observed dismally, was faring little better than she was in securing the opportunity to make sales.

By the time the counters and tables were draped for the night and the employees were dismissed, Antonia's back was aching, her eyes were burning from the dyes, lint, and dust, and she was in no mood to have to deal with Remington Carr. But when she exited the employee's entrance wondering where she could get a cab to take her home, she spotted Remington's carriage waiting on the street and felt a treacherous burst of gratitude inside.

He must have been watching for her; he swung down immediately from the carriage and bundled her inside. As the carriage lurched into motion, he looked her over and grinned at what he saw. She sat straighter and sent a self-conscious hand to check her hat and hair . . . and regretted it instantly, as his smile broadened.

"A hard day, was it?" he said.

"I've had worse," she said tightly, looking out the window. "I can't imagine what you think you have accomplished by all this."

"I can't imagine either. Why don't you tell me?" he said, leaning back against the soft leather seat and folding his arms. "What did you learn about men's work today?"

She frowned as she thought about it. "I learned that men's work is tiresome, grueling, and largely indistinguishable from women's work," she answered testily. "I dusted, swept, cleaned, polished, and put up with impossible people, mostly managers and staff. I could have stayed home and done the very same things. Do you know—that idiot department head, Hanks, wouldn't allow me to count linens in his department? Apparently he thinks women have defective heads when it comes to numbers."

He winced. "Unfortunately, not everyone in my employ shares my profound and ever-enlarging respect for womanhood. What else?"

His words, though lightly spoken, echoed through Antonia with unexpected impact. In that moment her ideas about him and his views on women's rights underwent a palpable shift. He *did* respect women, though in a way she hadn't recognized as respect until now. He insisted they should have the right to work, to learn, to be independent and take care of themselves outside of marriage. And that new recognition of his decency and fairness released a well-guarded warmth in her.

"I also learned that working outside the home can be difficult for women," she continued, her spirits rising, "not because they cannot do the work, but because of others' attitudes toward them. If a woman needs or wishes to work for pay, to support herself and be independent, then she should be allowed to do so without some old fossil like Hanks degrading or berating her. I have to say, today's experience has quite converted me to your school of thought."

"It has?" His grin faded.

"Most certainly. I see clearly now that many women need never marry at all," she said, beaming vengefully. "Marriage is indeed an inequitable institution . . . one that constrains and burdens women unfairly. If a woman chooses not to marry, then she should be allowed to train and work to support herself, independent of men." His face was as readable as a newspaper headline; he was genuinely alarmed by her adoption of his "enlightened" views.

"Hold on, now. I never said . . ." But he *had* said marriage was onerous and inequitable. "I never said women should . . ." But he *had* said that unmarried women should give up the notion of marriage. "I have never said that a woman had a right to choose or not choose marriage," he declared adamantly.

"That's true." Her smile broadened. "But since you have widely championed that freedom for men, I'm sure that was just an oversight on your part." There *was* a bit of justice in the world, she thought, relishing the sight of him with his ears aflame and his face dark with the knowledge that the duality of his standard was showing.

"Or perhaps the newspapers and magazines just neglected to print it," she continued, smiling softly. "That is another thing I learned today: you cannot trust the newspapers to present the whole or unbiased truth."

He fastened on those words and she could see him analyzing and interpreting them. "You saw the article," he concluded, trying to decide if it was good or bad.

"I did." She paused to censor her words before she revealed any part of the outrage that vicious bit of scandalmongering had generated in her. "And I must say, your lordship, I wouldn't have guessed that you and that odious *Gaflinger's Gazette* had so much in common."

"In common? How is that?" he growled.

"You both have a way of being miserably wrong, even when you're right."

Remington sighed quietly while she settled back into the seat and into silence. But he brightened when it occurred to him that the day hadn't been a total waste if it led her to admit that at least on occasion he was right.

Promptly at eight-thirty the next morning, Remington's carriage appeared in the street outside Paxton House. Antonia was determined to ignore it this time. In one short day she had experienced enough of "men's work" to last a lifetime. But the wretched coach remained in the street until a quarter past ten and once again drew attention—from news writers, delivery lorries, a local constable, and several irate neighbors who felt that street access to their houses was being impeded.

The tsking and tutting outside the small parlor finally pulled Antonia from her desk. When she emerged and strode for the front door, intent on sending the carriage and driver packing, she found Aunt Hermione in the front hall, dressed for an outing and holding *her* hat and gloves. In short order Hermione had harnessed her forward momentum and propelled her through the clutch of news writers and straight into the open carriage. They were under way before Antonia recovered enough to protest. In the cross seat Hermione sat with a cherubic smile.

"Put your hat on, dear," Hermione said, thrusting it into her lap. "The blue goes perfectly with your eyes."

When the carriage stopped, Antonia was surprised to find herself being handed down onto the street before the Emporium. Standing not three yards away was Remington, with a watch in his hand. He glanced at her and at the timepiece, then shook his head. After giving his driver instructions to take Hermione on to his offices, where his Uncle Paddington awaited her, he took Antonia by the elbow and propelled her toward the employee entrance of the store.

"We shall have to do something about this tardiness of yours."

"This is low," she said irritably, wresting her arm from his hand and walking ahead a pace. "Employing my own aunt to belay and kidnap me. You do seem to bring out the worst in people, your lordship." From the corner of her eye she saw his smug expression fade and felt a twinge of satisfaction. "This is positively the last time. After today my obligation to you is finished."

"Two weeks, Antonia, not two days," he declared.

"Two days in this place is the same as two weeks . . . believe me," she said crossly, quickening her step and hurrying up the steps and through the door without looking back.

The hidebound Mr. Hanks was positively choleric when she appeared in his department—more than two hours after store opening. He spent some time berating her lack of diligence and industry. Then he ordered her to remove "that ridiculous bonnet," handed her a dust cap, and set her to washing the front windows. She spent the better part of two hours standing in the middle of a huge display window, in blistering sunlight, breathing ammonia fumes. She was so miserable, she scarcely noticed the people stopping to peer into the window . . . or the fact that a number of them wore brown bowlers and carried notepads.

It was approaching dinnertime before she was able to finish and return to the sales floor. Davidson greeted her with a wan smile and, over the course of the next hour, introduced her to a number of the other young clerks. They didn't seem a bad lot, individually, but their comradeship evaporated the instant a customer came into view.

Antonia found their competitive attitude and blatant self-interest unsettling. From her largely menial tasks she was able to observe their quiet jostling for sales and resulting commissions, and noticed the subtle flow of favor toward certain junior clerks, who were not assigned tidying duties. Then, just when they were due to go to dinner, Davidson was approached by a fashionably dressed gentleman who had a number of purchases to make. She watched with growing pleasure as Davidson ably assisted the customer and suggested a number of related items the man found desirable. It would be his first large sale and would make a wonderful contribution to his "marriage fund."

But Antonia was not the only one watching. The department head, Hanks, and the senior clerks were also taking note of the mounting total. Just when Davidson was about to finalize the sale and collect the payment, Hanks stepped in and directed the customer and his sizable purchase to one of the senior clerks for writing up. Davidson was forced to step away and watch the commission go to another clerk. Antonia was stunned by the injustice of it, but was even more shocked by Davidson's attitude toward what to her would have been a lethal blow.

"That's the way it is, sometimes," he said, swallowing his disappointment along with his bread and cheese as he shared his cold dinner with her over a barrel in the stock room. He shrugged. "There'll be another sale."

"But it's not fair," she declared. "You needed that commission."

He gave her a pained look. "Harrison needed the commission too . . . he's got four children to feed." When she frowned and folded her arms, he smiled. "We all need the money. Most of the seniors have wives and families to support, and the juniors—Easley has two younger brothers to feed, and Bayless is taking care of his sick mother. Look, I don't mind competing in a contest where everybody does his best. I can hold my own in a fair fight." He scowled. "What's bad is when the department heads mix in and play favorites. That means you never know if your sale will be snatched out of your hands and all your hard work will go for naught." After a thoughtful silence he straightened and his boyish smile reappeared.

"I lost this time. But the next time I'll win because I'll work that much harder. Take a lesson, Paxton. You have to be able to take a few knocks and come back again. You have to learn to take it like a man."

She didn't want to take it like a man, she thought, when the dinner break ended and she was plunged back into the tension of the sales floor. She wanted to take it like a woman—rather, like a mother—so she could take the rest of them by the ear, make them say they were sorry, and make them promise to behave in a more civilized and charitable manner. Competition. Ugh.

But as the day wore on and she watched the other clerks on the floor, she began to think about Davidson's view of it as a contest that was sometimes won, sometimes lost. Gradually she began to see Harrison in terms of four hungry little mouths, Easley as a diligent older brother, and Bayless as a dutiful son. Each man on the floor was driven by responsibilities, which made their striving pressured at times, but at least more understandable.

Slowly, she was drawn into the spirit of competition herself and began to think about her own desire and ability to compete in their contest. What would be wrong with showing them she could be just as clever, skillful, courteous, and persuasive?

Late in the afternoon she found herself stuck in the shoe department, polishing glass cases and feeling overworked and irritable and abandoned. She was drafting a few choice words to say to Remington Carr when he dared show his face to her again, when a very stout matron in a dark print dress and excessively feathered hat entered the department. There was a flurry of motion around the woman, and it took a moment for Antonia to realize that it was a number of jostling, gyrating children.

She watched as the woman paused to examine first one ladies' shoe, then another, giving each a disdainful look and dropping it back onto the display. When the woman finally hit upon a shoe that seemed to meet her standards and looked around for assistance, every clerk in the area seemed to have disappeared. It seemed exceedingly odd to Antonia, for only moments before, they had been tripping over each other in order to help another well-heeled matron.

The woman called several times, "Clerk! I say, clerk!" then declared in great pique, "Really, I should expect better service here!" The department head came up behind Antonia and tapped her on the shoulder, ordering her to wait on the customer. Surprised by this rare opportunity, she plunged in to offer the woman her help.

"No, no—this one is much too narrow!" the woman insisted when Antonia had helped her wedge her foot into the shoe. A display of boxes on a nearby counter went toppling as two of the woman's children pulled on it. Antonia discreetly pulled the small boys away and asked them not to touch things. They darted around the counter, and as she horned the woman into another pair of shoes, she saw them, joined by a sister, climbing up the shelves against the wall. She ordered them down and finally had to pluck them bodily from the shelves, knocking several shoe boxes onto the floor.

By the fourth pair of shoes, both Antonia and the bench where the woman sat were groaning silently. Between the woman's impossible demands and her children's atrocious behavior, Antonia was fast losing what was left of her composure.

"No, of course not—much too high a heel!" the woman declared, tossing yet another shoe back at Antonia. "A person could break her neck on a stair runner in such heels. I want something stylish. And sensible. And reasonable."

Antonia was about to tell her to get a stylish, sensible, and reasonable foot first. But a glimpse of the department head standing at the edge of the area, scowling, made her hold her tongue.

As the woman's frustration in not finding a proper fit escalated, she became increasingly irate. When Antonia hooked the buttons of yet another shoe onto her foot, she flinched and howled, claiming Antonia had jabbed her foot with the button hook and declaring that she'd never received such shoddy and incompetent service in her life.

Antonia pushed wisps of hair back out of her face, planted her hands in the small of her aching back, and suggested vehemently: "If you don't like the service, perhaps you'd better take your business somewhere else!" Gasping at Antonia's insolence, the woman struggled to her feet and made a straight line for the department head to express her outrage.

Just at that moment one of the woman's boys reached the top of a free-standing display shelf and succeeded in pulling the entire thing over with him. Some of the shoes went crashing through the glass top of a display counter, and the sounds of shattering glass and a child's scream brought people running from everywhere to see what had happened. Turmoil ensued as the woman came rushing back through the department, screaming that her baby had been killed. The manager came running after her, calling for help; and the other children froze, then began to wail with fright.

The boy was found on the floor, at the side of a nearby counter, crying but uninjured. The mother picked him up, pressed him to her ample bosom, and turned on the manager in a high rage.

"It was all the fault of that upstart girl—that shop creature!" she railed. "Insolent thing—she stood there insulting me while my poor dear baby was teetering on the brink of disaster—why, he might have been killed on that dreadful thing!"

Antonia was seeing everything in red and feeling the urge to mayhem rising, when the woman demanded they compensate her for her distress and fire Antonia. The tensions and accumulated outrages of a very long day erupted in a volatile blast, and she launched herself at the woman's back, intent on having at least one handful of those absurd hat feathers as a souvenir of the coming fight. But something—someone—grabbed her by the waist and held her back.

Try as she might, she couldn't get free, and soon she was pulled, struggling and flailing, away from that chaotic scene and through the nearest curtain. "Let me go—the old witch—I'll scratch her eyes out—" she growled, shoving at the arms clamped around her ribs and scrambling for footing.

The laugh that vibrated her shoulders and rumbled through her head was familiar, and she realized who held her the same instant he spoke.

Chapter

16

"Oh, no!" Remington said with a ragged laugh. "I can't have you attacking my paying customers bodily, no matter how irksome and irrational they are."

He carried her through a cavernous and deserted stockroom, between towering racks of shelves, past stacks of crates and barrels, and finally halted beside huge bales of fabric bolts. As soon as they stopped, she found the floor with her feet and managed to turn on him.

"She deserves it—did you hear what she called me?" She pushed back in his arms. "A shop creature! The moldy old crone blamed me because her foot was too fat for the shoe! And her pack of brats was climbing all over—" He began to laugh and she gasped. "It's not funny!"

"Yes, it is."

"It is not! She turned the shoe department upside down and tried to get me fired—don't you dare pay that awful woman a penny, do you hear?"

"She can't get you fired, sweetheart." His eyes danced in the dim light as he watched her righteous indignation. "You've never been *hired*."

She stared up at him in disbelief that gradually widened to include her own anger. Her skin caught fire as she realized just how seriously she had taken what was, after all, only part of a wager. What in heaven's name had come over her? "You really are a beast"—she shoved him without much effect—"forcing me to do manual labor, subjecting me to all manner of insult and injury—"

"Just as you did me," he countered wryly. "Thank your lucky stars that I'm not making you wear trousers and a board-stiff collar into the bargain."

She stilled in his arms, absorbing the warmth and certainty of him, feeling the rightness of his arms around her. Against her better judgment she looked up into his eyes. Desire rose, hot and vaporous, inside her, seeping through her body, gliding along her limbs, softening her bones. She could scarcely breathe.

"Do you know how luscious you look?" he murmured, lowering his head. He halted halfway down. "You know, the thought of you in a pair of trousers does have a certain *appeal*."

She stiffened. "You wouldn't dare."

"Wouldn't I?" he said, grinning in a way that made her heart beat erratically.

His mouth descended on hers, and for a moment she stood motionless beneath his kiss, drinking it in, stunned by the liquid pleasure that poured through her. His kisses were like nothing else she had ever experienced. Each contained the same immediate and powerful intimacy, the same lush and compelling delight of the very first one. And yet each felt somehow unique and just created, filled with limitless new possibilities. That, she realized dimly, was what she felt vibrating in and through her: possibilities—a whole universe of emotion and sensation and experience yet to be discovered between them.

Her arms circled his neck as she gave back what he had just given her, parting her lips, molding her body to his, opening to his deepening explorations. When he stooped to lift her into his arms, she was too weakened to resist—or to recall why she wanted to. He bore her back onto a pile of fabric bolts and suddenly she was lying in his arms, feeling his hands on her, directing them to the well-guarded mounds of her breasts. Through layers of apron, bodice, corset cover, corset, and chemise, she could still feel the heat of his hands. Her blood rushed to absorb it and focus it into the tautly contracted tips of her breasts, where it ignited a low, sweet burn.

The silence around them grew heavy with expectation as the exotic scents of dyed fabrics, cedar shelving, and straw-stuffed barrels blended with the sweet musk of woman and the tangy scent of male arousal. His hands raked her sides feverishly, seeking passage through her garments as the intensity of their kisses deepened. Then he pressed against her hip, undulating slowly, and every part of her body seemed to thicken and swell with awareness of him.

She felt the liquid warmth of his kiss on her closed eyes, her ears, her neck, and felt it stop at the barrier of her collar. He kissed her chin, her throat, then met that same obstacle. As her fingers flew to the buttons of her bodice, they found access blocked by the bib of the heavy apron she wore, and she gave a groan of frustration. Pushing him back, she sat up and reached for the ties of the apron at the back of her neck—then froze halfway through untying them.

The shift from horizontal to vertical caused those intoxicating pleasures to drain from her senses, and, looking around, she realized where she was and just what she was about to do. Good Lord—in a dingy, ill-lit warehouse of some sort, lying on a lumpy pile of fabric bolts—she was about to strip her breasts bare and surrender what was left of her virtue to a man she wouldn't trust to give her the correct time of day!

Horrified, she scrambled back across the bolts and slid down the side of them, struggling to assert some control over her rebellious desires. Her hands trembled as she untied the apron strings, and when the apron was halfway off, she felt his hand on her upper arm and looked up to find he had slid closer and was staring at her with a look that contained roused passion and emotion.

"Antonia—" he said, breathing hard, searching the alarm in her eyes. What he saw there caused him to hold back the question he had been about to ask and to substitute another. "Well, what do you think of men's work thus far?" He released her and slid from the bales, too, brushing his trousers and straightening his vest and tie.

"I think it is beastly, exhausting, and grossly unfair. I don't know why anyone in his right mind would do it," she said, folding her apron, then smoothing her bodice and the front drape of her skirt.

"Necessity, perhaps?" Remington suggested.

She looked at him and found his gaze filled with wry interest and a surprising bit of understanding. "It's not so much the work as the way it's done . . . all that wretched competition. But the worst part is the favoritism. One very bright and promising young clerk made a large sale today, only to have it taken from him and given to a senior man— at the department head's whim. I was so furious. Poor Davidson. Where is the point of working hard, if it all gets taken away from you in the end?"

"Ummm." He leaned his shoulder against a shelf and crossed his arms, looking thoughtful. "And what would you do to change things if you were the store director?"

"I would pay them all a fixed wage—no more commissions," she declared.

"And which wage would that be?" he asked, stroking his chin. "The wage of a senior clerk who has a large customer clientele and works through dinner to increase his earnings, or the wage of a junior man who spends most of his time chatting up the office girls and loafing in the store room?"

"Well . . ." She huffed with annoyance. "Halfway between the two."

"So . . . you would make the hardest-working clerks take a reduction in pay, while giving a raise to others who scarcely earn what they receive now?"

She blinked. "That's not what I meant. I meant . . ." It seemed a bit more complicated, said aloud, than it had seemed in her mind. "It might not sound fair, put that way, but then neither does the way the department heads show favoritism and take sales from some clerks to assign them to others."

"There has long been a seniority system at the Emporium," he said, considering it. "Most shops and mercantile establishments are organized that way."

"Well, it's unfair. If there has to be competition, then it ought to be free and open . . . with each man keeping what he earns."

"Sounds reasonable. Let's say that we put that into effect tomorrow. Who could possibly oppose something as straightforward as that?" The look on his face said it wasn't a rhetorical question. Who indeed? It didn't take her long to see the problem.

"The department heads, all the senior clerks, and, I suppose, a number of junior clerks who have the heads' favor. . . ." She listed them on her fingers and realized where he was leading. "You're saying it wouldn't work. They would resist the change and do things their own way, regardless." Fighting the urge to surrender, she squared her shoulders. "But it could work. As the owner you could insist, and if insufferable old fossils like Hanks didn't like it, they could always go somewhere else."

He laughed and his eyes shone as they flowed over her. "More problems, I'm afraid. 'Old fossils' sometimes have considerable influence with customers; trust and confidence in merchants takes a while to build with customers. Also, replacing workers and training new people can be expensive business. . . ."

"I can't believe it is impossible to improve working conditions in your store," she said, impatient with his genial pessimism.

"Not impossible. Just difficult. And in ways you probably didn't anticipate . . . perhaps couldn't anticipate until you've been in a position of making such decisions." He smiled and reached out with one finger to lift a stray wisp of hair back from her forehead. "Congratulations. You've just had another taste of men's work. My work, in fact. Lots of ideas, lots of possibilities, all with problems attached. How do you like it?"

She stood looking at him, feeling the hard edges of her determination against him softening dangerously. For a moment she glimpsed the complexity of the world he inhabited and began to see men and their work in a new light. Men had to compete—within constraints that sometimes frustrated their best efforts—and often with the knowledge that others depended on them. Suddenly she was bombarded by conflicting feelings, wanting to know more, yet afraid of what learning more would mean to her.

Suddenly his face, his eyes, were all she could see.

"Is there a way to change it?" she said softly, drawn to the power and certainty of him, seeing him as a knowledgeable and powerful man in a man's world.

"It can be changed, but it will take time. People have to adjust, even to freedom and fairness. It's not easy to change a lifetime of habits and attitudes. It usually takes something important—something a person wants a great deal—to get him to change." The warmth and longing in his gaze said that he had found that something. . . .

If it hadn't been for Davidson strolling back through

the stockroom, calling her name, she might have acted on the wild impulse trembling her limbs just then. The young clerk spotted her with someone and came hurrying over . . . only to halt with his jaw drooping as he recognized her companion. Rescued from her own reckless impulses, she hurriedly introduced Davidson to his noble employer, then fetched her hat and declared she was through with the mercantile trade.

Remington caught up with her as she left by the front door of the store, and he escorted her to the carriage waiting down the block. As he made to help her in, she paused on the step.

"Don't you dare send this monstrous vehicle for me tomorrow morning," she insisted, staring disapprovingly at the seductive opulence of the coach's interior. "If I ever have to travel to your offices again, I'll hire a cab."

Paxton House was charged with tension when Antonia and Hermione returned home that evening; Antonia felt it the moment she walked in the front doors. Eleanor and Pollyanna were waiting to usher them into the drawing room, with news that they had a guest for supper. There on the center settee, in a cluster of anxious faces, sat Alice Butterfield Trueblood, another of Antonia's former protégées, her dark eyes filled with hurt and evidence of tears recently shed. The sight caused Antonia to halt.

"Lady Toni!" Alice pushed to her feet and stood wringing pale hands until Antonia's tension melted and she came forward with open arms.

"Alice! How good to see you!" She enfolded the young woman with a fervent hug. Alice's presence there during the supper hour spoke volumes to Antonia, but she had to ask, all the same. "What brings you here?" Alice made a noise of distress against Antonia's shoulder, and Antonia gave her a comforting pat. "Was it my letter?"

Alice nodded, and when she pulled away, one look at Antonia's sympathetic expression made her burst into tears. "Oh, Lady Toni—it's so awful—"

Antonia led her back to the settee and listened as she poured out the story of a marriage gone wrong. It had begun with such promise: Alice had been certain Basil Trueblood loved her, and she had done everything womanly possible to make up to him for the involuntary nature of their vows. But from the start nothing she did was quite elegant enough, precise enough, thorough enough, or good enough to please him.

"The roast was too rare one time and overdone the next. The table linen wasn't white enough, there wasn't enough starch in his shirts, the bedsheets were too stiff, and I let the tea steep too long," Alice said, sniffling and dabbing at her eyes. "My perfume had too much jasmine, my posture needed improving, I didn't have the silver polished to a proper sheen, my laughter wasn't quite musical enough, I didn't choose the proper wine with supper, the curtains I selected were a half shade off color, and even . . ."

"There there," Hermione said, patting her in encouragement.

"Even in our marriage bed I never seemed to do anything right. He criticized my affectionate nature and said I wasn't . . . *ladylike* . . . in my conduct toward him." Tears of shame rolled down her cheeks.

Antonia had heard enough. "The mean-spirited wretch! Well, you don't have to withstand another minute of it. You can come back to stay with us here."

A chorus of agreement broke the tension in the room; it was exactly what they had hoped she would say. But all were a bit surprised to have Camille Howard edge forward with tears in her eyes and a heartfelt offer.

"She can share my room." She smiled at poor Alice, then at Antonia. "We'll have a lot to talk about."

Supper that evening was a bit more festive than usual, with two new but familiar faces at the table and lots of stories to share. The subdued pleasure carried into the drawing room afterward, where Victoria played the pianoforte, Alice sang, and Molly and Aunt Hermione led several others in a scandalous dance-hall song or two.

Just as they were pushing back the chairs to make room for an impromptu reel, Hoskins appeared at the drawing-room doors with a scowl etched deep into his brow.

"A caller, madam," he intoned crossly.

"At this hour?" Antonia said, somewhat out of breath from the exertion of moving chairs. "It's late for visitors, Hoskins—"

The old butler opened his mouth to speak, but out came a feminine voice. "Oh, please, Lady Toni!" Hoskins started and glared at someone just behind his shoulder. With a grumble he threw the doors open, and there stood a voluptuous, thirtyish woman with a rounded face set with soft eyes. She was biting her lip and looking desperate indeed.

"D-don't you know me, Lady Toni? Aunt Hermione? It's Margaret. Margaret Everstone."

"Of course we know you, Margaret!" Antonia hurried to greet her, taking her hands and drawing her into the midst of the group. "What brings you here this hour?"

"I got your letter, Lady Toni, and I—I just—"

Through tears and reassurances and occasional outbursts of anger, yet another tale of marital woe came tumbling out.

"Albert Everstone," Margaret began furiously, "is the stingiest man that ever walked God's green earth! He's so tight, he opens old envelopes to write letters on. He won't go to church for fear he'll have to put something in the collection, and lately he has taken to wearing the same drawers for a week just to save on laundry bills!"

There were gasps and groans as her harrowing tale unfolded. And when she was through, another valise was carried up the stairs, and Paxton House had given shelter to yet another wife who had fled nuptial turmoil . . . and returned to the penitent generosity of her matchmaker.

At that same hour, in the bar of White's Club, Bertrand Howard and Basil Trueblood sat at an out-of-the-way table, staring morosely into tumblers of Scotch.

"Just like that," Howard said with bewilderment. "Not a word of warning. Just gone. Went to stay with a friend, she said. Truth be told, I didn't know she *had* any friends." He lifted his gaze to Trueblood, who shook his head in sympathy.

"Good riddance, I say," Basil muttered, tossing back another drink of liquor. "Mine left me a damned note. Says she can't live with a man who picks apart everything. I am a reasonable man, Howard, God knows. It's not my fault the woman cannot suffer even the smallest criticism. She was always puckering up over something or other . . . and then her eyes would get all red and her nose would swell up like a strawberry . . . and she would make that annoying little 'eek-eek' sound whenever she cried. Well, it was enough to rile any sane and reasonable man"—he looked to Howard for confirmation—"wouldn't you say?"

"Ohhh"—Howard came out of his reverie with a scowl and lifted his glass—"abs-solutely."

For a while they just sat staring off into the distance, drinking, not speaking.

"To top it all," Trueblood ventured miserably, "the

woman made four spelling errors in the wretched note she left me. I'm probably well rid of her."

"We're well rid of them, all right. Wives are nothing but trouble." After a moment Howard rubbed his face and sighed, "I just wish I knew where she had gone."

A booming voice called their names, and they looked up to find Albert Everstone bearing down on them across the bar. The portly MP was red-faced and his neck veins were at full swell—he was more exercised than they had ever seen him. He rushed over to the table, flung himself into a chair, and snatched up Trueblood's glass, downing the contents in one desperate gulp.

"What's got you in such a lather, Everstone?" Trueblood demanded irritably.

"She's gone, the wretched scattergoods!"

"Who is gone?" Howard sat straighter, scowling at him, then at Trueblood.

"My wife—Lady Spendthrift!" Everstone roared, flinching afterward from the stares his outburst brought their way. Lowering his voice to a pressured stream, he bent forward and slapped a folded note onto the table. "Got home a bit ago and found this propped on my empty dinner plate. Not a scrap of supper to be seen . . . just this note. And on brand-new paper!"

When they reached for it, he snatched it back and jammed it into his vest pocket. "The woman tried to spend me blind, I tell you. Always had her hand out. Money for food or replacing perfectly good linens or paying some worthless quack of a doctor, over a bit of nothing. Now she's upped and left me. Gone." He poured himself another drink in Trueblood's glass and downed it.

The heat of the Scotch gradually drew the venom from his manner and his words. He sank back into his chair as the fact of his wife's leaving was finally sinking in. His anger drained, leaving him genuinely shaken.

"Took just her clothes," he murmured. "Didn't even take the hot-water bottle I gave her last Christmas. I checked." After a long moment his shoulders rounded and his voice lowered to a rasp. "Paid more'n nine shillings for that clay pig."

Howard jerked his head toward Everstone and gave Trueblood an unsettled look. "His wife, too? Good Lord—it's an epidemic."

"What's an epidemic?" Everstone looked up.

"Wives leaving. Mine did, and Trueblood's, too. Now yours. And the worst is, we don't even know where they've gone."

"Well, I damn well know where mine went," Everstone said irritably. "Hotfooted it straight back to Lady Matrimonia, she did. Said so in her note."

"Back to Lady Antonia?" Howard murmured, the awful sense of it dawning. His gaze connected with Trueblood's, and both pairs of eyes widened as the impact of their wives' destination sank in.

"Lady Matrimonia giveth"—Trueblood groaned—"and Lady Matrimonia taketh away."

The headlines that greeted Londoners the next morning ranged from the absurd to the erudite. But the one that was most eagerly awaited—from the paper that always seemed to beat the others to the story of the earl and the widow, *Gaflinger's Gazette*—was simple but devastating:

THE LADY FORCED TO DEGRADING LABOR!

The notorious earl was not content with compromising Antonia Paxton and dragging the lady's name through the scandal-mire, the article asserted. He continued to harass her, besieging her at her house, dragging her off the streets

. . . demanding that she fulfill an ill-begotten wager that any gentleman of conscience would have forgotten the instant the question of the lady's honor was raised in public.

Worse yet, the sources of this information were beyond reproach: a number of correspondents from leading newspapers, an MP, a Bank of London executive, and the scores of Londoners who had passed by Carr's Emporium on the previous afternoon. The article related in lurid, moralizing detail how the good widow was put on degrading display in the shop windows, and lingered with outraged sympathy on how pale and drawn she appeared, and how bravely she held back her tears of shame.

The women of Paxton House read the *Gaflinger's* account and were speechless as Antonia entered the dining room for breakfast that morning. She felt their eyes searching her, and halted, checking her buttons, her hair, and her bustle with a frown of confusion.

"What is it? Have I forgotten something?" she asked.

"Are you sure you're all right, Toni dear?" Aunt Hermione said with a worried look. "I should have stayed with you yesterday, I know, but I honestly thought—"

"What *are* you talking about?" Antonia poured herself a cup of tea at the sideboard and carried it to her chair at the table. She set it down and took the paper Eleanor offered her, frowning at the sight of that vile masthead. But her eyes widened when they fell on the article about her. As she read the outrageous account, she paled, her jaw loosened, and she sat down on her chair with a plop. The others exchanged worried looks as they watched her shock turn slowly to outrage.

"How dare they?" she erupted, cramming the paper into one hand and shaking it as if she could somehow dislodge and rearrange those hideous words by physical force. "Distortions, misinterpretations, and outright lies— every bit of it!"

"It is?" Pollyanna said, melting with a relief that was shared by the others around the table.

"Well, of course it is! You don't honestly think Remington would be capable of such callous, ruthless—" She halted, reading in their faces that they had indeed thought it. It escaped her, momentarily, that she had thought it as well, and as recently as yesterday. Just now all she could think was that her ladies had worked side by side with him, entertained him, and shared their stories with him, and they should know better. Looking around at their wary gazes, she realized that if they believed such stuff just because it was printed in the wretched newspapers, then how much more would other people, who had never set eyes on him?

"Remington Carr is most certainly an arrogant, devious, and relentless man," she declared, coming to his defense. "But he would never force a woman into brute labor . . . without a very good reason."

Antonia's sentiment, however, was not shared by the occupants of London's leading residence. A number of papers bearing accounts of the earl's ungentlemanly behavior had found their way into the family apartments of Buckingham Palace. Try as they might, there was no way the queen's daughter, secretaries, and personal staff could keep her from seeing at least one of them.

"Wha-a-at?" she roared, coming up out of her chair. "He's done what?"

"Apparently he's insisted the lady fulfill her part of that 'Woman Wager,'" her secretary said, grimacing at the sight of his sovereign's rising ire. "He has put her to work. Men's work, according to some; brute labor, according to others."

"The ignoble churl." Victoria strode to the window and narrowed her eyes as she looked out over the busy courtyard, as if to pierce the distance and rebuke the offending earl. "He continues with his hideous campaign to revile and degrade both that unfortunate lady and all other members of her sex by association. It would seem our wishes and our expectations regarding his nuptials are being ignored." Her round face took on the aspect of rose granite.

"He had best beware . . . or he shall find the rope we give him just long enough to *hang* him."

Promptly at nine o'clock that morning, a cab drew up before Paxton House, and the driver announced that he was there to convey the lady of the house into the City. Antonia deliberated a much shorter time than previous mornings before changing into a tailored gray skirt and fitted jacket and selecting her best black velvet hat and matching Swedish kid gloves. Aunt Hermione declined to accompany her, saying there were too many things that demanded attention at home, and so Antonia entered the cab alone.

But inside that hire coach she found Remington waiting with a satisfied look that made her cheeks heat. "Only an hour," he said, glancing at his watch and tucking it back into his vest pocket. "Considerably better than yesterday," he added, dropping his voice to an intimate murmur. "I do believe we're making progress."

"Don't count on it, your lordship," she said, straightening her spine. "I simply don't think either your reputation or mine could withstand another embarrassing incident just now."

"Well, there is a way to be sure there are no further incidents, Antonia," he said, letting his eyes drift over her.

"Indeed there is," she said tartly, knowing just where *that* comment was leading. "I could move to Pigworth on Taunton and wear a bag over my head in public."

He threw his head back and laughed—a free, deep-chest sort of sound that caught Antonia by surprise as it invaded her skin and hummed along her nerves. She couldn't hold back her smile, though she did manage to turn it toward the window. When he sobered, he settled a searching gaze on her.

"Marry me, Antonia," he said quietly.

She looked at him and found him relaxed against the seat. Only his eyes hinted at the intensity behind that question.

"No," she said, turning away to look through the smudged cab window. For some reason she felt a need to soften that rejection. "Marriage has nothing to offer a woman in my situation."

"Nothing?" he said with a hint of exasperation.

"Nothing I don't already have."

"Except passion," he said with a sensuous husk to his voice that made her very glad she wasn't looking at him. After a moment she heard him expel a heavy breath that might have been either disappointment or disgust. "And, of course, protection."

"Neither of which I need."

They had come full circle, and in a mercifully brief time they arrived at the offices of Carr Enterprises. She escaped the tension of the cab, only to find herself thrust into a very different kind of tension inside the offices. The casual air of the other day was gone; everything was brusque and quick this morning. There were decisions to be made and deals to be transacted. Antonia felt a subtle change in Remington, a watchfulness, a tension, as if he were somehow at the edge of his senses, continually poised on the brink of reaction.

Markham and Hallowford and the others she had seen yesterday asked to have a word with Remington straightaway. He informed them he would be leaving soon, to escort Mrs. Paxton out to New Market and the site of the Sutton Mills construction; but they prevailed upon him to delay his trip. There were several urgent matters concerning the Sutton Mills transaction that required his personal attention. He thought a moment, looking at Antonia, then came up with an alternative plan. He escorted her down the hall and introduced her to another kind of work for the morning: learning the indispensable new skill of typewriting. He assigned a young man named Collingwood to instruct her, then disappeared into his office with his managers.

Antonia sat staring at the mechanical contraption before her with a dubious expression. It was a black metal box, cut away on one side to reveal a maze of long finger-like levers that were fitted with round tabs bearing the letters of the alphabet. Collingwood leaned over her shoulder, fitted his long fingers to the "keys," and punched several of those tabs. Levers jumped up and smacked a paper wrapped around a rolling pin, and in a moment she was staring at her name in neat black letters: MRS. PAXTON. She smiled and looked up at Collingwood.

"Can I try?"

He showed her how to press the keys, then how to place her fingers on the proper letters, and asked her to key some additional words. Out of her deepest recesses came words and she typed them, once, twice, then again and again, each time with more confidence and precision. After a few moments she paused and held up the paper to find that she had typed the words "MARRY ME" fourteen times.

Collingwood sputtered and reddened and she shrank and blushed . . . and snatched the paper out of the machine. "I-I think I should try again. Something else."

He nodded and nervously began to talk as he fitted clean paper into his machine. "They say the queen hates these machines . . . won't allow typewriting in her sight. But, it's the coming thing, you know. They're even training women to be typewriters, now. The government has a program to teach young ladies to do it. They say women have good fingers for it—what with all the fine work they do and such. And Carr Enterprises is right in the thick of it—we have a school for typewriters, too."

Antonia typed "YOU DO?" by pressing one key at a time. She pointed and he read it, then smiled.

"We certainly do. A number of the factory girls take the classes after work each day."

She typed: COMMENDABLE.

And he laughed, delighted. They carried on that rather unusual conversation for a few minutes, with Antonia's responses getting longer and more involved. And finally Collingwood decided that she was a good candidate for real training. He showed her how to hold her hands and which keys to strike with which fingers, then gave her several words and phrases to practice without looking at her hands.

The minutes slipped by and quickly became one hour . . . then two. Antonia was so intent on her work that she scarcely heard it when young Collingwood announced it was time for his dinner and excused himself. On the periphery of her senses she detected a drop in the noise level in the offices, but dismissed it. Minutes later she heard a faint click and felt a draft of air; the door had closed. Then someone touched her shoulders and she gave a startled cry.

"No, don't let me disturb you," Remington said, spreading his hands over her shoulders, resting them there. It was an unusual touch, intensely personal yet devoid of sexual content. "Collingwood says you're coming along very well."

"He's a good teacher," she said, trying to contain her runaway heart. "It's a little like playing the piano, only here you make words and sentences instead of melodies. It's . . . interesting." She both heard and felt the rumble of his laugh, and realized he was leaning against her chair. She felt him sliding down, probably to his knees.

"I can make it even more interesting, sweetheart." His low murmur near her ear set her tender fingertips tingling. He slid his hands down her arms and lifted her hands to the keys again.

Her fingers splayed over the keys and his fingers slid over hers, curling, fitting themselves to their curve. Slowly, deliberately, his fingers coaxed hers to press the keys, one at a time. Over and over he stroked her fingers; over and over she yielded him control. She could feel his body pressing against her back, his breath moving her hair and brushing her ear. She could feel the warmth of his body melting her determination . . . turning it into a deepening pool of desire.

Then he stilled, and after a moment drew his hands back up her arms and rested them on her shoulders.

"Read it," he whispered into her ear.

She managed to scroll the paper up and focus her eyes on it. There, in bold type, were the words: DO YOU LIKE THIS?

She sat staring at them for a minute, feeling tension collecting, then releasing. And she put her hands to the keys again and typed: YES.

She could almost feel him smiling. He slid his hands down her sides, warmly caressing her waist, asking, "And do you like this?"

She typed: YES.

He blew softly in her ear, and then nibbled it, and finally tongued it with long, luxurious strokes. "And this, sweetheart? Do you like this?"

YES.

He slid his hands up her corseted ribs to her breasts and circled his palms over them slowly, again and again. "And do you want more of this?"

YES.

Then his fingers found her buttons and gingerly pried them free. She could scarcely breathe as her jacket parted and her blouse buttons began to give. Finally her chest was bare, and his gentle, rousing fingers dipped into the cups of her corset to tease her nipples. She squirmed against the chair as he rolled them between his fingers and thumbs and managed to vibrate cords of sensation that reached down into her warming, tightening hollow.

"And this," he murmured raggedly into her ear, "do you want this to stop?"

Of habit she typed: YES.

His hands withdrew from her aching breasts with a caressing stroke, and she nearly choked on her dismay. She opened her eyes and was mildly shocked to see her half-bare breasts. But she was even more surprised when her eyes focused on the three little letters that had put an end to the luscious pleasure she had been experiencing. Y-E-S.

She groaned silently. Why did he have to choose now to begin taking her refusals seriously?

"One more thing," he said quietly, leading her fingers back to the keys. With his fingers guiding hers, they typed out: DO YOU LIKE ME YET?

She paused, feeling confused and excited and power-fully drawn to him. Here, in his world, he seemed the most reasonable of men. The most forward thinking and capable of men. She liked the loyalty he inspired and liked the way he put his values to work as policies in his businesses. And on a personal level she liked the way he laughed and the way he teased, and the way he was trying to make up for the hurt she had suffered. She had to admit . . . she was beginning to really *like* him.

She typed out "Y-E-S" again.

He spun her around by the shoulders and his eyes were glowing and his face was dusky with both arousal and pleasure. He leaned forward, staring at her mouth, and she parted her lips, expecting a hungry and penetrating kiss. What she got was a quick brush of promise. Dismayed by how easily he had raised her sensual responses, she snapped straight on the chair and frowned at him. He smiled mischievously.

"Button up, sweetheart. I'm supposed to be taking you out for a bit of dinner." His gaze dropped to the silky rose crescents peeping above her corset. "And if you sit like that much longer, I may change my mind and make you the main course instead."

She liked him. It was a simple thing, really, he thought. More friendly than passionate. More affectionate than sexual. But it was vastly more pleasurable to him than anything else he had experienced with her, from the sweetness of her bed to that delicious little typing exercise. *She liked him.* That knowledge kept him smiling all through luncheon.

She liked him. It was a very complicated thing, really, she thought. It was a little bit companionship and a little bit passion. It was some part desire and some part respect. And it was infinitely more dangerous than anything she had experienced with him before—including their abandoned loving in his bed. *She liked him.* And despite her worry over what it meant, she couldn't help returning his smiles.

Antonia's intention of avoiding another incident notwithstanding, another imbroglio was lurking just around the corner, literally. Returning from dinner, they spotted a small crowd in the street at the south entrance to Remington's building. Antonia tensed and slowed, and Remington paused outright. Both squinted against the sun, trying to make out what was going on.

There didn't seem to be any checkered coats or oversize bowlers in the group, but that small relief was undercut by the puzzling predominance of skirts and ladies' hats and signboards in the crowd. As they approached, they realized that the group was listening to someone speak. A woman's voice carried high and clear above the gathering, punctuated periodically by feminine calls of agreement and the waving of signs and jiggling of placards. It was a gathering of women.

And from the sound of them, angry women.

"They must not be allowed to make women into mere chattel!" the speaker was saying passionately. "They must be held accountable for their abuse of women, for their use of women as voiceless drudges or as receptacles of their vile pleasures—" Remington recognized the tenor of the words and one or two of the faces, but it took him a moment to place them, and that was just one moment too long.

"There he is now!" a woman at the edge of that group of radical suffragettes shouted, galvanizing the others. She lurched toward them, pointing, and a score of faces followed her. "And he's got a woman with him!"

"That must be poor Mrs. Paxton!" shouted another.

The women rushed to meet them, and before Antonia could do more than shrink back against Remington's side, she was engulfed by women pushing and shoving, shaking fingers and fists, and venting their anger in the most alarming invective.

"There you are—you foul, heathen beast—you monstrous deceiving *man*!" a dignified-looking woman in black declared, shoving a fist under Remington's nose.

He drew back and tried to pull Antonia along behind him through the crowd, but they angrily pushed him back and refused to let him escape.

"You've shown your true colors at last!" shouted another, thrusting her round, florid face into his. "All this time pretending to be a supporter of suffrage . . . an emancipator of women . . . a devoted equal rights-er!"

Ugly cheers greeted that. Remington tried to speak up and rebut the shocking charges being made against him, but he was drowned out by a third woman shouting:

"Touting emancipation—all the while abusing and degrading women—forcing them into bondage to serve your vile urges! We knew all along you were a fraud—and now you've proved it!"

"Fraud." "White Slaver!" "Oppressive Male." "Carnal Beast!" Jeers flew out of the crowd like rotten tomatoes. Antonia felt Remington flinch as if struck and looked up. His face was red and his chin was tucked defensively. But his eyes were dark and turbulent—disbelieving.

With widening horror she realized that he was totally unprepared to respond to such unexpected feminine virulence against him. He was a man who had gone against his peers and colleagues to champion women's suffrage and equality. He had published articles and made speeches in the Lords demanding equal treatment for women. He was a man who had begun education and training programs in his business concerns to allow women to better their lot in the workplace. Whatever Remington's motives, no man in all Britain had sided more vehemently against the "chains" that bound women to dependent and subservient roles under men. How could they possibly think he—

"Take heart, sister!" someone called, as the attention shifted to her. "Come with us—we'll help you!" "Rise up, sister, and strike off the shackles of male oppression!" "Don't let him degrade you—force you into degrading labor—speak up!"

Through the din and the buffeting Antonia realized that this was at least in part about *her*. They thought she was being abused, and they had come to confront him because of what they read in the cursed newspapers! She did speak up.

"Stop this!" Her heart pounded wildly as she burrowed her way in front of him and faced them. "Stop it! How dare you attack his lordship on the street like a lawless pack of ruffians?" There was a stunned pause for a second; then someone from the back shouted:

"He attacks women on the streets—it's no more than he deserves!"

"That's not true!" she shouted, trembling with righteous anger. "And I should know—I'm the one he was supposed to have attacked! The vile newspapers printed a pack of scurrilous lies, just to sell papers!" She took advantage of their surprise to seize his arm and draw him with her toward the building and safety.

"He forces women to degrading labor—he treats women like thralls!" came another charge. "He made you work like a drudge—held you up to ridicule—"

"I work for him as a result of a wager—freely and of my own blessed will! It's between him and me! And if you want to know how he treats women in his businesses, why don't you ask the young women in his factories and businesses—ask them about their reading classes and typewriting programs—"

Anger choked off the rest, and she turned and pushed and shoved her way through the frustrated crowd of women, with Remington right behind her. Behind them she could hear desultory rumbles and confusion. Calls of "dupe" mingled with "poor misguided creature" as she glared at the women blocking the door until they moved. Then she turned to the others again.

"Go home—all of you. And if you really want to know what Remington Carr believes about women, I suggest you come and talk to him civilly, as mature, rational women who believe in the decency and dignity of womanhood!"

She shoved her way past the women just inside the doors, and by the time the red haze cleared from her senses, she was on the steps, nearing the third floor and encountering a cordon of men across the stairs. Most were clerks and officials of Carr Enterprises who had organized to keep the women from invading their offices, and when they saw Remington with her, they let her pass. Partway down the hall she realized she was still holding Remington's arm in a fierce grip and released him.

"It was those bloody wretched newspapers—that Rupert Fitch and his lot," she said furiously, stopping to look up into his face. "I cannot believe the way otherwise reasonable people accept everything they read in black and white, without a moment's pause." She felt a surge of righteous rage and blurted out, "Abusive, bullying, oppressive —a white slaver, for pity's sake! How dare they say such things about you?" The crack of tension in his face and the beginning of his smile made her realize that until very recently *she* had thought such things about him, too—had used some of those very words to describe his behavior toward her.

Somewhere along the way her attitude had begun to change.

"I mean—about me," she added hastily, lowering her scarlet face and tucking her chin. She headed down the hallway toward his office doors, stunned by her vehement defense of him. He certainly didn't need her protection— he was a man of the world, a man of power and privilege. He was virtually invincible. If anyone needed protection here, it was she. And what she needed protection from was *him*!

She quickly found Collingwood, and for the rest of that very long afternoon had to face both the memory of his

face that moment in the hallway and the sensuous suggestion of the typewriter's tapping keys.

The women were long gone from the lobby when Remington escorted her downstairs late that afternoon. The
only remnant of their harrowing encounter was a discarded
placard lying just outside the door. As they waited on the
steps for the cab that would take her home, she found it
difficult to look at him. He watched her avoiding his gaze
and read in her manner the confusion that the day's events
had stirred in her. He fought an almost overwhelming urge
to pull her into his arms, telling himself it was best not to
press too hard.

But as he helped her into the cab, he couldn't resist
holding on to her hand for an extra moment. Her gaze
sought his, and he could see roused feeling in her eyes.

"Trust me, Antonia," he said softly. Then he pressed
something into her hand and stepped down off the cab,
swinging the door shut.

Halfway down the block she opened her hand to find
another silk-covered button in her hand. Her button. He
was slowly returning them to her, as reminders of her
passion for him. She sighed and squeezed her hand and
eyes shut.

As if she needed reminding.

Chapter

17

Tension greeted Antonia the instant she stepped through the doors of Paxton House. Hoskins's usual air of skeptical deference had been replaced by a hostile glower. He took her gloves and hat and jerked his head toward the drawing room.

"Might just as well hang out a shingle . . . damned charity house for runaway females," he muttered, shuffling off. "Women comin' out the windows a'ready. . . ."

Hoskins's testy mood and the sound of high-pitched voices coming from the drawing room prepared Antonia for what she would find in her main parlor. The three recent additions to her household, along with Pollyanna, Eleanor, Prudence, and Molly, were clustered around the sofa on the street end of the drawing room, listening raptly to a distraught young woman in an expensive figured-silk dress. Antonia paused for a moment just inside the door, registering the presence of yet another of her protégées: Elizabeth Audley, who had married Lord Carter Woolworth.

"She never let me suggest a menu or change a drapery or even speak with the laundress about the linen," Elizabeth was saying in an aggrieved voice. "I found her in my room once, going through my personal things . . . she reads my dressmaker's bills aloud, in front of Carter . . . and she intercepts invitations and turns away callers before

I get to see them." Tears of righteous anger were spilling down her cheeks. "His mother makes my life a misery, and Carter never takes my part. She snaps and snarls at me and he just turns and walks away."

Eleanor looked up from comforting Elizabeth and saw Antonia standing by the door. "Lady Toni! Look who's come back to us."

Antonia managed to smile.

As it happened, Elizabeth wasn't the only Bentick bride to return to Paxton House that day. Delicate Daphne Elderston, wife of Lord Richard Searle, had arrived that morning, bag and baggage. When she learned Antonia was home, she hurried in to see her with a tale of a volatile husband whose storms and drafts of temper regularly trembled the roof timbers. Antonia graciously accepted both women into their midst and was grateful to learn Aunt Hermione had negotiated amicable sleeping arrangements for them.

The supper table was quite full that night, set with five extra places. The atmosphere was thick with emotion, which occasionally erupted into nervous laughter or tears. After supper the group divided in two, the older ladies in the drawing room and the younger women in the upstairs parlor—where Antonia found them sharing their tales of woe. She watched from the door as they compared the miseries of a spineless mama's boy, a skinflint, a perfectionist, a tyrant, and a man who scarcely acknowledged his wife's existence.

Had she made any matches that had ended happily? Were any of the thirteen marriages good and loving unions? Being treated like a servant or a troublesome child, having no property of your own, having no say in the most basic decisions of your life, being allowed no opinion of your own—was this what marriage was really like?

She retreated to her rooms, thinking of her own marriage. It hadn't been like that with Sir Geoffrey. He had been generous and honest and honorable . . . and so much *older*. And as she stood looking at her bed, remembering the way Remington had climbed up in it, she allowed herself to wonder what kind of husband he would make.

He seemed warm and generous with those close to him. But then, those closest to him had always been men. She had seen only too well how cold and inaccessible he became when demands were made on him by a woman. What would he be like when the problems and troubles and needs of life descended? Would he ruthlessly seize control, or lose his temper and bully and demand, or grow impatient and dismissive as he had with that Hillary woman and the infamous Carlotta? And what would he do if he had children? Odd—she knew that his Uncle Paddington loved and wanted children; she hadn't a clue how Remington truly felt about them.

Not that she needed or wanted to know, she told herself sternly.

She found herself staring at the row of buttons down the front of her blouse, thinking of what he said as he put her in the cab. She found her black gloves on her dressing table and tilted them to let the button he had returned to her roll out into the palm of her hand. *Trust me.*

After all she had seen and heard, after all that had happened between them, how could she? And why did she still want to so badly?

The ladies of Paxton House were settling in for the night— a few still talking or reading, most preparing for their beds —when there came a fierce pounding on the front doors. Hoskins, who had already retired for the evening, was slow to respond, and the ever-increasing racket roused the entire population of the upper three floors of the house. Ladies in night robes and slippers poured down the steps and onto the gallery at the rear of the main hall. When Antonia poked her head out of her room and learned what was happening, she snagged her jacket and headed for the entry straightaway.

Hoskins, with a many-branched candlestick in one hand and an empty, upturned one in the other, ambled through the hall, grumbling to himself. He placed the lit candles on the hall table to wait for Antonia to arrive. Eleanor, Pollyanna, Molly, Gertrude, Maude, and Prudence trickled down the stairs after Antonia, looking mildly alarmed at these odd doings. The sounds of feminine voices buzzed excitedly around the high-ceilinged hall as Hoskins threw the lock and opened the door.

Into that hive of femininity burst three intrepid males with fists and shoulders flexed defensively. They halted to take their bearings, disoriented by the candlelight and shadows and the clamor of so many women's voices. "Here —you can't barge in here like that!" Hoskins bellowed, tottering forward, brandishing his candlestick.

"It's all right, Hoskins," Antonia said, hurrying forward to restrain him. There in the light stood Albert Everstone, Basil Trueblood, and Bertrand Howard, reeking of two-day-old shirts and recent whiskey.

"Where are they?" Everstone demanded. "Where's my wife, woman? I demand to see my wife!"

"And mine. I know she's here!" Trueblood declared hotly, looking up at the bevy of women around the gallery. "Alice—you come down here this minute—I'm taking you home!"

"Camille!" Bertrand Howard followed Trueblood's lead. "I have a few words to say to you! Show yourself!"

Antonia felt a bolt of outrage racing up her spine as she heard their half-drunken demands. For the second time that day, in defense of those she cared about, her hands clenched, her face reddened, and her shoulders swelled with righteous fury. As she stalked forward, she was transformed from a mere female into the fire-breathing dragon that had once descended on them as they sat in a woman's bed.

"How dare you enter my house under cover of darkness and threaten and bully my guests!" She advanced on them, her eyes glowing eerily in the candlelight.

"W-we come to get our wives and take 'em home where they belong," Everstone declared, falling back a step and looking to the others for support.

"They belong to us now," Trueblood declared. "You saddled us with them!"

"And we want them back," Bertrand Howard said, from behind the others' shoulders.

"Well, you cannot have them!" Each word seemed ripped from the bottom of her soul. "Your wives, gentlemen, want nothing further to do with you. They are not your property or chattel; they do not *belong* to you! From this day on they and they alone will decide where and to whom they belong. They have left your callous, indifferent, and despicable clutches for good reason. And in doing so, they have allowed me to redress the wrong I have done in shackling them to the likes of you."

She forced them back a step as she advanced on them with feminine anger burning brightly at her core.

"Go home and count yourselves the most fortunate of men. For this day you are relieved of the burden of an unwanted wife. Hoskins, the door!"

"I won't stand for this!" Bertrand Howard declared, darting around her for the stairs, shouting, "Camille— come down here!"

The others moved to join him but stopped dead in their tracks as they watched him run into a line of older women, standing shoulder to shoulder on the stairs, in their night-clothes. Before their disbelieving eyes the women descended, step by step, a formidable wall of experienced femininity forcing Howard back and down the steps.

"You won't get away with this! Can't keep us from our own wives—there's laws, you know!" Albert Everstone shook his fist at Antonia, but only as he was backing toward the open door.

"There's also justice," Antonia said with regal poise, sweeping them before her, out the door. "And that's exactly what you're getting right now."

The doors slammed shut and the locks were thrown again.

It took some time before the household settled once again into the night and into a jittery stillness. In the hush of their darkened room, in the sleepless hours that followed, Camille Howard smiled to herself and whispered to Alice Trueblood:

"Did you see that? They came for us."

Women Protest Earl's Depravity!

The headline that greeted London the next morning, on the front page of *Gaflinger's,* was sensational in the extreme. But the titles other papers gave their articles were not much better. "Earl Unfair to Fairer Sex," "Suffragettes Protest Earl's Actions," and "Women Demand End to Degrading Labor!" were among the more restrained assessments applied to the incident.

Apparently there had been a few checkered coats and brown bowlers in the crowd outside Remington's building, after all. They had scrupulously recorded every word said, but had been considerably less conscientious about presenting those words in the context in which they had been uttered. A number of the stories were spiced with the shocking mention of "white slavery," "bestial carnal activities," and of women "attacked" and "kept shackled."

Antonia saw the *Gaflinger*'s headline at breakfast the next morning and could scarcely eat a bite afterward. She paced the small parlor downstairs, until several of her Bentick brides invaded the room, looking for a place to do some stitchery. She excused herself and fled to the study, where she picked up a feather duster and began to dust some of Cleo's memories, while trying to sort out her thoughts. After a few minutes Cleo came tottering in and found her staring at the much-dusted figurine of the beautiful waltzing couple.

"That's me and my Fox in Vienna, you know," she said loudly, coming to take it from Antonia.

"Yes, I know," Antonia said, watching the old lady's cloudy eyes collecting memories from the colors and lines of the porcelain statuette.

"How that man loved to dance." Cleo appeared to be sliding off into her memories, but came back to the present with a vengeance. "You ever waltz, Toni girl?"

"I . . . um . . . no," Antonia said, feeling unsettled by the admission.

"Ever seen the sun come up in a man's arms?" Cleo demanded in a softer voice. There was no room for evasion, despite the unthinkably personal nature of the question.

"I . . . no," Antonia answered after a minute, feeling her face grow hot.

"Ever been so wild in love that you felt drunk . . . without touchin' a drop?"

Antonia shook her head.

Cleo sighed and placed a knotty hand on her arm. "You got a lot of livin' yet to do, my girl. Don't wait forever." She raised that hand to pat Antonia's cheek. "None of us has forever."

Antonia watched her wander into the midst of her

memories and felt a haunting emptiness opening in her. *Taste life and savor it. Live.* That was exactly what Aunt Hermione had said to her, again and again. But coming from Cleo, it sounded almost like a divine imperative. *Don't wait forever.*

She stood by the door for a moment, watching the morning sun glinting on old Cleo's faded finery. Seized by a rising urgency that she couldn't explain and didn't want to examine, she called for Hoskins and ordered him to summon a cab.

"Don't need to go for one," he said with a disgusted look. "Been one sittin' outside the door for the past quarter of an hour."

Antonia flew to her rooms, hurriedly changed her dress, and soon rushed back down the stairs, properly hatted and gloved. She left word with Hoskins for Aunt Hermione—in case more of her protégées should arrive during her absence—then hurried out to the cab. And it was a genuine disappointment to find it empty.

Remington paced his offices, waiting for her to arrive and hoping that the incident yesterday and the hideous things they were saying about him in the papers wouldn't combine with her lingering mistrust of him to keep her away.

The women's demonstration yesterday had genuinely shocked him. He was used to people disagreeing with his radical notions of equality; he had certainly had enough slings and arrows flung his way. But it usually happened in print or on the floor of the House of Commons, and was generally done by stodgy old men. Until yesterday he had counted the suffragists among his allies.

Antonia had blamed it on the newspaper stories about them, and he realized she probably was right. He had ignored the news writers, assuming—in error—that a flame that wasn't fed would soon go out. He hadn't imagined that their wretched appetite for scandal was so tenacious it would find a way to feed itself. Nor had he counted on the possibility that others would take their absurd ramblings so seriously. Judging by the women's reaction yesterday, half of London now considered him a pillaging opportunist, a brutal oppressor of women, and a hopeless profligate!

God knew how many more demonstrations, rebukes, and outrages he would have to bear before Antonia finally relented and agreed to marry him. The fortnight the queen had given him was almost half-gone, and—

The queen. His stomach contracted sharply.

Did Britain's dour sovereign read newspapers, too? Victoria had been outraged, thinking him a despoiler of virtuous widows. He groaned and rubbed his cramping stomach. Now that he was publicly accused of attacking women in the streets and forcing them to do brute labor, now that he had almost been arrested and had women demonstrating in the streets against him . . . His face turned gray. She was probably screaming for his head on a spike!

Frantic to see Antonia and settle this thing once and for all, he stalked to the outer office, into the main corridor, and stood glowering at the stairs as if he could somehow make her materialize there. Then he retraced his steps, pausing to rake a glare over the accounting room, and then stopping by the door of the room where Collingwood labored over his typewriter.

"Your lordship." Markham approached him as he stalked into his office. "A moment, please. The gentlemen from the bank have not arrived to finalize arrangements for the loan on the Sutton Mills stock transaction."

Remington frowned; the good gentlemen of the Bank of England were *never* late. You could set a timepiece by them. As he thought of what might have caused such an unprecedented delay, he paled. There was nothing bankers liked more than newspapers—they positively devoured them of a morning! The *Gaflinger*'s morning headline popped into his mind: "Women Protest Earl's Depravity." There was nothing bankers liked less than "depravity," unless it was "depravity" exposed—*scandal*!

Just then the sound of voices in the outer office drifted down the hallway and through his open door. He held his breath, and there was Antonia's musical soprano. He went charging out of his office to greet her.

She was wearing her fawn-colored silk with its graceful panniers, and pert little bustle. He called her name, and when she turned, there were rows of new buttons down the front of her bodice. Her hat was a matching fawn-colored felt with a demiveil and pheasant and egret feathers. Her hair seemed a bit brighter, her form a bit curvier, and her aspect a bit more feminine in that delicate color.

He stood gawking, then reddened slightly and reached for his pocket watch. "Only a half hour late," he said huskily. "You show steady improvement."

"As do you," she said, removing her gloves one tantalizing finger at a time. Before he could react to that provocative statement, she had unpinned her hat and was swaying past him down the hall, headed for Collingwood's office. "I've decided I really may have a knack for business, after all. And I believe I should learn all I can."

Steady improvement. His heart gave a thump in his chest and started to beat again. And as he watched her disappear into the secretary's office, he felt as if he were not only running a footrace, but that he might also be winning . . . until Markham brought him back to earth.

"Should I send round to the bank and ask what is keeping them, sir?"

Remington came back to reality with a thud. "The bankers—good Lord." He scowled and thought for a moment. "Where the hell is Uncle Paddington? He could go to the bank and find out what's going on. He's an old school-mate of Sir Neville Thurston's."

"He hasn't been in for the last two days or so, your lordship," Markham said.

"Then send round to his town house—he's spent the last night or two there. Better yet, go yourself. Explain and tell him I need him to do a little 'banking.' He'll know what I mean"—he paused, then added—"I hope."

Antonia felt his eyes on her from the doorway, and her heart beat faster as she looked up. His arms were crossed, and he was leaning a shoulder against the door frame with a determined expression.

"I think it's time you were promoted. Come with me." He took her by the hand and led her into the conference room, where he seated her at the table and proceeded to lay out his diversified empire on the table, using the charts his staff had shown her two days ago.

As he talked, she watched his mouth move and her skin grew warm and sensitive beneath her bodice. She saw his hands move and his shoulders flex as he picked up one chart and laid down another, and she couldn't help wondering if he knew how to waltz. Her gaze fastened on his chocolate eyes, and she felt a sweet shiver and wondered if they had ever seen the sun come up while lying in a woman's arms.

"So you see, I have a good many assets," he said, laying the last chart aside.

"Yes," she said with a telling bit of thickness, "I can certainly see that."

"And I take a hand in the management of every one of my interests."

"Ummm," she said sweetly. "That must keep your hands very busy."

"Quite." He smiled nervously. "Though not too busy to

add additional interests . . . which brings me to my point. I am thinking of making an acquisition."

"Oh?"

"Something along the lines of a merger, actually." He settled one thigh on the edge of the table, half sitting, leaning toward her. "Something that would require considerable time and energy. A highly personal transaction. And I wonder if you might be interested in hearing more?"

He was testing the waters, asking her feelings about the possibilities between them. Her heart beat faster.

"I have no need of a *merger,* your lordship. In fact, a union of the sort you refer to would effectively strip me of all my assets and place all of my worldly property into other hands. Where women of substance are concerned, marri—*merger* always works to a man's advantage. By law the moment a woman enters into such an agreement, her property passes over to her husband in its entirety, and he is free to do with it whatever he wishes. Married women share this dismal lack of property rights with children, criminals, and the mentally insane."

"My desire for you is anything but fiduciary, Antonia."

"So you say, your lordship. But I am of a mind to think the law may have a bit of wisdom in it, after all. It is possible that there is something in marriage that drives women to desperate acts or renders them childish, imbecilic, and sometimes irrational." She smiled with a bit of mischief. "I suspect that thing may be *men.*"

Caught back, he was about to reply when Hallowford came rushing into the conference room, out of breath.

"Your lordship—thank heaven you are still here!" he gasped out.

"What is it, Hallowford?" Remington said, rising and frowning at the man's harried state.

"News from New Market. Bridgeman has made a preemptive offer to purchase Sutton Mills, and unless we can exercise our option and complete the transaction by week's end, the owner intends to accept Bridgeman's offer."

"He can't do that!" Remington declared, going rigid in an attempt to contain his ire. "We had an agreement. I was to buy controlling interest—convert the ownership to a stock basis and issue a solicitation for additional shareholders. The mills need an infusion of money and equipment in order to take advantage of the rising market for—" He halted and narrowed his gaze on something only he could see. "I believe I need to pay Sutton a visit—refresh his memory on just how binding a handshake can be. Hallowford, send round for my carriage."

He started for the door, turned, and caught Antonia by the hand. "Get your hat, sweetheart. You're coming, too."

The ride to New Market took the better part of two hours, and in that time Antonia watched Remington and his men, Hallowford and Evans, plotting out a strategy for confronting the waffling owner of the mill that was slated to become a pillar of Carr Enterprises' holdings. It was an ambitious project, socially as well as financially, for there was a certain reorganization involved that would permit a number of employees to participate in the ownership through the sale of earmarked shares. It was also a project in which Remington and his staff had already invested considerable time, money, and entrepreneurial pride. And now the entire project was threatened by the entry of a well-heeled spoiler into the picture. Loss of the project would mean the loss of thousands of pounds and of some face in the financial world.

"Sutton, my friend!" Remington said, boldly offering the fellow his hand when they were shown into the owner's offices. After handshakes and introductions they were offered seats and coffee, both of which they accepted. Then Remington came to the point. "I understand you've received another offer for the mills. Not surprising, really."

He glanced admiringly around him. "There is a great deal of opportunity here." Then he pierced the rotund and moist-faced Sutton with a sharp look. "What did surprise me was word that you were seriously considering it."

"Well . . . a man must . . . surely look to his best interests in such important matters," Sutton said, straightening and stretching his neck as if his collar bothered him.

"True," Remington agreed, with a smile crafted of burnished steel. "But a man must first look to his honor, else he will find others regard his word with the small respect that he shows for it."

What followed reminded Antonia of a chess match: move and countermove. A demand thinly cloaked. A concession adroitly made. A suggestion, then an assertion; provocation, then conciliation. She watched in fascination as Remington's mien went through every conceivable permutation of human emotion: anger, outrage, determination, calculation, condescension, pleasure, confidence, sympathy. It was a highly charged and competitive game. And in the end Remington won.

After two hours of wrangling, posturing, negotiating, the final price was fixed, and papers—which Remington had already prepared for a future meeting—were signed. They departed with an air of triumph . . . which gradually deflated as the carriage lurched along, carrying them back to London and to realities Remington dreaded.

He relaxed back against the seat, looking as if he'd just run a long-distance race. The aggressive posture eased and the mesmerizing force of his countenance drained. Only then did she realize he had been under great pressure, even while seeming confident and appearing to enjoy the fierceness of the negotiation.

"Congratulations, your lordship," Hallowford said, his shoulders slumping.

"Thank you, Hallowford," Remington said, expelling a

deep breath. "Now all we have to do is find the small fortune we have just promised to pay Mr. Sutton two weeks from today."

"Find the money?" Antonia asked, frowning. "Surely you have enough money. You're a very wealthy man."

"And most of my wealth is in property and investments. I don't keep hundreds of thousands of pounds just lying around, any more than you do."

"But why would you agree to buy it if you don't have the funds?" she asked.

He smiled ruefully. "Because it makes good business sense, believe it or not. And a great deal of business is done with borrowed money. Now all I have to do is convince the bankers that it makes good sense." He chuckled grimly at the confusion on her face. "Welcome to the world of high finance, Antonia. I won't ask you what you have learned from this little bit of men's work. From the look in your eyes I don't think I'd like the answer."

He couldn't have been more wrong, for the turmoil he glimpsed in her face merely reflected the upheaval occurring in her attitudes and the softening of her heart. Remington was engaged in a competition, too, she realized—one with larger prizes and more devastating consequences, but not so unlike the one faced by young Davidson. And like the clerks at the Emporium, Remington competed under the pressure of responsibilities, obligations, and expectations . . . from his co-owners, his employees, his backers, his bankers, and even the public at large. It suddenly struck her that to some extent, all men probably did so.

For all their apparent command and control of the world, men—even men of power and privilege like Remington—had their pressures and problems, too. If today was any example, the wielding of power and influence was not necessarily a pleasurable experience. And even in victory there were fresh obstacles and worries to contend with.

As she watched Remington relaxing back into the seat with his eyes closed, she was overcome with a great feeling of tenderness for him. She glanced at Hallowford and Evans, who seemed as drained by the experience as their employer, and realized it was a good thing they were in the carriage, too. If they hadn't been, she would have slid across the carriage and taken him into her arms to ease the strain in his face and frame . . . in a very direct and female sort of way.

When they arrived at Remington's office, it was pin-drop quiet at a time that would normally have been bustling with sound and movement. Markham was waiting in the outer office and shoved to his feet with a look of great relief when Remington and Antonia entered.

"Your lordship! Thank heaven you've returned." He hurried forward, then stepped back to give them room.

"What is it, what's happened?" Remington demanded, searching his assistant and trying to anticipate what had sent the usually unflappable Markham into such a state. The bank . . . his uncle . . . "Did you take Uncle Paddington to the bank?"

"He was not at home." Markham clasped and unclasped his hands, looking flushed. "His butler said he left yesterday and might not return for several more days."

"Gone?" Remington said, mildly alarmed. Uncle Paddington managed rather well in his local environs, but traveling outside London, and alone . . . It didn't bear thinking about! "Did his man say where he went?" Markham's high color drained visibly.

"Yes, my lord. To Gretna Green."

Remington was slow to catch the implications of it. "Gretna Green? Why on earth would he want to go there?"

Antonia was only slightly more perceptive. "Surely not the sort of place a gentleman of his age would go, even on holiday. Why it's a marriage mill . . . full of shopgirls and junior clerks who have run off together . . . and . . ." Something in her description of the place made her halt uneasily and look to Remington.

"That's all he said?" Remington demanded of Markham, shocked by the thoughts that sprang to his mind.

"That . . . and he left orders to have ice and champagne ready when he returned." Markham looked pained to have to add: "And oysters."

"Oy-sters?" Remington choked out, looking as if he'd been punched in the gut. "Gretna Green, champagne, oysters . . . For God's sake—the old boy's eloped!"

"Eloped?" Antonia's immediate reaction was disbelief, followed closely by a flare of anger. "Why, the bounder! Aunt Hermione will be crushed!"

"Crushed?" Remington turned on her in amazement. "Good God, Antonia—who do you think he's run away *with*? It can only be your aunt Hermione—he doesn't know any other marriageable women!"

Every bit of color in her face drained, too. "Don't be absurd. Auntie would never—" She halted, stunned. But Hermione *had*, at least twice before. In fact, she had something of a passion for elopements. Her last two husbands had both swept her away in the dead of night and carried her straight to . . .

"Dearest Lord!" She lifted her skirts and ran for her hat and gloves.

Remington grabbed his hat and was at her heels by the time she reached the stairs. "Where are you going?" When they reached the landing, he pulled her to a halt.

"I cannot believe she would do such a thing without a

word to me. She's at home right now—I'm certain of it." But she was apparently not so certain of it that she could refrain from seeing with her own two eyes, that Hermione was safely at home.

"I'm coming with you," he insisted, searching the anxiety in her face and sensing that what she discovered at home could have direct bearing on how she felt about him.

The ride from the City to the Piccadilly seemed to take forever. Lorries stalled in the streets and unexpectedly thick traffic delayed them. Each turn of the wheels beat like a muffled drum in Antonia's heart. When they finally reached her house, she lurched out of the cab ahead of Remington and raced up the front steps. Throwing open the front door, she called to her aunt and headed for the drawing room, where Hermione often sat doing needlework this time of day.

"Where is she?" she demanded of Pollyanna and Prudence, who looked up from their knitting with surprise. "Aunt Hermione—where is she?"

"Well, I don't know," Pollyanna said. "I haven't seen her since . . ." She frowned, unable to say just when she had seen Hermione last.

"I haven't seen her either," Prudence said. "Not since . . . was that yesterday morning? Why? What's happened? You look like you've seen a ghost—"

"She may be . . . m-missing," Antonia said frantically. "I have to find her!"

She rushed out into the hall just as Remington entered through the door she had left standing open. "Is she here?" he called to her, but she didn't seem to hear him as she rushed toward the stairs at the end of the hall. He went up the steps after her, and together they encountered Eleanor in the upstairs hall.

"Have you seen Aunt Hermione?" she demanded.

"Haven't seen her for some time . . . good to see you, your lordship!" Eleanor smiled at him.

Antonia rushed into Hermione's room, calling her name, and startled Daphne Searle and Elizabeth Woolworth, who jumped up from the bed and the settee with their mending in their hands. Antonia blinked, then stared at them.

"What are you doing in here?"

"This is where Aunt Hermione assigned us to sleep," Elizabeth said.

"She positively insisted we use her room. She said she would be sleeping elsewhere," Daphne added.

"When was that?" Antonia demanded furiously, going to the clothes chest and wardrobe, opening drawers and flinging doors wide.

"Well . . . yesterday morning, not long after I arrived," Daphne said, alarmed by Antonia's rising anger. "She said she knew you wouldn't mind my staying."

Antonia couldn't speak. She stood looking into a half-empty wardrobe. The truth seeped through her like the penetrating aroma of cedar that rolled from the chest. Aunt Hermione was gone.

"It can't be," she said, groaning. She began to pull things from the bottom of the closet and found Hermione's leather valise missing, along with her best clothes and shoes. Most of her jewelry, her underclothing, her best corsets were missing from her drawers, and the top of her dressing table was virtually clear . . . a telling detail. Hermione always liked her things sitting out in view, what she called "a healthy bit of clutter." But most devastating of all: the four miniatures that always sat on the top of her dresser, portraits of her beloved husbands, were gone.

"It can't be," she said, backing away from the sight of those empty drawers and hangers.

"What is it? What's the matter?" Eleanor asked from the doorway.

"Aunt Hermione has apparently eloped to Gretna Green," Remington answered with a broad smile. "With my Uncle Paddington."

Eleanor gasped and disappeared out the door. The sound of her voice calling the news to the other ladies drifted back into Hermione's room as Antonia stood looking at Remington's grin with growing horror.

"How can you smile at a time like this?"

"Because I think it's wonderful," he said, reaching for her. She shrank back, her eyes widening.

"It's not wonderful, it's horrible! Aunt Hermione— good Lord—at her age—" She darted for the door and was down the hall and around the gallery before he caught up and snagged her by the elbow.

Chaos was erupting all around them. Women were running up the stairs, down the hall, and along the gallery, converging on Antonia. "Is it true?" "When did you hear?" "How did you find out?" "Did they really elope?"

"We have to go after them—bring them back—talk some sense into them—" Antonia insisted, frantic to free her arm from his grip.

"We'll do no such thing," he declared, holding her back. "They're two mature, reasonably responsible people, and if they've decided to marry and live out the rest of their years together, then more power to them. Uncle Paddington has always needed someone, and I've never seen him happier than he is with Hermione. He's like a young boy again."

"No doubt he is," she snapped. "That's precisely the trouble. Young boys require care—lots of it—and Aunt Hermione has already provided more than her share. She worked her fingers to the bone for her precious husbands and had nothing to show for it when the last one died—not even a roof over her head." The pleasure he took in this awful elopement struck her as callous in the extreme. "She needs the trouble of another husband about as much as a mackerel needs shoes!"

"Trouble?" he said irritably. "Well, apparently she doesn't agree!"

"If not, it's because she isn't thinking clearly. She has property now, and a bit of personal freedom, and peace of mind—she doesn't need to have to cater to a man and truckle after his needs and be his unpaid servant, ever again. She doesn't have to put up with the annoyances and restrictions of marriage. She has me—I'm her family. I'll take care of her in her declining years, instead of making her work and worry herself into the grave caring for some old man!"

Remington stared at her with disbelief. "Work and worry and exhaustion—is that all you believe she'll have? Is that what you think marriage is about?" he demanded, releasing her. Then it struck him; was that what *her* marriage had been about—worrying over and taking care of a man more than twice her age? "If so, then it's no wonder you avoid it like the plague yourself," he said, running his hands back through his hair in frustration. "Has it not occurred to you that she might also find companionship and caring and laughter and warmth with my uncle? Did you never think that he's a wealthy man who could hire hundreds of servants and nurses to ease his final years . . . and hers? How is it that the Maven of Matrimony, the Avenging Angel of Marriage, and the Defender of Domesticity now speaks of marriage as if it is a *trap*?"

"Because it is," she declared fiercely, waving a hand toward the clustered faces of her Bentick brides. "Just ask them! I levered them into marriages with men of property and position and vigor, men who supposedly desired them . . . and still they found themselves ignored, deprived, overworked, and maltreated. I'll not allow that to happen to my aunt Hermione. She deserves better. She deserves to be here with me, where I can take care of her and keep her safe and secure."

"Ahhh, I see." He shoved his face into hers. "She deserves to have to stay here with you for the rest of her days, does she? Could it be you're just angry and frustrated at losing Hermione? Who is being selfish now, Antonia? I'll tell you this—I'm glad to have had a hand in introducing your aunt to my uncle. And I'm delighted that they've run off together like two starry-eyed adolescents!"

"You had a hand in—?" She stared at him as if truly seeing him for the first time. "You did it on purpose." Without giving him a chance for rebuttal, she built one conclusion on top of the other: "You deliberately introduced them, hoping to marry her off, didn't you? What was this . . . another of your nasty little schemes for revenge?" She was suddenly hurting, trembling all over. "Did you plan to marry them all off? To strip me of all my family? Who was next? Eleanor? Gertrude? Or maybe Maude?"

Turmoil broke out around them, everyone talking, reasoning, chiding, and pleading at once. Some took her side; some took his. But suddenly everyone in the house was on the gallery or the stairs voicing an opinion full force. That storm of emotions unleashed the anger and frustration that her suspicions generated in him.

"No, I did not *plan* this, Antonia!" he roared, clenching his fists as he towered over her. "It just happened. People do meet and do fall in love sometimes, without schemes or plotting or ulterior motives. But I wouldn't expect that you would know anything about that!"

For one stark moment her distrust of him met his anger at her.

Neither would give.

He turned on his heel and stalked down the stairs, weaving around the ladies who stood on the steps; in shock. The sound of the door slamming reverberated around the hall for a full minute. After another moment passed, in which not a breath was taken or expelled, turmoil broke out a second time.

In the midst of all that confusion, Cleo, who was near the top of the steps, grew agitated and confused, staggered, and then crumpled into a heap on the floor.

Antonia saw it happening and stood paralyzed with shock. She couldn't get to Cleo fast enough to keep her from hitting the floor, and couldn't free her frozen throat to cry out to another to intervene. Then time resumed its normal pace and a ripple of panic freed her voice and jolted her to action.

"Cleo!" she rushed to the old woman's side and lifted and cradled her head. "Cleo—can you hear me?" She thought Cleo might have groaned in response, but then she was still—so very still.

Reaching deep within for control she hadn't realized she possessed, Antonia began issuing commands, carving order out of the panic around her. She sent Hoskins for the doctor and directed others to help her carry Cleo to bed. In a short while they had Cleo in her bed and were bathing her aged face and smoothing her thin silver hair.

Moments before, rancor and frustration had driven the residents of Paxton House apart; now they were bound together by the hush of shared grief. A few of the ladies stayed in Cleo's room, waiting for the doctor, dabbing at tears. Others went to the upstairs parlor or down to the drawing room to talk in quiet tones of shock and disbelief. All waited anxiously, for there was not a resident of Paxton House, however long or brief her stay, who had not felt old Cleo's influence.

When the doctor arrived in a rush, Antonia met him at

the top of the stairs and bustled him into Cleo's room. He listened to Antonia's description, examined Cleo, and determined that she had suffered a stroke.

"How bad is it?" Antonia asked anxiously.

"Hard to say, really." The doctor wagged his head. "But the first forty-eight hours will usually tell. I'm afraid there's not much we can do but give it time." He left a few instructions with Antonia and said he would check back the next day.

And the vigil began.

Through the afternoon they watched and waited, giving her water and keeping her warm. Cleo's words of that very morning ran hauntingly through Antonia's head: *None of us has forever.*

The others came and sat in her room in shifts, but Antonia never left the old lady's side. In quiet moments she would talk to Cleo, pleading with her to get well and promising her all sorts of fanciful things if she did. As she watched Cleo lying so still, looking so frail and vulnerable, she began to feel that way herself inside. Vulnerable.

If only Hermione were here, she thought desperately. Hermione was one of those rare and special people who seemed to make wine sweeter, candles brighter, days sunnier, and hearts lighter wherever she was. Nothing ever seemed hopeless or impossible with her around. Hermione's presence in Antonia's life had somehow compensated for the disappointments and heartaches she had endured. Now the anguish her absence caused was so intense it caused a crushing tightness around Antonia's heart.

She looked down at the sparrowlike woman who was so light she barely made an impression on the feather mattress beneath her. She had lost Hermione. She had lost the fragile trust that had been developing between her and Remington. And now she was losing her beloved Cleo.

She had never felt so alone in her life.

The bar at White's was always noisy and crowded at nine in the evening, but it was especially so that night. Remington squared his shoulders with grim anticipation and forged into the room, meeting all eyes, both widened and narrowed, head-on. He was intent on having as many drinks, civilized or otherwise, as it took to get roaring drunk. There was a knot in his belly, a crushing weight in his chest, and several weeks' worth of frustration twitching in his frame. And there was no better way to get rid of all that than to put his knuckles into some annoying bastard's face. All he needed was a little Dutch courage and a few annoying bastards.

He didn't have to look very far.

In the corner, at the very same table where he had been recruited into their mad revenge scheme, sat five of the six men who had all but ruined his life.

His face was flinty as he strolled to the center of the bar and smacked the polished wood with an open palm, sending the clap vibrating through the room. Those intrepid enough to turn and glower glimpsed the violent glint in his eye and quickly thought better of confronting him. He ordered his usual brandy and tossed it back, savoring its potent afterburn.

Basil Trueblood lifted his gaze from the brown study of his drink and caught sight of him. He reddened and grabbed Carter Woolworth's arm, then Albert Everstone's. The sight of him positively galvanized them. They lurched to their feet and stumbled toward him. Remington braced and doubled up both fists, anticipating the delicious surge of satisfaction he would feel upon landing that first punch.

"Landers—where have you been?" Woolworth said frantically, then lowered his voice to a forceful whisper when several men turned to stare. "You've got to do something!"

"It's as much *your* fault as ours," Everstone declared, widening his stance to steady himself.

"If you had just married her and kept her on a short chain, none of this would have happened," Trueblood whined, glancing nervously over his shoulder.

"We cannot go to the courts without a public scandal," Bertrand Howard hissed with a desperate look. "And they have no family to appeal to—you're our only hope!"

Remington stared at their drink-flushed faces, stunned, his anger momentarily deflected by their bizarre charges.

"It's my fault? What in bloody hell are you talking about?" he growled, straightening, his shoulders swelling. "I ought to thrash the lot of you within an inch of your worthless lives for what *you've* done to *me*—invading my house in the dead of night and turning my life upside down—"

He smacked his glass down on the bar and made to leave, but they closed ranks around him, and Everstone got up the courage to grab his arm. Once he had it, not even Remington's steeliest glare could make him release it.

"Listen here, Landon," Woolworth said desperately, "you've got to help us. The Dragon's got our wives, and she won't let us talk to them or even see them."

"She admitted they were in her house. But when we tried to haul them home, she tossed us straight out!"

"You've locked horns with her before—you can find a way to make her listen!"

"They're our wives, goddammit! They belong to us!"

"Turned 'em against us, she did. And they up and left us."

"Let me get this straight," Remington said, anger outstripping his disbelief. "Your wives have left you? And it's somehow *my* fault?" He jerked free of Everstone's grip and vibrated with the urge to plant his aching fists in the middle of their strained and bloated faces. "You're mad—stark raving lunatics—the lot of you! I should have known two months ago—the minute you started blathering on about dragons and marriage traps—"

As he said the words "marriage" and "trap" in the same breath, he suffered an intense revisitation of the morning's argument with Antonia. She had gestured to some women he had never seen before—young women—and had spoken of their miserable marriages. She said they had fled overwork and maltreatment, callousness and indifference, in the marriages she had made for them.

"Good God," he said, staring at them, "they were *your* wives." As they looked at each other in confusion, he realized that part of Antonia's anger and distrust of marriage had come from the way these wretches had treated the women she had married off to them. And he knew if he didn't leave immediately—now—that he was going to do exactly what he had imagined doing when he set foot in the bar: plant his fists right in the middle of their infuriating faces.

"Well, I'd say you got exactly what you wanted, gents," he snarled. "You got rid of a bit of unwanted baggage and got your precious freedom back in the bargain." Shoving them roughly aside, he strode for the door.

They looked at one another for a minute, torn between red-eared chagrin and impotent fury. In the same moment each of them made the same decision, and together they scrambled for the door. Racing up the steps and into the lobby, they saw the porter handing Remington his hat and walking stick.

"Landon!" Everstone called out. "You can't jus' walk out on us!"

"Oh, but I can," Remington said with a furious gleam in his eye, donning his hat. "Watch me."

He stepped out into the street. And as the doorman stood holding the door for them, thinking they intended to exit as well, they did just that. Rushing out into the street, they spotted Remington headed for the cab stand two blocks down and lumbered after him, calling his name.

He heard them coming and quickened his step. Swinging up into an open cab door, he snarled his address to the driver. But before the door closed and the driver could get under way, his pursuers seized the horses and prevented them from moving.

"Drive on!" Remington ordered the driver.

"Dammit, Landon!" Everstone shouted. "You're to blame for the entire thing!"

"You've wrecked our marriages—you owe us!" Woolworth declared.

"You didn't marry her and put her out of business. Now we're paying for it!" Richard Searle gave the cab door a punishing thump with his fist. "Come down out of there and talk to us man to man!"

"Driver—there's a tenner in it for you if you get this cab moving now!" Remington snarled. With added incentive the driver slapped the reins sharply and the coach lurched forward, sending Howard and Trueblood—by the horses—skittering out of the way.

The five abandoned husbands stood in the street, panting, shouting, and shaking fists as the vehicle disappeared from sight. Then as their outbursts thinned and died on the silence, they wilted and stumbled back to the club, looking as if the stuffing had just been knocked out of them.

Behind them, in a darkened doorway near the street-lamp where they had besieged Remington's cab, Rupert Fitch stood with his yellow pad exposed. He checked his list of names to be sure he had them all: Everstone, Wool-worth, Trueblood, Howard, and Searle. But in truth, there was only one name that mattered: Remington Carr, Earl of Landon.

Fitch grinned to himself. Wagers with voluptuous wid-ows, midnight liaisons gone awry, virulent suffragette dem-onstrations, and now a juicy tale of marital carnage: the wrecked marriages of prominent men and accusations of responsibility. Who would have guessed three months ago that his intense and speculative scrutiny of the unorthodox earl's doings would bear such fruit? The man was a verita-ble gold mine—a whole career's worth of scandals and outrages walking around on two feet!

Fitch congratulated himself as he tucked his pad away and swaggered down the street. In his mind he began plan-ning how he would spend the bonus his editor had prom-ised if *Gaflinger's* sales jumped yet another five percent. He grinned. A few wrecked marriages ought to be good for at least *seven*.

Maybe he'd buy a new hat.

The offices of Carr Enterprises were ominously silent the next noon. There was not a typewriter "clack," a squeak of pen, or a rustle of paper to be heard. Words were ex-changed only in whispers, and everyone seemed to be walking on tiptoes.

Remington sat gazing at one calamity and listening to another. On his desk was the front page of *Gaflinger's*, bearing the headline:

SOCIETY MARRIAGES ON ROCKS—LANDON TO BLAME!

And standing before his desk was Markham, telling him that not only had the Sutton Mills loan been denied, but Carr Enterprises had been put on the "short list"— categorized with firms and concerns considered to be unacceptable risks. His stomach felt as if it were being crumpled in a fist, and his eyes felt hot and grainy from the sleepless and regrettably sober night he had just passed.

Things could scarcely get any worse. There was a crowd of outraged Methodists outside his offices all morning, protesting his flagrant sin and immorality. The building owner had paid him a call and insisted that Carr Enterprises sell back its lease immediately, and now there were news writers crawling along the building ledges, shouting questions at him through his office windows. His social reputation was in tatters, his financial standing would soon be lying in the gutter, and the scandals being attached to his name were enough to blacken the once honorable title of Landon for generations to come.

Purely hypothetical generations, he realized; no woman in her right mind would consent to bear children for a woman-attacking, suffragette-enraging, marriage-wrecking beast, even if it did entitle her to be called "m'lady."

But with all that, the thing that weighed heaviest on his heart was that he wouldn't be seeing Antonia . . . not today, nor tomorrow, nor perhaps ever again.

She didn't like him, she didn't trust him, and didn't need him. And in the four days she had spent in his world, he hadn't managed to change her opinion of him, or of marriage to him, in the least. To make it worse, the killing stroke to his hopes had been supplied by his own dear, dotty old uncle, who had managed to progress from "second childhood" to "second adolescence" and had fallen passionately in love with her aunt and eloped after only a three-day acquaintance.

Three days. He sighed. Things were apparently a lot less complicated at age seventy. People just got down to business and fell in love, and didn't let little things like pride, personal history, or social philosophy get in the way.

He slowly straightened and his eyes widened. They fell in love.

A house falling on him couldn't have had more impact.

He had fallen in love, too. Hopelessly, deliriously, inexplicably in love with Antonia Paxton. That's what this peculiar malady was that had him raging between fever and chills from minute to minute: love. He wasn't sure how he knew; he just *knew* . . . with every nerve in his aching body.

He buried his face in his hands and groaned. Oh, God, he was in trouble. He was in love for the first time in his life —and with a woman who didn't trust him enough to believe him if he said it was Tuesday!

And in eight short days, when his wedding announcement failed to appear in *The Times*, the queen was going to have his head on a platter . . . or something equally memorable and instructive to the lower orders.

Eight days, as it happened, was a rather optimistic estimate. That same afternoon the queen's keen ears detected the low hum of scandal vibrating through her personal audiences at Buckingham Palace. In an unprecedented move she withdrew to her sitting room and demanded that her secretary procure for her a copy of that scandal sheet, *Gaflinger's*. He didn't have to go far; there was a copy in the footman's boot, another in the undersecretary's desk, and a third being passed from pillar to post in the kitchens.

Victoria had him hold it up for her, so that she

wouldn't have to touch it, and donned her spectacles to peruse the headlines. She blanched. "Read it to me," she demanded. "I want to hear every single word."

Her color returned and deepened as she learned that several "leading gentlemen" had accosted the Earl of Landon in the street the previous night and accused him of wrecking their marriages. No names were given, apart from the evil earl's, but it was revealed that two of the men were prominent young lords and one was a well-known MP and Knight of the Garter. The queen's royal person puffed with outrage, and before he had quite finished the reading, she thrust to her feet and sent immediately for the prime minister.

Discovering he was in love was such a distracting and disorienting experience that it took Remington a while to recover his equilibrium. It was a measure of just how far off his game he was, that it wasn't until afternoon that he realized he didn't need a *good* reason to see her; any old excuse would do to get him inside the door. And those idiots last night had handed him the perfect way to get her attention. He could claim to be there to plead their case . . . and in doing so, plead his own.

On the way to her house he rehearsed several opening gambits and straightened his tie at least a dozen times. By the time he descended from his carriage and reached for the familiar brass knocker, his mouth was dry and his palms were damp. When there was no response, he imagined old Hoskins standing on the other side of the door with a belligerent glare, and set the side of his fist to the door.

When the door finally swung open, it was Eleanor who greeted him. Her eyes were puffy, her shoulders were rounded, and there was an air of exhaustion about her.

"Your lordship." She glanced anxiously over her shoulder. "I'm afraid you've come at a bad time."

"I have to see her, Eleanor." He sounded a bit too desperate in his own ears and spoke louder. "And I intend to stand here and pound on the door until she sees me. I ran into a few of her former 'victims' last night and they told me that their wives . . . had left. . . ." He scowled, realizing that his words were having no effect.

"It's Cleo!" Eleanor blurted out, tears spilling down her cheeks. "She's dying!"

Remington felt as if he'd been sucker punched. His head snapped back and he found it difficult to draw breath. "How? What happened?"

"A stroke, the doctor says. It happened just after you left yesterday. Lady Toni has been with her all night . . . won't leave her side."

Remington pushed the door back himself and entered, heading straight for the stairs at the rear of the hall. Eleanor trotted along after him, directing him to Cleo's room. In the hallway he passed Molly and Maude and Prudence and Pollyanna. Each met the distress in his gaze with shared misery and reached out to give his hand a squeeze as he passed.

In Cleo's room he found Antonia bending over Cleo, bathing her face. For a moment he stared at the old lady's small form in the middle of the large bed. Without the liveliness of her eyes and the restless, birdlike energy of her movements, she looked gaunt and drawn, every bit of her more than eighty years. Emotions deep inside him wrenched painfully tight.

Antonia heard someone moving behind her, straightened as if her back were aching, and looked around. She froze at the sight of him.

"Antonia," he said softly. She was wearing the same dress she had worn yesterday, and she looked as tired and rumpled as it did. It was all he could do to keep from pulling her into his arms.

"What are you doing here?" she whispered in choked tones, searching his face, unable to believe her senses. She was terrified of moving, afraid of discovering that he was only a hysterical vision conjured by her pain and longing. Just the minute before, she had been wishing with all her heart that she could see him, and touch him, and feel that precious surge of sensual energy that he always generated in her.

"How is she?" he asked, ignoring her question. He paused by the foot of the bed, then slowly worked his way up the side of it to Antonia.

"There's no change," she said just above a whisper. "She hasn't awakened."

Every step he took seemed to force air into her chest, to make her breathe deeper, and to pour much-needed strength into her wilted spirit. His eyes were soft in the dim light, and the subtle spice of his soap mingled with the scent of his starched shirt in her head. He looked so genuinely concerned, so caring, that her knees weakened and she had to work to remain upright.

"Are you all right?" he said, putting out a hand to steady her. "When did you sleep last? Have you had anything to eat?"

She shook her head, nodded, then looked up, confused. His touch and her hunger for the solidity and surety it offered combined to overcome her pride. It felt as if she had been here forever, worrying, praying, tending Cleo. And now that her spirits were at low ebb, he appeared and all she could think was that she wanted to curl up against him and feel his warmth all around and through her.

"Toni," he said softly. And then because he couldn't help himself, because he was aching inside, too, and because he needed to touch her as much as she needed to be touched just then, he took the risk of a lifetime. He reached out to cradle her face in his hands. He held his breath.

And she didn't pull away.

Her eyes closed as she absorbed his touch, letting the solace of it pour into her aching heart.

"Why don't you get some rest? There are plenty of others to sit with her."

"No, I want to stay. I need to stay," she whispered, feeling tears seeping between her lashes.

"Then I'll stay, too."

He left no room for negotiation. He simply stayed through the rest of the afternoon and into the evening, watching, waiting with her. He helped to bathe old Cleo's face and raise her head for a drink of water. And as night came on, he removed his coat and spelled Antonia in the chair by the bed, holding the old lady's cool, reedy hand in his.

Unconsciously, he adopted Antonia's curious habit of speaking to the old woman, despite the fact that she was half-deaf and asleep. He told her about the new shows and plays being staged in the Vauxhall and Covent Gardens and promised to take her to one when she woke up. He reminded her that she had a lot of responsibilities; memories to dust and stories to tell. And as the night deepened and gloom settled over the chamber, he glanced at Antonia and told Cleo that she was worrying Lady Toni half to death and that she'd better stop this nonsense and wake up, so Lady Toni could get some rest.

It was a good thing Antonia had her arm around the post at the foot of the bed; without its support she would have slid to the floor as his words weakened her knees. He saw her wilt and had his arms around her in a minute, transferring her dependence from the bedpost to his arms.

"Lean on me, sweetheart." He pulled her close and held her, giving her his strength and, in a more subtle way, offering her whatever else she might need from him. Neither heard Eleanor slip out and close the door behind her, leaving them alone.

The feel of his arms around her released her tears, and her shoulders trembled as she cried against his chest. He lifted her into his arms and carried her to the wing chair in the corner. Settling her on his lap, he cradled her head against his shoulder and caressed her hair and back with soothing strokes, giving her what comfort he could.

"I'm so afraid of losing her," she murmured into his collar. "I couldn't bear it."

"I know," he said, realizing with some surprise that he did indeed know. There was a soft spot in him for old Cleo, who, if her stories could be believed, might even have been his mother. And he sensed those feelings were a pale shadow of the pain he would feel if it were Uncle Paddington lying there, so still and cold.

"She won't die, sweetheart," he whispered against her hair, his voice thick with emotion. "She'll be all right, I promise you."

She lifted her head from his shoulder with a small, forgiving smile that said such promises were not his to make. Her eyes and nose were red from crying, and her lips showed the marks of her teeth. In that moment she was part angry child, part grieving woman, part hurting lover. And the ache crushing through his chest was for all three. From his depths rose a powerful urge to comfort her, to protect her, to merge his turbulent feelings with hers . . . and in that union, to make something that would last through the hurt and loss.

He took her face between his hands and brought his lips to hers. Sensation flowed, heightened by awareness of pain, fermented into a river of rich and complex pleasure . . . filling empty places, assuaging sorrow and loss and disappointment . . . both past and present.

Her head slanted and her lips parted. She drank him in, seeking his warmth and vitality, sliding her arms around him and pressing her body against his. Uncertainty and fear receded to the edges of her mind as his kisses washed softly through her, caressing her raw and tender nerves with each loving motion, healing, binding up her frayed emotions.

For a few brief moments she wrapped herself in him, reveling in the feel of his hands on her body, in the hardness and latent power of his frame. Her fingers slid over his collar and tie and loosened them. His skin was smooth and hard underneath, and as she caressed and kissed what she could reach of him, she drew strength from the familiarity of him.

Their kisses lightened, becoming nips and brushes of intimacy as they reached a mutual boundary. And together they settled into a passion-warmed but companionable embrace that was somehow different from anything they had shared before.

"She says such things. And somehow, coming from her, words seem wiser and truer than when others say them," she said. "The other day she asked me if I'd ever waltzed. When I said I hadn't, she said, 'Don't wait forever. None of us has forever.'" Tears welled in her eyes again. "I'm afraid she was right."

"That doesn't mean she is out of time altogether," he said quietly. When she looked up, he was gazing at Cleo. "Talk to me, Toni. Tell me about her."

Antonia laid her head against his shoulder and began to talk. She told him about meeting Cleo and bringing her home, and about the old lady's early encounters with Hoskins, the neighbors, and the workmen who came to build shelves in the study. She smiled, warmed by the memories, and lulled by his presence into surrendering some of the anxiety she held so tightly. He was right; talking somehow eased the pain.

As one hour passed, then another, they took turns checking Cleo, giving her water, and holding her hand. His warm smiles and unswerving confidence in Cleo's powers of recovery were a tonic for Antonia's strained emotions. When he repeatedly insisted she sit for a while and rest, she finally relented. And the last thing she saw as her eyes closed was Remington holding Cleo's hand.

Some time later she awakened with a start, in a mild panic. She couldn't find Remington at first in the dim candlelight, but as she shoved to her feet and hurried toward the bed, she stopped, staring at the sight of him.

He was sitting on the bed, his back braced against the headboard, with Cleo wrapped in a comforter on his lap. He was cradling her in his arms the same way he had that day in the study. His head was tipped back against the bedstead and his eyes were closed. At the sound of her movement they opened and fastened on her.

"What are you doing?" she asked. But she knew somehow before he answered.

"She asked me to hold her before when she was cold. And she seemed . . . so cold a while ago. . . ." He ground to a halt, looking a bit vexed by his own reasoning. He wanted to warm and comfort her, and that seemed the most direct and comforting way . . . the way Cleo had once chosen herself.

Antonia smiled through the tears collecting in her eyes. She knew in that moment that she was wholly, madly, and hopelessly in love with Remington Carr. And this one breathtakingly tender moment—feeling this overwhelming, exhilarating surge of love and affection and pride in him—would be worth all that had gone before and all that would come after. In all her life she had never known anything as powerfully sweet and enthralling as the emotion swelling in her breast. And she realized she'd probably been in love with him since the first time she'd seen Cleo in his arms.

"You don't think I should?" he said, frowning lightly, watching the play of powerful emotion across her face and praying that at least some of it was good.

She went to the bed and climbed up in it beside him, stroking Cleo's face.

"I think it's exactly what she would want. She always did like handsome men. And you, Remington Carr, are without a doubt the handsomest man I've ever seen."

"I am?" The tension drained from his expression, and he gave her a smile that was nothing short of dazzling, even in candlelight. Especially in candlelight. "That's a good thing to know."

They sat like that for some time holding hands, holding Cleo, and feeling they had turned a corner.

The gray light coming in around the covered window said it was nearly dawn. Eleanor crept back into the room and paused, confused by the sight of Antonia and Remington sitting in the bed, holding Cleo on their laps. Her gasp of surprise jolted them to awareness, and Antonia slid quickly from the bed.

While she tried to explain, Remington returned their patient to her bed and tucked the covers around her. Then, as he turned away, he caught sight of her lips moving. He whirled back and sank to his knees by the bed, calling her name.

"Her lips moved—I saw it! Cleo—Cleo can you hear me?"

Antonia and Eleanor rushed to his side, holding their breath, their eyes fixed on Cleo's face. After an agonizing delay and more prompting from Remington, the old lady's eyes fluttered and her mouth moved.

Galvanized, they all began to call to her, coaxing her

back to them. After a few moments her mumbles became clearer.

"C-come back . . . n-naughty F-Fox . . . I'm cold."

"Cleo—" Antonia cried, squeezing the old woman's hand. "Can you feel my hand? Do you know who I am?"

Cleo's eyes fluttered open and she seemed a bit confused. But after a bit she seemed to grasp that Remington wasn't Fox, that she was in her bed, and that she was going to be all right. Before she drifted back to sleep, she did manage to say "Toni," and Antonia threw her arms around Remington in an outburst of joy.

Ever a man to make the most of a possibility, Remington covered her mouth with his, kissing her fully and passionately until she broke away to beam up at him through tears of happiness.

"I have to tell the others! They've all been sick with worry!"

In mere moments the room was filled with women in robes and dressing gowns, hugging and laughing and wiping tears. Remington was roundly hugged and patted and cried on, just as if he were one of them. And it didn't occur to him for a moment that he wasn't. But when Antonia made the round of joyful embraces and returned to him, he felt her soft curves pressing his side and it finally did occur to him. And he decided that being just "one of the girls" wasn't quite enough. He took her by the wrist and dragged her toward the door.

"What are you . . . ?" Antonia said, looking up at him. "I can't leave—someone still has to stay with her."

He turned to Eleanor, who was by the door. "You'll sit with her, won't you? Toni is exhausted and I'm going to put her to bed . . . and then go home."

Eleanor nodded with glistening eyes, and Remington pulled Antonia out the door and down the hall to her room.

Something in the deliberate way he closed her door behind them and turned the key in the lock sent a shiver up her spine. When he came toward her, she caught her breath at the sensuous light in his eyes.

"I thought you were putting me to . . ."

"Bed. And so I am." He ripped off his vest, shed his suspenders, and pulled the studs from his shirtfront while she stood watching, stunned. Every movement telegraphed his intentions, and he watched her eyes widen as he jerked his shirttail from his trousers and opened his French cuffs.

"And you were going home," she managed.

"Oh, I will . . . sooner or later." He flashed a wicked grin. "Buttons, sweetheart. I've waited a long time for this, and you'd better get busy if you want to keep that lovely dress in one piece."

She began to fumble with her bodice buttons, hesitantly at first. Her heart was beginning to pound and her body was flushing with warmth. He was going to make love to her. And—oh, Lord—and she was going to make love to him—to the man she loved with all her heart!

Her fingers flew over her buttons, eagerness interfering with skill. She felt his eyes on her as she jerked the buttons from their loops and quickly dropped the bodice and started on her belt and skirt. Layer after layer hit the floor: skirt, petticoat, corset cover, and—with his help—corset. Then there were shoes, garters, and stockings, and in a shocking burst of rebellion, those white silk drawers with their pink satin ribbons.

She looked up to find him stepping out of his trousers, naked as the day he was born. And she gasped. The enormity of what he was about to do—not to mention the enormity of what he was about to do it with—froze her in place with her arms wrapped protectively over her breasts. For all her bravado and marital experience, she had still never seen a man's fully naked body in her life. The sight was fascinating, terrifying, and somehow humorous, all at once. She bit her lip and watched in guilty fascination as he strode to the bed, threw back the counterpane and comforter, and turned for her.

She was standing there with her eyes as big as saucers and her arms clasping her body as if it were on loan from a vestal virgin. He gave her an indecently appreciative smile and braced with his hands on his hips, letting his hungry gaze roam her bare feet and pale legs and settle on her glaring white chemise.

"Off with it, sweetheart." His voice was a seductive growl. "I have no more secrets from you, and I think, by now, I'm entitled to see the gift without the wrapping."

She blushed and, when he made a move toward her, backed a step. "I'll just . . . leave this on . . . if it's all the same to you."

It wasn't all the same to him. But he studied her trim ankles, her shapely calves, and her reluctance, and decided to let it go for now. He reached out his hand and waited for her to put hers in it. He hadn't realized his heart had stopped—waiting—until her touch started it again. With a wonderfully wicked and joyful laugh, he pulled her into his arms and poured a kiss over her mouth that ignited a flame in her blood.

"Love me," she said between whiskey-hot pulls of his mouth, "until I'm drunk with it."

"I intend to," he declared between voluptuous bites of her neck. "And this time I won't care if the queen herself walks into the damned room!"

By the time he sank with her into the center of that soft feather mattress, all he could think about was the sweetness of her mouth and the ripening hunger of her frame beneath his. And all she could think about was the heat of his skin against hers and the delicious determination of his body above hers. Each kiss, each touch, bore a quiet ferocity, a defiant joy at being alive and whole and together at last.

Soon he peeled open the placket of her chemise, lowered his head, and dragged long, liquid kisses over the curves of her breasts, up her throat and across her mouth. The trail of liquid fire he left both chilled and burned her skin. As she shivered with response and reached for him, she felt him lifting away from her and sliding down her body. She opened her eyes and gasped as his chest settled provocatively over her lower legs, trapping them, and he laid a kiss on her bare thigh, at the edge of her chemise.

"What are you . . . ?" She tried to sit up, but he pushed her back down with a sensuous growl.

"Close your eyes, sweetheart, and just enjoy."

Shocked by the sight of his head at her bare knees, she was grateful to do as he suggested. But to her surprise, the veil of darkness that closed over her sight somehow heightened her other senses. His mouth against her thigh felt as if it were reaching through her very skin. Pools of heat formed in her muscles, collecting the liquid sensations he was pouring along the curve of her leg. And he added tantalizing flutters and sensuous raking motions that caused her to hold her breath.

With exquisite patience he proceeded up the slope of one thigh and then the other, nudging the fabric farther up her leg with each brush of his lips. Then he paused and slyly pushed the back of her chemise up, using her own responsive movement to free it beneath her. When his kisses resumed on the curve of her hip, she squeezed her eyes tighter and tried not to give in to the urges that were trembling her limbs and slithering through her body.

Ah, but he wanted her to give in to them; he demanded she surrender to them unconditionally. And when he nuzzled the curls at the base of her belly, she gasped and squirmed, part in protest, part in invitation. His tongue darted along that sensitive groove and found her aching center. Almost before she realized what he was doing, he had moved on.

Inch by delicious inch, her chemise retreated up her body: along her waist, up her ribs, and over her breasts. He literally kissed it from her, collecting and savoring every responsive movement of her body along the way. She writhed and undulated, exploring some sensations, begging others. Her hands flew over his bare shoulders, her fingers wound through his hair, and as he gradually stretched out over her body, her legs entwined with his, exploring his own long, muscular limbs.

She opened her eyes and found him staring down at her, his eyes black and hungry in the soft, filtered light. And as she watched, transfixed by the hunger in his face, his mouth reached her breast and fastened possessively on her nipple. She gasped, watching the movement of his mouth against her . . . suckling, teasing, nipping her tightly aroused flesh.

Suddenly every muscle in her body was hot and primed; she had to move, to find his body with hers. She tugged at him, whispering, "Now . . . now . . . now . . ."

He curved over her, molding to her, settling hard into the hollow between her parting thighs. He fitted himself against her and began to move, rasping her sensitive flesh, varying each thrust, watching her response. And when she wrapped her legs around him and arched against him, whispering his name again and again, he realized the time had come, drew back, and entered her.

She stilled, holding her breath, then met his second thrust, and his third with strained, seeking motions. It was familiar and yet so very different . . . the fullness, the liquid heat, the ripples of sensation, the sweet burning that was like an itch permeating her flesh. Only that divine contact, only that searing penetration could relieve her need, and she tightened her legs around his, welcoming him, claiming him, taking him deeper. Suddenly he was there . . . all of him . . . hers . . . hot, driving. When he stilled within her, she still felt a pulse of movement. Through the churning roil of sensation came the realization that it was his heartbeat . . . within her . . . joined to her.

She went still and opened her eyes and lifted his head from her shoulder to look into his eyes. Could he feel hers, too? In all her life she had never imagined the intimacy of that moment. Breast to breast, bodies joined, hearts pounding . . . it was as if they were one body, one flesh.

"Two hearts, beating as one," she whispered, unaware she had said it aloud, or that Remington would know both what it meant and where it came from.

But he did know. He sank his arms beneath her, cradling her head in one of his hands. "I feel yours, too, sweetheart. Come with me . . . now. . . ."

Then he joined their mouths and began to move within her.

Long-denied hungers flared and drove them together with an intensity that defied all attempts at control. They arched and strained, reaching for each other, exploring the depth and breadth of pleasures both had waited a lifetime to experience. She rippled and writhed beneath him, abandoned to all but the sense of him and the delicious tension mounting in her body. Quicker, closer, harder they pressed, until she was caught by a torrential updraft that flung her aloft, through barriers of self and sensation.

Her senses shattered, releasing her from her body and propelling her into realms of pure emotion, pure being. And as she soared, filled with brilliant, expanding light, she felt him rising and taking flight with her. The boundaries of self dissolved, and for a time they mingled without the encumbrance of thought or even action. In the pure essence of love, each knew completely and was completely known.

And as they slowly returned to their senses, quaking with release, shuddering with pleasure, each knew beyond all doubt that they were loved.

Remington slid onto his side, turning her with him, sheltering her heated body against him as the passion-storm passed. He grinned at the feel of her bare skin under his hands as he stroked her.

"Ah, sweetheart, you feel so—" But as he drew back to look at her, he found her eyes closed and her body suddenly limp against him. She was exhausted. He smiled and brushed her hair back from her damp face, pressing a kiss on the end of her nose. And in moments he was asleep, too.

Antonia awakened some time later to an exquisite ache in her loins and the compensat-
ing warmth of a large, hard body pressed
against her shoulder, hip, and thigh. She looked up to find
Remington propped on an elbow against her, watching her
sleep. His eyes were that soft chocolate color she loved and
were half-closed to match the half smile he wore.

"I thought maybe you'd sleep the rest of the day," he
murmured near her ear, his hand skimming her waist.

"What would you have done if I had?" she said sleepily,
running her fingers over his face, tracing the slope of his
nose and the plane of his cheek.

"I would have stayed here the rest of the day, watching
you." He looked deep into her eyes. "Watching over you."

She felt a glow of sunlike warmth inside and tilted her
head to look at him. "When I looked up and saw you
standing in Cleo's room . . . I don't think I've ever felt so
grateful to see anyone in my life." She closed her eyes and
nuzzled her face against his bare chest. "I'd already lost
Aunt Hermione . . . I was so afraid of losing Cleo, too."

He smiled at her kittenish movements, then wrapped
his arms around her and drew her close, settling into a
more thoughtful mood.

"You will, you know." When she opened her eyes and
looked up at him quizzically, he took a heavy breath. "You

will lose her someday, Toni. She's lived a long and interesting life, but she won't live forever. I don't think she even wants to."

She sat up abruptly, disturbed, and he sat up with her. "Toni?" After a moment he turned her face back to him. "They're all old ladies, sweetheart. What will you do when they're gone?"

She looked up at him with her emotions reeling. What would she do without them? They were her family, her life. She felt as if the bottom had suddenly dropped out of her heart. They would die one by one and leave her . . . alone.

He stroked her face to bring her gaze back to him.

"I'll be here with you, sweetheart. Tomorrow, next week, next year . . . year after year . . . just as I was last night."

As he was last night, when she needed him. The thought flowed through her with the clinging sweetness of honey. *She needed him.* It wasn't frightening or diminishing at all, certainly not in the ways she had feared. She needed him as she needed the air she breathed and the food she ate, like sunlight and laughter and warmth. She had needed him last night, and he was there to comfort her, to share her worry and heartache. Now he was here to share her joy and pleasure. And there was no other in the world with whom she could share the powerful and soul-rending things that had just passed between them—not Hermione nor Cleo nor any of her ladies. She had not even shared such things with Sir Geoffrey, who had been her husband.

Somehow she understood: these were feelings and experiences shaped into loving acts by the love she bore him. It was her love for him that made the difference.

He watched her coming to terms with it and held his breath, hoping that he had said enough, and not too much. The soft melancholy of her face slowly gave way to a sweeter expression, a glow of acceptance, then a loving look. And he knew it was all right.

"I was wrong. I do need you, Remington Carr."

It was more than all right, he realized. He grinned and kissed her, wrapping her in his arms and sinking back onto the bolsters with her. But the joy in him was too exuberant to be contained in just kisses. He felt like running, jumping, shouting—like squeezing her to him until her body melted into his. He pulled her harder against him, his eyes snapping with sensual energy.

"Let's see, now. You've decided you like me. And you need me. What's left? Oh, yes. *Trust*." A pulse of pleasure darkened his eyes as he ran his hands down her body and felt her shiver of response. "I think we may have dispensed with that little objection to me as well."

"We have?" She blushed as she recalled her vehement charges against him. "You think I trust you now?" It was a question she asked herself as much as him. "And what gives you that idea?"

"This, sweetheart." He glanced down at her bare body, pressed intimately against his. He dragged his fingers up the side of her hip, across her waist, and over the tightly contracted tip of her breast . . . watching the flow of his fingers and appreciating the lush territory they covered.

Her gaze followed his, watching his hand, feeling the delicious rivulets of sensation that trickled from his fingertips through her skin. What made him think . . . ? Then it struck her, she was seeing *bare* skin. Stunned by the sight of his hand caressing her bare breast, she lay motionless, watching, feeling, and realizing that somewhere in the fury of their loving he had managed to coax her out of her chemise as well as out of her inhibitions.

"Ohhh—" She tried to cover herself, but he caught her arm and redirected it around his side. Then she tried to roll away, but he stopped her by sliding his body over hers.

"Sweetheart, it's a little late for modesty. I've already made more than a passing acquaintance with your naked self. And with your encouragement, I might add. Look at me." Slowly she opened her eyes and found herself looking up into his frankly admiring gaze. "You're beautiful, Antonia . . . your face, your eyes, your body. And I love looking at you. Where's the harm in that?"

It was easier to ignore her nakedness with him covering her like a blanket, and she calmed, though her face and entire breast felt as if they were on fire. "I'm not sure it's quite decent, somehow. I would just feel better with . . ." She glanced away.

"With a few buttons between us?" he finished for her. "The sainted Geoffrey never saw you without your clothes, did he? Tell me, Toni. And I won't ever mention it again." When she wouldn't answer, he began to worry. "Toni, did he hurt you?"

Her tension eased as she recognized the protectiveness that had shaped his question. She shook her head.

"No, Geoffrey was a kind and gentle man . . . just very . . . modest."

"He made you wear a nightgown," he supplied, adding on impulse: "with lots of buttons."

She blushed and looked away, uncomfortable. But in the sheltered confines of her bed, with his warm, solid body pressed intimately against hers, she felt the urge to confide what she had never spoken of to anyone.

"After a while he declined to visit my bed—" Her eyes clouded with a memory that caused her to draw back. "Never mind. It's not important now."

"It is if it troubles you. He left your bed? What on earth could have happened to make him abandon making love to you?"

Some of the hot color drained from her face and she

tried to push him off her. "I really don't see what that has to do with you . . . or us."

"What was it, Toni?" He refused to release her, sensing from her agitation that he was close to the truth. "Did he make you do things you found repugnant?"

"No, he didn't," she said irritably, trying again to lever him to the side and slide from beneath him. It was no use. The more she tried to escape, the more determined he became. She halted and finally gave him what he demanded.

"He wanted me to *not* do things!"

"To *not* do . . . what things?" It took him a moment to realize what her adamant silence meant. "You mean *that* thing?" he said, eyes widening as he recalled her reaction to her first taste of pleasure with him, and her shamed confession that she had reached a climax before. "You reached a climax and he didn't want you to?"

Again her silence confirmed his supposition. It shouldn't have astonished him, but it did. He knew that many men believed it was detrimental for their wives to respond during sex . . . said it ruined their character, made them loose and unruly and untrustworthy. Such men saved their caresses and lubricious attentions for the already "ruined" Hillarys and Carlottas of the world, while their wives got only dry, miserable duty in their beds.

"The old fool," he said, looking at her with disbelief that slid quickly into anger. "He left your bed because of that?" Her nod was barely perceptible.

"I didn't agree with his decision, and one night I went to him and I . . ." She blushed from the tips of her breasts upward as she recalled that night in her husband's room. Sir Geoffrey had stood watching her as she . . . "unbuttoned my nightdress and showed myself to him, hoping to . . . to . . ." She couldn't say it and so he did.

"Seduce him." He nodded. "And?"

"And I managed to humiliate both him and myself. I had never seen him angry before that night. He buttoned me up, from neck to toe, and sent me straight back to my room like a . . . a . . ."

"Naughty child," he supplied. "And you stayed 'buttoned up' ever since." He began to smile. No wonder she had reacted so strongly when he cut off her buttons that day in the parlor! "Well, if you hadn't already guessed, sweetheart, I don't share his modesty or his restraint. I don't mind being seduced in the least. And on occasion I have been known to behave like a naughty child myself." With a grin that was some part relief, some part rebellion, he pushed up onto his elbows. "Come with me, Lady Antonia."

He rolled from her and from the bed, pulling her up with him. She squirmed and resisted, blushing furiously as he dragged her across the floor and stood her in front of the pier glass. Shocked, she twisted and shoved at his arms, but he tightened them forbiddingly around her waist and ordered her to look at herself. She clamped her eyes shut and he chuckled and began in sultry tones to describe her to herself.

"God—you are a piece of work, Antonia Paxton. Look at those, long, silky legs . . . ummm . . . trim little ankles . . . strong, sleek thighs." His hand joined the exploration as he reached her hip. "Extraordinary curves . . . a soft little belly . . . sweet curls . . ." He brushed them with his fingers, and she groaned. "Very nice waist, Antonia . . . and then some of my favorite parts . . . your lovely breasts." He held her against his body with his elbows, freeing his hands to cup her breasts. "Round and soft . . . just made to fill my hands . . . and those long, pouty nipples . . . tight little swatches of velvet. Ummm, how they make you squirm. I do like the way you squirm, sweetheart."

She went still and caught her breath as he rolled her nipples back and forth between fingers and thumbs. Her knees gradually weakened and the fight drained from her as she surrendered to his hot words and tactile persuasions. On impulse she opened her eyes, filtering the sight of her naked body through her lashes.

Then with his seductive words flowing into her ear and his supple hands flowing over her body, she opened her eyes wider, and still wider. She looked at herself, then at the tantalizing outline of his body behind hers. His strong arms wrapped her, his agile hands cupped and caressed and skimmed her body with sensuous assurance. And the sight of him claiming her nakedness both unnerved and reassured her.

She dragged her gaze up the legs in the mirror, then over the hips, up the small waist and to the full, rose-tipped breasts. She met his eyes in the mirror. They were glowing with pride and desire and not a little mischief.

"What do you think? Isn't she the most beautiful naked woman you've ever seen?"

She blushed and laughed with an edge of embarrassment. "She's the only naked woman I've ever seen."

"Well, she's not the first I've seen . . . though I admit some have been on French postcards—ow!" She had jabbed his ribs with her elbow, and he straightened and grinned. "Well, I told you I was naughty sometimes."

He turned her around and pulled her hard against him, with their sides to the mirror. "Look at us." Thigh to thigh, breast to breast, they stood looking at the softly merged lines of their bodies in the glass. They were like a statue or a painting, one of Winterhalter's sylvan romps.

"Any time you want to 'unbutton' in my presence, sweetheart, feel free."

Feel free. That was exactly what she was doing and she liked it—the sound, the feel of it, the way it resonated through her body, bringing her to life. She stepped out of his arms and swayed across the room to the bed, sensing his eyes on her as she stretched her arms wide, rolled her shoulders, then arched her back and wiggled her hips, trying out her new freedom.

"I think I like this," she said, turning to him, drawing him toward her with a sultry look. Nakedness was not all she was trying out, he realized. "What if I come to like it too much?"

"I believe that was precisely what old Sir Geoffrey was afraid of," he said huskily, watching her hands gliding down her sides and then up her ribs, brushing the tips of her breasts. He saw the flicker of pleasure in her eyes and felt his temperature rise. "I'll try to see that you get loose and libidinous only in my presence." ·

"And how will you manage that?" she said, squirming seductively, and watching the effect it had on him.

"By keeping you . . . busy," he said, feeling his throat tightening at the way she was twitching her hips, moving to some internal rhythm.

"Ummm . . . I like being busy." Her eyes darkened to an alluring midnight-blue. "But what if I'm not busy enough? What if I get unruly and loose and wicked? What if I get . . . out of control?"

"Every husband's nightmare," he breathed softly, unable to pull his eyes from the erotic movements of her hands over her body. He felt a sudden pang of sympathy for knotty old Sir Geoffrey. The old boy hadn't had a prayer of keeping up with her, and obviously knew it. "Believe me, sweetheart, I have never suffered the illusion that I have ever been in control of you."

"Ummm." She halted, her eyes half-closed, her arms wrapped around her just beneath her breasts so that she looked like the veriest temptress he had ever seen, French postcards or otherwise. "What if I decide to take up a placard and demand the vote?" As she swayed across the room, he watched her legs flex and her hips swing provocatively. Then she stood in the middle of the clothes they had shed and demanded, "Or what if I decide to take up wearing trousers?"

He felt the bedpost at his back and leaned heavily against it, watching in heated fascination as she reached for his trousers and, with an eye on him, held them open. First one pale leg, then the other, sank inside the black legs of his trousers as she raised them to her waist. With her lip caught between her teeth, she worked the buttons, then released the trousers, letting them sink so that they caught on her hips. She laughed softly and bent to roll up the bottoms so she could walk. Catching sight of his starched collar and tie on the floor, she wrapped them around her throat and swayed to the mirror to tie his tie. With the collar in place beneath a creditable knot, she turned this way and that, watching his reaction in the mirror.

"Well, what do you think?" She strolled seductively toward him, his trousers hanging just below her navel, her throat bound in his proper collar and tie, and her breasts and body bare between the two. His eyes went black as he watched her hips wriggling inside his trousers, watched her breasts jiggle with each step, and saw the way his hard collar circled her neck and forced her chin up to a provocative angle. She was rebelling against years of sexual constraint, and he knew it.

"I believe you said something about making me wear trousers and a stiff collar. How would I look?"

She turned slowly, letting him look her over, tempting him. She had no idea just how tantalizing she looked or just how close he was to ripping those trousers off her body. He snagged her arm as she swayed into reach. Pulling her against him, he let her see the desire she ignited in him, then pressed her trouser-clad hips hard against his swollen desire, making her feel his arousal.

"When you dance, sweetheart, you have to pay the piper."

She laughed softly, letting her desire show in her eyes, too. "Take whatever payment you want, piper." As his hands slid feverishly over that collar, down her bare breasts and waist, to squeeze her buttocks through his trousers, she groaned softly and thrust her pelvis against his in a slow, grinding motion. "I'm not through dancing."

He crushed her lips beneath his and felt her explode slowly in his arms.

Together they toppled onto the bed, kissing, straining close, arching hungrily into each other. He fumbled with his fly buttons and finally laughed, admitting he had never had to undo pants on somebody else before. She laughed and helped, peeling open the placket to reveal a slice of silky abdomen. The contrast of his half-open trousers and her pale skin was the most erotic thing he'd ever seen. He leaned down to trace that seductive V with his tongue.

Shortly, his trousers lay in a heap by the bed, and his body was sliding onto and into hers with the same liquid motion. They moved together in wild, changing rhythms: frantic and lustful one minute, light and playful the next. They rolled and writhed and teased and laughed, exploring and celebrating their closeness even as they did their passions. And this time, as sensation and response built, they held each other tightly and went tumbling one after another into wild, churning waves of pleasure that carried them onto the broad shores of release.

It was dusky in the room when they awakened. Antonia gave an involuntary moan as she sat up. Every muscle in her body was aching; it felt as if she'd been pounded.

When she extracted her legs from his and tried to slide across the bed, she halted and turned a look of distress back over her shoulder.

"What is it, Toni?" he said, rising onto his elbow, his voice concerned.

"I feel like I've been pummeled . . . all over," she said with an agonized look.

He laughed and pulled her back onto the bed. "I know just the thing to help that. Lie down . . . facedown."

Frowning uncertainly, she obeyed, and he began to rub and knead her aching muscles, turning them to butter under his strong hands. After a while he had her sit up, and she found most of the soreness gone. "That's wonderful," she murmured, giving him a gentle kiss.

"You see?" he said, holding her with only a smile. "You trust me."

She stared into his eyes, hoping she wasn't making a huge mistake.

"Heaven help me, I do trust you, Remington Carr."

His smile widened and took on a triumphant curl, then he glanced at the window. "Would you look at that? The sun is going down. You've slept the day away, lazybones." When he turned back, she caught his eye with a wicked look.

"I haven't exactly *slept* the day away," she said flirtatiously.

She led him into the bathroom that adjoined her bedchamber. Between kisses and playful caresses, they managed to wash and brush hair and don clothes. She was loath to let him take his trousers back, until he promised to bring her a pair of her own the next time he came.

The next time.

The idea lay suspended on the air, between and around them, as they finished dressing. She sat down at her dressing table and picked up her brush, looking at her glowing face in the mirror and feeling a chill stealing into her limbs. He must have seen her response, for he came up behind the bench and went down on one knee.

"There will be a next time, and a time after that," he said quietly. He felt her stiffen as he said, "We will have a lifetime of 'next times' . . . when we're married."

"Married?" she whispered. A chill swirled through her like the draft from an open door, starting with her feet and rising. For a time she had thought only of here and now, keeping thoughts of the future and the cost of her pleasure at bay. "I didn't say anything about marriage. . . ."

Disbelief mingled with irritation in his words. "Come, Antonia, don't be stubborn. What have we been doing all morning—all day?" When she just sat, gripping her brush and looking paler by the moment, he turned her to face him on the bench. "I don't know about you, but I've been making love to the woman I want to marry."

She wanted to say that she'd been making love to the man she loved, but somehow couldn't. To say it would be to give him rights with her, would give him power over her and her future. He wanted that power—he had already begun to claim it . . . assuming she would marry him because he wanted it to be so, absorbing her into his expectations and his desires. She felt herself sliding, being pulled toward something in which she would have little say, and that feeling of powerlessness frightened her the way nothing else could. Something deep in the pit of her stomach began to quiver, and dread collected in her throat to keep her from speaking.

She was terrified of being caught up in a disastrous marriage, but just as frantic at the possibility of losing him. All her life she had dreamed of feeling this way . . . of loving someone with all her heart . . . of having someone to share her time and her ideas and her passions. The conflict in her was almost unbearable. She took a deep breath and made herself say it.

"I don't want to get married, Remington."

With an aching heart she watched the frustration turning to anger in his face.

"Dammit, Antonia, I thought we had put what happened that night behind us. I've done everything I can to prove myself to you. And you even admitted that you need and want me, and even trust me—"

"It's not you," she said, taking hold of his shirtsleeves, willing him to understand. "I'll love you—every day and every night if you want. I'll share my bed with you, my table with you, my time with you. But I don't know if I can marry you."

"Good God—what *do* you want?" he demanded, glowering. "To be my mistress?"

"A mistress is a kept woman—I would never be 'kept' any more than you would 'keep' me. I have my own household, my own means, and my own responsibilities. I suppose that would make me . . . your lover."

"Lover? I don't want a *lover*—I want a wife! And I want a home. And babies, dammit—a whole houseful of babies. And I want it with *you*! I want to marry you and give you my name, and carry you home with me, and barricade the doors against the whole crazy world. Don't you understand? I want to walk down the street with you, to make you the center of my home and my heart, to have people point to that ravishing creature with the auburn hair and say she belongs to the Earl of Landon." He knew the instant he said it he had made a mistake.

She blanched and shot to her feet, feeling more alarmed with each word he spoke. "Belong to you? I don't want to *belong* to anyone. If you want me, Remington Carr, I'm afraid you'll have to settle for me as a lover." When he shoved to his feet, she paced away before he could take hold of her.

"I'm not being stubborn or vindictive, I swear to you. It's just that I've seen so many marriages . . . and none of them good. I don't know of any that have endured with anything akin to caring and affection and even companionship. None. Remington, don't you see? I'm responsible for thirteen marriages—"

"Thirteen?" He choked on the word as it came out.

"Yes. And even as we speak, *five* of those women are here, under my roof. They fled marriages with men they believed they loved and thought loved them. God knows how many more of the thirteen will return to me over the next weeks."

She was speaking of the wives of her White's Club victims, he realized with a start.

"Well, for God's sake, Antonia, send them home . . . back to their husbands . . . make them work it out!" he declared, running his hands back through his hair.

"I can't send them back," she insisted. "You have no idea what wretches I matched them with. Albert Everstone is so miserly that he actually counts the pieces of bread Margaret eats . . . Bertrand Howard goes for days without speaking to Camille . . . Lord Woolworth's vicious old mother runs his house with an iron fist and doesn't hesitate to wield it against poor Elizabeth . . . and Basil Trueblood seems to think his wife isn't a lady unless she has ice in her veins—says her kisses are too 'warm' to be decent. I could go on and on!" She came close, her face filled with anxiety.

"Men change when they get married," she said miserably. "They grow cold and distant and jealous of their time and money. They begin to think of their wives as conveniences or possessions or objects meant to decorate their lives. And I suppose women change, too—they begin to keep houses not homes, and become fixed on things and appearances and status. Marriage changes things between people, even between people who love each other." She paced away, clasping her hands, then turned, praying he would understand.

"I don't want to be a possession or an object or a convenience to you, Remington."

He stared at her, his face dusky with frustration and his eyes glowing hot.

"There's no danger of your becoming a 'convenience,' sweetheart. You're the damned most *inconvenient* woman I've ever known!" he bellowed. He stalked to the bed, shoved his arms into his coat, and tugged his vest down into place. With fire in his eyes he headed for the door and turned the key in the lock. Pausing in the open door, he looked back and jabbed a finger at her.

"I'm going to marry you, Antonia Paxton, if it is the last thing I do in this life!"

He strode down the hall and down the stairs, where he bade good evening to a wide-eyed Eleanor and shocked Pollyanna on the steps. In the entry hall he asked old Hoskins to retrieve his hat and walking stick, and saw the narrow, speculative look in the butler's eyes. He braced as the old boy thrust his hat and cane into his hands. But as he shuffled away, Remington clearly heard him say:

"Lucky bastard."

Out on the street, striding for the nearest cab stand, Remington didn't feel like a lucky bastard. Despite a whole day of wild, unbridled passion, he was feeling twitchy and deprived and a little desperate. He had never dreamed he would find himself frantic to convince a woman that free, unencumbered, and unbridled passion wasn't enough—

that she belonged in his home, bearing his name, his children, and his adoration, as well!

It was guilt, that was what it was. As the heat drained from his temper, he saw it all too clearly; she felt personally responsible for trapping women in marriages that hadn't worked out. Thirteen marriages. Good Lord. Now she was terrified of a bit of celestial retribution—getting trapped exactly the way she had trapped others, in a miserable marriage. And she had five sterling examples of the dismal fate that awaited an ill-conceived marriage, right under her nose. He stopped dead in the middle of the street. Everstone, Woolworth, Howard, Trueblood, Searle . . .

Those whiny, annoying bastards! They had wrecked his possibilities with Antonia before, with their selfishness and resentment, and now they were doing it again!

As he stood there in the street, he grew steadily more outraged. In order to marry Antonia, he would have to get those women out of her house and back home with their wretched husbands . . . and make them seem happy as clams. The glint of cunning entered his eye as his mind raced.

Those miserable wretches, the ruined bachelors of White's Club, were going to shape up and become model husbands by week's end—or he was going to know the reason why!

The barman at White's stood staring at the figures draped miserably over the corner table. "Ye'd think they was planted there," he mumbled to himself as they waved to him, ordering another bottle. He stepped out from behind the bar, empty-handed, and strolled over. The odor of stale liquor, stale cigars, and frustrated male heat was overpowering. "Beggin' yer indulgence, sirs. But ain't it time ye went home? Ye been here goin' on three days. Go home to yer wives"—he winced discreetly—"and yer razors."

Trueblood raised bleary eyes and a stubbled face to him. "Wives? What wives? We don't have wives . . . anymore."

"No one to go home to," Howard said miserably, raking a hand through his hair.

"And no supper," Everstone added. "She fired the cook when she left."

"No clean shirts," Trueblood said dolefully, giving his linen a pained sniff.

"No lady things clutterin' up my shaving sink," Searle mumbled.

"No one to talk to over supper—except Mother," Woolworth said morosely, staring into his dwindling drink. "And a damned cold bed at night."

There were several murmurs of agreement with that, and the barman wagged his head in disgust and returned to his place behind the bar.

"No reason to go home." Howard summed it up in a whisper: "Her blue eyes won't be there."

"Can't bear to see that hot-water bottle I gave her," Everstone mumbled.

"No more singing. Haven't heard a note of music since she left," Searle moped.

"Left her needlework," Woolworth muttered. "I found a nightshirt she was embroidering with my family crest, for me."

"There you are." A powerful voice startled them out of their doldrums.

They looked up to see Remington Carr bearing down on them with a fierce expression. To a man they stiffened and edged back from the table. But he halted and stood staring at them from a few paces away, looking as dapper, energetic, and determined as they looked disheveled, exhausted, and dispirited.

"Ye gods—look at you," he said with a wince. "You're pathetic. When was the last time you had a shave, Howard?"

Howard thrust to his feet and shook an unsteady finger. "Well, you're to blame—you and Lady Matrimonia. It's a criminal offense, you know, interferin' in a man's marriage —I checked. A man's home is a sacred thing . . . an' a man's wife is . . . is . . ."

"His property?" Remington supplied with a sardonic look. But before they could agree, he continued: "His chattel, perhaps? His goods? His convenience?" His eyes glittered as he came to stand at the edge of the table. "God— no wonder they've left you. If I were a female, I'd have thrown myself on a Catherine wheel before I'd have let them yoke me up with the likes of you. You're little more than savages in disguise."

"See here, now—" "Strong talk, Landon—" They stiffened in their chairs, outraged at his high-handed manner. He leaned over the table, into their midst, his eyes narrowing as he scalded and silenced them with the same look.

"But this is your lucky day, gentlemen. I'm going to help you. I want your wives out of Antonia Paxton's house and back in yours by week's end. To that end I'm here to see that you become exemplary husbands."

"Exemplary husbands?" Woolworth said, offended. "What the hell do you know about being a *husband*, Landon?"

"More than you, apparently. For I know that a man should never let his mother run his house, harass his wife, and ruin his marriage, Woolworth," Remington declared with a piercing look at the young peer, who reddened and moved his jaw soundlessly.

"And I know enough not to pinch pennies and flog

pounds with a woman . . . keeping count of the very food she consumes, Everstone."

"Damn you, Landon—that's entirely out of bounds!" the burly MP sputtered.

"I certainly know enough not to go for days without speaking to the woman who shares my bed, Howard," Remington continued, undaunted by their outrage.

"It is none of your affair who I speak to—or when!" The young bureaucrat shoved to his feet again with his fists clenched.

"And I know that a warm, affectionate woman in a man's bed is a blessing, not an embarrassment, Trueblood."

"How dare you say such a thing to me?" Phlegmatic Trueblood roused himself to a tepid display of indignation. "My wife is a lady in *all* respects."

"She's a woman first, Trueblood. They all are," Remington said, emphatically. "You pleaded for my help the other night. Well, I've decided to give it to you. I'm going to help you woo and win your wives back to your sides, starting first thing tomorrow morning. You're going to be gracious and interested and generous to a fault. You will take them chocolates and flowers and gifts." He silenced Everstone's grumble with a javelinlike glare of warning. "And you're going to talk to them, and *listen* to them, and treat them like the women they are. With any luck you'll have them back by week's end, and I can get on with my own marriage."

Their eyes bulged and they lurched to their feet, demanding all at once: "Marriage?" "What marriage?" "You're getting shackled?" "You—the Bastion of Bachelorhood?" "To whom?"

"To Antonia Paxton," he declared, smiling defiantly at the horror that bloomed on their faces. "I claimed the Dragon's heart after all, you see. But I decided to keep it for myself."

. . .

That night, as the morning edition of *Gaflinger's Gazette* was put to bed and the offices finally emptied out, Rupert Fitch donned his spanking-new bowler hat and stepped out onto Fleet Street. He paused for a moment on the steps, to search his pockets for a match, intending to light a cigarette. There was a fair amount of traffic on the street, so he paid no attention to the coach slowing and stopping a dozen feet away.

Out of that coach sprang three burly men, who seized Fitch and wrestled him toward their vehicle. His hat and cigarette went flying, and his notepad was jerked from his pocket. At the door they pounded a fist in his gut, to quiet him, then stuffed him into the coach and carried him off into the night. A moment later the street was quiet and empty . . . except for an unburned cigarette and a pricey bowler hat that a carriage wheel had squashed flat.

It was a harrowing ride for the little news writer. They trussed him up and shoved him down onto the floor of the coach. In the darkness, struggling for breath, he lost track of time. It seemed forever until the rattling of the coach stopped and he was hauled out, shoved through a doorway, trundled down a hallway. In a bare room lighted by a single kerosene lamp, he found several inquisitors waiting. They shoved him down in a chair and shone the lamp in his face, temporarily blinding his dark-adjusted eyes.

"So you're Fitch." A huge man with a nasty scar down the side of his face bent down to stare into his eyes. "Got a few questions for ye, Fitch." With a wicked gleam in his eyes, he raised a sharp blade and moved it menacingly toward Fitch's face. The news writer squealed with terror, but the steel merely slid between his skin and the cloth to cut away his gag.

The big fellow smiled nastily and stepped away. He was

replaced by a smoother, more gentlemanly looking fellow in expensively tailored clothes.

"Here, here, Mr. Fitch. We mean you no harm. We are agents of Her Majesty's government, and we've a few questions to ask you. Cooperate with me, and you won't have to deal with Mr. Ajax, there." Fitch saw the glint of the big fellow's blade in the shadows and swallowed hard. But whatever Fitch lacked in courage and scruples, he more than made up for in brass.

"Wh-what's in it for me?" he croaked out.

The gentleman's cool smile faded to a look of menacing scrutiny. "Your reward will be the satisfaction of doing your duty to your sovereign queen."

Fitch nodded and groveled and tried just once more. "It's just that—I'm sure I would remember quicker, say, if I knew there was a story in it somewhere for me." Fitch's heart nearly pounded out of his chest as he waited for the gentleman to respond. After a look at others standing in the shadows, the gent jerked a nod of agreement and it was settled.

"You wrote a story a day or so ago, alleging that the Earl of Landon was accosted in the street by several men," his questioner declared. "According to your report, they claimed that he had wrecked their marriages and they demanded reparation. We want the details, Mr. Fitch. Including the names of those poor, unfortunate gentlemen."

In a short while Fitch told them everything he knew about the "evil earl," naming names, fabricating and embellishing where the truth seemed a bit lackluster, weaving a tale in which truth, half truth, and lie were so skillfully intertwined that he himself forgot where one stopped and the other started.

When he finished his inventive recounting, he quickly found himself out on the street once more—missing his change purse, his notepad, his new hat, and facing a very long walk to his lodgings.

But despite those losses he was whistling, for he had in his possession the germ of a story that he knew would set all London on its ear.

"You damned well better be right about this," Everstone grumbled, tugging at his collar and shifting the beribboned box and the flowers he held from one sweaty hand to the other. "These cursed flowers cost me—"

"Dammit, Everstone, I've warned you about this cheese paring of yours," Remington whispered, glaring at the portly peer from the corner of his eye. "It's what got you into trouble in the first place."

"For mercy's sake, Everstone, do as he says and cease this endless caviling over every penny," Trueblood added, wincing at the pathetic little nosegay of violets he held and sending a hand to scratch beneath his vest. "It's most undignified."

They stood in the entry hall of Paxton House the next morning, waiting for old Hoskins to fetch Antonia. The two husbands were justifiably nervous as they recalled their last encounter with the Dragon in this same hall. At the sound of their voices, a number of Antonia's ladies appeared on the stairs and the gallery above them. Remington called greetings to them and asked after Cleo. They returned his greetings and assured him the old lady was improving, but cast suspicious looks at his companions.

Antonia hurried from the dining room to greet him, but

stopped the minute she set eyes on Everstone and Trueblood.

"Antonia, you look beautiful this morning," Remington said, striding forward to meet her while covertly motioning the others to remain behind. And she did look magnificent, her hair swept up into a fall of burnished curls, wearing a dusky-blue satin dress that exactly matched the color of her eyes. No black-banded purple, no midnight-blue, no gloomy gray. It boded well for his enterprise.

"What are *they* doing in my house?" she demanded, staring at the men who had taunted her as she sat in Remington's bed, then had dared invade her house to reclaim what they deemed their marital property.

"I've brought them to see their wives, Antonia. They have no right to ask favors of you, I know. And so I appeal on their behalf to your good graces . . . asking only that you grant them the same fairness and mercy you showed to me. A man is capable of a change of heart, after all. And I believe their wives will find them genuinely changed men."

"You presume a great deal on my regard for you, your lordship," she declared, transferring her glare to him.

"I know I am taking a risk," he said, lowering his voice and seizing her unoffered hand, holding it between his own. "But I would hazard your anger and a great deal more for a chance to help these gentlemen win back the wives they so desperately miss. People can change for *better* in a marriage, too . . . not just for *worse*." His smile contained a caress she found irresistible even when she looked into his eyes and saw his thoughts working behind them.

He had something else in mind; she could feel it. And it didn't take a genius to deduce that it had something to do with convincing her that marriage wasn't a hopeless bargain. Forewarned was forearmed, she pacified her better sense.

Sending Hoskins for Margaret and Alice, she led the

others into the drawing room and, by her own refusal to sit, kept them all standing and shifting nervously from foot to foot.

It wasn't until the women arrived that Antonia deigned to look at the errant husbands. Everstone was dressed to the nines and clutching a prettily ribboned box and a massive bouquet of spring flowers. But her eyes widened as she examined Trueblood. He looked like a ravaged man: hollow-eyed, rumpled, and with several days' growth of beard on his face. The way he gripped the pitiful sprig of violets he had brought clutched unexpectedly at Antonia's heart.

Margaret and Alice stood just inside the door, arm in arm, lending each other support for whatever lay ahead. Antonia joined them, inserting herself between them, and ushered them forward.

Silence descended as Everstone and Trueblood nodded to their wives with uncertainty and a bit of embarrassment. "I should like a private word with you, Margaret," Everstone said, scowling.

"Anything you have to say to me, Albert Everstone, must be said here and now. I'll not be a private shame to you any longer."

"And the same goes for me, Basil Trueblood," Alice said to her husband, though her eyes were wide with distress as they searched his disheveled form.

"But surely it wouldn't hurt to draw aside for a few minutes." Remington saw his scheme unraveling before his eyes and tried to intervene. "Surely these matters of the heart are . . . rather delicate."

"Matters of the heart?" Margaret said, looking accusingly at Everstone.

"Of course," the bluff MP said, reddening under his collar. "Why else would I have spent good brass on such stuff as this?"

He shoved the flowers toward her, but she hesitated,

searching his eyes. The desperation she saw in them led her to accept that offering. With a softening expression she buried her nose in the flowers and headed for one of the settees in the center of the large room. Everstone followed and settled stiffly on the edge of the seat beside her, gripping the gift box he held with one hand, and his knee with the other.

"Are those for me?" Alice said quietly, staring at the bedraggled nosegay Trueblood was gripping as if it contained the keys to the kingdom.

"What?" He started and came back to the present, coloring hotly. "Oh, well . . . yes. They're not the freshest . . . they're a bit wilted and the color is already fading. I pulled out the worst ones . . . and I know it looks a bit spare. . . ." He caught a glimpse of the emphatic look Remington was giving him from across the room and realized he was rambling. Taking a deep breath, he held out the flowers. "But I know you love violets more than any other flower . . . and I specifically wanted to bring you violets . . . and these were all I could find. I scoured the city, I swear . . . money was no object. . . ."

She accepted them and looked down at the fragile blossoms. They were a little faded and more than a little wilted and still warm from the heat of his hand. But the fact that they were her favorite flower had eclipsed their imperfection, and to Alice that made them the most perfect offering that perfectionist Basil Trueblood could have made her. She tucked her chin and headed for the sofa near the settee.

Remington heaved a quiet sigh and braced; those opening moves had shown him just how far they had yet to go. And the distance seemed to lengthen as he watched Antonia standing between the two couples, scrutinizing the entire process with a scowl. Neither couple spoke for a time, and Remington rolled his eyes and finally settled himself on the settee beside Everstone, who looked like a bullfrog ready to jump. He nudged Everstone's arm once, then a second time before Sir Albert glanced at him with a resentful glare. After an exchange of vehement looks, Everstone recalled the package in his hand and offered it to Margaret.

"Oh—and I brought you this, too," he said in gruff tones. "I know you wanted it last Christmastide." He looked down at his thick, brawny hands and muttered, "Heard about it often enough." He cleared his throat. "Go on . . . open it up."

With a wary look Margaret removed the multicolored satin ribbons from the box and opened it. Her countenance glowed with tender pleasure as she pulled out a mahogany music box, inlaid with ivory. "It's exactly what I wanted . . . the very thing." She ran her hands over it lovingly, then raised eyes to him, which, six months after Christmas, still bore traces of hurt. "You gave me a hot-water bottle, instead, Albert. With the price still attached. Nine shill—"

"I know how much it cost," Everstone said gruffly, avoiding the others' judgmental eyes. "Won't do that again. If you'll just come home, Margaret. With the cook gone, the maid's quit, I've had to eat at the club every night and it's dashed expensive." Remington gave him a vicious nudge. "Not that I mind a little expense, mind you," he said, shifting irritably. "Gettin' to be a regular spendthrift, I am. Flowers an' music boxes is only the start. I'll loosen up more if you'll come home, Margaret. I been thinking it over, and I could give you an allowance, like you said . . . to run the house and buy what you need. It'd be like your own money."

"*Like* my own money" she said, her spine straightening and her mouth drawing into a tight line. "But it wouldn't *be* mine, would it?"

"I meant—"

"I know what you meant. But, Albert, I can't live like that—having nothing of my own, a slave to your pinchpenny ways, feeling like a servant in what should be my own house." She hugged the music box to her breast and her chin trembled.

"Aw, Margaret," Everstone said with a huff of exasperation, "come home. I want you home."

"Why, Albert?" she said, raising her eyes to him, searching him.

"I . . . miss you." If he hadn't looked quite so pained by the admission, it might have had a greater effect. She was about to decline when he reached out to touch her hand and she felt the powerful persuasion of his warmth. "Say yes, Margaret. Come home with me today, now. I'll change. I swear it."

She glanced at Antonia, who had withdrawn to the fireplace and stood with her arms crossed, reminding her with a determined look that she needn't go, now or ever. Wavering, Margaret took a breath and then set both her mind and her chin.

"Not today, Albert. I must have some time to think on it."

Antonia had watched Remington prodding Everstone and realized that he had something to do with the tight-fisted MP's visit, and probably more than something to do with the gifts. Now she watched as he rose and shifted his attention to Alice and Basil Trueblood, while appearing simply to stroll the room with his hands shoved into his pockets.

"What's happened to you, Basil?" Alice finally had the nerve to say. "You look so . . . tired." And so unkempt, and so dispirited, that she was genuinely alarmed.

"I can't seem to sleep in our house of late and have been spending nights at the club," Trueblood said dolefully. "It's hideously noisy till all hours, and there is never any hot water for shaving, and the linen is frightfully coarse and common—one should really expect better—"

Remington settled on the end of the sofa, at Trueblood's back, and covertly gave him an elbow in the ribs. Trueblood started and reddened.

"But that hardly compares with the discomfort of not seeing your dear face across the breakfast table," he asserted, looking genuinely distressed, then began to slide again. "Or with the fact that I haven't had a decent meal at home since you left. Cook burns everything just to spite me. And that snippy upstairs maid can't or won't recall where you sent my shirts out to be laundered . . . and she forgets to press my trousers and refuses to empty or clean my shaving basin. The thing's so filthy I can't bear to—"

Remington gave him a sharp nudge that made him snap upright. "I-I mean . . . I miss you, Alice. I suppose I never realized how much you do to make my life better. You seem to have a mind just made for working with menials, and for dealing with all the flotsam and jetsam of life—" Another, even more emphatic jab from Remington forced a gasp of surprise from him.

"Your lordship." Alice leaned around Basil to address Remington directly. "You needn't continue. I know what Basil is like." Then she sat back and turned her haunting blue eyes on Trueblood. "Nothing is ever good enough for you, Basil . . . or clean enough, or quiet enough, or starched enough, or proper enough."

"That's not true. You're proper enough, and quiet enough and clean enough. I miss you, Alice. I miss your little misspelled notes by my breakfast plate. I miss your off-key humming as you write letters or do your lady stitching. I miss the way you lay out the flatware wrong on the table and the way your eyes get puffy when you cry over a sad song. . . ."

Remington sighed with resignation and propped his chin on his hand, against the arm of the sofa. Antonia watched his eyes close and saw his pained expression as Basil Trueblood rattled on with his list of hopelessly unflattering compliments. She couldn't help smiling just a little. He had obviously expected more from this visit. It seemed to really matter to him that Everstone and Trueblood reclaim their wives.

He must have felt her gaze on him, for he looked up just then and caught her staring at him. His slow, wistful smile was irresistible. She let the warmth she was feeling rise into her face, while memories of his loving began to stir powerfully in her. It was a minute before she realized he was standing and speaking, responding to something Hoskins was saying to her. Then he turned to her and the sense of it righted in her head: the butler had announced more callers.

"Who?" She scowled at Hoskins. "Who, did you say?"

"Lord Woolworth, ma'am." The old butler looked down at the cards he held, squinted, and shoved them out to full arm's length. "Also a Lord Richard Searle . . . and that Mr. Howard fellow . . . him of the excessively sharp revers."

She turned on Remington, who took his time meeting her eyes. "The rest of them, too? What would you have done if I had tossed the lot of you out on your coattails?"

"I had faith that your fairness and good judgment would rule," he said, producing a smile that was both mischievous and endearing. And she knew he lied. He wasn't counting on her head, he was counting on her hopelessly soft heart to win his battle for him. And it looked as if his faith in it hadn't been misplaced.

No sooner had Everstone and Trueblood bade their wives good-bye and departed, than she found her drawing room being invaded by three more men she had sworn never to allow through her door again. The sight of them stirred a confusing mix of feelings in her. Each carried flowers, each wore his most dashing clothes, and each greeted her with a blend of trepidation and grim deference.

Again she let them stand and shift uneasily while she sent Hoskins for their wives. Elizabeth, Daphne, and Camille arrived forthwith, their faces flushed becomingly and their eyes bright. When they glimpsed Antonia's erect, crossed-arms posture, they halted in the doorway, shoulder to shoulder. They were sensible and clever and capable, Antonia thought with some pride. But they were also warm-hearted and forgiving. She glanced at the handsome faces and brimming bouquets of flowers they faced, and she sighed, preparing herself for the worst.

With considerable dignity they accepted the flowers and refrained from eyeing the boxes under their husbands' arms. Richard Searle held out his hand to little blond Daphne expecting to escort her to a seat, but she surprised him by withholding it.

"Come with me, Daphne," he said emphatically. "I have a few things to say to you . . . in private."

Daphne's pale perfection grew a bit paler, but she lifted her chin and made herself say: "You have already said a great deal to me in private, Richard. For now, anything you have to say to me must be said in public . . . or at least before my dearest friends."

"Now, Daphne," he ground out with an edge of warning, his face and shoulders swelling with bruised pride and irritation.

"No!" she shouted fiercely, startling him back a step. "I said *no* and I meant it!" she continued forcefully. "I'll not suffer your wretched outbursts of temper in silence anymore, Richard!"

Everyone in the room stood as if bolted to the floor, their ears ringing. When the sound died away, he stood in complete shock, fumbling for a response. She reddened slightly, seeming a little unsettled by her own blast, then took herself in hand. Crossing her arms over her chest, in imitation of Antonia's adamant pose, she lowered her voice.

"I am sorry, Richard, but I thought you should learn the way it feels to be yelled at before others—the servants, your family, even waiters in restaurants. It is not a very pleasant experience."

"I . . . well . . . I . . ." Searle's face set like granite and his tongue seemed to have turned to stone as well.

"I'm quite sure you don't raise your voice to your gentlemen friends, Richard. And I believe I deserve at least the respect you would show to them." She steeled herself. "Are you willing to talk with me as if I am a reasonable being?"

All of his carefully prepared speeches had been blasted out of his head. He nodded and, in a desperate move, handed Daphne the flat box he carried. When she accepted it, he seemed to find his tongue. "I thought you might like to have some music to sing by." He gestured to the box. "I got you some. I . . . miss your singing."

Daphne met his darkened eyes, gave him a wary but warming smile, and put out her hand. Together they moved to a settee near the window.

Antonia watched them go, feeling oddly reassured. Of all the brides that had returned to her, she would have judged Daphne the most tender and vulnerable. Daphne's firm stance with her overpowering husband left Antonia feeling there might actually be some hope for them all to better their lot.

Lord Carter Woolworth stepped forward and handed Elizabeth a small package, asking her to open it. She did so with trembling hands and found a printed note card inside. "Read it," he said quietly.

"Lady Penelope Woolworth, Countess Dunroven, is receiving guests at Dunroven Hall, Kewes, Sussex," she read aloud. For a moment she stared at it, frowning, uncertain what it meant.

"Not that she will have many guests," Woolworth said, edging closer. "But if she entertains, it will be there, or nowhere. She no longer lives in my house, Elizabeth."

Antonia watched Elizabeth's tenuous smile as she settled on the settee by the pianoforte with him. Then she turned back in time to see Bertrand Howard removing a pair of thick spectacles from his pocket and donning them. Camille watched him in astonishment.

"I think you should know . . . you are looking at a new man, Camille," he said in a dry voice. "I have taken to wearing spectacles. I have probably needed them for some years. Vanity kept me from wearing them . . . the same way vanity kept me from seeing you."

Her jaw dropped. "Bertrand, are you saying your eyesight is bad?"

He swallowed hard and plunged ahead. "I don't always scowl because I'm displeased, Camille. Sometimes I am simply squinting in order to see better. I didn't mean to look through you. Sometimes I just couldn't see that you were there at all. And that is the most inexcusable of wrongs . . . not seeing you."

Camille blinked, disarmed by his admission, and by the thickness of the glass that magnified his eyes and made him look owlish and a bit comical. She pressed her lips together to prevent a laugh, and it was a minute before she could speak.

"Do you expect me to believe you ignored me— wouldn't speak to me or take me anywhere, or introduce me, or simply talk with me—because you couldn't *see* me?"

"It's the truth, Camille . . . in part." He squared his shoulders and admitted: "The other part is that I'm just a terrible bonehead."

Camille stood looking at him, watching his discomfort,

sensing a new sincerity in his manner. "Yes, you are a bonehead. A very infuriating and annoying and self-absorbed bonehead." As she spoke, he held out a small, delicately wrapped package to her. She accepted it hesitantly and at his urging opened it.

Inside was another pair of spectacles. She frowned and held them up.

"I don't need spectacles, Bertrand Howard. There is nothing wrong with *my* eyesight."

"I know, Camille," he said, moving closer. "You have lovely eyes, splendid eyes. But I would like you to wear these lenses when you are looking at my faults." He winced appealingly. "They make everything look smaller."

Surprise melted Camille's reserve and she allowed herself to smile. And they were soon seated on the middle sofa, talking.

There were no blinding revelations, no wrenching reconciliations in the drawing room that afternoon. But as Antonia showed the gentlemen out and then watched the Bentick brides climbing the stairs with hopeful faces, she realized they had made a start at reworking and reclaiming their loves and their lives. As she turned toward the drawing room, she saw Remington standing in the middle of the room, watching her through the doorway, and she went soft inside.

"It was you, wasn't it?" she demanded as she joined him. "You were responsible for the flowers and the gifts and the speeches." His ears reddened and a small guilty smile appeared. Irresistible smile. Irresistible man. "Those spectacles . . . they had to be your idea. They were just the right balance of the absurd and the touching. And you probably told Trueblood not to shave for several days, so he'd look *perfectly* pathetic." She couldn't hold back the smile tugging at the corners of her mouth. "Lord, what a devious man you are, Remington Carr."

He took her into his arms and kissed her deeply.

"Not devious enough, apparently," he said against her lips. "I'm still a bachelor. And it feels as if I'm going to be the last bachelor on earth."

She escorted him upstairs to see Cleo, and after a short visit he declared that he had to leave. He had work waiting at his offices and intended to stop by Uncle Paddington's town house to see if the newlyweds had returned yet. Promising to send word if he found them at home, he gave her a quick kiss and warned that he and the husbands would be back the next afternoon to continue their courtship. It was as good as an admission that this scheme was indeed a "courtship" . . . and that its true object was her heart.

And he was gone before Hoskins could say, "Smug bastard."

With Antonia's kiss still warm on his lips, Remington went straight to his offices, where he spent a miserable afternoon. The bank had called in several of his "call notes" and proved reluctant to discuss the situation with him. He managed to set up an appointment with Sir Neville Thurston for the following morning, then left his offices, feeling a bit grim despite the day's personal successes. He stopped by Uncle Paddington's house and found him expected home later that evening. Deciding not to wait, he promised to call first thing the next morning and headed home himself.

With his mind set on a hearty supper and a bit of port, he relaxed back in the seat of his carriage, considering the possibility of creeping up the back stairs of Paxton House, to Antonia's room, without being seen. He sighed as he thought of the intrigue and tension involved. How much better it would be to have supper across the table from her, to share a bit of wine with her, and then to take her by the hand and lead her upstairs to their marriage bed . . . where no one would disturb them until noon unless they permitted it.

How long would it take, he wondered, for her to understand that it was meant to be and give herself up to the idea of marrying him? He had only five days before the queen's deadline. He told himself there was a reasonable chance that he could get her to agree to an engagement in that time. Perhaps the queen's expectations could be fulfilled by an engagement announcement. And in any case—how much damage could the queen do him in two or three days' time?

The front door of his house swung open, and he handed Martin, the underbutler, his hat, gloves, and cane. "You have visitors, sir," Martin said, looking a bit harried. "In the drawing room."

Remington's footsteps rang off the marble floors and reverberated around the marble walls of the huge entry hall. It was odd that Phipps wasn't there to meet him, he realized—just as he pushed back the half-open doors and spotted the butler sitting on a straight chair, being restrained by two burly men. Up from the nearby sofa sprang two others dressed in dark suits and holding black bowlers in their hands. As he lurched into the room, glaring at them, Phipps tried to rise, calling out: "I'm so sorry, your lordship. There was nothing I could do!"

They pushed him down onto the chair again, and the doors slammed shut behind Remington. He whirled to find two uniformed constables brandishing nightsticks, blocking his avenue of escape.

"Remington Carr, Earl of Landon?" One of the two men in suits came toward him, looking him over with a pugnacious thoroughness.

"I am the Earl of Landon," he answered with scarcely

contained outrage. "And who the hell are you . . . to barge into my house and lay hands on my butler like this?"

"I'm Inspector Gibbons of Scotland Yard. It is my duty to place you under arrest, your lordship, in the name of the queen." He jerked his head, ordering the two toughs who held Phipps to release him and seize Remington instead.

"What?" Remington was too stunned to react at first, and they seized him without much of a struggle. "You must be joking—on what grounds?"

The inspector waved a Queen's Bench warrant, then tucked it back into his breast pocket and rocked up and down on his toes. "There's a list of 'whereases' and 'where-fores' as long as my arm, your lordship. But they all boil down to 'corruption of public morals.' Take him away, gents."

"This is an outrage!" Remington declared fiercely, planting his feet to resist, his patrician pride at full swell. "I demand that you unhand me—or, better yet, that you convey me straight to Buckingham Palace! I demand to be permitted to speak with the queen!"

"Oh, I don't think she'd want to be seein' you, your lordship," the inspector said, unimpressed by Remington's invocation of noble privilege. "It was *her* and the PM what brought the complaint in the first place."

___

The next morning Antonia spent time in the small parlor, listening to the hopes and fears of her Bentick brides, and steadying them on their course of action. It was clear that their husbands' visits the day before had made a great impression on them. Though none were ready to pack their things and go home, all were hopeful that some accommodation might be reached that would allow them to return home and to build the kind of marriage they wanted.

"We don't know what we would have done if you hadn't allowed us to come and stay for a while," Camille summed it up, speaking for all of them as she squeezed Antonia's hand. "You've been so good to us all. We only hope you find happiness yourself someday, Lady Toni."

"Amen to that," came a familiar voice from the doorway.

Antonia looked up with her heart in her eyes to find Aunt Hermione in the doorway, smiling. "Auntie!" She bounded up and threw her arms around Hermione, and it was some time before she could bring herself to let Hermione go, even to ask some of the questions she was dying to ask.

"You look wonderful—positively glowing," Antonia said, then looked around her aunt. "And Sir Paddington? Is he here, too?"

"He brought me here, then went on to Remington's offices. He's needed about some awful banking mess or other. We arrived later than expected last night."

Antonia held her at arm's length and looked at her with remnants of heartache visible in her eyes. "Are you happy, Auntie?"

"Oh, yes, Toni dear. Paddington is all I could possibly want." Then she got that mischievous twinkle in her eye. "And a bit more." Antonia laughed and ushered her back out into the hall, sending Camille to tell everyone Hermione was home. Halfway to the drawing room she remembered and halted, taking Hermione by the hands.

"It's Cleo, Auntie." She took a deep breath. "She was taken ill . . . a stroke."

Hermione paled and had to steady herself against Antonia.

"Is she . . . ?"

"She's recovering, but won't be allowed out of bed for a while. She'll want to see you, I know." They hurried up the stairs to Cleo's room and found her awake and strong enough for a few hugs and a few tears.

"You did it, eh?" the old lady said, clutching Hermione's hand and squinting as she looked her over. "And it's good, from the looks of you. You youngsters." She shook her head fondly. "I said you should follow your heart."

"And I took your advice, Cleo," Hermione said, patting the older lady's thin hand. "As usual, you were right. You know, I'd almost forgotten how nice having a man around can be." Then she cast a glance at Antonia. "I just wish we could get Toni to listen, as well. She needs a man in her life. And love. And babies."

Antonia stood with mild irritation, watching the two old ladies flaunting their conspiracy while giving her an oblique lecture on life. Apparently Hermione had asked the older woman's advice about marrying again, and Cleo had advised the "youngster" to do it. "You knew. And you kept it from me," Antonia declared, scowling at Cleo, who gave a papery cackle of a laugh.

"Wouldn't want Hermie here to go without, just because you choose to, girl."

Antonia sputtered for a response while Hermione laughed.

Word had spread quickly through the house that Hermione had arrived, and everyone dropped their work and came running to greet her and to hear all the details of her romantic adventure. They collected in Cleo's room, so she could hear as well, and Hermione began to tell her story. Secreting her bag out the kitchen door, the mad rush to Gretna Green, the vows spoken in a small parish church, the flowers Paddington had picked for her along the way, the old family ring with the magnificent ruby that he had given her—duly admired by everyone present—and the romantic wedding supper after . . . it was like something from a young girl's dream. And Hermione seemed somehow more youthful from having lived and recounted it.

"Your Paddington sounds splendid," Eleanor said mistily.

"Well, I know one thing," Gertrude said, dabbing at her eyes with the corner of her apron. "Ye mus' bring 'im around for supper some night so we can meet him."

Hermione beamed at their good wishes and their open invitation to visit them. Antonia thought she detected a trace of mist in her aunt's eyes and mentioned that Hermione must want to see about the rest of her things. As the others went back to work or hurried off to prepare a special luncheon, Antonia went with her aunt to pack.

In Hermione's room a silence settled between them, which deepened with every garment and knickknack they placed on the bed to be packed. Then Antonia turned from retrieving an old beaded reticule from the bottom of the wardrobe and found Hermione standing in the middle of the floor, clutching an aged scrapbook to her chest. Her rosy face and rounded form were filled with emotion. Watching her, Antonia felt tears welling and swallowed to clear her throat.

"Why, Auntie? Why would you run off and get married?"

Hermione smiled at her through a prism of tears. "When you love someone, you want to be with them. And I'm head over heels for Paddington. He's so droll and well traveled and interesting. Do you know he was in India the same year my Stephen and I were? We must have just missed meeting at the viceroy's ball. And he has the most handsome silver hair and the gentlest hands. . . ." She trailed off into realms of feeling that were difficult to put into words. Then, after a moment, she came back to the present. Searching Antonia's face, she shook her head at what she saw.

"And frankly, Toni dear, I got a little tired of waiting for you to get on with your life so I could get on with mine."

Antonia drew her chin back and her eyes widened. Aunt Hermione had been waiting for *her* to get on with her life, so that she might get on with . . . locating husband number five?

"No offense, my dear. But just because you've no taste for 'footsie' doesn't mean that no one else does. And I'm not getting any younger. When the chance for love comes along, I take it." She smiled with just a hint of rebellion that Antonia had seen in her face before, but hadn't recognized as that until now. "I always have, you know."

Antonia wobbled to the bench at the foot of the bed and sat down hard. Hermione joined her and gently put an arm around her shoulders. "I love you with all my heart, Toni. You're the child I was never able to have. It hurts me to see you alone. What will you do with the rest of your life, dear? There's so much more to living than stitchery and charity work and taking tea in the afternoon. And if my marrying will give you a nudge to do something more—"

Hoskins appeared in the doorway just then to announce: "Sir Paddington Carr is here to see both Mrs. Fielding-Carr and yourself, ma'am. He says it is urgent."

Antonia and Hermione left both their packing and their conversation unfinished to hurry downstairs to see Paddington. They found him in the entry hall pacing, red-faced and stomping this way and that, looking as if he were ready to explode. When he looked up and saw them, he did just that.

"Hermione—Antonia!" He came rushing toward them, his whole being a'quiver with outrage. "Hell's fire—pardon th' French—" he declared, looking a bit confused, caught unexpectedly between the ordinaries and the extraordinaries of life. "They've arrested Remington on some charge or other, and he's in jail!"

"Arrested him?" Antonia suddenly had difficulty drawing breath. "Dearest heaven—what for?"

It was Hermione who had the presence of mind to pull them into the drawing room and sit them down to learn what Paddington knew, which wasn't very much.

"Phipps, Remington's butler, hotfooted it to the offices first thing this mornin', sayin' the boy's been placed under charges. They came to his house last night . . . Scotland Yard, he said. Waited for him all evening, and arrested him on the spot, the minute he set foot in the door." Here Paddington paused and looked a bit confused. "Something about consumption of the queen's morals . . ."

"Consumption? Morals?" It made no sense . . . until the gears of Antonia's mind finally kicked into motion. "Do you mean—dear Lord!—*corruption of public morals*? Was that it?" It sounded like a serious charge. Heart-stoppingly serious.

"No—*the queen's* morals," Paddington said, scowling at the way it sounded. "The queen was definitely involved . . . her and her 'national fibers.' Something about his being 'under her mining' and weakening some of her 'timbers' . . . Dashed if I can figure when or how he might have fiddled with her blessed fibers. . . ." He halted, straightened abruptly, and looked startled as the pieces finally fell into place in his head. "Good Lord—Remington's being accused of meddling with the queen's morals! Damned scoundrels—accusing him of such dastardly business. Why, I doubt he's set eyes on the old girl in years!"

Antonia blinked, watching Paddington grapple to make connections that were being made all too clearly in her own mind.

"Not the *queen's* morals . . . the *public's*!" She groaned and reached for Paddington's sleeve. "The queen is accusing him of corrupting public morals—that has to be it. But why? What could he possibly have done to make her accuse him of such a thing?"

Neither of them could answer her, and the only way to learn what had happened was for Sir Paddington to hurry down to Scotland Yard and demand to know the reason for his nephew's detention. Distraught as she was, Antonia did think clearly enough to advise Paddington to call first on Remington's solicitors and insist that they accompany him to police headquarters. Remington most certainly needed legal help.

Uncle Paddington was suddenly back to full capacity and set upon a solid course, at the peak of his form. But as he reached the front doors, Antonia felt a towering surge of anxiety and called out to him.

"Wait, Sir Paddington—give me a minute to fetch my hat and gloves. I'm coming with you!"

Scotland Yard, the headquarters of the Metropolitan Police, was a stately old building that was indeed constructed around a yard—a courtyard set in the middle of London. It was the place that prisoners were taken for questioning and to await trial. As Antonia's and Paddington's carriage neared the center of London, the streets were clogged with cabs, carriages, carts, and people on foot. Waiting for the traffic wore on Antonia's nerves; every minute seemed precious and time was wasting.

She glanced at Paddington, beside her on the seat, and found him staring worriedly out the window. Across from them in the carriage was Denholm Herriot, one of the leading solicitors of King's Inn, and Remington's chief legal counsel. He was a moderately tall, balding man whose eyes were lively and whose wise countenance usually inspired confidence. Just now he was the picture of distress. When Paddington had explained Remington's situation and asked for his opinion, he judiciously refrained from offering one, except to say that a morals charge was a criminal offense and was never pressed lightly—certainly not against a man of Remington's standing. And he said that if there was a trial, it would likely be held at the Old Bailey.

A criminal offense. The words lay like a smothering weight on Antonia's chest. And *trial.* The word itself meant "ordeal." They would put Remington on the prisoner's dock and have people come and testify as to his . . . what? Immorality? How could anyone possibly think Remington a corrupting influence? He was one of the most decent, responsible, and moral men she had ever met!

They spoke little as they inched along through the late-afternoon traffic. Then Paddington straightened, leaned toward the window, and lowered the glass to listen to something. Antonia craned her neck to see and realized he was staring at a newsboy who was barking out the headlines on a street corner. It was time for the afternoon editions, and something in one of the headlines galvanized Paddington. He whistled and waved the boy over to the carriage, tossing him a shilling and stretching down to snatch the paper. He snapped it open, and as she read over his shoulder, Antonia was hit by a sickening wave of horror. The headline read:

EARL ARRESTED ON MORALS CHARGE!

Gaflinger's had not only scooped every other paper in town, it had also scooped Remington's own legal representatives. For there, in lurid black and white, was a list of the charges against him and a version of the circumstances that had prompted them. ". . . charged with the corruption of public morals, a case brought from the very highest levels of Her Majesty's government and the palace itself," Paddington read aloud.

As Antonia listened and stared at that obscene headline, she felt a rising fury generated by yet another distorted and sensationalized story about him—and in that despicable rag, *Gaflinger's.* Trembling with impotent anger, she realized that those wretched reports and the ill will they had stirred against him had finally accumulated to an intolerable weight. And that weight had set the slow but inexorable wheels of the justice system into motion against him.

It was the cursed newspapers! First the stories about the "Woman Wager," then the humiliating revelations of that awful night when the Bentick husbands invaded his house, then that business of his attacking women on the streets . . . Her heart beat faster with the recall of every absurd but still damaging piece of scandal press. They had gleefully reported that he forced her into degrading labor, and had women demonstrating against him in the streets—which they then reported with vicious whispers of "shackles" and "male oppressor" and worse. Then, finally, came the last straw: allegations that he had wrecked numerous marriages!

The stormy history of their courtship and the demise of his good name could both be traced in the headlines of *Gaflinger's*. And because good people, well-meaning people, believed the things they read in hallowed shades of black and white, many now believed Remington was an immoral beast and a woman-abusing cad, a man determined to destroy the nation's moral fiber by attacking its most basic institution, marriage. Why, if she didn't know the truth, she would probably be screaming for his neck in a noose herself!

The carriage stopped and the driver jerked open the door. Antonia felt like something of a criminal herself as she mounted those steps, knowing she was the reason Remington was locked up.

The main hall was filled with officers in uniform and a motley consortium of people—some poor and some well-to-do; some decent and some dangerous looking; witnesses, complainants, and those accused of crimes. They approached a sergeant sitting behind a counterlike desk to ask directions, and he sent them up the stairs to a busy waiting room with yet another desk with yet another bobby in uniform. They gave their names and stated their desire to see the Earl of Landon as his legal representatives. The officer looked them over, then focused a suspicious gaze on Antonia.

"You the wife?" he demanded.

She reddened. "No, I am . . . a friend."

"Sure ye are." The officer gave her a sardonic look before turning back to Sir Paddington and Herriot. "You two" —he gestured to them—"come with me."

She looked at them in confusion. "Wait—where do I go?"

"Over to one o' them chairs," the officer said, pointing to several empty chairs on the far side of the waiting room. "You'll have to wait for 'em here."

"But I came to see the earl, too," she said emphatically, and was relieved to hear Sir Paddington affirm and support her intention. The officer wasn't impressed.

"Don't let no females in to see the prisoners . . . except wives. If you ain't his wife—you don't go in. Them's regulations." He wheeled and strode off, and Herriot and Sir Paddington assured her they would look into it, then hurried after him.

Her face burned as she watched them go. She felt demeaned and dismissed and, at first, too devastated by the prospect of not seeing Remington to be angry. But after a moment the anger struck. What sort of stupid regulation kept women from visiting their—their what? Lovers? Her legs felt a little weak, and she made her way to one of the straight wooden chairs that ringed the walls.

Wives had rights. Lovers didn't. They had legal rights —to live with a man, to have children with him, to share his name and bed and company. But in her years of widowhood she had forgotten the more subtle rights of custom that society conferred on married women: the right to be with a husband wherever he was—even in a hospital or a jail or a court—and the right to claim his welfare as her own: to see to his needs and comfort and safety. Marriage was a special claim that allowed a wife access to her husband day and night, in good circumstances and bad, in good health and illness, in times of joy and sorrow.

And she had none of those rights with Remington. She wasn't his wife.

Paddington and Herriot emerged nearly an hour later, looking overheated and irritable. They collected her and hurried down the steps. "Did you see him?" she asked, her fears rising at the grim lines of their faces. "Is he all right? Tell me—"

"He's well enough," Paddington said, offering her his arm. "Brought 'im up in chains, though. Nearly gave poor Herriot here a stroke."

"It's a disgrace—a pure outrage," Herriot declared with quiet fury. "Manacles on a peer of the realm, a member of the House of Lords! I'll see a few boxes are rattled over this, I tell you." After a moment he expelled a hard breath and calmed. "They won't release him without an appearance before a magistrate. I've already sent word to Kingston Gray —he's one of the finest barristers in London. I'm sure he'll defend Lord Carr. But the first order of business is to get him released from this cursed place."

In the carriage on the way home they remembered to give her Remington's regards and informed her that the papers had been regrettably accurate: the charges were indeed twofold. The first was that he had promulgated immoral and seditious views with the intent of undermining the accepted values of society with regard to marriage. Tied to the first charge, strengthening it, was the charge that he had contributed directly to the disruption and demise of five specific marriages.

"Dear heaven—they're blaming him for breaking up the marriages of Lord Woolworth and Sir Albert Everstone and the others!" she said in disbelief.

"They've drawn the charges cleverly," Herriot said solemnly. "All they have to do to prove the first is to produce copies of the articles and papers he has written and call upon the records of the Lords. He has been quite vocal in his opposition to marriage; the evidence is irrefutable. And for the second charge, I suppose they will bring witnesses."

"But he had nothing to do with their marital troubles," Antonia protested. And if anyone should know the truth of the matter, she should. "How could the queen and her government bring such charges based on headlines in a scandal sheet?"

Paddington scowled, thinking about that. "The boy hasn't been in the queen's good graces for some time. She hates talk of female emancipation . . . won't countenance the notion of women working in trade or in the professions. Some months back she banned him from her presence because of his female politics. Didn't seem to matter much. Nobody ever sees the old girl anyway. This nonsense in the newspapers about his breaking up marriages must have been the last straw."

"But a newspaper cannot testify in a . . ." Antonia looked anxiously at the solicitor. "Does that mean the husbands will have to testify against him in court?"

He pulled a document halfway out of a leather briefcase he carried and scanned it. "I would assume these men—Woolworth, Everstone, Searle, Howard, and Trueblood—will be called as witnesses for the Crown."

"Is there no way we can keep them from testifying?" Paddington asked, looking uneasy.

"Not if they are subpoenaed by the court," Herriot said. "And what crown prosecutor in his right mind wouldn't order them to appear? They would make his case." Herriot sighed and stuffed the documents back into his case.

They fell silent for a time, until Antonia's fears got the better of her.

"What will they do to him if he is convicted?" she asked in a choked voice, fearing the very answer she sought.

"Probably send him to prison for a time. Reading Gaol, or some such," Herriot answered dismally.

"B-but people go into Reading Gaol and never come out again," she said. Her own words jolted her.

Remington. The possibility that she might never have him in her arms or make love with him again was crushing. She loved him with all her heart and wanted to spend her hours, days, and years with him. Lord—why hadn't she told him that? Why hadn't she just thrown her arms around him the other day in her room and told him that she loved him? What if she never had another chance to say it?

They rode the rest of the way to Herriot's office in deep silence.

When she arrived home, the atmosphere of Paxton House was thick with tension. Her ladies hurried from all over to hear what had happened, and their reactions ranged from indignation to despair, to righteous fury. The rest of the afternoon and into the evening, Antonia paced and wrung her hands, and her ladies and her Bentick brides waited and worried with her.

She had never felt so helpless in her life, knowing that Remington was in trouble, knowing he needed her, and feeling there was nothing she could do about it. The thought that all of this might have been avoided if she had just agreed to let him "rescue" her was never far from her mind. Her refusal to marry him had placed him in awkward situations again and again, and now *he* was the one in need of rescue. And it would take much more than a marriage vow to save him.

After a simple cold supper that evening, she came across a small gathering of her ladies in the servants' hall, just off the kitchen. She was about to walk in on them when she heard Gertrude say: "Lady Toni's a clever one. She turned 'is lordship around, right enough. Now she'll think of somethin' to help 'im."

The words closed around her heart like a fist. Help him. If she only could. But all afternoon she'd gone over and over it, only to reach the same despairing conclusion: she wasn't a lawyer, and she had no power to affect his case or to change the foul opinions that wretched newspaper had sewn in the minds of people. And she couldn't even see him to give him her support. She had never felt so powerless.

"I jus' wish there was somethin' I could do to help," Gertrude's voice penetrated her thoughts. "I feel so bad. If I hadn'ta talked to that snake Fitch—"

"It wasn't your fault, Gertrude," Eleanor's voice reassured her. "You couldn't have known that he'd betray your confidence like that."

"What confidence?" Antonia stepped through the door, surprising them. "Gertrude, you talked to Rupert Fitch?" The ample cook's shoulders rounded.

"Didn't think it would do no harm." She shook her head miserably. "He was alwus hangin' around the kitchen door, talkin' nineteen to th' dozen."

The story came tumbling out: an offer of coffee here, a bite of pie there, a generous helping of flattery, and a slick bit of journalistic—or was it male?—guile. Soon Gertrude had let down her guard and begun to talk, revealing the developing *tendre* and her hopes for a match between Antonia and Remington. Then on that fateful night nearly two weeks ago, she had told Fitch about Remington leaving, and he went to Remington's house, where he witnessed the sordid spectacle of Antonia's humiliation.

They sat for a moment in silence when Gertrude finished. She looked so miserable that Antonia put an arm around her. "It's all right, Gertrude. It was Fitch, not you."

"Something ought to be done about that man," Pollyanna said fiercely.

"Somebody ought to take him down a peg or two," Molly agreed.

It was hard to say where the idea came from; it seemed to rise independently in several minds at once. And that simple fact seemed to destine its expression.

"*We* should do somethin' about him," Gertrude spoke

their common thought. "I'd give a month off'n my life to watch that worm wring and twist."

They began to talk at once, and somewhere in the midst of those deliciously vengeful suggestions for Fitch's comeuppance, Antonia felt her heart beating faster and her spirits lifting. She was a woman who got things done, a woman who took on challenges and put actions where her beliefs were. She was a clever, contriving woman, and it was high time she began to act like it!

The next afternoon Hermione arrived to stay with Antonia while Paddington and Herriot went to Scotland Yard to see about Remington's release. Antonia had packed a hamper to send to Remington, and no sooner had Paddington and Hoskins lugged it out to the coach than she was already planning another. Half of the ladies of Paxton House gathered in the kitchen to help make food and treats to send to him. The activity made the waiting easier, somehow. A knock came at the kitchen door and she opened it herself, thinking it was the ice man or the boys who hauled away their refuse.

She found herself staring at Albert Everstone and Carter Woolworth, instead. They looked harried in the extreme, and when they saw her, they paled and braced.

"Did you hear? About Landon?" Woolworth spoke for the pair, then glanced over his shoulder and shoved Everstone into the kitchen ahead of him. Wrenching the door from Antonia, he shut it behind them.

"Of course we've heard." She eyed them irritably, stepping back.

"The papers say that they've named us in the charges against him. They say we blame him for wrecking our marriages!" Woolworth declared.

"They're calling our marriages wrecks—it's a nightmare!" Everstone groaned. "Our names will be splattered all over the papers—think of the scandal!"

"It's worse than a scandal," Antonia said, watching their moans of self-pity with rising ire. "The prosecutors will subpoena you and demand that you testify against Remington in open court."

"T-testify?" Everstone said, his eyes widening. "But I don't want to testify!"

Woolworth looked stunned. "If they get us in the witness box, there's no telling what they'll demand to know about our marriages . . . and about Landon." He looked at Antonia with growing alarm. "How can we explain without—good God—we'll be finished!"

"I agree you can't testify," Antonia said, folding her arms and engaging their eyes, letting them feel a bit of the Dragon's heat. "For if you do and you help send him to prison, it might be a very long while before you get your wives back."

"You—you can't do that!" Everstone bellowed. "You can't keep them from coming home!"

"She wouldn't have to," came a voice from the doorway. The men turned and found Margaret and Elizabeth standing just inside the kitchen door: "If you testify against Lord Carr, none of us would be of a mind to come home for quite a while," Margaret said.

"You'll just have to refuse to bear witness against him, Carter," Elizabeth said gravely. Both women nodded, and as the men looked around the kitchen, they spotted other brides here and there around the kitchen worktable nodding too.

Just then Hoskins appeared in the doorway behind Elizabeth and Margaret to announce: "Beggin' your pardon, ma'am. More of them 'husbands' at the door."

Taking Woolworth and Everstone in tow, she hurried up the stairs to meet them. Howard, Trueblood, and Searle were every bit as horrified at the prospect of testifying. And they brought more disturbing news: the subpoena servers were already out and about. Trueblood had nearly bumped into a pair of them hanging around his front door. He had ducked out of the way in time to keep from being seen, thinking they were probably news writers. But they had been dressed better, and he heard one of them say something about "serving him the paper."

"If they can't find you, they can't subpoena you," Antonia said, realizing that at last she had a way to help Remington. "What you need is a place to hide for a while."

She paced and thought and examined each suggestion they made. Hotels were too easy to check, their country houses and clubs were too obvious, and none of them could afford to involve their relatives. They were at a loss until Hermione, who had sat listening to it all, suggested:

"What about Remington's house? Paddington was just saying that he ought to look in today, to let the staff know what is happening. The house is empty except for staff. And who would think to look for Remington's accusers in his own house?"

It was nothing short of brilliant.

Antonia smiled for the first time in more than two days.

A knock came at the kitchen door of Paxton House that same night, and Gertrude crept through the half-darkened kitchen to open it. In stepped Rupert Fitch, in his natty new pin-striped coat and black bowler. "Hello, gorgeous," he said, doffing his hat with a glint in his beady black eyes. "Got your message. Now what's all this about 'needin' to see a bit of justice done'?"

"Aw, Rupert," Gertrude said, sniffling and looking at him as if he were the light of her life. "It's terrible—what that man's done to our laidy Toni. It's jus' one scandal after another. She's plum heartsick." She buried her nose in a handkerchief and took a deep, shuddering breath. A moment later she dabbed at her eyes. "Will ye help 'er, Rupert? Will ye listen to 'er side o' the story and see its gets told straight in the newspapers?"

"Her side, you say? Th' whole story?" He could scarcely contain himself. "Of course, Gertrude," he said wrapping a cozening arm around her. "You just lead me to her and I'll see it all gets written and reported, straight 'n' true."

"Oh, thank ye, Rupert!" Gertrude's joy was utterly sincere. "I knew I could count on ye!" She looked around, searching for some way to repay his largess. "Say—have ye eaten? I've got a tasty stew and some berry pie, and I expect I could find a spot o' wine."

Fitch grinned. He never got food like Gertrude's cooking. Hell—he scarcely got meals at all! A scoop of a story and tasty victuals all at the same time—tonight was indeed his lucky night. He sat down to eat and drink while Gertrude hurried upstairs to fetch Lady Antonia. He finished his food, but couldn't help going back for seconds, and then third helpings of that delicious blackberry pie. He had settled back at the table for a bit of a smoke when Lady Antonia appeared, looking pale and distraught and, oh, so lovely.

Fitch pulled out his yellow pad and his most solicitous manner, and as she began to speak of the way the earl had provoked her to that vile Woman Wager, he began to scribble notes.

"Are you writing it all down on that little pad?" Lady Antonia asked, her sapphire eyes wide and so very innocent.

"I take notes first, then I'll write out the full story later," he said.

"Oh. And will the story be in the paper tomorrow?" she

asked with the most musical lilt to her voice. He felt a curious rumble in his stomach and sat straighter.

"You bet it will." That made him stop to think: to be sure of a good spot, he'd better warn the night editor that he had a late-breaking scoop for the front page. He asked Lady Antonia if she had a footman or anyone who could carry a message to his paper, and she said her butler would do so. He promptly wrote out a note and handed it to the old boy, who shuffled off to deliver it.

"Now, where were we?" Fitch asked. And as he poised his pencil over the pad, he felt a growl of discomfort in his belly. By the time he had written two or three pages of notes, his belly was heaving and cramping. At five pages of notes it felt as if someone were tearing him in two. He grabbed his stomach and held tight; then, when he couldn't bear it, he jumped up and headed for the back door.

They found him doubled over in the service yard, where he had emptied his stomach, and they helped him back inside.

"Dearie me," Gertrude said, frowning. "I hope it wasn't nothin' ye ate."

Fitch gamely declared he was feeling better and sat down to continue. But in two minutes he was rolling on the bench by the table, clutching his belly and groaning.

"I hope that stew weren't a bit offish," Gertrude said, going to sniff the pot.

Fitch asked to lie down a moment, and they helped him into the servant's hall and onto a bench by the hearth. He had never felt so bloody awful in his life. And before long he was ready to embarrass himself yet again. Afterward he opened his eyes to find several women standing around him, with solicitous smiles.

"Feeling awful, Mr. Fitch? That's a nasty bit of something you've got," one said.

"Like comin' to like, I reckon," said another.

"You needn't worry about a thing. We'll take care of you," said a third.

Then Gertrude's face appeared in his swarmy vision . . . smiling with a vengeful glint. "A pity you won't be able to finish Lady Toni's story, Rupert. But I tell ye what." She patted him. "We'll just finish it for ye."

Squalling with both pain and alarm, Fitch tried to rise. "You can't . . . do that!" But he quickly found himself on his back, writhing in pain.

"Oh, it's no trouble," Gertrude said with a smile of genuine pleasure. "After all ye done for us . . . we owe ye one."

Chapter

22

The next morning the headline of *Gaflinger's* read:

The Widow Tells Her Story!

And under the byline of the infamous Rupert Fitch was the tantalizing subheader: "Allegations Against the Earl Totally Unfair." The lengthy article reported an interview with Lady Antonia Paxton, the lovely widow who had challenged the Earl of Landon to the wager that had set London's tongues a'wag. And there was plenty in the report to set tongues wagging anew: the lady's discussion of the earl's early skepticism, praise for his diligence in performing the "women's work" required of him, and the tantalizingly worded evidences of his gradual change of heart.

Through it all the insightful Fitch glimpsed and reported Lady Antonia's deep-felt respect for the earl—especially in the face of the hideous things that were being said about him in the papers. And with a final, dramatic flourish, Fitch detailed the lady's horror and heartache at the ugly rumors that had been stirred in the papers about her personally, as a result of an unfortunate story involving another infamous pair of the London elite. In an unprecedented act of journalistic sensitivity, Fitch admitted that he was the very writer who had reported that story and offered her a gallant apology for the distress its vagueness had caused her.

The article was an immediate sensation. *Gaflinger's*—whose editor had been flabbergasted by Fitch's story, but in desperation to fill the space he had held, had printed it anyway—had to go back to press with an afternoon edition to supply the demand for papers. Not a small part of the sensation was the hint of even greater revelations the next day, when a second article was promised.

Antonia sent Hoskins out to buy several copies of the paper, and shared one of them with Rupert Fitch, who had been installed in an unused servant's room on the fourth floor of her house. He had begun to recover and felt well enough to take nourishment. Whether from the food or from the sight of the article he hadn't written, he quickly suffered a relapse into the illness that had struck him down the night before.

Once again Antonia helpfully put pen to paper to help him meet his deadline.

Fitch's article, sensational as it was, had stiff competition from reports in the *Telegraph* and the *Evening News*, both of which quoted the earl's solicitors as saying that he was being unfairly prosecuted for his political and social views, and that the earl was far from the radical opponent of marriage that he was painted to be. Opinion articles resurrected the notion of the Woman Wager and speculated on whether doing women's work had changed his attitude toward women and marriage. And the papers ran companion pieces analyzing and discussing his published papers, from an Oxford don, a leading suffragist, and an expert in social theory from the Royal Society for the Study of Eugenic Living.

Then the following morning Rupert Fitch's second article appeared, and the speculation raised in the other papers was satisfied by yet another scoop by the gritty little correspondent. Newsboys selling *Gaflinger's Gazette* were fairly mobbed by people eager to have a copy of the piece titled:

THE "WOMAN WAGER" WON BY THE WIDOW!

According to Fitch, the infamous wager was conceded by the earl to the widow and—even more spectacular—it had resulted in a true change of heart in the archbachelor. And the article divulged that Lady Antonia, seeing the great change in him toward women and marriage, had agreed to fulfill her side of the bargain of her own free will.

Then came what the entire countryside had waited for: the revelation that the Earl of Landon had actually proposed to Mrs. Paxton, offering her his protection in the light of certain damaging publicity. The article detailed how she had tearfully declined, not wishing to burden the gallant earl. And in a disarmingly candid statement, she declared that the earl had proved to be a man of honor and generosity and great kindness. She had nothing but the highest respect and the warmest regard for him, and she was distraught at the government's attempt to malign and discredit him.

In the palace the queen's ear for intrigue detected the buzz of scandal, and when she demanded to know what was afoot, Fitch's article was produced by her red-faced secretary. Victoria sat listening to it, growing more choleric by the paragraph.

"Enough!" she said, waving her secretary to a halt. "That poor creature, Mrs. Paxton, having such lies attributed to her. We are to believe that Landon proposed and she declined—what fools do these news writers think we are? It's clear he's paid the little wretch to print it, hoping to draw sympathy in his favor. Well, it will not work!" She picked up her drawing pad and continued sketching the nude figures frolicking by a stream in a scene from her favorite Winterhalter painting. "Sympathy or not, he's a scandal and an embarrassment to the Crown, and I want to see the immoral beast get exactly what is coming to him."

In his jail cell, still awaiting his release, Remington read the article that Paddington had brought him, and sat stunned for a moment. He couldn't imagine what had gotten into the venomous Fitch—or where he had gotten hold of such stunningly accurate information—unless it was from Antonia or someone in her household. But after a moment he jumped up on his rickety bed and leaned his ear toward the barred window. As he listened, he fancied that he could hear on the wind the sound of the queen once again screaming for his head on a platter.

"Six bloody days in that hellhole!" Remington declared the minute the coach was under way. He looked back at the crowd they left behind and the news writers running after them, still shouting questions. Then he settled irritably back into his seat, scratching vigorously beneath his coat. "I think I've lost half a stone and I'm sure I've got fleas! What took so bloody long?"

Herriot and Uncle Paddington explained the monstrous delay: finding a magistrate who would handle the request for release. Remington's case was a political hot potato and no one wanted their fingers burned. Then there was endless wrangling over the requirement of bail money, which was a callous attempt by the liberal element in government to show that the courts were unbiased and no respecters of person. When bail was finally agreed, it had taken a while to collect the shocking amount of money required to guarantee his appearance in court.

Both prosecution and defense had pulled out all the stops, employing stall tactics and shouting matches—all that on just the matter of his freedom for the two days that remained until the trial started.

The explanation only served to deepen Remington's irritation. "How dare they require surety of me—I'm a sitting member of the Lords!"

"Our point exactly," Herriot said tersely. "The papers have taken note, I'll tell you, and it's raised a bit of a stir. A stroke of luck for you, actually."

"It is?" Remington snarled, burrowing back into the seat.

"Absolutely, my boy," Paddington inserted, handing him a newspaper with a headline reading:

OUTRAGEOUS BAIL REQUIRED FOR LANDON!

Beneath it was a subheader declaring: "Does Government Prosecute or Persecute Controversial Earl?"

"The papers have come down on your side. Called it irregular and vindictive. The *Telegraph* and *Evening News* both have said it was the queen's undue influence, and that, since she doesn't 'bother' with public life, she ought not to 'bother' the courts, either. The Lords passed a bill of protest, and there have been a number of fiery speeches in the Commons."

"There have?" Remington scanned the paper and his tense frame relaxed. "This is certainly a novelty—seeing my name in the papers without the words 'radical,' 'woman hater,' or 'depravity' linked to it."

It was dusk when they arrived at his home. There was a small crowd of news writers loitering on the street outside. As the coach slowed to enter the carriage turn by the front steps, the writers swarmed after it, waving and shoving to get onto the steps ahead of him. He battled his way toward the doors, growing steadily more indignant at their relentlessness and furious at the way they invented what they couldn't—

"Come on, yer lordship—give us *somethin'* to print!" one called out plaintively.

It struck him like a bolt out of the blue, stopping him in his tracks. They invented things because they needed something to publish. Then why didn't he just give them something—something *he* wanted to see in print?

"You want a quote? Then try this," he said, turning to them with a calculated smile. "These charges are totally spurious . . . brought to punish me for speaking my mind and publishing my views." He struck a pose of subtle drama. "We enjoy a vigorous and independent press in Britain, one that promotes and encourages the exchange of ideas. But it will not remain free much longer if we who dare to think new thoughts and publish them are arrested for being a danger to society.

"I have dared to ask questions about that most basic of institutions: marriage. And in my questioning I have learned a great deal. When I walk into that courtroom a few days hence, I alone will not be on trial. The institution of marriage will stand trial with me." He paused. "Now, if you will excuse me, I would like a bath and a bit of decent food." He managed a wry smile. "Scotland Yard accommodations, gentlemen, leave a good bit to be desired."

They tossed additional questions at him, but he turned and shoved his way past them and through the opening doors. They stood outside for a while, watching, hoping he would relent and speak again. But when one correspondent decided simply to use what the earl had already said and left, the others saw him hurrying off to his paper and soon followed.

"My lord!" Phipps met him looking uncharacteristically flustered. "How good to have you home, my lord! We didn't expect you so . . . that is . . . we thought . . ."

He took the hat Remington held because he hadn't wished to put it on with his hair so filthy.

"A bath, Phipps. And while Manley is preparing it, I want something to eat," Remington ordered, heading straight for the stairs leading down to the kitchen. "Whatever you have on hand will do—I'm famished. I'd have starved if it hadn't been for Antonia's hampers. Uncle Paddington, show Mr. Herriot where the liquor is."

"Really, my lord—" Phipps hurried along after him, paling a bit more with every step Remington took. "Truly, I can bring you a tray in just a few minutes—"

Remington went charging into the kitchen before he could be stopped. But once there, he stopped dead. At the table—his kitchen table—were five faces he had sworn to put his fist through the very next time he encountered them.

"What in hell are you doing here?" he demanded, stalking toward them with his fists clenched.

"We're . . . we're . . ." Trueblood put down the glass in his hand and backed away from the table.

"Eating," Everstone supplied, pushing back from the table and rising, his cheeks bulging with ham and roast potatoes.

"I can see that!" Remington roared. "What in God's name are you doing in *my* kitchen eating *my* food?"

Woolworth swallowed what was in his mouth with some difficulty, then shoved to his feet. He glanced at the others and then squared his shoulders manfully and confessed: "Dodging subpoenas."

Remington closed his eyes for a moment as he gathered strength. His association with these pathetic "ruined bachelors" had proved to be the very low point of his life—and with each new encounter that point seemed to sink a bit lower. This was probably yet another catastrophe in the making.

"Let me get this straight," he said, suddenly fixing them with a glare. "You're hiding in my house . . . from the people who are trying to serve you subpoenas to testify against me?" When they nodded, he momentarily lost control.

"Good God—wherever did you get such a harebrained idea?" he thundered. It was Woolworth who assigned the blame.

"From Lady Antonia."

"She and her aunt thought that this would be the last place they would look for us . . . and since you weren't here . . ." Howard tried to explain.

Remington closed his eyes. Antonia. He should have known. Devious woman. First she worked a little magic on Fitch to turn things around in the newspapers, and now this. Maddening woman. Interfering woman. Delicious woman. She was undoubtedly worth every bit of trouble he was going through to win her.

Paddington and Herriot came rushing downstairs to see what all the commotion was about and halted behind Remington, wide-eyed at the sight of five gentlemen sitting in his kitchen in shirtsleeves and braces. Remington came to life, snatching up a slab of bread and a hunk of ham and somebody's glass of wine, then ordering the lot of them upstairs, to sort it all out. When introductions were made minutes later in Remington's study, lawyer Herriot went perfectly gray in the face.

"Dear Lord—these are the men named in the charges against you!" When Remington nodded, he grew frantic. "Then you've got to get them out of here! If they're found here, it will look as if you're trying to influence their testimony!"

As Remington stared at the lawyer, his mind raced. Then a slow, inexpressibly wicked smile stole over his handsome face.

"Oh, no! You cannot let them stay," Herriot declared, watching a scheme being born in Remington's expression. "It's . . . irregular . . . possibly *criminal*!"

"So is the government's case against me," Remington responded. "And perhaps it's time to fight fire with fire."

When asked to relate how it had all come about, the five husbands spun yet another tale of their marital woes. Their conjugal fate had now been linked to the success of his defense, they informed him. Their wives, under Lady Antonia's influence, refused to come home to them until he was free.

"What are we to do, Landon?" Woolworth demanded, looking shaken. "If we testify, our marital troubles will be splattered all over London! I'm already on thin ice with my family—my uncles have already paid me a call over this business with my mother. I can't stand another brouhaha."

"If we don't testify—it will look as if we've something to hide!" Trueblood whined.

"Because we damn well do!" Everstone ground out. "I may have to stand for reelection at any time. Can't have my troubles with Margaret made grist for the political mill—I'd be finished!"

"And if we do testify, our wives won't speak to us for months—years!" Howard declared. "This just gets worse and worse! You've got to do something, Landon!"

"On the contrary, gentlemen," Remington said, settling into the chair behind his desk, munching his ham on white bread and looking perversely pleased. "This time I'm afraid it is *you* who will have to do something."

"Us?" Searle said, nearly choking on the word. "What can we possibly do?"

Remington gave them a perfectly devious smile.

"Testify, gentlemen. You can testify."

The courtroom, Number One Court of the Old Bailey, was packed, and had been from the moment the doors opened, the morning of the trial. News writers, liberal Lords, conservative MP's, curious socialites, placard-carrying suffragists, outraged clergymen, and even a few ordinary citizens jostled for the standing room at the side of the gallery. A similar crowd—with the addition of pickpockets, protesters, constables, and roasted-nut vendors—filled the corridors outside and spilled out into the street. This was a sensational trial, and there wasn't a person in London who didn't wish to be there to see the proceedings.

That large and increasingly unruly crowd greeted Antonia and her ladies as they arrived. One of the news writers recognized her as she stepped out of the cab and rushed to question her. In seconds she was beset on all sides by people shouting questions, spouting scripture, chanting suffrage slogans, waving signs, and even offering her money to endorse face cream! She managed to reach a bobby, and he helped clear a path so they could enter the building.

Remington's solicitor was waiting outside the courtroom and spotted her above the crowd. With some effort they showed their passes and made it down the steps to the front of the gallery, where Aunt Hermione and Uncle Paddington had saved them front-row seats. Antonia took several breaths to steady herself, then straightened her hat and smoothed the bodice of the creamy-yellow shot-silk dress that Florence and Victoria had spent half the night updating. She had chosen to wear something cheerful and easy to spot, so Remington could see her from the prisoner's dock—that is, assuming that he wanted to see her.

She still hadn't seen him since his release nearly two days ago. Paddington brought word that he was closeted with his solicitor and barrister, planning his defense. He also brought her a personal note from Remington, which thanked her for all her help and support and assured her that he was doing well. She had read and reread it, trying to find meaning between the lines and finding only blank space instead.

Was he furious with her? Did he not want to see her? She had lain in her darkened bed the night before, aching for him, wishing he would materialize out of the dark to love her and reassure her. Why wouldn't he come, or at least ask her to come to him? Through the long night she had been tortured by what he had said the last time she had seen him: he didn't want a lover . . . he wanted a wife. Was it possible that after all this he didn't want her anymore?

Now as she sat in the courtroom, waiting to see him for the first time since he left her bed more than a week ago, she was terrified that he would turn in her direction with a cool, polite smile and look right through her.

Below them the floor of the court was filling with black-robed barristers and their associates. They bustled back and forth, shuffling papers, exchanging briefs, and covertly preening their robes and wigs. At the front of the paneled court loomed the judicial bench, behind which three high-backed chairs sat awaiting the clerk's cry and the arrival of the three justices.

Remington appeared a short while later, accompanied by barrister Kingston Gray, who would present and argue his defense. Remington's impeccable dove-gray morning coat and black silk tie were an elegant counterpoint to the sea of black robes on the floor of the court. There was an audible, and decidedly feminine, stir when he looked up and swept the gallery with a searching glance.

His eyes settled on Antonia, and he stilled, staring at her, absorbing her with his eyes. Dark eyes. Irresistible eyes. But eyes that gave little clue to the emotions behind them. Her heart stopped. And then he smiled at her. It was a small, speaking smile, but for the life of her Antonia couldn't make out what it was saying.

He turned back to confer with his counsel before allowing warders to escort him to the prisoner's dock. Then a hush of expectation fell over the venerable Number One Court. A moment later the crier entered and called out: "Oyez, oyez, oyez. All manner of persons that owe suit and service to this court of the Central Criminal Courts, draw nigh and give your attendance!"

The bewigged and scarlet-robed justices took their seats behind the bench. Antonia reached for Aunt Hermione's hand and stared at Remington as the clerk of the court rose to read the charges against him. He seemed composed and outwardly confident as they detailed his crimes against the Crown and state.

". . . Remington Carr did advocate and promulgate ideas injurious to both the common moral will and the common good, to wit: views and opinions denigrating that most sacred and beneficial institution which is the foundation of society and which has been ordained for humankind by the Almighty Himself: marriage," the clerk read in stentorian tones. She vibrated with the urge to stand up and shout the little wretch down. "That Remington Carr did actively seek and contribute toward the destruction of at least five existing marriages . . . and through the injuries inflicted upon their unions, he did attempt to do injury to all other marriages by association."

As if feeling her eyes on him, Remington let his gaze wander to Antonia. After the third or so time that their eyes met across the courtroom, Antonia felt the coil of anxiety in her loosen. What he could not say in a display of emotion, he seemed to say with the frequency of his glances. He thought of her. She still mattered to him. She felt a little dizzy with relief. By the time the prosecutor began his opening argument, she was able to sit straight and focus on the proceedings.

The case boiled down to a very simple and very ugly situation, the lord prosecutor declared. The Earl of Landon despised marriage and had written about it, spoken about it, and avoided it personally. He had denounced it as an unfit association and advocated that people refrain from it, if unwedded, and abandon it, if already wedded. Then he had carried his views one unforgivable step further, by attempting to destroy the marriages of five prominent men.

The dignified Kingston Gray rose to make his opening argument, and a hush fell over the gallery. The Earl of Landon had only dared to express what virtually every bachelor on the face of the earth had felt at one time or other, to one extent or another—that marriage was an inequitable and archaic institution, which should not be permitted to tyrannize the lives of both men and women any longer. People ought to have choices besides marriage, he believed. And he had written and spoken his opinions in a decent, orderly, and scholarly manner that had harmed no one. In due time the facts would exonerate his client.

Opening the testimony, the prosecutor called a series of witnesses dealing with the publication of Remington's various articles on marriage. Large sections of his clear, pungent articles from the *Spectator,* the *New Statesman,* and *Blackwood's Magazine* were read in the court, establishing the fact that he advised the unmarried to stay unmarried and those married to live as if they were not married: men and women each responsible for themselves, at least with regard to work and financial support. Next, the prosecutor presented two renowned social theorists who were asked to give their assessment of what would happen to society if people were to take seriously Lord Carr's dangerous advice.

As expected, they declared that a chaotic and dangerous situation would result: unstable marriages, difficulties between men and women, children abandoned to the streets, immorality and sloth, and the eventual collapse of the society as it was currently known. It was damaging testimony from well-credentialed and creditable witnesses.

When it was time for cross-examination, the distinguished Kingston Gray rose, grasped the lapels of his robe, and demanded to know of these learned witnesses whether they knew of any other such advice on marriage, from any other source. Each denied knowing of any creditable thinker who had dared attack marriage in such a heinous and shortsighted manner. Kingston Gray smiled and handed the second witness, an Oxford professor, a book, asking him to read a marked passage.

". . . Art thou loosed from a wife? seek not a wife.
But and if thou marry, thou hast not sinned; and if a virgin
marry, she hath not sinned. Nevertheless, such shall have
trouble in the flesh: but I spare you.
But this I say, brethren, the time is short: it remaineth that
both they that have wives be as though they had none . . ."

There was a murmur through the court as the antique-sounding words were read, falling with familiarity on the more educated ear. Kingston Gray asked the professor if he was familiar with the passage, and the gentleman swallowed hard and reddened, saying that he couldn't recall . . . he might have heard it somewhere before.

"Does not this writer advocate that those who are unmarried stay that way?"

"Well, yes—"

"And does not this writer go on to advocate that married persons should behave as if they are unmarried?"

"Yes, I suppose, but—"

"Would you look at the title of that book, sir, and tell

the court just what radical and dangerous text it is that exhorts people to such godless and antisocial behavior."

The professor looked at the title, turned scarlet, and fairly choked on the words.

"The Holy Bible."

Volleys of laughter, murmurs, and gasps of outrage burst forth from the gallery, as Kingston Gray retrieved his book and raised his voice to address the court in booming tones. "A most radical and dangerous bit of advice from that most radical and seditious thinker, St. Paul the Evangelist. I submit to the court that his book was written nearly two thousand years ago . . . and these words have been read and discussed countless times over the intervening centuries . . . without crumbling the foundations of our civilization or making the slightest inroad against what St. Paul deemed the 'necessary evil' of marriage. Ideas, my learned justices, are powerful things. But only if people take them to heart and put them into action. There is no proof that my client's, ideas—however shocking—have damaged society or its members in the least."

There was another outbreak of reaction in the gallery: cheers and boos and generally rowdy approval for Kingston Gray's clever gambit. As the prosecutors huddled in conference and the justices conferred among themselves, the bailiffs moved to restore order in the gallery.

When things quieted, Antonia found herself growing tense with expectation and dread. The second half of the prosecutors' case revolved around the testimony of the five men who had accused him of wrecking their marriages. They were not present in the courtroom, but then neither had been the "expert" witnesses just called.

As the delay progressed, there seemed to be some consternation on the part of the prosecutors, who begged the court for a recess in order to confer with their next witnesses. Seeing that it was approaching one o'clock, the justices agreed to their request and went them one better, adjourning court for midday recess.

Antonia wilted with relief. She looked down the bench to her Bentick brides and lifted crossed fingers that they understood full well. She cast Remington a wistful look across the way as he was being swept away by his solicitors. Then she went with her ladies to eat at a restaurant, though —in truth—the only thing she hungered for was a few short, sweet words with Remington.

After midday recess, the crier announced the justices, the court convened, and the prosecutor called his first witness of the afternoon.

"Lord Carter Woolworth, present yourself to the court and be sworn in."

Antonia tensed. She had been expecting this. As the seconds labored by, she watched the doors below . . . and nearly fainted when one opened and Carter Woolworth stepped inside!

Steadying herself with a grip on Aunt Hermione's arm, she leaned forward to look down the bench at Elizabeth Woolworth. The young woman's face was pale and her eyes were dark with distress as she met Antonia's gaze. Then together they watched him take the witness box and swear to tell the truth. Antonia felt her stomach sink and closed her eyes.

Carter Woolworth glanced up nervously at the gallery and smiled at his blanched wife. And he proceeded to answer the prosecutor's questions about his association with the Earl of Landon.

"We were at school together, some years ago. Harrow. We went on to Oxford together but hadn't seen each other for some time, until of late."

"Let me ask you, your lordship, to recall the events of the night of June seventeenth. Were you or were you not on the street outside your club, White's, on St. James Street between nine-thirty and ten o'clock?"

"Was I?" Woolworth looked a bit taken aback. "Well, if you say so, sir . . ."

"No, *I* do not say so." The prosecutor struck a determined pose. "*You* must say so. Were you or were you not there, sir?"

"Truly, I . . . cannot recall. I usually have a few drinks at my club. Or more than a few. A fellow loses count . . . along with a few other faculties." He tossed a grin toward the gallery, and laughter broke out.

The prosecutor glared at the young lord and tried a different tack. "I submit to you that you may have been on that street at that hour . . . and involved in an altercation with the earl. . . ." Kingston Gray objected and was upheld. The prosecutor decided upon a more direct approach.

"Have you or have you not accused Remington Carr of destroying your marriage?"

Woolworth's amicable facade dropped like a wet curtain. "My marriage, sir, is quite healthy. Why on earth should I accuse a friend and a gentleman of destroying it?"

"Is it not true, my lord, that you and your wife are currently separated?"

"Ye gods—you see how these cursed rumors circulate." Woolworth grew quite indignant. "My wife is currently visiting a lady friend whose aunt is seriously ill. She has taken time out to come to court to support my testimony." He pointed to the gallery. "There she is. My wife, Elizabeth."

As the barristers and justices raised eyes to the gallery, Elizabeth could do nothing but smile weakly, redden, and nod. The prosecutor was vexed in the extreme. "Have you or have you not discussed the problems of your marriage with the earl?"

"I have. Though I believe to call the normal and usual adjustments of a bachelor to wedded life 'problems' might be painting it a bit thick. The earl initiated certain questions and discussions on the subject . . . during which I was pleased to impart to him whatever wisdom I had gained on the subject of matrimony."

Antonia's jaw dropped, and she leaned forward to glance at Elizabeth, whose eyes were wide and shocked. Wisdom? He had tutored the earl on matrimony?

"You expect the court to believe you tutored the Earl of Landon on marriage?" The prosecutor's face was crimson and the veins in his temples were throbbing visibly.

"I cannot answer for what the court believes, sir. I only know that I have spoken at length with the earl, giving him my views of matrimony. You see, I was—how shall I say it? —a reluctant bridegroom. I had been a bachelor until my thirtieth year and feared the adjustment to family life." He fixed his gaze upon Elizabeth, in the gallery, and his face softened with a smile.

"But I needn't have feared. My wife is a wise and understanding woman, who has helped me to learn that most primary of lessons: that a man must leave his father and *mother* and cleave only to his wife, as scripture teaches." Elizabeth slid to the edge of her seat and gripped the railing before her, watching him declare to her—before God and the government of Britain—that which she most longed to hear.

"A man and his wife become one flesh, it is said, and together they must make their fortune and their way through the ups and downs of life. Thus, the love and affection of a wife supplants those other loves and loyalties in a man's heart. And in time that love grows and that union bears the sweet fruit of family life. Especially when a woman is as loving and gracious as my dear Elizabeth."

There were tears in Elizabeth's eyes as Gray declined to cross-examine and Woolworth was excused from the witness box. She rose and went to meet him at the far aisle. They stood for a moment, staring into each other's eyes; then he offered her his arm and she let him lead her out.

Antonia watched them threading their way through the crowd and felt her heart give a single heavy thud, then race a moment later to make up for lost beats. She had little time to think about what it all meant, for when she turned back, she heard the bailiff calling the next witness. "Sir Albert Everstone . . ."

Forewarned by Woolworth's testimony, the prosecutor took a stern approach right from the start with Sir Albert. But Everstone also had difficulty recalling the events of the night in question. And no matter how the prosecutor phrased it or belabored it, he could not seem to recall more than having a few drinks with his old school chums, Landon included. Then came the questions about the rocky state of his marriage.

"A scurrilous lie, sir," Everstone blustered, looking ready to throw down the gauntlet. "Why, my wife and me are the very picture of wedded bliss."

"How can that be, sir, when you are separated from her?" the prosecutor challenged him.

"Who dares make such a scandalous charge, sir? and on what grounds? My wife is visiting a friend . . . the lady, in fact, that stood up with her at our wedding. And she has returned recently to attend this court today. There she sits" —he pointed to the blushing Margaret—"in the gallery now. My dear wife. I'll take exception with any man who casts aspersion upon my marriage, sir!"

"Did not the Earl of Landon interfere in your marriage by speaking out against the restrictions of married life and trying to persuade you to leave your wife?"

"He never did, sir! And I'll take any man to task who says he did. Landon is a decent chap and a good friend. We did discuss marriage, on numerous occasions. And I was pleased to give him the benefit of my experience." He paused and shifted his gaze to Margaret, in the gallery. His gruffness muted, while the urgency of his manner intensified. Margaret leaned forward to meet his gaze and clasped her hands, pressing them to her lips.

"You see, I too went into harness a bit laggardly," Everstone explained, drawing sympathetic male laughter from the spectators. "I'm known for being a bit close with a coin, and I will say that I feared marriage would be a most costly undertaking. Was quite right about that, sir . . . costly it is. Requires all a man has got. But I had not reckoned with the yield I would gain on that investment."

"Which is?" the prosecutor demanded, following the line of Everstone's gaze to the gallery. The sight of Margaret's face, filled with heartfelt emotion, infuriated him.

"The profit is . . . all a woman has inside her. As the good book says: 'Who can put a price on a virtuous woman? Her price is far above rubies.' And my Margaret is the pearl without price." His stern expression melted into a tentative smile as he saw Margaret smile lovingly at him. "Told Landon all that when he asked. I said a man is meant to give his wife worldly goods, to share all he has with her. Teaches a fellow generosity and largeness of heart. It's easy to give to a woman like my Margaret . . . who gives a lot back."

Recognizing the futility of his efforts, the prosecutor yielded to the defense, who had no questions. The justices dismissed Everstone, and the prosecutor asked for a moment to confer with his associates. While they were in conference, Everstone walked up the side aisle to the row where Margaret sat, and extended his hand.

Margaret rose with tears in her eyes and joined him, placing her hand in his and proudly walking out with him.

Antonia watched in confusion. Good Lord—the things they were saying! They had taught Remington about cleaving to their wives and sharing their worldly possessions? It was absurd . . . preposterous. . . .

She turned to stare at Remington and found him looking at her with a subtle twinkle in his eye. That knowing glint said that he was somehow responsible for their unexpected testimony—if it could rightly be called "testimony." It was more like a shameless and irresistible bit of wooing, done at great risk, in front of an entire courtroom. By testifying as they had, Woolworth and Everstone had both proclaimed their own willingness to change and addressed openly the problems that lay at the heart of their marriages. And in so doing they had reclaimed their wives.

She let the surprised pleasure in her heart rise into her eyes as she looked back at Remington. What a deliciously devious man he was. By testifying as they had, they had also reduced the government's case against Remington. When Remington looked away, she realized the prosecutor was addressing the bench, and came alert.

"Your honors, we must ask the court's indulgence to add one more witness to the list. He has not yet been found, but we hope to locate him shortly. There is considerable discrepancy in testimony here, and this witness should help us get to the bottom of it."

The justices conferred, then announced they would allow it, providing it did not result in undue delay. "And the name of this witness is?" the chief justice demanded.

"Rupert Fitch, your honor. He is a news writer for *Gaflinger's Gazette*."

Antonia froze, thinking of the little wretch lying ill, abed, asleep, on the uppermost floor of her house. What would they do if they couldn't find him? Would she be breaking the law by not coming forward with him? He was certainly in no condition to testify. . . .

"Meanwhile, your honors, the Crown calls to witness Mr. Basil Trueblood."

With dread settling over her shoulders, she watched Trueblood fend off the prosecutor's bullying questions about his "ruined" marriage to declare that he, too, had been reluctant to wed, but was now the most content of married men. In marriage, he declared, he had learned a great deal. In spite of the florid-faced prosecutor's insistence that it was not necessary to tutor the court, Basil forged ahead to enlighten the Queen's Bench, just as he had his friend, the Earl of Landon. But in truth, his eyes directed every word he spoke, not to the justices but to the pale, slender beauty who sat anxiously in the first row of the gallery, watching with her heart in her eyes.

"Marriage, you see, is a union, a partnership of two woefully imperfect creatures. But, according to the wisdom of the Divine Plan, when these two flawed and incomplete beings join, a wondrous thing happens . . . and that thing is called love. And that love grows to cover and then to change those imperfections. And in the course of loving, even the faults, blemishes, and defects of our beloved become dear and precious to us. None of us is perfect, fortunately. For if we were, we would have no need of each other." His lanky face brightened with a smile formed just for Alice. "And if I have learned anything in my short marriage, it is that my dear wife, Alice, however imperfect, is still *perfect for me.*"

Antonia watched Basil claim his weepy bride and escort her out the door. She blinked back the mist in her own eyes and sent Remington a wondering smile.

The agitated prosecutor, sensing the futility of calling his final two witnesses, rested—with the stipulation that he could reopen his case for the testimony of Rupert Fitch, as soon as the news writer was found.

The justices, taking note that it was nearly five o'clock, bound over all witnesses and recessed until the following morning. As the spectators filed out of the court, news writers descended upon Antonia and Remington, who had no opportunity to speak to each other. Antonia gave him a last, longing look as she watched him being inundated by ravenous newshounds. Then she went home with her ladies and spent the evening writing Rupert Fitch's account of the trial.

The gauntlet outside the Central Criminal Court was even more formidable the next morning. The crowd was larger and included a number of rowdy elements that hadn't been there the day before: Fabian reformers, trade unionists distributing leaflets, ladies' temperance-committee members, patent-medicine salesmen hawking their wares, and adolescent boys with leftover Christmas crackers. The air was filled with the clamor of the crowd and the calls of newsboys passing among the crowd with their morning editions.

TESTIMONY TURNS IN LANDON'S FAVOR!

That *Gaflinger's* headline, written by the incomparable Rupert Fitch, was followed by a subheader reading: "Kingston Gray Brilliant!" The *Telegraph*'s headline assigned the credit elsewhere:

St. Paul Testifies for the Defense!

Other papers presented a somewhat more equivocal opinion of how the testimony was running, some quoting Remington, some St. Paul. But it all served to heighten interest in the trial and to make it just that much harder for Antonia and her ladies to fight their way through the crowd into the courthouse and the courtroom.

Once seated, Antonia looked for Remington and finally spotted him entering through the prisoner's door. He looked up at her with a warmer and more tactile smile than yesterday, and the sight of it set Antonia's heart racing. She returned his daring visual caress, pouring all the love in her heart into a brief, dazzling smile.

In an outlandish move Kingston Gray opened the defense by calling the prosecution's two unused witnesses. Mr. Bertrand Howard took the stand to testify that Remington Carr had taken him aside after his recent nuptials to give him an excellent bit of advice. And when asked to relate that advice, he fixed his rather squinty gaze on his bride of three months, Camille, and declared: "Marriage is a partnership built upon companionship. It involves the blending of lives, of families, of friends, and of ideals. And such a blending can occur only by the spending of time and effort." Here he softened remarkably in both voice and demeanor, gazing at his Camille. "But such sweet effort it is, such divine toil . . . to be ever in your beloved wife's company, to hear her voice, to see her smile. It is the work of heaven here on earth." He paused, then added, "The sharing of my hours with my dear wife is the crowning joy of my life."

The prosecutor glowered at him on cross-examination.

"Do you mean to say that Remington Carr, the same man who wrote that marriage is 'an onerous and inequitable union,' advised you to view marriage as a partnership? a sharing? a joy?"

"I meant to say exactly that," Howard said, looking puzzled. "Did I not do so?"

Lord Richard Searle took the stand next to testify that his marriage was not, as had been suggested, destroyed. He went on to say that Remington Carr had spoken to him on more than one occasion about the fact that marriage was "a safe haven from the storms and wintry blasts of life and fortune. And my dear wife, Daphne, is the very calm after the storm. She is the mate to my temperament, an anchor in the gales of my own blustery nature. Marriage, at its best, leads us to grow, to become better men. We strive to improve ourselves"—he stared at his wife in the gallery, with undisguised adoration—"to make ourselves worthy of those to whom we owe our hearts."

The prosecutor was so insulted that he just kept his seat and with a furious hand waved away his right to question the witness.

Antonia watched Howard and Searle reclaiming their wives and looked with pride at the empty seats on the bench. She knew full well who had done the tutoring and who had done the learning. And as she understood that the words came from Remington, she absorbed them into her heart. Marriage was cleaving to the beloved through good and bad times; it was a sharing and a giving that enlarged the heart; it was spending the days and nights of life together; it was changing to accommodate the beloved—growing past prejudices and imperfections.

She was so filled with her own tumbling, reckless thoughts, that she scarcely heard the next witness being called. Hermione nudged her, and when she looked up, both her aunt and Sir Paddington were staring at her with widened eyes. She frowned, then looked around to find Eleanor, Prudence, Molly, and Gertrude all looking at her with something akin to alarm.

And then she heard the crier's voice: "Mrs. Antonia Paxton, present yourself to the court and be sworn in."

Chapter

23

The crier called her name once more, before the summons and the shocked faces of her family and friends finally penetrated her disbelief. She was being called as a witness, to speak in Remington's behalf! She stood up, hearing the clamor of the other spectators and the comments of "She's the one!" and "They've called the widow!" that were flying through the crowd. With her face aflame she made her way down the steps at the side of the gallery.

When she stepped into the witness box, her knees buckled. She was facing nearly a hundred people—solicitors, barristers, spectators, news writers, and curiosity seekers. And they would hear every word she was forced by her oath to say.

"Explain to us, please, Mrs. Paxton, how you met the Earl of Landon," Kingston Gray instructed her. "And what happened between you that night."

"We met at the home of a mutual friend," she said, her voice dry and tight. Gray poured her a glass of water and she gratefully accepted it. Her heart was all but pounding out of her chest as she continued. "And I challenged him to a wager."

"Why did you do that, Mrs. Paxton?"

"Because I believed he needed . . . a comeuppance." A furor of excitement broke out at the rear of the gallery.

This was what the spectators had come to hear: the story of the wicked earl and the virtuous widow!

"And why did you believe that, Mrs. Paxton?" Gray continued.

She swallowed hard. Why would he ask such a thing of her? She groaned silently, afraid to look at Remington. "Because I had read some of the things he wrote in magazines and newspapers, and I thought they were horrid." There was such a reaction in the gallery that she thought it best to explain. "He didn't seem to think much of marriage or women, and I thought it would be useful to . . . educate him."

"To change his mind about both women and marriage," Gray clarified, and she nodded. "Tell us, Mrs. Paxton, what was your personal opinion of the earl when you issued that challenge?"

She blanched. Did he really expect her to answer that? His steady regard said that he did. "I thought he was arrogant, prejudiced, unfair, and"—she swallowed and made herself say it—"callous, narrow-minded, and insufferable." The reaction in the gallery was immediate, and the justices had to call the bailiffs to enforce order. She looked at Remington again and found his eyes glinting with amusement.

"Yet this callous, arrogant, and narrow-minded earl accepted your wager, did he not?" Gray continued, when things had quieted. When she answered "Yes," he looked pleased and continued. "Tell us . . . what did this wager require?"

"He was to do an average woman's work for a fortnight. And if, at the end of that time, he had changed his mind about women's work and women, he would support the Deceased Wife's Sister Bill. If he had not, then I was to do an average *man's* work for a fortnight." Kingston Gray struck a pose below the witness box.

"Who won this wager?" he asked.

"I did. He ceded the wager to me before the two weeks were quite finished."

"He ceded the wager . . . in effect, admitting that he had changed his attitude toward women. And did you believe him?"

Here at last was a chance to say something positive. "Yes, I did."

"Why?"

"Because I had seen his work over the course of two weeks, and I believed he had learned a great deal." She looked at Remington, met his eyes, and saw in them the depth and breadth of the man she had come to know.

"I had seen him up to his elbows in dishwater. I saw him scrubbing and polishing floors until his knees and hands were raw, and I saw him struggling with a needle and thread, learning to mend linen. I saw him learning to purchase food on a budget, to beat rugs, and even to clean out the necessaries." There was muffled laughter at that, and she blushed, but did not take her eyes from him. "And I saw him listening to the ladies of my household, learning that women were not dependent, clinging, contriving, or indolent, as he had been wont to perceive them. He learned that women can be trusted, can be resourceful, kind, compassionate, and generous." She ground to a halt and looked down at her hands on the tall railing before her.

"Interesting, indeed. Then it would be fair to say that your opinion of *him* changed also."

"I believe so," she said.

"Mrs. Paxton," Kingston Gray said, smiling in such a disarming way that she was caught totally off guard by his next question, "has the Earl of Landon ever proposed marriage to you?"

She gasped silently. If ever there was a time to faint, this was it. And yet there she stood—with her eyes wide, her knees turning to jelly, and her hands icy inside her gloves—without a vapor in sight!

"Yes," she managed to say.

"How many times?" he said. She glanced at Remington and found him watching her with his eyes luminous and his frame tensed and focused on her. And she suddenly understood—this was to show Remington's change of heart toward marriage. She took a deep breath and answered as best she could.

"I haven't . . . kept count," she said.

"More than once, then?" When she nodded, he continued counting. "More than three times? More than five times?"

"Perhaps four or five times." There was a clamor in the gallery and she clung to the railing for support, feeling a bit stunned by her own admission: Remington had proposed marriage to her at least four or five times. And every time he had meant it. Suddenly the questions came fast and furious.

"And you refused him those four or five times. Why? Was it because you find him loathsome and personally repugnant?"

"No."

"Is it because you find him callous, arrogant, prejudiced, and narrow-minded?"

"No," she said, glancing at Remington, wishing with all her heart she could take back those refusals.

"Was it because you found him greedy or miserly or dishonorable?"

"Certainly not."

"Was it because you believed him insincere in his desire to marry you?"

Her answer was so hushed that everyone in the courtroom leaned forward in their seats to hear. "No."

Gray nodded. "Would you please look at the defendant,

Mrs. Paxton." She stiffened and leaned heavily against the railing as she turned to Remington. His dark eyes reached out across the court to touch her and search her response, while his lawyer stopped her heart with a simple question:

"If he proposed to you here and now, Mrs. Paxton, would you accept?"

"I object!" The prosecutor was on his feet in a heartbeat, while the courtroom erupted around them. "Your honors—this is an outrage! The Crown objects to these tawdry theatricals! None of this is relevant to the charges—"

"But it is entirely relevant to the earl's defense, your honors!" Kingston Gray intoned in a commanding voice, above the chaos he had unleashed. "The earl's willingness to marry Mrs. Paxton is proof that he is not and never has been universally opposed to matrimony!"

Conferring with his associates, the chief justice banged his gavel and declared, "Objection overruled!"

But when some measure of order was restored, Gray glanced at Remington, then turned back to Antonia, who stood with her eyes lowered and her cheeks crimson and withdrew the question. He rested and took his seat, leaving Antonia in the hands of the hostile prosecutor.

"Just one question, Mrs. Paxton," the choleric prosecutor said, spitting out each word. "If you truly believed he had changed his opinions of women and that he was sincere in his proposal . . . why did you not marry him?"

Antonia lifted her head and took a deep breath. "For the best reason in the world, sir: because I did not want to be married."

"You, a known advocate of marriage and women's place in the home . . . did not wish to marry?" He faced the justices to pose his question to them, even as he posed it to Antonia. "*Why* did you not want to be married?"

"I believe that is *two* questions, sir," she said, thinking frantically for an answer that would not reflect on Remington. And she hit upon a surprising truth, albeit a half truth. "Because I had been a widow for some time and am used to managing my money, my time, and my household as I please. I found the idea of surrendering my considerable property and my right to direct my own affairs intolerable."

"It had nothing to do with the earl or his views of women or marriage?"

"It did not," she said with all truthfulness. "It had to do with *my* views of marriage . . . and men."

"Specifically with your opinions of *one man,* did it not?" The prosecutor, sensing a possible stroke for his side, grew impassioned. "Since it was Remington Carr you refused, it must be Remington Carr you objected to in some way. Just what was your opinion of the earl when you rejected his repeated proposals, Mrs. Paxton?"

Antonia drew a deep breath and told the absolute truth. "I believed the earl to be a complex and interesting man, an honorable, clever, and often considerate man. I believed him to be a man of strong principle and strong passions, who put his principles into action in his business and financial concerns." That raised a murmur in the court. "I found him desirable and utterly fascinating. But I did not wish to marry . . . him or anyone. I confess; I had come to see marriage as something of a trap that deprived women of their freedom and property. I, too, had a great deal to learn."

She scarcely recalled the trip across the courtroom and to her seat. All she knew was that another two steps and her legs would have given out. Paddington and Hermione put her down between them on the bench and held her icy hands. A moment later the justices were adjourning the court for the midday recess. She recovered enough to catch the smile Remington aimed in her direction and watch him exit with Kingston Gray.

"Did I do all right?" she asked Hermione and Paddington as they fought their way through the courthouse crowd.

"You did just fine dear," Hermione said, patting her hand.

"Excellent. Top-notch," Paddington said, then frowned slightly, looking a bit confused. "Now . . . were you testifying for or against him?"

There wasn't much testimony left to hear, Paddington told them when he came back to the gallery after conferring with Remington's lawyer. "That's good," Antonia said limply. "I don't think I could stand much more. When do you think they'll hand down a ruling?"

Paddington shrugged. "Tribunals sometimes rule straightaway, sometimes choose to deliberate. Hard to say."

And it was harder still to say how the evidence and testimony was being viewed from the bench. The justices' faces looked as if they were carved of stone. Even during the most unruly outbursts from the back, they scarcely raised an eyebrow. Both prosecution and defense would have to wait until the judgment was handed down to hear the justices' opinions.

When the court was reconvened, the chief justice asked the prosecutor whether his final witness, Rupert Fitch, had been located. The prosecutor shifted and stalled and asked for a bit more time. The justices granted it, providing they could locate him before summation of arguments. Then they instructed Kingston Gray to call his next witness. He called Remington Carr, Earl of Landon to the stand.

Antonia sat straighter, watching Remington move from the prisoner's dock to the witness box. He looked a bit solemn as he took the stand and swore to tell the truth. When he looked toward Antonia and she smiled, some of his aristocratic reserve seemed to melt and he became more accessible.

"My lord, we have heard much made of your previous views on marriage . . . and of your change of heart regarding matrimony. Would you please tell the court, in your own words what the intent of your writings on marriage were."

"It was my intention to raise questions and to provoke thought . . . in some small way to contribute to the debate on the idea that women should be granted full legal rights and responsibilities as citizens under the law. It was also my aim to express my opinions freely and responsibly."

"And in light of what you have learned and experienced over the past month, would you retract any or all of your writings and speeches on the matter?"

"I would not retract them." Remington paused. "I would *revise* them."

"To what, my lord? Would you revise your stand on the emancipation of women?"

"I would not. Though my reasons for believing in it have certainly changed." He glanced at Antonia. "But I would most radically alter my writings about marriage."

"What do you say of marriage now, my lord?"

Remington grew thoughtful, then glanced at the justices before pinning his gaze on Antonia. And the courtroom settled into a hush.

"I have been wont in the past to judge marriage by its worst, rather than its best, examples. Of late I have come to see the folly in judging a thing solely upon its deficits. I pray the good justices hearing my case share that insight." Gentle laughter swept the gallery, damping the instant he continued.

"Marriage, I have learned, is not a cold, social abstract;

it is a warm, living encounter between two people. Yes, it has societal ramifications . . . but if the relationships between married couples are good, then the resultant harmony can only be good for society at large. In these last weeks I have discovered marriage to be all those things that you have heard described by my friends earlier. Marriage is cleaving to one another first and always, sharing time and resources and the events of life, bearing with another's imperfections, supporting one another in times of triumph and defeat, and sometimes making sacrifices for the good of each other. But I have also learned more." And he gazed at Antonia with his heart in his eyes, willing her to see, making her know that he was speaking for her . . . to her.

"Marriage is not ownership of another, but a partnership . . . a full and equal partnership, built on mutual trust and need, on respect and affection. But it is a partnership where the two become one . . . one flesh, one heart, and at times even one mind. It is a joining in which giving everything that is in you somehow never leaves you feeling empty. A dear friend of mine describes a loving marriage as 'two hearts beating as one.' And she couldn't be more right."

A friend. *Cleo.* Antonia felt a shiver and came to the edge of her seat, clasping the railing before her. She watched him calling to her, resurrecting memories with his gaze, and with his words. As he continued to speak, she focused tightly on his face, and the rest of the courtroom gradually faded to the edges of her awareness.

Suddenly she could see in his dark eyes reminders of a thousand "touch me's" he had said without speaking, of the endless words of desire he had poured into her ears and sent wrapping around her heart . . . of cherries and cream, of buttons clattering across the floor, of red wine and candlelight, of corsets and trousers and ties. She could see "I need you" glowing in every line of his face. She could hear "I want you" clinging to the underside of every word he uttered. She could feel again the gentleness of his hands as he caressed and comforted her and pleasured her.

"Marriage is holding each other into the night, drying each other's tears, letting passion flow to sweeten the bitter knowledge that you do not have forever . . . only now."

He was recalling the same thing—that night when they sat with Cleo. She felt again that wild, precious swell of love in her heart.

"Marriage should be a nest, not a cage. It can ground us and make us more stable, while freeing us to explore the depths and heights of our hearts."

She understood somehow: the rootedness, the stability that marriage could provide, and the paradoxical way it could allow a heart to soar, to stretch, to become.

"Marriage forces you to look at who you are and what you believe. It makes you think beyond yourself, grow beyond who and what you have been. It enlarges your experience, your ideas, and your heart . . . by two."

And that was exactly what she felt . . . her heart had enlarged . . . grown . . . filled with . . .

"Marriage can be hell on earth—or heaven. And the thing that makes it one or the other is love. Love with the right person. And I never would have known that if I hadn't gone to Paxton House."

In the silence she felt him reaching for her, felt the pull of him in the very marrow of her bones. Through his testimony he had recalled all that had happened between them and had poured it out across the landscape of benches and robes and trappings of governmental power, using it to woo her in a shameless and breathtaking courtship. She pushed to her feet and stood gripping the gallery railing.

"My lord," Kingston Gray said in a solemn voice, "that is indeed a marvelous statement. But the true test of your views on marriage must be whether or not you will marry yourself. Given the chance, would you marry?"

"In an instant. You see, I'm very much in love with the right person. I'm in love with Antonia Paxton." Remington watched Antonia's glowing face and saw the tears collecting. Her chest was heaving, like his. He could see the emotions swirling in her beautiful blue eyes and warming her rosy skin . . . he had touched her with his words. But would it be enough? He took a ragged breath and then took the biggest risk of his life.

"Toni, will you marry me?"

For just one second she was frozen. Joy, disbelief, anxiety, relief—she was paralyzed by the explosion of feeling inside her. Then from behind someone gave her a nudge, and she heard the choked word: "Go!"

And she started to move . . . to the aisle . . . down the stairs . . . blinded by tears but guided by unfailing instinct. She didn't care that they were in Court One or that the one she was rushing to embrace was on trial . . . all she knew was she had to be with him, to touch him, to hold him when she said *yes*.

He flew out of the witness box and opened his arms just in time to catch her and her exultant: *"Yes—yes—yes. I'll marry you!"*

He picked her up and whirled her once around, laughing. And when her feet touched the floor, his lips touched hers and it was somehow just like the very first time he had kissed her. The softness, the wonder, the warmth of her engulfed his senses. She was life and sustenance and pleasure, the woman meant to complete his heart.

For that moment nothing else mattered; not the courtroom erupting in joyful turmoil, not the justices furiously banging their gavels and sending the clerk for more bailiffs, not even the prospect of being convicted or the specter of being parted. And it was some time before Remington heard his name being called and raised his head, though he refused to relinquish his hold on her.

"Your honors!" the prosecutor was bellowing, "this is an outrage! They've made a mockery of the court and the legal process! The Crown requests an immediate ruling and a conviction!"

"Your honors!" Kingston Gray matched his volume in a powerful, booming bass voice. "We ask the tribunal to understand the special circumstances of this case . . . to right the injustice already done to the defendant, and to set aside the charges and exonerate Lord Carr of all wrongdoing!"

Remington and Antonia looked up to find three hot-eyed magistrates glaring down at them. "Order!" the chief justice roared, banging furiously, then pointing at the pair of lovers with a gavel that was trembling. "You—both of you—stay right there! Bailiff—see that no one so much as moves a foot!"

The justices withdrew to the rear of the bench and could be seen arguing heatedly for several minutes. Antonia looked up at Remington with a worried expression and mouthed the words, "I'm sorry. I just had to hold you." He smiled and lowered his head to her ear.

"I love you, Toni, and you love me. What else matters?"

She slipped both arms around him, heedless of the glares and gasps around them. "I do love you, Remington Carr. With all my heart. And I'm going to marry you."

"Even though I'm not the last bachelor on the face of the earth?"

She laughed and let her face fill with the love rising from her heart. "You're my last bachelor . . . that's quite good enough."

Minutes later the justices returned to their places, looking stern and forbidding as they banged for order. Attention quickly focused on the bench, and on the justices' obvious displeasure. Remington released Antonia and together they faced the bench, with Gray beside them.

"We have reached a unanimous decision, and rather than delay and waste more of this court's valuable time, we will deliver the ruling and pass sentence now." He looked down his nose and down the bench to the glowing pair of lovers. "In the first charge the evidence is ponderous and convincing. It is the finding of this court that the defendant is *guilty* of advocating and promulgating ideas injurious to both the common moral will and the common good, to wit: views and opinions denigrating the holy and majestic institution of marriage."

Guilty. The verdict staggered Antonia. She looked up at Remington and found his face set with equal parts of determination and dread. She slipped her hand in his and tried to ignore the clamor of outrage coming from the gallery.

"Order!" He hammered for silence again and got a lowering of the roar from the back instead. "And in the matter of the second charge, the Crown's evidence is found woefully insufficient. The defendant is found not guilty."

Remington looked at Antonia with a bit of relief, then squeezed her hand.

"Now as to the sentence. A prison term is generally called for. . . ."

Antonia's stomach sank.

"However, seeing that there were special circumstances in this case . . . and that the miscreant has already been more than rehabilitated, we have decided upon a more fitting sentence. Remington Carr, Earl of Landon, this court sentences you to life—in marriage with one Mrs. Antonia Paxton. The sentence to begin this very day, in this courtroom." And he bent down over the bench toward them with a bit of fire in his eyes. "And may God have mercy on your souls."

Remington broke into a stunned grin. "I believe, Your Honor, He already has."

In seconds they were being hugged and embraced by Paddington and Hermione, who fought their way through the bailiffs to stand up with them. The justice sent for the rector of the church down the street and gave them a few moments to prepare. Antonia's ladies were permitted down on the floor of the court with them, and among them they managed to find something old, something new, something borrowed, and something blue. Some romantic soul outside located a flower vendor down the street and sent a nosegay of flowers through the crowd and up the court to Antonia.

By the time they were ready, the rector arrived, the special license was issued, and in a few short minutes they were indeed married. For better or worse. For richer or poorer. In sickness and in health. For the rest of their lives.

There was hardly a dry eye in the courtroom when he took her gently in his arms and kissed her.

Shortly, they were barraged with handshakes, hugs, and congratulations. Among those who came down to wish them well was Sir Henry Peckenpaugh and his wife, Rosamund Garvey Peckenpaugh, the sixth and last of Antonia's Bentick brides. She hugged Antonia and answered Antonia's question of how she was getting on with a beaming smile. "Henry and I are . . . expecting," she whispered. "And, Lady Toni, it's made us do a lot of thinking and talking. It's getting better every day." Antonia laughed, feeling her spirits rise at the realization that perhaps some of her protégées had found happiness. It seemed the perfect thing to set her own happiness in her new marriage.

Together they fought their way through the crowd to the church down the street to register their vows, then managed to find a cab and escape to Remington's house for a while. Antonia's ladies, the Bentick couples, and Hermione and Paddington went with them. And with Gertrude's help Remington's overwhelmed cook managed to put on a simple but tasty wedding dinner. Toasts were drunk, music was made, and Remington's mansion was duly explored and admired by the ladies of Paxton House. But when it came time for the guests to leave for their respective homes, the host and hostess were missing.

Paddington roused himself to go look for them, but Hermione pulled him back down on the settee. "Don't bother, Paddington dear. I'm sure they're somewhere perfectly safe . . . learning to play footsie."

The sun was high in the sky the next morning when Antonia awakened in her grand new bed . . . to the feel of something sliding sinuously over her naked hip. It felt wonderful, and she knew without opening her eyes who was responsible. After a few delicious moments she opened them and found Remington tantalizing her skin with a lock of her own hair. She turned from her side onto her back, smiling up at him.

He was wearing the most indecent smile—something between saturated with pleasure and ravenously aroused. "Wake up, Countess. I have a present for you." He took her left hand and placed on her ring finger an exquisite cut diamond set in an intricate bed of gold and polished rubies. "It was my mother's ring . . . and my grandmother's. It has been worn by several generations of Landon countesses. I didn't expect ever to give it to anyone."

"It's breathtaking," she said softly, her eyes shining as

she turned her hand to admire it. Then she glanced flirtatiously at him from beneath lowered lashes. "If I'd known there were so many benefits to being your countess, I might have said yes to you earlier."

"It would have saved me a bit of grief, sweetheart. You know, of course, that the queen—" But he halted. Maybe he'd save the news of the queen's marriage ultimatum for another time. He quickly substituted: ". . . may never receive us at court."

"I'll try to bear up under the disappointment." She laughed wickedly and turned toward him, rubbing the side of his bare leg with her foot, luxuriating in the sensual feeling it roused between them. "I just hope we won't be totally shunned."

"I suspect we'll live it all down . . . in thirty or forty years," he said, nuzzling her shoulders and drifting up her throat toward her mouth. She frowned and bit her lip and he looked up to see the beginnings of real worry in her face.

"Constance Ellingson will probably be the only one who will invite us. . . ."

Remington groaned as if in pain. "That settles it—I won't be stuck with Lady Constance and her interminable soirees. As soon as it's decently possible—in two or three months, when the season is well under way—we'll throw a huge, lavish ball to celebrate our marriage. And their curiosity about the beautiful and sensuous Countess of Landon and the ravening, depraved beast she rescued by marriage will overcome their proper and prudish impulses. They'll come. And they'll see how you've tamed and changed me. And we'll be positively in demand." He grinned down into her glistening eyes. "Sound better?"

"Ummm. Much." She slid her hands over his chest, admiring her ring, then transferring that admiration to the smoothly muscled skin beneath it. She kissed his chest lightly, then with soft, lingering strokes of her tongue.

He rolled onto his back, pulling her atop him, and as his hands slid over her bare back and buttocks, he murmured hotly, "Come here, Countess, and let me thank you once again for making a married man of me."

Epilogue

Landon House was richly decorated for the Christmas season, resplendent with fragrant pine boughs and crimson velvet ribbons, and warmed by the light and the scent of beeswax candles. A quiet evening's entertainment was under way in the great drawing room, while Phipps and his staff laid out a simple buffet in the dining room.

Antonia sat in her favorite crimson tea gown—the one that still covered her greatly expanded stomach—listening to Victoria Bentley's strong, clear voice leading the others in Christmas carols. In recent months she had cut back on her entertaining a great deal—her sole concession to impending motherhood. She glanced around the room and felt her heart swell at the sight of her Paxton House ladies sitting like aged cherubs among their other guests. She had insisted they continue on at Paxton House in her absence, though in truth they were at her house in Hyde Park nearly as much as they were at home.

There had been a number of changes since her marriage a year and a half before. Cleo had finally joined her beloved Fox Royal, after another severe stroke the previous winter. Old Hoskins had decided to retire, on generous pension, only to become the caretaker in a monastery. The ladies of Paxton House had taken in three more widows, and now Eleanor and Pollyanna oversaw the day-to-day running of the house. Paddington and Hermione had decided to travel and spent the better part of the last winter on the Mediterranean. This year they were waiting until after Christmas and the imminent birth of Antonia's baby before making the journey to their rented villa in the south of France.

Remington slipped into the room, spotted Antonia, and tiptoed to the back of the group to join her on the settee. He put an arm around her and pulled her close, giving her a lingering kiss. His lips were that odd combination of outer cold and inner heat that spoke of his long ride home in an ill-heated carriage. He had spent the day visiting his Sutton Mills project and whispered an apology for the delay.

"That narrow bridge . . . traffic was terrible," he whispered, taking advantage of the fact that the others hadn't seen him yet to nuzzle her ear.

"Ummm. I shall have to speak to my local MP about the disgraceful condition of this nation's roads," she said with a hum of contentment. Then she glanced at Albert Everstone, who was downing yet another glass of champagne. "Later, however. How were the mills faring?"

"Your investment is doing splendidly. With the new machinery they'll double production easily." His eyes glowed as he toyed with a strand of hair from the nape of her neck. "Clever woman, deciding to strike a deal with that handsome fellow from Carr Enterprises and loan him the money to clinch the deal."

"Clever man, agreeing with your wife's insistence that she keep her property in her own name and handle her own investments. She's made you money, you know."

He chuckled and glanced around before claiming her lips with a good bit more than fiduciary interest. "She's made me more than money," he whispered, staring into her eyes. "She's made me happy."

And that happiness had been responsible for Remington's wholehearted support of the Married Women's Property Act, passed a year ago. He was still working to provide support for women's suffrage and emancipation, though with an entirely different motive from before.

She caught sight of Phipps standing in the doorway, scouring the room for her, and waved silently to him. Remington sat straighter and released all but her hand as the butler hurried over with a look of dismay.

"I'm so sorry, my lord." He wrung his hands. "But there is someone here to see you. I've told her you are busy, but she is most insistent."

Remington's eyes narrowed at the word "her." "Who is it, Phipps?"

The butler winced. "Miss Hillary Fenton, sir."

"Damn." Remington set his jaw and made to rise, but Antonia grabbed his sleeve and held him back.

"Remmy dear," she said in a falsetto voice. "I'll handle it."

Soon she was floating through the center hall toward the morning room. Shortly, Hillary arrived—in a state, as usual. One glimpse of Antonia and she halted just inside the room. "It's you. I specifically asked to see Remington." She huffed irritably and put away the handkerchief she had ready.

"Good to see you, too, Hillary. What is it this time?" Antonia said with a tart smile that was more warning than pleasantry.

"It's the Christmas money. The settlement-house roof developed a major leak, and we had to use the Christmas money to fix it." Since Remington's marriage Hillary had been converted to the cause of downtrodden women and had thrown herself body and soul into the redeeming work of helping the poor, unfortunate women who had fallen prey to the appetites of men. She was a member of the board of the Magdalen Society. "Our funds are so short we can barely provide food, much less a decent Christmas dinner. And some of the women have children. Oh . . ." Out came the handkerchief after all, and she dabbed at her eyes. "It breaks my heart to see the little ones going without."

Her sidelong look—half-accusing, half-imploring—had been perfected through long years of employing feminine wiles to get what she wanted from men. This time it fell to Antonia's middle. Antonia was going to be a mother, it said. How could she bear to think of any child in need?

Antonia stood there, feeling protectively and motherly and embarrassingly blessed by happiness and good fortune —which was exactly what Hillary had intended. She usually drew a hard line with Hillary and Carlotta and their theatrics and demands, and Remington was content to let her handle them, woman to woman. But it was Christmas. And the thought of any child in need was difficult to bear.

"How much?" Antonia said, planting her hands on what was left of her waist.

Hillary brightened instantly. "Five hundred should do."

"Five hundred?" Antonia gasped. "That's enough to buy a dozen children clothes and food for a year."

"Yes, it is," Hillary said with a look that, for the first time in Antonia's memory, held a genuine bit of warmth and concern. "And I'll see that it does."

Antonia sent Phipps for her bank book and wrote out a draft.

"Thank you, Antonia," Hillary said warmly, before retreating behind her inner walls again. "Well, I must be off and leave you to your precious party."

As the sound of Phipps letting Hillary out the door drifted back down the hall, Remington stepped into the room.

"That a girl . . . be tough with them. Let them know

they can't wheedle and manipulate and push you around," he said, quoting her. As she glowered at him, he chuckled and came to take her into his arms and kiss the scowl from her face.

"She caught me in a weak spot . . . children and Christmas," she said a bit sheepishly. She raised her mouth to his and sighed as he kissed her lavishly. "If she shows up next year on December twentieth, I'll let you handle her."

He grinned and escorted her back toward the drawing room, feeling a bit mischievous. "You know, I've been thinking," he teased. "Hillary is a nice name for a little girl. . . ."

Antonia stopped in the center hall and grabbed him by both sleeves, scorching him with the fire in her eyes. *"Not Hillary!"* she demanded, with such force that he burst out laughing.

"Well, we'd better think of a name soon. She'll be here before we know it."

"I already have a name." She released one sleeve and touched her mounded stomach. "I've been meaning to bring it up. It's not very fashionable, but it has wonderful associations for me . . . and I think for you, too."

"Oh?" He drew her into his arms again. "And what name is that?"

"Cleo," she said, then bit her lip, watching his reaction. The sudden luminosity to his eyes made her catch her breath. And for a brief moment they felt a curious, glowing warmth waft through their senses and wrap around their shoulders. Memories, the past, dragged across the strings of their joined hearts.

"Cleo it is, sweetheart," he said softly.

And he kissed her.

Author's Note

I hope you enjoyed Antonia's and Remington's story. If the substance of their conflict seemed oddly current to you, it may be because, in a very real sense, history repeats itself. It was in the middle-class drawing rooms of London, in the 1880's and 1890's that the question of a woman's rightful place in the world was first asked.

Discussion of "The Woman Question" was prompted in part by an increasing number of well-born women in England who found themselves raised to the Victorian expectation of woman as "wife, homemaker, and mother," but without any prospect of marriage and with no means of support. As Antonia states, well more than half a million women in England found themselves in just such straits. The reasons for this state of affairs were a shortage of eligible men and an increasing reluctance toward marriage among middle- and even upper-class men. Marriage for such men would have meant trading a comfortable bachelor existence for the restrictions and comparative penury of marriage; their time and salaries would have had to stretch to meet the needs of a wife and, eventually, children.

Thus, embarrassingly large numbers of respectable women who had been indoctrinated in the Victorian ideal of womanhood were left adrift in society. The advertisements Antonia read from *Cornhill* were indeed taken from old issues of *Cornhill Magazine*. All are regrettably genuine. Notices and ads seeking employment or merely "a place to sleep and a bit of bread" were a regular feature of the newspapers and magazines and are to modern ears pathetic in their appeals. Presumably, claims of being uneducated, abandoned, and unable to do anything of value were meant to evoke pity in their readers. I am indebted to my sister, Sharon Stone, head of the English Department at Granville High School in Ohio, who uncovered these excerpts while doing research for her master's thesis and generously shared them with me. It was, in fact, her research into Victorian women writers and our discussion of the debate ignited over these "surplus women" that generated the idea for this book.

In popular publications and in scholarly tracts of the 1880's, questions were raised about the morality of women working outside the home and on ways these unmarriageable women could be made self-supporting. Just what—politicians, social theorists, and reformers asked—could these surplus females actually *do*? Their proposals for appropriate "female labor" run the gamut from simpleminded to chilling.

The 1880's–90's and 1980's–90's bear yet other striking similarities. Both eras feature a woman of dignity and bearing sitting on an embattled British throne—and waiting in the wings of both is an heir whom the public and the media fear will destroy the monarchy. I have depicted Queen Victoria as my research shows her to have been at this stage of her life: reclusive, obsessed with her widowhood, and—for a female monarch—surprisingly hostile to women in any role outside the home. She actively opposed higher education for women, and enlisted her prime ministers in the fight against women in the professions. She insisted that a woman's lot was to be a wife and mother, yet paradoxically bore a great distaste for marriage—called it "a trap which young girls would never allow themselves to fall into, if they knew what was in store for them."

Another shared feature of both eras is the eager and sometimes unscrupulous British press. The great newspapers of the day were largely reputable and printed news for the middle and upper classes. But there were numerous weeklies, journals, and "ha'penny papers" (precursors of the tabloid journalism rampant in Britain today) that catered to the burgeoning "underclass" of readers—working-class people who were becoming literate as a result of the Elementary Education Act of 1870. But, of course, love of scandal knows no boundaries of class or rank, and these scandal sheets found their way into the poorest tenement and into the palace itself. The despicable Rupert Fitch has real-life counterparts on both sides of the Atlantic today.

As to the heart of the story: the views of men's and women's roles and of marriage are purely mine. I have long believed that men and women have much more in common than not. And while our biological and social roles often seem to take us in different directions, we are brought together again and bonded to one another in marriage . . . sharing strengths and weaknesses, experiences and abilities, sorrows, dreams, and hopes. It is in the grace of a good and loving marriage that we can find the encouragement and the freedom to risk and to grow . . . to become that which is written in every fiber of our beings . . . that which we are meant to be.

About the Author

Betina Krahn lives in Minnesota, with her physicist husband, her two sons, and a feisty salt-and-pepper schnauzer. With a degree in biology and a graduate degree in counseling, she has worked in teaching, personnel management, and mental health. She had a mercifully brief stint as a boys' soccer coach, makes terrific lasagna, routinely kills houseplants, and is incurably optimistic about the human race. She believes the world needs a bit more truth, a lot more justice, and a whole lot more love and laughter. And she attributes her outlook to having married an unflinching optimist and to two great-grandmothers actually named "Polyanna."